KT-172-965

Judith Lennox spent most of her childhood living in a remote part of the Hampshire countryside. The family home, which had once been a game-keeper's cottage, was at the edge of a wood. There were nightingales and orchids, but no neighbours, shops, mains water or electricity.

Judith escaped via university and a variety of jobs to the comparative civilization of Cambridgeshire, where she now lives with her husband and sons. Her most recent novels include *The Secret Years*, *The Winter House*, *Some Old Lover's Ghost* and *Footprints on the Sand*, which are also published by Corgi Books.

Also by Judith Lennox

THE SECRET YEARS
THE WINTER HOUSE
SOME OLD LOVER'S GHOST
FOOTPRINTS ON THE SAND

and published by Corgi Books

THE SHADOW CHILD

Judith Lennox

CORGI BOOKS

THE SHADOW CHILD
A CORGI BOOK : 0 552 14603 X

First publication in Great Britain

PRINTING HISTORY
Corgi edition published 1999

3 5 7 9 10 8 6 4 2

Copyright © Judith Lennox 1999

Set in 10/12pt Sabon by
Phoenix Typesetting, Ilkley, West Yorkshire

Corgi Books are published by Transworld Publishers,
61–63 Uxbridge Road, London W5 5SA,
a division of The Random House Group Ltd,
in Australia by Random House Australia (Pty) Ltd,
20 Alfred Street, Milsons Point, Sydney, NSW 2061, Australia,
in New Zealand by Random House New Zealand Ltd,
18 Poland Road, Glenfield, Auckland 10, New Zealand
and in South Africa by Random House (Pty) Ltd,
Endulini, 5a Jubilee Road, Parktown 2193, South Africa.

Printed and bound in Great Britain by
Cox & Wyman Ltd, Reading, Berkshire.

To Ewen, Alexis and Dominic

PART ONE

A BIRTHDAY PICNIC

Picardy – July 1914

CHAPTER ONE

There were six tiny buttons on each of his boots. When she bent to fasten them, Charlie flung his arms round her head and cried, 'Allie, Allie, Allie!' and beat her with his fists. Charlie Lanchbury was two years old, and plump and adorable. Alix swung him up in her arms and covered his face with kisses.

She looked out of the window, down to the courtyard of the chateau, where Uncle Charles was handing Aunt Marie into the Daimler. Alix could see her three young cousins, Ella, May and Daisy, all wearing matching white muslin dresses tied with pink sashes. It was May's, the middle Lanchbury sister's, ninth birthday. The entire Lanchbury family – Uncle Charles and Aunt Marie, the four children, their Boncourt grandparents, and Alix herself – were to go on a picnic.

'Stand *still*, Charlie.' His red-gold curls were tickling her chin, making her giggle. She tried to straighten the rumpled tips of his lace collar, but he wriggled out of her grasp and tottered around the room, shouting, ''Ord! 'Ord!'

The afternoon sun gleamed through the window panes, marking bright squares on the polished wooden floor. When Alix picked up her sketchbook, a leaf of paper floated to the floor. It was a drawing of her father and mother standing on a quayside, huge handkerchieves pressed against their faces, their oversized tears forming a comical puddle round their feet. The sketch was entitled, 'Mr and Mrs Gregory, seeing their daughter Alix off on her travels.' It was signed AJG, her father's initials.

Alix had hardly felt homesick during the entire two months of her holiday in France: she had been too busy, and too entranced by the difference of it all. It was her first holiday with her Lanchbury cousins; at fourteen years old it was her first holiday abroad. Yet, looking at the cartoon, she felt a sudden pang.

Crawling around the room on her hands and knees, she peered beneath tables and chairs.

'Help me find your sword, Charlie, or we'll be late.'

She discovered the toy sword hidden inside a box of wooden bricks. Charlie jumped up and down with excitement, and toddled across the room to her. ''Ord,' he said, and beamed, a wide smile patched with tiny pearly teeth.

'Sword,' Alix corrected him gently, and, pulling the ribbon from her own dark, curling hair, she tied it round the middle of his velvet-covered stomach, and fixed the small wooden sword inside. He held out his hands to her, and she carried him to the window. All around them, as far as the eye could see, the fields of northern France shimmered in the midday heat. Alix hugged Charlie's small, warm body against her own. Then she grabbed her hat and ran outside into the sun.

In the motor-car, she kept her sketchbook and pencil in the pocket of her dress. The book was almost full, only a few empty pages left. And all *sensible* drawings, nothing like the pictures that had got her into such trouble at school. Her stomach still lurched at the memory of being summoned to Miss Humphreys's study and seeing, spread out on the headmistress's desk, her cartoons of the members of staff at Ashfield House. Miss Turton, the hockey mistress, red-faced and stout-calved; Miss Bright (history) peering over her pince-nez. Her teachers' most prominent characteristics magnified and mocked. Her drawings, scribbled in the margins of rough books or on the pages of autograph books, made the other girls laugh; they traded lemon drops and bull's-eyes in exchange for a cartoon. Miss Humphreys, though, had not laughed. Retribution had been swift and unrelenting. Alix had not even been allowed to say goodbye to her friends.

The most awful thing – and Alix, no longer noticing the pale gold of the passing French countryside, gave a small sigh – the most awful thing had been the bewilderment and disappointment on her parents' faces when they had arrived to take her away from school. She had hated herself for letting them down. The second most awful thing had been her realization that she herself must have left the sketchbook in the school cloakroom. Added to the mislaid galoshes, dancing tunics and fountain pens that had haunted her brief career at Ashfield House was that final, self-incriminating carelessness.

A few weeks after her ignoble exit from school, Alix's mother had received Uncle Charles's letter. 'So kind of Charles and Marie,' Beatrice Gregory had said. 'They've offered to take you to France with them. They take the four children there each summer to stay with Marie's family.' Mrs Gregory had frowned. 'I'm not sure . . . fourteen is so young . . . and we really should look for another school. But Nanny Barnes is unwell, you see, so she can't go.' Some of the strands of grey hair that escaped incessantly from Mrs Gregory's coiffure fell over her creased brow. 'Marie asks it as a favour. You would be expected to help with your little cousins, of course, Alix. I'm not sure . . .'

The motor-car driven by Robert, the Boncourts' stable-boy, jolted on the cobbled road. Charlie wriggled on Alix's lap as she remembered the promises she had made to her mother. I'll be as good as gold, I'll take care of all my belongings, and I'll never argue or complain. She would have promised anything to be permitted the adventure of travelling to France.

She had kept her promises, by and large. She had only once stuck out her tongue at Ella, when Ella, inspecting the contents of her suitcase, had said, 'Cotton gloves, Cousin Alix! We always have kid or lace. Mama says that only governesses and ladies' maids wear cotton gloves.' And she had only lost her temper once, when she had overheard Aunt Marie whisper to Mme Boncourt, 'Alix's father is a schoolteacher. Beatrice Lanchbury married beneath her – frightened that she would remain an old maid, I suppose.'

Now the Boncourts' chateau and its surrounding fields were far behind them. The level plains of Picardy were sheened with ripening corn and dotted with poplars. Heat gathered in the motor-car's open-sided cab.

Five-year-old Daisy whined, 'Are we there yet?'

'Course not, silly,' said Ella.

'I'm hungry.' Daisy's face crumpled.

'There'll be plenty of nice food at the picnic, dear,' said Mme Boncourt comfortingly. 'Though I always think French food is so rich for little tummies. Such a pity Nanny couldn't come. Nanny made such lovely rice puddings and egg custards, didn't she?' Mme Boncourt, who was kind and vague and fat, beamed at Alix. 'You are enjoying your little holiday, aren't you, Alix dear?'

Alix thought of the Channel crossing and the golden sands of Le Touquet, where they had stayed for the first three weeks, and the sleepy French villages, and the verges embroidered with scarlet poppies and blue chicory. And she pictured the splendour of the Lanchburys' lives – Aunt Marie's exquisite silk gowns, and the servants who waited on their every need. And the motor-car, of course. Until last month she had never travelled in a motor-car.

'It's been *wonderful*,' she said vehemently. She hugged Charlie closer to her, breathing in the clean, soapy scent of his skin, kissing the top of his head.

Alix drew the picnic table, and the servants setting it out. She began to draw Robert and the nursemaid Louise, who were half hidden beneath the trees, but Charlie threw himself onto her lap, seizing her pencil and jabbing at her sketchbook.

''Nake.'

'Snake? Charlie wants to draw a snake?' Alix guided the pencil, clutched in his chubby fist. Sinuous curves crawled over the paper.

''Nake,' he said again, and pointed at the trees. 'Over dere.'

'You saw a snake? Over there?' Alix stood up, dusting fragments of dried grass from her skirt. 'Let's go and see.' She held out her hand to him.

Pink and white flickered among the green and black of the forest as May and Daisy, ahead of them, darted through the trees. The conversation of the adults, sitting in the shade, retreated into the distance, the timbre of their voices curiously flattened, as if the tall trees or the summer heat itself smothered their words.

'. . . could visit dear Amelie in Paris.' Mme Boncourt's voice.

'But the harvest . . .' M. Boncourt, unlike his wife, spoke in French.

'Of course, Felix. I had forgotten. Of course we must wait for the harvest.'

'The Kaiser's army may not do so.' Mr Lanchbury paused in his pacing of the boundaries.

'Really, Charles.' Mme Boncourt gave a little laugh. 'I don't think things have reached quite that pass.'

'Of course you don't. I have always thought, *belle-mère*, that you make optimism into an art form.'

Charlie tugged Alix's hand, pulling her deeper into the woods. Distantly, Uncle Charles added, 'I should like to have left tomorrow. We must return to England early in view of the . . .' and then he was out of earshot, and Charlie was whispering, ''Nake, Allie, 'nake.'

She shivered when she saw the coiled shape in the dried leaves. Then, looking again, she laughed and said, 'It's only an old snakeskin, Charlie. See, there's nothing there.'

Squatting beside her, he poked the sloughed-off skin with the tip of his sword, overturning it. Gently, Alix pulled him away. 'Leave it, Charlie, leave it alone. Let's find your sisters, shall we?'

He padded ahead of her through the trees. *We must return to England early*, Uncle Charles had said. Suddenly, Alix longed to be home again, showing her father her sketchbook, telling her mother about the vast, airy rooms of the Boncourts' chateau, crammed with gilt and velvet furniture, and describing to her Aunt Marie's gowns, with their froth of lace and baby ribbon that

14

whispered as she walked. Alix knew that if she had been walking through these woods with her father he would have told her the names of the tiny white flowers that quivered in the undergrowth, and he would have recognized the song of the bird that perched in the highest branches of the trees. He would have known which snake had sloughed off the skin that had alarmed Charlie, and he would have shown Alix how to draw a picnic table whose legs appeared to be made of wood, and not rubber.

The only horrible part about going home would be leaving Charlie. Charlie had been Alix's principal charge during her eight weeks in France. He had attached himself to her on her very first day with the Lanchburys, kneeling beside her on a bench on the deck of the steamer, watching the boat's white wake stain the steel-grey waves. In the hotel at Le Touquet Charlie had refused to sleep unless Alix tucked him in; on the long train journey to Amiens he had sat still only when Alix had hugged him on her lap and told him stories. She loved him with a fierce, unexpected passion; she had never cared much for dolls, and she had thought, somehow, to find her two-and-a-half-year-old cousin equally dull. But she had discovered that it was a delight just to hold him, to feel his weight in her arms, and to press his fine, silky curls against her face when she bent to kiss him.

After the picnic (ham and jellied chicken, apple tarts and a vast, pink birthday cake), Alix helped the girls make daisy chains. Ella, May and Daisy lay on the grass, pressing their thumbnails into the green, juicy stalks. Charlie played around his mother's skirts, poking with a plump, dirty finger at the ladybird that climbed laboriously from blade of grass to clover leaf.

Mme Boncourt held out a hand so that her husband could help her from her chair. 'I must go home, Marie dear. It's so hot, and I'm feeling quite faint. I'll travel in the dogcart with the servants. I'll not spoil your day.'

'Maman—'

'Hush, Marie. I prefer to travel in the dogcart. Motor-cars are such nasty, dirty things.'

The servants were arranging the hampers and rugs in the dogcarts. Uncle Charles, tossing Ella's ball smoothly from one hand to another, said lazily, 'If you are to go home now, *belle-mère*, then be sure to take that wretched nursery-maid with you. She does nothing but flirt with the stable-boy.'

'*Charles*. Little pitchers—'

'Alix will look after Charlie, won't you, Alix? We'll have a game of cricket. Find some sticks, Ella, for stumps.'

'It's past their bedtime . . .' A vague gesture of a white-gloved wrist. 'We should go home, Charles.'

'Nonsense, Marie. On such a glorious evening?' Uncle Charles jammed the sticks that Ella had found into the grass. 'Alix, Daisy and myself in one team. Ella, May and Charlie in the other. May shall bat first because it's her birthday.'

The dogcarts carrying the servants and the Boncourts and a sulky Louise disappeared down the lane. The cart-wheels sent up clouds of dust. Uncle Charles bowled, and May lashed out with the bat. The ball soared into the undergrowth, and Charlie clapped his fat hands together, and Ella shouted, 'Run, May, run!'

Uncle Charles bowled again and again. The little girls' feet pattered on the hard ground. The sun slid towards the treetops, a burning globe. The ball, hurtling down from an overbright sky, slipped between Alix's palms.

'Butterfingers,' said Uncle Charles sharply.

The click of ball against bat marked the passing moments. The trees became black silhouettes against a darkening sky. Charlie, supposedly fielding, had crept back to his mother and was sucking his thumb. Every now and then Aunt Marie reached down and silently pushed his hand away from his face, but after she had sat upright again the thumb slid back into his mouth. Soon, Alix thought, Uncle Charles would notice that Daisy had become red-faced and tearful, that Ella's sullenness had turned to aggression, and that even May's sunny disposition had begun to falter. Yet the ball continued to rise up into the air, and Uncle Charles continued to harangue them to run faster, try harder.

The last wicket fell. 'Bowled,' said Uncle Charles, smacking his hands together. 'My team's game, I think.'

Dark shadows licked the grass. The Lanchburys gathered up bat and ball and discarded hats and gloves. Daisy's pink sash trailed greyly in the dust, and Charlie, when his mother pulled him to his feet, quivered with weariness. Walking back to the motor-cars, Ella and May argued.

'It's *my* turn to go with Papa,' hissed Ella.

May showed her teeth. 'It's *my* birthday. Papa *said*.'

In the back seat of the Boncourts' car, Alix cradled Charlie in her lap while Daisy huddled against her. The wheels jolted on the baked earth. Charlie's lids drooped slowly over his cornflower-blue irises. A languor had seized them all.

Fields and streams drifted by. Oil-lamps gleamed in cottage windows, and the last rays of the sun lit with gold the flowers in a roadside shrine. I shall remember

17

this evening for the rest of my life, thought Alix. I shall remember the scent of the dust and the grass, and the way the poppies on the verge bend and sway as the motor-car passes, and I shall remember the way Charlie smiles as he dreams.

Reaching a village, they stopped. Faces flickered in the dim light, staring curiously into the car. Charlie sat up, blinking. Ahead of them, the Daimler had also come to a halt.

Aunt Marie approached the car. 'Papa says that you had all better get out. The motor-car . . .' She drew away, her white glove slipping from the rim of the door, one hand to her face, fingertips fluttering against her veiled mouth.

They clustered together on the cobbles. May cocked her head to one side. 'I can hear music,' she whispered. There was the distant sound of fiddles and drums. 'Papa, I can hear music.' She ran to the corner of the street, peering into the darkness.

'The radiator's overheated,' said Mr Lanchbury. 'We must wait for it to cool down.'

'Papa, there's a *fair* . . .'

Not quite in rhythm with the music, Uncle Charles tapped the rim of his straw boater against his thigh. 'A fair, you say? We may as well go and see.'

'*Papa!*' May clapped her hands together.

'Charles . . . it's so late . . . and a little country fair . . .'

'You may remain in the motor-car if you wish, Marie.' Charles Lanchbury began to stride down the narrow alleyway.

The journey from the picnic glade seemed to have revived them. May skipped, and even Ella smiled. Reluctantly, Marie Lanchbury followed after them, Charlie scampering beside her.

The street debouched into a small square. In the centre of the square a bonfire burned, illuminating both the market stalls and the people gathered beside them. Dancers pirouetted around the bonfire and in one corner of the square a carousel was turning. May, clutching one of Alix's hands, ducked through the press of bodies, heading towards the dancers. Daisy's small paw gripped Alix's other hand. Looking back, Alix saw Charlie, half hidden by his mother's silk skirts, hypnotized by a juggler's soaring coloured hoops.

'*Beautiful*,' said May. The word was a sigh of delight. Her rapt gaze focused on the gypsy dancers.

'Allie, Allie, Allie!' Charlie cannoned into her knees, almost knocking her over. Alix scooped him up in her arms.

Ella, running after him, said, 'He wants you to see the monkeys.'

'Monkeys?'

'There's a man with two little monkeys. You hold the monkey and he plays a tune, and you give him some money.' Ella, head down, forced a path across the square.

The monkeys' tiny, sad faces peered out from beneath knitted bonnets. May and Ella cradled them like babies as the hurdy-gurdy turned, a melancholy drone. Charlie stroked a wrinkled paw with his own plump finger. Alix handed a few coins to their owner, who slid them into a greasy leather purse.

Next to the organ grinder was a sweet stall. Charlie tugged Alix's hand, begging for a lollipop, but she shook her head.

'I've no money left, Charlie. There's your mama – run and ask her.'

On the stone steps in front of the *mairie*, Alix sat

down and took out her sketchbook. Fragments of the Lanchburys' conversation drifted over the shouting and laughter of the crowd and the jingle of tambourines.

'. . . must not touch my gown with such sticky fingers, Charlie. I *said* . . .'

'It's not *fair*. She has more than me. *And* she held the prettiest monkey.'

'. . . fail to see why we must mingle with such people. It's not like you, Charles. I realize that you wish to . . .'

'I want to be a ballerina. When I grow up I'm going to be a ballerina.'

Alix wanted to be an artist when she grew up. She had confided her ambition to no-one yet, knowing that she must choose the right moment to persuade her parents to let her go to art school in London.

When her sketchbook was full she stood up. Every page was crammed with drawings. Looking around, Alix realized that she could no longer see the Lanchburys. As the night closed in, the fair had become insubstantial, made of shadows. It had started to rain, a fine drizzle that gave the cobbles a gleaming, oily sheen. Uncoiling inside her was the fear that the Lanchburys had forgotten her, that they had driven back to the chateau without her. Alix tried to recall where they had left the motor-cars. Down that side street, surely . . . or had it been along that alleyway? She began to run. The rain stung her eyes. Then a hand grabbed her wrist and she spun round. An old woman jabbed at the lines of her palm with a calloused fingertip. Alix heard a gabble of words, but could not in her panic recall any French.

'She wants to read your palm, Cousin Alix. She's a fortune-teller.'

'*Ella*.' Alix felt dizzy with relief. 'Where were you? I was afraid I was lost.'

'The others are going back to the motor-cars. Papa sent me to fetch you. He's very cross. He says that it's late and you must hurry.' Ella glared at the old woman. '*Allez vous en*, won't you? *Pas de l'argent. Allez vous en.*'

The rain became heavier. Alix could see Uncle Charles's hat, bobbing above the crowd, drops of rain drumming against the brim. Aunt Marie was surrounded by villagers, a flicker of ghostly-pale silk. Alix's thin cotton dress clung damply to her shoulders, and for the first time that day she felt chilled. The villagers surged around the motor-cars, curious fingers reaching out to touch them. May and Ella's shrill cries soared above the chatter and laughter.

''S not fair! It's *my* birthday!'

'*I'm* the eldest! *I* should go in Papa's motor-car!'

'Papa said—' A scream. 'You pinched me! Cousin Alix – Ella pinched me!'

'Beastly little girl—'

A louder howl. 'She stamped on my foot! Ow, ow!'

'Good God, you two are not fit to leave the nursery.' Uncle Charles's cold voice cut through the rain. 'As for you' – he turned sharply to Alix – 'don't just stand there. See to them.'

'Go with your mama, Ella,' said Alix quickly. 'May can come with us.' Ella, triumphant, threaded through the crowds towards the Daimler.

Alix steered May towards the Boncourts' car. May beat at her with her fists. 'Not fair!' she howled. ''S *my* birthday!' Rain plastered May's hair to her scalp, and her pale blue eyes were furious.

'Oh, *May*!' Alix wiped the tears from the little girl's eyes. 'We'll have a nice time,' she coaxed. 'We'll play I Spy.'

May flung herself face down on the back seat, threw her hands over her ears, and sobbed. Alix peered around the inside of the car. No Charlie. Just Robert, in the front seat, smoking a cigarette, his eyes half closed, humming to himself.

Suddenly anxious, Alix touched Robert's shoulder.

'Robert, where's Charlie?'

Robert shrugged. 'In the Daimler, I expect, mademoiselle.' He stubbed out his cigarette, climbed out of the car, and turned the starting-handle.

There was the sound of small feet on the cobbles. Alix spun round. Daisy scrambled into the seat beside her. 'Not going with Ella. Ella's horrid.'

'Daisy, where's Charlie?'

Daisy, her thumb in her mouth, mumbled, 'With Mama,' and curled up next to her sister. Back in the driver's seat, Robert pressed the accelerator, and the engine roared. Rain battered the cobbles; many of the passers-by had begun to run to escape the downpour. Kneeling up, Alix peered through the darkness and the rain. Her fingers touched the door handle. She could not, among the milling crowds, see Charlie. And the Lanchburys' Daimler was already driving fast out of the village, forcing its way through the throng, its rear window a black, opaque mask.

Robert, too, began to head out of the village. Raindrops pounded against the roof of the car, and May sobbed noisily. Without Charlie, Alix's arms felt empty. Daisy had slid into the footwell and was already asleep. Alix's eyes, too, had become heavy. When she closed them, random scenes from the day fluttered behind her lids. The drive through the sunsoaked countryside. Charlie, brandishing his toy sword in the wood. The monkey, with its lost, sad eyes.

May's tears had died away, replaced by slow, hiccupping breaths. Though Alix would have liked, like Daisy and May, to sleep, she did not seem able to. Though she ached with exhaustion, disjointed images continued to flicker through her mind. Whenever she began to drift off to sleep, something – the cry of a bird, the alteration in pitch of the engine as Robert changed gear – woke her. When the motor-car drew to a halt, she opened her eyes, expecting to see the lit windows of the Boncourts' chateau. But instead, through the curtain of rain, she caught sight of a railway-engine, wheels and pistons churning, a long line of carriages tagged behind it, heading along the track that crossed the road ahead of them.

Robert spoke. Alix blinked, shaking her head.

'*Soldats*,' he repeated. 'Soldiers.' He gestured to the carriages. Through the endless passing windows, she glimpsed the bright reds and blues of the French uniforms.

'Soon, I am a soldier,' said Robert proudly. 'I shall fight for my country. No more driving. No more cleaning stables.' He threw back his head and laughed.

The train continued on its way, a long black and yellow serpent heading north. Alix could not see the Daimler. The road was empty.

At last, she fell into a deep, dreamless sleep. Parking in the forecourt of the Boncourts' chateau, Robert had to shake her shoulder to wake her. Sleep sucked at her, trying to claw her back. She glimpsed Charlie's toy sword, abandoned in the footwell of the car, and picked it up. She saw the Daimler, parked on the gravel. May and Daisy, stumbling with exhaustion, trailed beside her into the chateau. Alix ran upstairs, sword in hand. The nursery was dark, the nightlight unlit. She sensed as soon as she stepped into the room that it was empty, yet still she glanced inside the cot, and saw the plumped-up pillow, the turned-back sheet, and the nightshirt, neatly folded.

For the remainder of the night, for the remainder of her life, the conversation with Aunt Marie echoed inside her head.

Where's Charlie? I wanted to kiss him good night.

Charlie? Charlie was with you.

No, Aunt Marie. Charlie went . . . and then the first glimmering of dreadful possibility, and the scratchy sound of her own voice repeating, *Charlie went with you. Charlie went with you.*

They were in the drawing-room. Aunt Marie had taken off her hat and veil. The gilt mirror reflected the dawning fear in her eyes.

'*Ella* was with us.' Marie Lanchbury pressed a bell. Her hand shook. 'Only Ella. You are mistaken, surely, Alix.'

When Louise came into the room, Aunt Marie spoke to her. Louise shook her head. 'I was going to bath the girls, madame.'

'No, Louise. You must bring them downstairs immediately. And you must fetch Mr Lanchbury.' Marie Lanchbury's small, tapering fingers clasped and unclasped the pearl brooch she wore at her throat. 'In the village . . . the village with the fair . . .'

The room filled with people. The three girls, Uncle Charles, the Boncourts. No Charlie. In the blink of an eye, the turn of a head, Alix knew that she must see him, clutching May's hand, or peering out from behind Grand-père Boncourt's legs.

Their voices echoed, staccato and disbelieving.

'Left behind?'

'The village . . .'

'What nonsense. How can he have been left behind?'

'Where's Charlie? I want Charlie!'

'Such a cry-baby, Daisy . . .'

'He was in the other motor—'

'No, Charles, no!' Marie Lanchbury's voice rose in a shriek. 'He was *not* in the other motor! That's what I am trying to tell you!'

A silence. Then, '*Bon Dieu.*' Mme Boncourt sat down heavily.

'He's not in the house?'

A whisper. 'I believe not, Charles.'

'Who saw him last?'

'In the village . . . He liked the bonfire . . .'

'Bonfire?'

'There was a fair, *Maman*. It was very crowded . . . dreadful people . . .' Marie Lanchbury's voice jerked and shook. 'Gypsies, Charles. There were gypsies!' Her twitching fingers returned to the brooch, ripping it from the fabric. 'Gypsies steal children, don't they!' She broke off, staring at her husband. 'Charles – Charles – you must go back – you must look for him . . .' Her words became incoherent, choked with dry sobs.

'Charlie was with Alix,' said Ella. 'She took him to see the monkeys.'

Where's Charlie? Charlie was with you. Their faces turned to her, and their eyes focused on her, as they waited for her to speak. The room was silent except for Aunt Marie's rasping, spasmodic breathing.

Memories entangled. Gripped by a rising panic, Alix could not recall their order. A plump finger stroking a monkey's wizened hand. A paper cone, and sugar round Charlie's mouth. Before the monkeys? After? She muttered, struggling to clear her thoughts, 'I was drawing . . . I sat down on the steps . . .'

'*Drawing*!' Uncle Charles took a pace towards her. 'You were *drawing* . . .'

'But Charlie . . . *where* . . . ? Tell us, Alix!'

'I couldn't see anyone. I got lost. Ella found me.' She spoke in short, sharp, frightened gasps. 'We went back to the motor-car.' She screwed up her eyes. She *must* remember. Had she seen Charlie in the crowds, hurrying back through the rain? Had she glimpsed him, a flash of blue and white and copper curls, among the people milling round the cars?

She pressed her clenched fists against her forehead. 'Ella and May were arguing. Ella went in Uncle Charles's motor-car. I told May to get into Monsieur Boncourt's car.' Suddenly, she looked up at them. 'Daisy came – yes, that's it, Daisy told me that Charlie was in Uncle Charles's car.'

'Daisy?' Mr Lanchbury glared at his youngest daughter. His voice was harsh. 'Daisy? Is that true? Did you tell Alix such a thing? Did you tell her that Charlie was in the Daimler with us?'

Daisy's thumb was in her mouth. Her eyes were dark and frightened, her hair a tangle of silver. She shook her head.

There was a peculiar sound. A low, unnerving moaning. Aunt Marie's eyes were wide and staring as she rocked to and fro. Her fingers clawed at her hair, pulling tortured clumps from her neat coiffure.

Alix flinched as Uncle Charles turned towards her. No-one had ever before in her entire life looked at her like that. Such cold loathing.

'You can't even admit your carelessness, can you? You try to pass the blame to your little cousin. You promised to look after Charlie. Don't you remember? *You* promised to look after him.' Charles Lanchbury addressed his wife. 'I shall go back to the village immediately. Charlie must still be there. Don't worry, Marie – I shall find him.'

Alix knelt on the window seat, pressing her face against the pane. During the uncountable moments of waiting the house had fallen silent. She leaned against the glass, unmoving. Her hair had fallen over her face, but she did not flick it back. She knew that Charlie would be found. Why should he not be found? Someone in that great crowd of people would have noticed a small child, lost and alone. Someone would have taken care of him. She felt calm; there was just a peculiar ache beneath her ribs. When Charlie came home it would go.

She flickered between sleeping and waking. She saw a little boy, stumbling through woodland. His face was stained with tears, and his clothes were muddy and torn. Branches reached out to him, and the high canopy of leaves knotted overhead, excluding the sky. Naked roots tripped his small feet. Dark pools, slippery-edged, lay beside the path.

If Charlie is found, God, I'll never be naughty again. I'll never draw silly pictures, and I'll always be obedient. I'll go to church every Sunday. If Mother says I can't go to art school, then I won't fuss. I'll stay here quite still until Charlie is found. I shan't move at all. I shan't sleep. If I don't move, then he'll be all right. *Gentle Jesus meek and mild, look upon a little child . . .* Her fingertips pressed against the glass. Every beat of her heart said his name.

She heard the sound of car wheels on gravel, and saw the motor-car, a blaze of light, drive into the forecourt.

A word echoed through her head: *please, please, please, please* . . .

Everything seemed to be happening very slowly. Uncle Charles was climbing out of the Daimler. There was no child in his arms. Uncle Charles had driven, Alix told herself, so Charlie must be with Robert. But Robert's arms were empty too. So Charlie was asleep in the back of the car. *Please please please.* The two men walked into the house.

Alix slid off the window seat. Her legs felt stiff, and her heart made its alarming drumming noise. She walked slowly down the wide, curving stairs, holding the banister.

Uncle Charles's voice. 'Nothing, I'm afraid. Not a sign.'

Grand-père Boncourt cursed.

'I've spoken to the *gendarmes*. I'll go back at dawn – scour the countryside . . . it's so dark now . . . We *must* find him, Felix. I thought it best to—' Uncle Charles, looking at the stairs, broke off.

Alix walked down to him. She touched his sleeve. 'Let me come with you, Uncle Charles. Please let me come.' The cloth of Uncle Charles's jacket was rough beneath her fingers, and there was a strange feeling in her head, as though the bones of her skull were pressing too close together. 'I know Charlie . . . I know the sorts of places he might go . . . He may have gone into the woods . . . did you look there? He may be hiding . . . he likes to hide. Take me with you. Please.'

Charles Lanchbury's mouth twisted into a grimace. When he turned round, Alix's hand fell away from his sleeve. Afraid that he might hit her, she took a step back. But instead, stooping beside her, he spoke.

'You promised to take care of him. We should never

28

have entrusted our son to someone like you. Never.' His warm breath caressed her face.

Alone in the empty nursery Alix moved among Charlie's belongings, the tips of her fingers lingering on the cheek of a rag doll, on a toy engine's carved funnel. She glimpsed in the unshuttered window her own reflection: her crumpled dress, her blotched face, her wild hair. *You promised to take care of him.* In a corner of the room she curled herself into a ball, her forehead pressed against her knees, her arms folded over her head. Her grief, her guilt, suffocated her. When she closed her eyes, in the moment before she gave herself up to the darkness, she saw a small child running through a forest, his bright red-gold curls like small, dancing flames, dimming as the woodland closed round him.

PART TWO

DANCING IN THE DESERT

1918–1925

CHAPTER TWO

Their footsteps sounded unnaturally loud on the polished wooden stairs. Neither Derry nor his father spoke as they followed the blue-uniformed nurse. The silence of the place made Derry want to tell raucous, distasteful jokes, or to run through the dimly lit corridors, shouting. Churches always had a similar effect on him. The odour of disinfectant that permeated this building reminded him of the scent of incense.

As if she had read his mind, the sister looked back and said disapprovingly, 'It's the patients' rest hour. You wouldn't normally have been allowed to see Lieutenant Fox at this time of day, but as you have travelled some distance . . .'

At the end of the corridor, she opened a door. Derry caught a blurred glimpse of a man lying in bed, a dark-haired nurse standing beside him. He imagined weeping abscesses, blackened extremities, and his stomach lurched. He heard the sister say: 'Why are you here, Gregory? And why are the blinds up? The patient is supposed to be resting.' With a whirr a blind was flicked down and the room darkened.

'My fault, sister,' said Jonathan placatingly. 'My

wretched leg was giving me gyp, so I asked Nurse Gregory if she could do anything.'

'*Miss* Gregory, Mr Fox,' corrected the sister, but her voice had softened slightly. 'Very well.' She said to the younger nurse, 'When you have finished here you may clean the sluice room.'

'Yes, Sister Martin.'

'Half an hour, gentlemen, and then the patient must rest.' Sister Martin left the room.

Derry shut the door behind her. Miss Gregory pulled up the blind and the pale winter light washed back into the room.

Jonathan said, 'Her bark's worse than her bite,' and Derry thought he detected a sceptical raising of Miss Gregory's eyebrows. She had interesting eyes, a dark, censorious green.

'How terrific to see you both,' said Jonathan. 'Father . . . Derry . . .'

'How are you, old man?'

'I'm very well, Dad.'

Mr Fox touched his elder son's shoulder. 'How's the leg?'

'Much better. Better every day.'

'I brought you some grapes. They're from Mrs Winstanley's hothouse. Most generous of her . . .'

Derry made himself look properly at Jonathan. The wavy golden hair, the tanned face and smiling blue eyes (Jonathan, of course, would manage to smile when his leg had almost been blown off) were all unchanged. The blankets were folded back: Derry forced himself to look at his brother's wounded leg. It would be bearable, he told himself, if he viewed it with scientific curiosity. The green-eyed nurse had gone back to her work.

He asked, 'Have they got all the bits of shrapnel out?

What if some of it ends up stuck in the middle? Do they just leave it there, or do they cut—'

'*Derry*,' hissed his father.

'The doctors always try to remove all the debris. Or the wound may become infected.' Miss Gregory's voice was low and scornful.

'I was unconscious when they did most of it,' said Jonathan. 'Out like a light. Lost a day and a half.' He frowned. 'Odd to know that it's all over. I keep thinking I'll have to go back. Every morning, when I wake up, I have to remind myself that it's over.'

'You did your bit.' Cautiously, Nicholas Fox patted his elder son's shoulder. 'I'm proud that one of my sons was able to do their bit. Your king and country are proud of you, too, Jonathan.'

Derry went to the window and, leaning against the sill, looked out. Fallowfield nursing home had, before the carnage of 1916, been someone's palatial country home. Velvety green lawns, now patched with ploughed squares growing rows of vegetables, extended as far as the open countryside of the South Downs. Beneath dank and dripping trees small groups of soldiers gathered, some in bath chairs, others on crutches. This entire great house, he thought, was populated by men who had done their bit.

The green-eyed nurse tucked the blankets neatly around her patient. 'Does that feel any better, Mr Fox?'

'Infinitely better. You are an angel.'

Miss Gregory's features softened. Then she left the room.

Derry let out a breath. 'Are they all like that? Harpies, I mean?'

'She's very sweet. Her—'

'"Her bark's worse than her bite,"' repeated Derry.

'If you'd been born in a different age, Jon, you'd no doubt have said the same of Lucrezia Borgia . . . or Bloody Mary . . . or . . .'

Jonathan smiled. Nicholas Fox said sharply, 'Do be quiet, Derry, if you have nothing sensible to say.' He pulled a chair over to Jonathan's bedside. 'Tell me about France, old chap. Tell me everything.'

'I'm a bit tired, actually, Father. I'd love you to talk to me. Where's Mother? Couldn't she come?'

'Your mother hasn't been too well, I'm afraid.'

Jonathan looked anxious. Mr Fox hastened to reassure him. 'The doctors don't think it's too serious. A return of the trouble she had last year. But she sends her love.'

'And you must send her mine.' Jonathan lay back on the pillows. Beneath the tan, his face was pale and strained. 'Tell me about home, Father. How's business?'

'I keep busy. Campkins still appropriates many of the more profitable cases, I'm afraid.'

Campkins was a rival firm of solicitors. Jonathan made suitable noises.

'I have always believed that they have undue influence,' added Mr Fox. 'Reginald Campkin's elder brother was Sir Lionel Fripp's land agent. Though, with Ronald gone, Reginald may find it hard to take on as much work as us. We may hope for a more equitable balance, perhaps.'

'Ronald Campkin died at the battle of the Lys,' explained Derry.

'Three daughters . . .'

'Might give you the edge, Dad.'

'When you are well, Jonathan . . .'

'Poor old Ronnie . . . never too bright, but . . .'

'The business could do with a younger man.'

'. . . dashed convenient of him to have stuck his head in front of that sniper.'

There was a short, shocked silence. Then, '*Derry!*' cried Mr Fox.

'I could do with some fresh drinking water,' said Jonathan quickly.

'Why will you' – Nicholas Fox's face was purple – 'why will you persist in deliberately misinterpreting me?'

'I only meant,' said Derry innocently, 'to point out that if one gloats over Mr Campkin's lack of business prospects, one must necessarily also appreciate the efforts of the German sniper who finished off his son.'

Nicholas Fox rose to his feet. Jonathan gestured to the flask on his bedside table. 'Do you think . . . ?'

Derry tucked the flask under his arm and left the room. He was at the end of a long corridor. Some of the doors leading off the corridor were open, and some were shut. As he walked, he tried not to glance through the open doorways. Yet his gaze seemed dragged to them, and besides, whatever he saw was unlikely to be worse than the horrors that he imagined. Hearing moaning, he walked faster.

The place was a maze of narrow passageways and twisting flights of stairs, and he soon realized that he was lost. White-capped nurses scurried by, looking stern and purposeful. A fur-coated woman was pushing a patient in a bath chair: her son, presumably. The man's legs were covered with a blanket – no, *leg*, Derry corrected himself; the blanket dipped horribly where the second leg should have been. He flattened himself against the wall, allowing room for the bath chair to pass, and then went on, searching for a bathroom, a kitchen, anything with a sink and a tap. He found himself longing for fresh air; glancing out of a window he imagined walking across that frost-tipped lawn and filling the flask from the fishpond. Then, hearing running water, he peered round a door. Not another sickroom, thank God. Some sort of washroom.

He opened the door fully, and saw Miss Gregory standing beside a large sink.

'I wasn't sure what a sluice was . . .' Derry saw a towering column of chamber pots. 'But I guessed it was probably something unpleasant.'

Her snapping green eyes focused on him. 'Can I help you, Mr . . . ?'

'Fox,' he reminded her. 'Derry Fox.'

'Yes.' She frowned. 'No. 17's brother.'

'Is that how you think of them? As numbers?'

She turned her back to him, and plunged her hands into the soapy water. 'That way,' she said, 'when they die, I don't mind so much.'

He looked at her. She was of average height but rather thin, with sharp, bony shoulders, and red hands and wrists – from the hot water, he supposed. Her thick, wavy dark hair was tucked under an un-flattering cap.

He asked curiously, 'Why are you Miss Gregory and not Nurse Gregory?'

A newly washed chamber pot thumped onto the draining board. 'Because I'm a probationer, not a trained nurse.'

'Is that why you get this sort of job?'

'My, what a lot of questions, Mr Fox.' Her sleeves were rolled up, and he saw the muscles stand out in her skinny arms as she scrubbed at the china with a brush. 'But, yes, that's why I get this sort of job.'

'Why don't you train to be a nurse, then?'

'Because I'm not old enough.'

'Ah,' he said. 'Another one.'

She paused for a moment, drying her hands on her apron, and then she turned and looked at him. 'What do you mean, "another one"?'

He shrugged. 'Like me. Too young for it.' He took a packet of cigarettes from his pocket and offered it to her. She glanced at the door, and then nodded. He lit two cigarettes, handing one to her, and explained, 'I was eighteen in May. Call-up's eighteen and a half – November. A month ago, just as the war ended. I think that our generation – yours and mine – is always going to be insignificant. A sort of just missed generation. You know, not quite witnessing events of world-shattering importance.'

She inhaled her cigarette and said, 'So?'

'So we'll probably never know quite what to do with our lives, and we'll probably never come to anything much.'

'Does it matter?'

'It does,' he said mildly, 'to me.'

There was a silence. He felt that she was assessing him. Then she said, 'Did you want to be a soldier?'

'It's not that. I should have been very bad at it, I expect, and they might not have taken me anyhow because I had pneumonia as a child. And besides, it would have meant following in big brother's footsteps, and I think I've had just about enough of *that*.'

'Don't you like your brother?'

'Of course I do. He's kind and honourable and brave and generally everything a man should be.'

She stubbed out her cigarette in a saucer, and turned back to the sink. 'You make that sound like a disease.'

'Not at all.'

She held out her hand. 'Give me the flask.'

He watched her carefully fill it with water. Handing it back to him, she said, 'You should be proud of your brother, Mr Fox. He's in pain all the time – did he tell you that? He never complains, and he never loses his temper. You should be proud of him.'

At dusk, walking around the grounds of the nursing home, Alix remembered what Derry Fox had said to her. *We'll probably never know quite what to do with our lives, and we'll probably never come to anything much.* And she had said, and meant, *Does it matter?* and he, with a blink of night-dark eyes, had replied, *It does to me.* When he had left the room, she had reflected that these days she thought little about anything other than her aching back and her sore feet, and the impossibility of getting through her work in the allotted time, and the importance of avoiding Sister Martin.

A twig snapped behind her, and she looked round. She smiled.

'Captain North.'

'Miss Gregory.'

Captain North had been a patient at the nursing home for almost two months. He was tall and thin, with gentle eyes and brown hair that had begun to grey at the temples.

He glanced at the book Alix held in her hand. 'Were you sketching? I won't interrupt you.'

She shook her head. 'I thought I might, but the light's not good enough.'

'What are you drawing? Those hideous rhododendrons?'

They were standing at the edge of the shrubbery. She smiled. 'They're not very picturesque, are they?'

'I suppose they'll look splendid in the spring, when they're in flower.'

'I don't think that either of us will be here in the spring, will we, Captain North?'

'I suppose not.' He looked at her. 'What will you do?'

'I've no idea. I've really no idea.' *We'll probably never know quite what to do with our lives.* Derry Fox's words remained with her, unsettling her.

'You look cold, Miss Gregory,' he said. 'Shall we walk?'

She strolled beside him through the trees. Sister Martin, if she saw them, would be disapproving. Fraternizing with the patients, Miss Gregory. She could make a country walk sound akin to prostitution. Sister Martin's opinion, Alix reminded herself, might not matter much longer.

They headed up the slope through the woods. Alix slowed her habitual quick footsteps so that Captain North would not become tired. When they emerged from the trees and stood on the ridge, she saw the wide sweep of the South Downs, and beyond the sea, the first stars dappling its waters.

'I never know,' he said thoughtfully, 'which view I prefer. The woodland, or the water.'

'Oh, the sea,' she said. 'The sea. I hate the woods. So dark and dreary.'

He looked down at her. He had a kind, patrician, intelligent face. Shrapnel scars pitted one side of his jaw.

'Now that, Miss Gregory, is the first time I have ever heard you express any strong opinion about anything.'

She did not reply. After a while he said, 'I beg your pardon. I didn't mean to offend you.' Another short silence. 'Would you let me see your sketchbook? I used to draw myself, you see, but this wretched arm . . .'

The right sleeve of his jacket was pinned emptily across his breast. Alix felt ashamed of her moodiness. She offered the book to him. 'Of course. But they're not very good, I warn you.'

He turned the pages. There was just enough light left to see. Some sketches were pencil, some pen and ink.

'These are quite splendid. The summer house . . . you've caught the shading of the statuary very well. And this tumbledown cottage.' He paused. 'Who taught you perspective?'

'My father,' she said. 'He taught me everything.'

'He must be a very talented artist.'

'He *was*,' she corrected him. 'He died six months ago.'

'I'm sorry.' He glanced at her. 'You must miss him a great deal.'

'I don't really have time to miss him,' she said, and, reclaiming her sketchbook, began to walk again. 'I'm always busy.'

'One makes oneself busy, doesn't one?' Captain North had quickened his pace to draw level with her. Below them, the full moon was perfectly mirrored in a circular dew pond. 'I lost my father in 1914, and my elder brother last year. Since then, even when I've been on leave, I've tried not to let myself have time to think.'

She heard his breath rattle wheezily in his chest as he struggled to match his pace to hers. She stopped, one hand on his remaining arm to steady him.

After a while he said, 'That's the trouble with this place. Far too much time to think.'

Beneath her palm, she felt him trembling. 'We should go back to the nursing home, Mr North,' Alix said gently. 'It's late, and Sister Martin will have my guts for garters.'

*　　*　　*

That night, she dreamed of him again. She was dressing him: the velvet tunic with the lace collar, and the matching velvet knickers. Six tiny buttons on his boots. When she knelt down to push the buttons through the eyelets, the leather seemed to melt through her fingers. She reached out to him, but he retreated, just as he always did, dissolving into the shadows until he was no more than a red-gold curl, and a flicker of silver sword . . .

She sat up, clawing for breath. Her room-mate groaned irritably, 'Oh, for God's sake, Gregory, put a sock in it, won't you?' and turned onto her side, pulling the blankets over her head.

When her panic had subsided, Alix climbed out of bed. She knelt at the window, pulling back the curtain, resting her forehead against the cool glass. She rubbed at her lids with her fingertips, but they were dry. She didn't cry for Charlie. She hadn't cried since 1914.

Since she had begun to work in the nursing home, Alix had realized that back then she had had some sort of breakdown. She recalled the same symptoms in her fourteen-year-old self as she now saw in the shell-shocked soldiers at Fallowfield. Nightmares of a particularly unpleasant kind, that insinuated themselves into one's waking hours. The patients saw dismembered corpses and fallen comrades, all the horrors of the trenches in the green lawns and quiet gardens of the nursing home. Alix herself had, four years ago, glimpsed little Charlie Lanchbury everywhere. Shadow children had hidden behind the trees in the garden, and had flitted through the crowds in the market place. In the park, she had seen him, over and over again: a flicker of sunshine through the trees, the gentle rhythmic movement of a swing. Yet whenever she had reached out to him he had dissolved, shimmering into invisibility.

Except for those visions, she could remember little of the months that had followed her return to England. She had survived because she had learned to shut away her memories of that summer behind a closed door in her mind. Her parents had colluded in her forgetting. Her father had forced her to accompany him on long, exhausting walks; he had insisted she learn the name of every flower, tree, and bird, and with gentle but stern discipline he had made her draw every view, every building. She had realized after a while that he was trying to put other memories into her head, to fill the void that Charlie had left. Her mother had only once referred to the summer's dreadful events. 'You mustn't reproach yourself, Alix. You were too young for so much responsibility. We'll put it behind us. We won't speak of it again.' And they had not. The name of Charlie Lanchbury was not mentioned in the Gregory household. But Alix had wept bitter tears over her mother's words, understanding that she, like Charles Lanchbury, thought her to blame.

Other scars remained. She was warier now, less trusting. Least of all was she able to trust herself. She was content to clean her chamber pots and scrub her floors because you couldn't make mistakes at that. Half the money she earned she sent home to her mother. The Lanchburys and the Gregorys had neither spoken to nor seen each other since 1914. Charles Lanchbury blamed his sister's daughter for the loss of his only son, and in consequence he had neither attended Aylwyn Gregory's funeral nor lifted a finger to help his impoverished widowed sister. The chain of blame and loss was forged ever lengthier: Beatrice Gregory now survived on the pittance she earned by taking in dressmaking, and on whatever Alix could spare from her wages.

Now, she saw Charlie only in her dreams. Looking out of the window to the darkened lawn below, Alix made herself look back, filling in the gaps. She remembered little of the journey home from France to England, only the horror in Aunt Marie's eyes, and the bewilderment in the little girls'. Aunt Marie had not spoken throughout the entire journey. The loss of her son had broken her, reducing her to frozen, faltering helplessness, so that without her maid's assistance she could not have alighted from the train at Calais, but would have remained in the corner of the carriage, motionless, staring into her own inner darkness.

Uncle Charles had sent his family home because France was about to declare war on Germany. He himself had remained in France to search for Charlie, enlisting, he had explained as he said goodbye to his mute wife, the help of both the *gendarmerie* and the local population. But within a few weeks the Boncourts' chateau, the woods in which they had picnicked, and the village with the fair, had been trampled and broken by the Kaiser's invading army. Uncle Charles had returned to England without his only son. Hope had died then, and Alix had lain in her bed, curled in a ball, not speaking, not eating.

In the course of the last four years the Great War had blasted to mud and shell-holes the golden fields of northern France. Country folk had been forced to leave their farms and villages as warring armies had crisscrossed the plains of Flanders and Picardy. If there had remained any trace of Charlie – a scrap of lace caught on a branch, perhaps, or a six-buttoned boot abandoned in a ditch – then war would have long since erased any such clue.

Alix glanced at her watch. Five minutes past four. Less than an hour before the rising bell. She crept back into bed, pulled the blankets over her head, and sank immediately into a dreamless sleep.

After breakfast, Sister Turner took her aside.

'Special duty for you today, Gregory. No. 17 had a bad night – doctor's worried about him, thinks someone should sit with him.'

'Now, sister?'

'Now, Gregory. Run along then.'

'What's wrong with him?'

Sister Turner's plain, kind face creased into a frown. Jonathan Fox was everyone's favourite.

'They're afraid the leg is infected. He may lose it, you see.' She turned to go.

The blinds were drawn in room No. 17. Alix rolled them up six inches, enough to see clearly the patient lying in the bed. Jonathan Fox was awake, his eyes glittering feverishly, his face pale beneath the red stains along his cheekbones. Alix wrung out a cold flannel and placed it on his forehead, and said gently: 'Well, Mr Fox, so you're causing us all trouble again.'

He focused on her. 'Don't scold me, please, Miss Gregory. I've been scolded enough.' His voice was a hoarse whisper.

'I'm afraid you're to be punished. I'm to sit with you today.'

His mouth curled into a smile. 'What a delightful punishment.'

She perched on a stool beside his bed, and pressed the cool flannel against his hot face. He said after a while,

'Talk to me, won't you? I know it's a bore, and that I must be pretty dull company lying about like this, but I would like you to talk to me.'

'Don't you want to sleep?'

'Can't, I'm afraid. My head's full of such nonsense. Keeps me awake.'

'I expect you're a bit delirious, Mr Fox.' Alix racked her brain for something to talk about, and then she began to describe to him the meadows and woods that surrounded her Suffolk home, so that he could walk in his mind's eye with her through cool, leafy copses, and hear the rattle of the mistle thrush, and scent the rain on the damp beech leaves.

After a while he slept, and she fell silent, watching him. His long, dark gold lashes cast spiky shadows against his hollow cheeks. His hair curled in wet tendrils against his sculptured cheekbones. She wanted to stroke the damp locks back from his forehead, but she was afraid of waking him. She wondered how old he was . . . twenty . . . twenty-two, perhaps? No more, she thought.

After an hour or so he opened his eyes. 'Still here, Miss Gregory?'

'I'm afraid so. I told you, Mr Fox, you're to endure my company for an entire day.' She fetched a cup and straw from the bedside table.

'Jonathan,' he said, as she helped him sit up. 'Please call me Jonathan.'

'Then you're to call me Alix.' She put the straw to his mouth. 'Though if you use my Christian name in Sister Martin's presence, she'll probably dismiss me on the spot.'

After he had drunk, she read to him. She thought he looked a little better; he even ate a few mouthfuls of lunch. But as the afternoon wore on, he began to shift on the pillow, unable to find a comfortable position. When the nurse came to dress his leg, Alix noticed that his wound was red and inflamed.

When they were alone again, Jonathan said, 'You're frowning, Alix.'

'I was thinking about my mother's birthday,' she lied. 'I can't think what to give her.'

'Mothers are tricky, aren't they? I never seem to get it quite right. I gave my mother a terrarium – have you seen them? Dashed peculiar things, like little glasshouses, with half a dozen plants in 'em. But it made her asthma worse. Had to give it to the maid.' Jonathan's fingers plucked restlessly at the sheet. 'Tell me about your family, Alix.'

'There's just me and my mother,' she said, and smiled. 'It was nice to meet your father and a brother yesterday, Jonathan.'

'It was good of them to come,' he said. 'Quite a long haul.'

'Where do they live?'

'Andover.' Jonathan attempted to smile. 'I'm glad I wasn't sharing a railway carriage with Father and Derry on the way home.'

Alix recalled the friction she had sensed between father and younger son. 'Don't they get on?'

'They just rub each other up the wrong way. Some people are like that, aren't they? They don't mean anything. Derry's great fun once you get to know him. He just likes to fool about sometimes.' Jonathan looked fretful. 'I wish Mother had been able to visit. She's not well, Father said.'

Alix glanced at him sharply. She wondered whether Jonathan's anxiety about his mother had contributed to his relapse. She tried to reassure him. 'You mustn't worry about your mother, Jonathan. You must concentrate on getting well yourself.'

'She's always been delicate. We try not to disturb her, but it must be awful for her when we're all at home – three clumping great men, making a lot of noise and bother.'

'I'm sure your mother doesn't find you any bother at all.'

'I'm supposed to take after her.' Jonathan tried to sit up, reaching a shaking hand towards the bedside table.

'Let me.' Alix opened the drawer.

'The wallet . . . there's a photograph . . .'

She handed him his wallet, and he took out a small snapshot. 'Look, she's beautiful, isn't she?'

Alix looked down at the photograph. She thought that although Mrs Fox was indeed beautiful – fair hair, like her elder son's, piled on top of her head, and well-shaped, light eyes – there was a petulant droop about her mouth that marred her appearance.

'She's lovely.' Alix propped the photograph against the lampstand so that Jonathan could see it from the bed. 'You and your brother aren't at all alike, are you?'

'Dad's father was Italian . . . I suppose that's why Derry's dark. Dad changed his name, of course . . . he's a solicitor, you see, so it's better to be plain and English. Gives people confidence.' Jonathan's words were fast and indistinct. 'I'm supposed to join the family firm when I'm better . . . Derry, too, though I can't quite see it. Too dull for Derry, family solicitor in an English country town. Not sure he'd stick at it. Wants to make his name, you see. Me, I don't care for that sort of thing any more. At school . . . at school it was fun being head of house and captain of cricket and all that rot,

49

but now I don't seem to give a damn.' He glanced quickly at her. 'Sorry. My language . . .'

Alix took his hand in hers, stroking it, hushing him. After a while, he whispered, 'You won't let them take my leg off, will you?' and she looked at him, her heart pounding, hoping that she had misheard him.

But he said again, 'I couldn't bear it . . . hobbling around like a cripple. You won't let them take my leg off, will you, Alix?'

She found herself shaking her head, giving him the reassurance he craved, which was not hers to give. Eventually his eyes closed, and she sat watching him for a long time, not daring to move, certain that if she shifted as much as a muscle she would wake him.

Captain North said, 'I saw you from the window, Miss Gregory. I was looking for you. Can you spare me a moment?'

Alix was sitting outside the nursing home, perched on the edge of the terrace, her cloak wrapped around her as she watched the rain drip from the branches of the yews. She had gone off duty half an hour previously, and had needed some fresh air.

They walked to the summer house. The small wooden building was circular, beamed with rustic, bark-covered branches. Cobwebs slung their grey trapezes between the rafters. Sleepy spiders, undisturbed for years, took days to traverse the conical ceiling.

'So cold . . .' she said, clutching her elbows.

'I'll light a fire. Here, take my coat.' As he shrugged off his greatcoat, Captain North took a notebook from his pocket. 'I thought you might like a look at this. It seems only fair after you let me see your sketch-book.' He draped the coat around her shoulders, and then stooped in front of the stove.

Huddled on a bench, Alix turned the pages of the book. Images flashed before her eyes: a string of beads of pale shell, a vase ornamented with chevrons and waves, an eagle grasping a stag. She was transported from the cold, musty summer house to a different world. Here was a great stone building, pyramidal in shape, steps rising endlessly to its pointed apex, and there columns soared from rocky outcrops, and statues gazed proudly from ancient walls. She turned another page, and then snapped the book shut.

He glanced back at her. 'I say. They're not that bad, are they?'

She smiled. 'They're marvellous.'

'A bad day?'

'I had to special Mr Fox.'

'That young chap – the yellow-haired chap? Didn't he make it?'

'They are afraid he may lose his leg. And when I looked at these . . . and saw how beautifully you draw . . . I realized how awful it must be for you.'

He put more sticks into the stove, and the flames roared. 'What I mind,' he said, 'is not being useful any more.' He stood up, dusting his hand against his great-coat. 'I'm an archaeologist, you see. I mean – I *was* an archaeologist.'

'You found these things? The beads . . . the eagle . . . ?'

'The shell beads and the relief are from a site in Mesopotamia where I worked just before the war. We called it the Eagle's Nest, after the copper eagle. We'd been digging for months and finding nothing and then we began to make these marvellous discoveries. But the season ended, and then, of course, war broke out.'

'Will you go back?'

'Someone will. Not me. What would be the point?' He touched the empty sleeve of his greatcoat. 'My patron's trying to persuade me to set up another expedition next year, but I've refused him. I will not be a burden. I will not be a dead weight.'

Leaning against the window sill, Captain North took out his cigarettes and lighter. Alix, watching him fumble one-handed with the cigarette case, half rose to help him, but stopped when she caught the look in his eye.

'I can't *dig* any more, can I?' he said. 'And I can't draw. And one needs to be able to draw – cameras are so cumbersome, and besides, they can't capture the detail. Drawing's not a common skill. It's not easily replaced.' He fell silent for a moment. Then he said, 'I'm sorry – how tedious for you, after your tiring day. Smoke?'

He held out his cigarette case to her. Alix shook her head, but picked up the sketchbook again, and opened it at its final page.

'Tell me where this is, Captain North.' She looked down at the picture once more. The house, old and rambling and mysterious, was backed by woods and meadow.

'That?' When he smiled, his whole face lightened. 'Oh, that's Owlscote.'

The Foxes always went to the Winstanleys at New Year. Derry noticed that this year numbers were rather thin on the ground: influenza, or fear of influenza, he guessed. Bubonic plague might, Derry reflected, have kept the Foxes away. Nothing less.

They drank sherry and fruit cup in the drawing-room, and then a gong sounded, calling them to the dinner table. The food was dreadful, but he didn't mind that, he never thought about food much. Boarding school had taught him not to mind lousy food. That first the hors d'oeuvres (unrecognizable things sharing a cocktail stick with a prune), and then the fish course (a fragment of smoked haddock, curling at the edges), were served on a silver salver by a uniformed manservant irritated him far more.

He amused himself by guessing the Christian names of the various guests. The gentleman opposite with a nicotine-stained moustache ('Let me introduce you to Mr Farrell, who has just moved into The Beeches,') was obviously a Horace. And the woman with the black pearls at the far end of the table, who had a faintly exotic air, must be called something foreign. Christina, or Kezia, or Natalia.

After cheese and fruit, the women left the table, and Derry, seeing that otherwise he would become entrapped with his father and Horace and dreadful Mr Winstanley, said loudly, 'Fishbone,' and pointed to his throat, and dashed out of the room. Then he wandered around the house, which was large and overfurnished and damnably cold. At the back of the house was a conservatory. Condensation trailed down the inside of the windows. Derry opened a door and stepped inside.

A wall of damp heat struck him, and he coughed. A bored voice said, 'Close the door, won't you, darling, or this place will be as deathly as the rest of the house.'

He saw the woman with the pearls. Christina or Kezia or Natalia. He shut the door.

The conservatory was vast and fecund. A narrow stone path wound between banks of flowering shrubs and fruit bushes. 'Like Eden,' he said, looking around.

'It reminds me of home.' She was smoking, backed by a mass of cloudy blue flowers. 'Lima.'

'Peru?'

She focused on him.

'Geography's my favourite subject,' he said facetiously.

She exhaled a stream of smoke and held out to him her cigarette case. 'Gasper? Or aren't you old enough?'

'I'm eighteen,' he said, accepting a cigarette.

Her brows rose slightly. With a flick of her lighter she lit his cigarette. He could not guess her age, he was no good at ages. Slightly older than Mother, he estimated from the faint crêpiness about her throat and the small meshes of lines to the corners of her eyes.

'I always imagined South Americans to be dark-eyed,' he said. Hers were speedwell-blue.

'I was born in England. But I married a businessman who worked in Lima, and lived there all my married life.'

'Is your husband dead?' She was wearing black.

'Last May.' She touched the string of black pearls she wore round her neck. 'Rather Gothic, don't you think?'

'Splendidly.' He asked curiously, 'What was he like? Was he interesting? Do you prefer to be a widow, or not?'

Her brows lifted again. 'Such questions. Most people confine themselves to muted expressions of condolence. Still' – and she stubbed out her cigarette in a plant pot – 'since you ask, he was not in the least interesting, he was very dull. But because of him, I've seen interesting things.'

'Places or people?'

'Both. He was absent from home a great deal, so I was able to have an interesting lover. Don't look so shocked, my dear – what's your name, by the way?'

'Derry,' he said. 'Derry Fox.'

She smiled. 'My name's Sara Kessel. I was born Sarah,

54

but that's rather dull, isn't it? I became Sara when I married. It's important to reinvent oneself every now and then, don't you agree?'

'Absolutely,' he said fervently. Though it irked him that recently he hadn't been able to decide what to reinvent himself *into*.

'As for your last question . . .' Her eyes narrowed, chips of blue between darkened lashes. 'In some ways it's better to be a widow than a wife, and in other ways it's worse. One has control of one's own finances at last. I'm not in the habit of giving advice to young men, Derry, but if I were to do so, then I would tell you to become financially independent as soon as possible. Financial independence means freedom, you see. On the other hand' – she began to walk along the stone path; Derry followed her – 'on the other hand, one needs an escort, and people have a habit of taking pity on one and expecting one to appear at appallingly dull social occasions. Such as this evening.'

'It was excruciating,' he agreed. 'My father adores Mrs Winstanley because she's related to landed gentry. But she always makes me think of a teacake.'

'A teacake?' She paused, one hand resting on the trunk of a peach tree.

'You know – yellowish complexion, little dark eyes like currants, little dark mouth.'

'A teacake . . .' she murmured. 'I hadn't thought.'

He was suddenly anxious. 'Mrs Winstanley isn't a bosom friend of yours, is she?'

Mrs Kessel shook her head. 'A bosom friend? No. Not at all.' She glanced up. 'Pick me a peach, won't you, Derry? They're too high up. I can't reach.'

He found a foothold in the peach tree's twisted trunk, and reached up and pulled off a ripe peach. He handed it to her, and she bit into the velvety flesh, and closed her eyes, and said, 'Mmm. Divine.' A small dribble of peach juice trailed down her chin. He watched, fascinated.

'Bite?' she said, and held out the fruit to him.

He bit where she had bitten. 'Like Eden,' she said softly. Then the door opened.

'Sarah? Sarah, are you there?' Through the vegetation, Derry glimpsed Mrs Winstanley.

'Yes, Marion,' called Mrs Kessel. 'Over here. I'm just coming.' Then she whispered to Derry, 'My sister-in-law – Marion Winstanley is my sister-in-law.'

He felt his face go hot. A square of card was pressed into his hand. 'When you are next in Town, and fancy a teacake,' she added, and left the room.

Jonathan Fox caught Alix Gregory as she came out of the sluice.

'I'm leaving today,' he told her. 'Given the all-clear by the quack.'

Her face broke into a smile. 'I'm so pleased, Jonathan.'

'Leg's still a bit stiff, but I'll be A1 in a few months.' He delved into his greatcoat pocket. 'I wanted to give you this.' He took her hand, and pressed the small parcel into it.

'You shouldn't . . .' Her pale skin reddened.

'I know it's against the rules and all that, but I wanted to say thank you. I couldn't have borne hobbling about on a peg-leg. You pulled me through, you know.'

'Nonsense,' she muttered. 'Such nonsense.' But she looked pleased.

He watched her untie the string. He felt a momentary pang of anxiety for her, and he wondered what would happen to her when this place closed down. It was already, in the early February of 1919, half empty.

'Oh, Jonathan, it's lovely!' She cradled the tiny penknife in her palm.

'For sharpening your pencils, you know. Girls never seem to have a decent knife.'

'So sweet of you.'

He heard footsteps coming down the corridor, and said, on a sudden impulse, 'Write to me, won't you, Alix?' He scribbled his address on a piece of paper and thrust it into her hand. 'Please.'

As Jonathan left Fallowfield, the sun and blue sky gave the illusion of spring. As he climbed into the cab, he reflected that his anxiety had not only been for Alix, but for himself also. He had not spent more than a fortnight at a time at home since he had joined up towards the end of 1916. The nursing home had become more familiar to him than the drawing-rooms and gardens of the house in which he had been born. He had, after one and a half years of active service, become unused to family life, to civilian conversation, to women. Especially women. There had been no women at Fallowfield, only dragons or chums. Sister Martin had been a dragon, but Alix Gregory had become a chum.

On the train to London, Jonathan sat back and watched the countryside speed by, and tried not to think of anything. At Victoria, people jostled him, and his leg ached. He caught sight of Derry, standing by the barrier, and waved, and let the crowds carry him along the platform towards his brother.

'Where's Father?'

'Couldn't make it. Something came up at the office.'

Jonathan held out his hand; Derry ignored it and embraced him. 'I'll take your rucksack.'

Jonathan thought that Derry looked awful, worse than him probably. Dark shadows beneath his eyes, and a cough that he tried unsuccessfully to stifle.

'It's all right. I can manage.'

'Shall we lunch in London, or are you impatient to get back to the family bosom?'

'We'll lunch here, I think.' They headed out of the station.

They ate in a café on Vauxhall Bridge Road. Or rather Jonathan ate, and Derry pushed pieces of sausage and potato around his plate. This irked Jonathan after a while, so he said: 'What's wrong? Aren't you well?'

'Oh, I'm fine, fine. Apart from this stupid cough.' He smiled absently. 'People tend to dive for cover as soon as they see me – they're afraid I've got influenza.' He looked at Jonathan. 'I'm trying to make a decision, you see.'

'Tell me.' The waitress cleared their plates away; Jonathan ordered jam roly-poly.

'A friend suggested I call when I was next in Town.'

'Is that all?' Jonathan felt relieved. 'Go ahead. You don't need to hold my hand. I'm perfectly capable of getting home by myself.'

'Oh, I know. Head of house . . . Thingummy Prize for all-round manliness . . . medals. I do understand that a little train journey won't worry you, Jon.'

'Then go and see him.'

'Her.'

Jonathan poured custard over his pudding. 'Anyone I know?'

'Mrs Winstanley's sister-in-law.' Derry tapped at the edge of the table with a small square of card. 'I met her at New Year.'

'Decent of her to invite you.' Jonathan looked at his

younger brother. 'You don't have to go, Derry. I know you find that sort of thing rather . . . dull.'

'I don't think it'll be *dull*, Jon.' He grimaced. 'Just a bit terrifying.'

'Terrifying? Tea and scones and reminiscences?'

'The thing is,' said Derry, 'the thing is, I think that she'll expect me to go to bed with her.'

Jonathan dropped his spoon. The waitress, clearing the adjacent table, paused, straining to listen.

'If someone offers you a bite of a peach and talks about the Garden of Eden, that's what they mean, isn't it?'

Jonathan didn't know what Derry was talking about. He said quietly, 'Derry, I think you've got the wrong end of the stick. For heaven's sake . . . Mrs Winstanley's sister-in-law . . .'

'Sara. Her name's Sara. Rather nice, don't you agree?' Derry's eyelids lowered. 'And it's not that I mind – she was perfectly charming – it's just that I might feel rather out of my depth. I mean, it's one thing with a girl one meets in a pub – one knows the rules, after all – but with someone like that . . . well, it could be rather terrifying, couldn't it?' He clutched his stomach, and added plaintively, 'That's why I can't eat. I can never eat when I'm nervous. I'm afraid I'll be sick.'

Jonathan quickly pushed a glass in front of him. 'Have some water. That'll do the trick.' He sighed. 'Derry, I'm sure that you've got this all wrong. But if you don't want to call on this woman, then don't. It's quite simple.'

Derry sat for a while in silence. One long finger ran round the edge of the visiting card, crushing and fraying the corners. Suddenly he stood up.

'No, I must go. You have to make the most of

opportunities, don't you? If I don't go, then I'll always wonder what might have happened. And I couldn't bear that.'

After her interview with Sister Turner, Alix walked aimlessly through the nursing home. Fallowfield had begun already to acquire an unfamiliarity, the smallest sounds echoing in the vast, empty corridors, wheelchairs and bedsteads heaped gleaming and unused in side rooms.

She was supposed to return immediately to her duties, but she paused at Captain North's room, rapping on his door with her knuckles.

Edward North opened the door. 'Any news?'

'A week's notice.'

'I'm sorry. Come in, Alix.'

As the number of patients at Fallowfield had declined, Alix and Edward North had been thrown increasingly into each other's company.

She shut the door behind her. 'Sister Turner said that they intend to close Fallowfield by the end of the month.'

'I was given my marching orders yesterday.'

'They've found places for some of the nurses in other hospitals, but there's nothing for me. Girls who can scrub chamber pots are two a penny. Sister Turner was quite kind – I explained that I have to earn my living, and she suggested other jobs I could do.'

'What other jobs?'

'I could be a paid companion. I could work for a gentleman who was wounded in the war. Someone who needs someone to look after them – not nursing care, exactly, but to help them wash and dress, that sort of thing.'

'It sounds . . . dreary.'

'It would be *work*,' she said firmly. 'I thought I should start looking at newspaper advertisements.' Alix patted her pocket. 'Sister Turner's written me a reference.'

There was a silence, and then he said, 'Could you meet me at the edge of the woods after lunch, Alix? There's something I'd like to say to you.'

They had fallen into the habit of walking along the Downs together; she sketched a little, he enjoyed the fresh air and the open spaces.

'I'm supposed to be on duty.'

'You already have your reference.'

Alix smiled. 'Yes, I do. Very well, Edward. After lunch.'

When she had finished washing up the last of the pudding bowls, Alix threw her cloak around her shoulders before she ran outside. Hurrying through the damp pine needles that carpeted the wood, she caught sight of Edward North standing on the ridge, silhouetted against the puffy white clouds that darted across the horizon.

Hearing her footsteps, he turned and smiled and held out his hand to her, helping her up the last few feet of the slope.

'Are we walking to the dew pond or to the cliffs?'

'The dew pond, I thought. Too blowy for the cliffs.'

She took his arm. The long grass brushed at her legs, soaking the hem of her grey dress. Eventually he said: 'When we spoke this morning, Alix, about your future, you didn't mention the possibility of marriage.' He glanced at her. 'You're young and pretty. Isn't there anyone?'

'I'm afraid not,' she said lightly. 'Not a lovelorn suitor in sight.'

Gulls soared overhead, shouting raucously as they headed for the coast. 'I've often wondered,' he said, 'did you lose someone in France?'

She stiffened. 'What do you mean, Edward?'

'I don't mean to pry. Only I'd like to know . . . and you sometimes seem unhappy, that's all.' He sighed. 'I've lost people myself so I recognize the symptoms.'

They had reached the dew pond. Staring down at the circular dark waters, she took a deep breath. 'You're right, I did lose someone in France.' She stopped, unable to continue. She would never, ever tell anyone about Charlie. If she told Edward North, then he would look at her as Uncle Charles had done, judging her, utter contempt chilling his eyes.

'You don't have to tell me about it,' he said gently. 'I just needed to know . . . that much.' They began to walk round the circular rim of the pond. 'Most women want marriage and children, you see.'

'Not me,' she said fiercely. 'I shall never want children.'

He frowned. 'Never,' she repeated.

'In that case' – and she saw him rub his forehead with his fingers – 'in that case, I have a proposition to make to you. No . . . a proposal.' He closed his eyes for a moment, and then, opening them, said, 'I wondered whether you would consider marrying *me*.'

Alix heard herself gasp. She had, over the past few months, become fond of Edward North. But as a friend, nothing more. Her heart hammered against her ribs.

She began to speak, but he put up a hand to stop her. 'Please hear me out, Alix. Let me explain. I know I'm not much of a catch.' He grinned wryly. 'One-armed and my lungs shot to pieces by mustard gas. I'm hardly the answer to a maiden's prayer.'

'It's not that—'

'It's best to face up to these things, don't you agree? I'm crippled and I wheeze and I'm thirty-five years old. Whereas you are young and whole and healthy.' His eyes were fragments of granite, and the wind whipped the ends of his scarf against his thin face. 'You must understand that I'm not suggesting a conventional marriage. I'm not such a fool as to think you should want that. I'm proposing a marriage in name only – a marriage of convenience, I suppose.' He looked at her. 'Do you understand me, Alix?'

When she did not reply he said brusquely, 'There would be no children. No possibility of children. I wouldn't expect you to share a bed with me.'

'*Oh.*' She looked away from him, her face hot, staring down to where the dark water licked the grass.

'That's why I needed to know whether you wanted children. This is . . . a business proposition. Lord Maycross has written to me again.'

At last, she managed to speak. 'Lord Maycross?'

'Freddie Maycross is my patron. He financed our last expedition to Mesopotamia.' Edward grimaced. 'I almost wrote back by return of post to remind him that without my right arm I'm useless. But then I thought of you.'

'Me?'

'You could be my right arm, Alix. You could help me.'

She squeaked, 'But I don't know anything about archaeology! I don't even know where Mesopotamia is!'

He smiled. 'You wouldn't have to. I need someone who can draw and write. You can write, and you can draw beautifully. I also need someone whom I can train to handle the most delicate artefacts. You have kind hands, Alix. When I first came here – when I was very ill and in a lot of pain – you were always gentle, you never hurt me.'

'Edward, this is very sweet of you, but I can't—'

'You need to understand what I can offer you. I'm not rich, but I am comfortably off, so you wouldn't have to live hand to mouth as you do now. Nor would you have to waste your life working as someone's skivvy. And Alix, Alix . . .' He smiled. 'If you come with me, I'll show you sights that you'll never, if you remain in this country, see. Wonderful things. All the treasures of ancient civilizations. There's nothing like it.' His eyes gleamed, and she could hear the excitement in his voice. 'The unpeeling of history from the sand – it's like being bitten by a mosquito. Or swallowing a draught of opium. It takes you over, it fills your veins, it haunts your days and your nights.' He looked at her. 'And Owlscote, too. In time, one day, I would take you to Owlscote.'

'Your house?' She remembered the drawing in the notebook.

Edward seized a flat pebble and bounced it across the surface of the pond. The mirror images of clouds and sky broke up, fragmenting into glittering diamonds.

'I haven't been back since my brother died. Can't bear to, somehow. They never found Rory's body, you see. "Missing, presumed dead." Well, I was in the trenches long enough to know what *that* means. Blown to bits, swallowed up by the mud. And I feel . . . I feel *guilty* that I haven't brought him home. I feel ashamed. It was my duty, wasn't it, to bring him home, and I haven't. I've left him there. Alone. Lost.'

Alix said nothing, but saw in her mind's eye the recur-

64

ring image from her dream. A child wandering in a forest. Alone. Lost.

She heard Edward add, 'Owlscote's empty now. I should sell, but I can't face it, and besides, no-one's buying at the moment. So in a while, when I don't mind any more, I could take you there.'

'Edward,' she said again.

But he had begun to head back up the ridge. 'Don't answer me now, I beg you, Alix. Think about it. Tell me tomorrow.'

Derry had been staying with Mrs Kessel in her Belgravia flat for more than a fortnight, and she hadn't so much as touched him. He didn't know whether to feel disappointed or relieved. It was almost – *almost* – like taking a holiday with a splendid and rather exciting aunt. She took him to the theatre and to the ballet and to the cinema – she had a particular fondness for American films. In the wide, straight streets of Knightsbridge, she showed him how to drive her car, a sleek and glittering De Dion Bouton. She taught him to drink cocktails instead of fruit cup; he went with her to parties where barbarous syncopated rhythms blared from gramophones, and couples writhed and embraced in extraordinary and erotic dances. She taught him how to order dinner in the smartest of restaurants, how to choose the correct wine for each course, and how to tell the difference between Virginian and Turkish cigarettes. She liked to sit back and watch him speak to the waiter, or taste the wine. At first these things daunted him, and he could not eat a morsel of the rich, expensive dishes that arrived at their table, but after a while he got used to it and his nerves lessened. And at the end of each evening she bid him a chaste and proper 'good night', and retired alone to her bedroom, leaving him to the vast grandeur of the spare room.

He could not lose his habit of asking questions other people didn't ask. He couldn't always tell which questions would offend people, and which wouldn't. And besides, it seemed to him that if you chopped and censored your words to suit other people's tastes, then you never found out anything worth knowing.

At the opera one night, they shared a box with three people Sara Kessel had known in Lima. She introduced them to Derry: Raymond and Frederick and Luisa. Raymond said, 'Sara. *Darling*,' (in public, Derry always very decorously called her Mrs Kessel) and kissed her on both cheeks. Raymond insisted on sitting next to Sara, whispering to her throughout the first half of the performance, and every now and then touching her arm. At the interval he seemed to notice Derry for the first time.

'What are you?' A twirl of moustache, a patronizing glance. 'A nephew or something? Half term hols, is it?'

Mrs Kessel said, 'Derry is the son of my sister-in-law's solicitor, Raymond. He's having a little holiday in Town.'

'Splendid!' said Raymond heartily. His oiled hair, Derry noticed, gleamed in a similar fashion to his patent leather shoes.

The other couple were putting aside opera glasses and picking up bags, making ready to leave the box for the bar. Raymond, leaning towards Derry, murmured, 'Run along now, won't you, old chap?'

'Why?'

Raymond's brows twitched. 'I'd like a word with Sara. In private.'

'Why?' asked Derry again.

'Such curiosity,' said Raymond. He had gone crimson around the collar, just as Derry's father tended to do when he was angry. 'Run along, child. Sara and I are old friends, you understand.'

'Do you mean that you are lovers?'

'You little—'

'*Raymond.*' There was a warning in Sara Kessel's voice; Raymond subsided back into his seat. Sara turned to Derry. 'Perhaps you would fetch me my mantilla from the cloakroom, Derry. It's chillier than I expected.'

'I'd prefer to stay here. Raymond could get it.'

'My mantilla, Derry.' Her voice was cold, clipped.

At the end of the evening, they took a cab back to Mrs Kessel's flat in Wilton Crescent. In the taxi, she did not speak to him. When, in her drawing-room, she turned to him, he assumed it would be to tell him to pack his bags.

Instead, she said, 'How dare you? How dare you speak to a friend of mine like that?'

'Was he a friend? I had the impression you disliked him.'

Her eyes, the same shade of sapphire as her evening gown, narrowed. 'Even if I do, it was inexcusable of you to be so impolite.'

She unclasped her cloak, and with a snap of tiny pearl buttons unpeeled her gloves. Her back was to him as she poured herself a drink from the cabinet. He heard her laugh. 'I suppose you have progressed, Derry. At least now you're sufficiently at ease with me to disagree with me. You were such a white-faced little thing when you first came here that one just wanted to scoop you up and protect you from the world. You wouldn't say boo to a goose. But you seem to have found your tongue.'

'I'm sorry,' he muttered. 'He annoyed me.'

She turned to face him, raising her eyebrows. 'Are you rude to everyone who annoys you?'

He considered. 'Yes. Yes, I suppose I am.'

'Oh, Derry, Derry.' She shook her head. 'You must learn to dissemble. Shall I teach you that, too?'

He asked curiously, '*Is* he your lover?'

She crossed the room to him. 'That,' she said, 'is none of your business.'

'I apologize for angering you,' he said. 'Do you forgive me?'

Her expression altered; she gave a small shake of her head. Then she laid her forefinger against the side of his face. Her touch made him shiver.

'Don't you know, my dear,' she said softly, 'that I would forgive you *anything*?'

In the candlelight, her hair was a rich chestnut brown, threaded with light. Pulled back into a bun, it puffed around her face. Two tortoiseshell combs held it in place. He had always longed to remove the combs, to release the coppery strands from their imprisonment. He did so now.

Her hair tumbled, a shining mass of waves and folds, to her shoulders. He took up a handful, and kissed it. It felt like silk against his lips. He heard her sharp intake of breath, and smelt her sweet, powdery skin. He wanted her so much that it was a delirious agony to wait, yet he was forced to do so, fumbling through the carapace of buttons, fasteners, ribbons and whalebone, hurling aside satin, lace and linen, before he was able at last to bury himself in the soft, embracing flesh imprisoned beneath.

CHAPTER THREE

In the mornings, the cold seemed to eat into Alix's bones. She breakfasted on yoghurt and coffee, and then she set to work. She had knitted herself a pair of fingerless gloves which enabled her to begin to draw before the rising sun spilled across the desert, warming the freezing night air.

She drew the litter of pottery, flint and obsidian tools that the archaeologists' trowels had revealed from beneath their covering of dust and potsherds. The pottery was glazed green and painted with triangles and hatching, and the dark obsidian gleamed in the sunlight. Thousands of years ago, when this part of the desert had been fertile, the Euphrates had flooded, and the mud cast up by the swollen river had captured each small object, setting it in stone.

Now, the barren wastes of the desert spread out to either side of the encampment. Mirages shimmered on the horizon. When Alix had first come here her dreams had each night populated this wilderness with hills and valleys and trees, as though her imagination could not tolerate such emptiness.

'Mrs North?' Fleetingly, a hand touched her shoulder. 'I say, Mrs North?'

She looked round and smiled. 'I'm sorry, Mr Keates. I was miles away.'

'Coffee?'

She shook her head. 'I'll just finish this.'

But when she was alone again, she put aside her sketchbook and sat for a moment, her knees hunched up to her chin. Alix *North*, she reminded herself. You are Alix North. She thought back over the past year: her leaving of the nursing home in early spring, followed by the long, uneventful months at home, living with her mother once more. She remembered her wedding day in August. The register office ceremony had been followed by a quick lunch in a quiet restaurant. A week later she and Edward had set out on the long journey from England. They had caught the Continental Express to Naples, then a steamship to Alexandria, another ship to Basra, and finally a horse-ride from Basra to the archaeological site at the Eagle's Nest. The digging season had begun in September, as soon as the intense summer heat had eased.

Alix touched the gold wedding-band on the third finger of her left hand. She had lost weight since she had travelled to Mesopotamia, and it moved loosely between her knuckles, a poor fit.

In December, Lord Maycross, Edward's patron, visited the site.

The previous evening Edward had said, 'He'll want to dig.'

Tony Keates, grimacing, had muttered, 'Then we'll find him somewhere where he can't do too much harm.'

The aeroplane touched down on the sand in the late afternoon. Ochre clouds formed around its fragile, trembling wings. Lord Maycross climbed out of the cockpit, wearing a cream-coloured linen suit and a crimson silk cravat. Strands of white hair escaped from beneath his leather flying helmet. He shook Edward's hand.

'Terrific work. Terrific work, my dear boy.'

As Edward showed Lord Maycross round the site, Alix sat in the shadow of the tent, inking in the pencil drawing she had completed that morning. The other men continued to work on the excavation: Tony Keates and Duffy Hardwick, who had known Edward since Oxford, Philippe Levasseur, whom Edward had met in Egypt, and Robin Pennant, an American photographer. The Arab workmen lounged in the shade. Alix was the only woman on the site. The men treated her with cautious, distant respect. She was Mrs North, never Alix. When, in the evenings, she heard them talking and laughing round the campfire, she remained in her tent, writing letters, combing the dust from her hair.

To celebrate the arrival of their patron, they dined together at a trestle table spread out under the stars. Halfway through the meal of stewed lamb and rice and dried fruit, Lord Maycross stood up.

'I should like to propose a toast.'

Duffy Hardwick drummed his glass on the table. 'To lost cities and incomparable treasures.'

Someone cheered. Lord Maycross said, 'Not at all. To the bride and groom.'

Glasses chinked. 'Tell me how you met, dear boy,' said Lord Maycross. 'I always enjoy a good romance.'

'Alix was looking after me in the nursing home,' explained Edward.

'Was he a good patient, Mrs North?'

'Very amiable.' Alix remembered Edward's long

71

walks around the grounds of Fallowfield. 'But restless. He wouldn't sit still.'

'Hasn't changed a bit.'

'Always a damned slave-driver.'

'Had you an interest in archaeology before you married, Mrs North?'

'Not really,' she admitted.

Lord Maycross looked sentimental. 'True love, Edward, old chap, that's what it is. Following you to this godforsaken place. You're a lucky fellow.' He raised his glass again. 'True love.'

Later, Edward caught up with her as she walked back to her tent. 'I'm sorry, Alix. Embarrassing for you, all that.'

She shook her head. 'It doesn't matter.'

'Freddie's a good fellow, one of the best. But tact's not his strong point.'

'Really, Edward, it doesn't matter.'

There was a silence. Following her into the tent, he said suddenly, 'I sometimes think that I've put you in a rather invidious position.' He scuffed the dust with the tip of his boot. 'Do you *mind*? Do you regret it? Coming out here, I mean?'

Alix lit the oil-burner and measured out a precious spoonful of the tea her mother had given her before she had left England. She looked out at the stars. They shivered, bright diamonds pinned to a black velvet cloth. 'Oh, Edward,' she whispered, '*look* at it. How could I possibly mind?'

After dinner each evening, Lord Maycross insisted they play games. Charades and consequences, acrostics and riddles, the desert dark and featureless to every side of them. Kim's game, with a blue bead, a sliver of copper and a clay flower among the spoons and coins and fountain pens arranged on the tray. 'Goddamn parlour games,' muttered Robin Pennant under his breath. 'Probably taught them by his goddamn *nanny*.' Yet he, too, stared at the tray, committing its contents to memory.

And they danced. Waltzes and foxtrots, tangos in the desert, to the music of the gramophone that Freddie Maycross had brought with him from England. Alix's feet slipped in the sand; a bubble of laughter rose in her throat as she was passed from hand to hand. Empty wine bottles lay discarded beneath the trestle table. The smoke from their cigarettes curled into the night air.

Before Lord Maycross's arrival, they had been six people, separated by experience, nationality, sex. He had altered them, subtly, almost imperceptibly at first, his clumsy benevolence rubbing off on them, infecting them, joining them together. Call me Freddie, he had said to Alix on his first day at the site, shaking her hand, bruising her bones. And she herself was now Alix, no longer Mrs North. She had become, she realized, a part of something.

Freddie insisted on joining in every aspect of the excavation. Edward and Tony winced as he leapt into delicate earthworks and knelt in the dirt, hacking at the sand with his trowel, whooping with delight at every shard of pottery. He would, Alix thought, have shaded in her pencil lines if she had let him. He had a habit of standing behind her, watching her draw. In anyone else she could not have borne it. Though her pencil faltered in his shadow, she did not snap at him. To be unkind to Freddie would have been like being unkind to a child.

Neither could she lie to him. When, yet again, he became sentimental about her marriage to Edward, she put down her sketchbook, linked her arm through his, and suggested a walk.

In the shadow of the clay-brick walls that were emerging from the sand, she told him the truth.

'It's a marriage of convenience, you see, Freddie.'

He did not believe her at first. 'Don't know what you're talking about, dear gel.'

'I didn't want to get married, but Edward insisted. He said that we had to marry, or my reputation would be ruined.'

'Can't go gallivanting around the world in the company of half a dozen fellers without tongues beginning to wag, y'know, Alix.' Lord Maycross glanced at her. 'But you're fond of the dear chap, aren't you?'

'We don't *love* each other,' she said firmly.

'People make such a fuss about love these days. If a chap likes a girl a lot and thinks she's pretty, that's good enough for me.'

'Edward needed someone to help him with his work, and I needed a job. All those other things – love . . . and passion – don't come into it.'

He looked unconvinced, so she added, 'Edward says that if I meet someone else, then he'll give me a divorce.'

Lord Maycross wiped his forehead with his handkerchief. 'Divorce? No need for that. Messy business, divorce. Have a love affair, that's what I do. Much simpler.' He took a flask from his pocket and offered it to her. 'You and Edward are both brainy, serious sorts of fellers. Marriage of convenience . . .' Lord Maycross tutted. 'Such nonsense.'

They began to dig at the far corner of the site. The Arab workmen hauled away the heaps of sand that had gathered around the brickwork. Steps emerged in the desert, the treads great slabs of white limestone. The wind got up, swirling sand back around the excavation, in one spiteful breath threatening to hide once more what had taken them weeks to uncover. Alix knelt in the sand, her head bent, drawing. The wind wrenched the paper and tugged at her straw hat. Edward circled the site, his features swathed in a white silk scarf, calling directions to the workmen. When he squatted beside Alix, looking through her sketches, she saw the excitement in his eyes.

The wind died down over the next few days, and they began once again to clear away the sand. Between the stairs and the wall they found treasures: columns of wood inlaid with mother-of-pearl, copper reliefs of bulls and eagles, fragments of mosaic. Delight animated Edward's features, and there was passion in his voice when he spoke about the artefacts to Alix. He ordered the erection of tents over the excavation, and they prepared the remainder of the relief for lifting. Alix helped Edward remove the fragments of mud and sand that adhered to the brittle metal. The copper crumbs shivered at his clumsy, left-handed touch, and he flung aside his trowel. This bloody *arm*, he muttered, as he walked away. Hearing him coughing, she turned round and saw that he was leaning against the staircase, bent double.

Edward did not appear at dinner that night. Alix heard him coughing before she drew aside the flap of his tent. He shook his head when she offered him codeine and morphine, so she made lemon and honey, propping him up with cushions and pillows so that he could drink.

He grinned. 'I feel like one of the Sumerian kings. I should click my fingers and call for dancing girls.'

He looked, she thought, exhausted. 'Perhaps,' she

said diffidently, 'perhaps you should rest, Edward. Take a few days off.'

'I can't. There's too much to do. By the end of May it'll be too hot to dig. Freddie will only finance the next season if things look promising.'

'You should eat something.' Alix stoned dates, cutting them into small pieces, offering them to him.

He smiled again. 'King Hammurabi, surrounded by his attendants.'

'*Silly.*' Though she, too, smiled.

'Did you read that book I gave you? Hammurabi's law-codes?'

'So harsh, don't you think?'

'Not for the times. They were comparatively enlightened for the times.' Edward sat back on the cushions, and quoted, 'The fine for breaking a bone was sixty shekels of silver . . . the fine for cutting off a foot was ten shekels of silver.' He paused. 'What price for the loss of an arm, d'you think, Alix?'

What price, she thought, for the loss of a child. She turned aside and began to tidy up the tea things.

She heard him add, 'The inheritance laws were pretty civilized. A widow was entitled to live in her husband's house until she herself died. Widows don't always receive such justice nowadays. I've left you Owlscote, you know, Alix. Altered my will before we left England.'

'Edward—'

'There's no-one else. I'm the last of my family.'

She said tightly, 'I didn't marry you for *that*.'

'I know you didn't. And it's probably more of a burden than a gift. But still, it will be yours.' He was silent for a moment, looking at her, and then he said, 'I want you to have it, Alix. I can't think of anyone I'd rather have Owlscote after I'm gone.'

'You shouldn't talk like that, Edward. You'll prob-ably live till you're a hundred.'

He frowned. 'I suppose I should have sold the place, but I couldn't quite bring myself to. Can't bear to go back there, and can't bear to get rid of it – ridiculous, isn't it? I should have taken you there before we left England, Alix, and then you'd have seen that it's not much of a bequest. I expect there's bats in the drawing-room by now. The house has been empty since Rory died in 1917, you see.' Edward narrowed his eyes. 'Though it's been through worse. The Civil War . . . the Black Death . . . There's supposed to've been settle-ments on the site from Ethelred's time.' He saw her incomprehension. 'Ethelred was an Anglo-Saxon king. Didn't they teach you anything at school?'

'I was expelled.'

His eyes widened. 'Truly?'

'Truly. When I was little, I went to a school in the village. A dear old lady taught me needlework and re-ligious knowledge. Then I was sent to boarding school, but I was expelled after a term.'

'What did you do?'

'I drew some unflattering pictures of the teachers.'

He let out a croak of laughter.

'After I left, my father taught me drawing and nature study. So, you see, I never learned any history.'

He took her hand. 'I enjoy hearing you talk, Alix. Just listening to your voice makes me feel better.'

So she read to him. In the cramped enclosure of the tent she sat beside him, turning the pages of the book. When, after a while, his head lolled against her shoulder, she remained where she was, her eyelids eventually closing, sleeping curled against him.

*　　*　　*

Alix drew the mosaic, making a precise map of the tesserae set in the dried mud. Half a dozen white birds took flight against a darkened sky. Fragments of mosaic were scattered over the floor of the excavation. She tried to fit them together, to complete the pattern. Like a jigsaw puzzle, she thought, a vast jigsaw puzzle in which half the pieces were missing. Edward, fully recovered now, worked beside her, his sharp eyes seeing connections when hers failed to. His excitement was infectious, and she too felt triumph and pleasure when fragment after fragment fell into place. They worked late into the night, the light of their torches illuminating the patterns in the desert. The immensity of the past they uncovered began to put her own past into perspective. The long days were a blur of exhaustion and happiness.

Lord Maycross left for London, taking one of Alix's sketchbooks and an inlaid clay flower with him. She walked with him to his plane. After he had climbed into the cockpit, he leaned over and called down to her: 'The feller's madly in love with you, y'know.'

She thought she had misheard him through the rumble of the engine, and the wind, nuzzling around the camp like a hungry animal. She cupped her hand round her ear.

'I said,' he bawled, 'that Edward loves you.'

Tony Keates was making ready to turn the propeller. Alix stepped back. Her words – *ridiculous*, Freddie – were lost in the roar of the engine.

She watched the tiny dragonfly rise up into the sky. She did not return immediately to the excavation. Pausing on the perimeter of the encampment, she remembered how Edward had taken her hand in the tent, and how his head had fallen against her shoulder as he had slept, and how she had rested her cheek against his silky hair. And how he had said, *I've left you Owlscote.*

Now, when he knelt beside her, she noticed when their elbows touched, and when their fingers brushed against each other as they sorted through the tesserae. Her skin burned, contacting his. Sometimes, in the evenings, when they were talking and laughing after dinner, she turned and looked at him, and saw that he was watching her. When he read to her, she became unable to concentrate on his words, but was aware instead of the fall of her own hair against her cheek, and the curve of breast and hip. She loved to hear the murmur of his voice, and to feel his gaze, flickering from the page and back to her. Alone in her tent, she looked into her small handmirror, studying each part of her face separately – nose, eyes, mouth – unable to fit them together, unable to decide whether or not they were pleasing.

Digging deeper into the solidified mud, they came across a limestone statue of a man. An inscription was carved into the back of the statue. That night, they celebrated, drinking champagne and eating tinned caviar beneath the vast, empty desert skies.

'To Mesanepada . . .'

'. . . King of Ur . . .'

'Mentioned in the Sumerian King-List, you see, Alix.'

'Dates this place for us.'

'Good old Freddie will cough up the cash for next season.'

Freddie had left his gramophone behind. 'Roses of Picardie' played over and over again, its scratchy little notes almost lost in all the silence. Alix danced with each of them in turn. She saw herself reflected in Tony's blue eyes and Robin's brown. Duffy gripped her hard around the waist, Philippe's long fingers caressed the back of her neck. Alix took Edward by the hand, pulling him out of his seat. 'Not much of a dancer,' he said. 'Never was, and with this . . .' He grimaced, his palm flat against his empty sleeve. She said nothing, but smiled, drawing him to her. Their footsteps marked out the waltz. Dizzy with champagne, they stumbled, laughing. When she raised her head, he kissed her. Closing her eyes, she seemed to sink in dark delight, deeper and deeper. Treasures surrounded her, glittering and hypnotic.

He pulled away from her. 'I'm sorry. I beg your pardon, Alix. The champagne . . .' He began to walk away, but she ran after him, calling out to him.

'Edward . . .'

He turned, pausing momentarily, glancing back at her.

'I'm sorry, Alix,' he repeated. 'I know . . . I know *that* wasn't part of our arrangement.'

Again, he strode away from her. She caught up with him at the edge of the encampment, where the light of the fire was swallowed up in the empty darkness.

She said clearly, 'The arrangement doesn't suit me any more, Edward.'

He stared at her. In the starlight, his eyes had darkened to slate-grey. She curled her hand into his, and leaned her forehead against his shoulder, and whispered again, 'The arrangement doesn't suit me any more.'

He groaned, and his fingers fell away from hers. He swung round, his hand reaching for the small of her back, pressing her to him. '*Alix*. Dear Alix – do you mean it?'

Her answer was to press her lips against the hollow of his throat.

'I cannot believe—' He broke off.

She looked up at him. 'What, my darling?'

He said simply, 'That you could love me. I cannot believe that I could be so fortunate.'

'I love you, Edward. I love you.' She said the words over and over again, laughing, proclaiming her newfound joy to the empty sands and skies.

They went back to Edward's tent. She could feel the fast beating of his heart, and smell the faint salty scent of his skin, and hear, in the immense silence of the desert, the rustle of button and cloth. His palm swept slowly across her naked skin, and his fingertips caressed her breast, her nipple. His mouth pressed against her face, her neck, her body. There was a fire growing inside her, consuming her, that she must learn how to put out. And when he kissed her smooth, rounded belly, she flung her head back, closing her eyes, unable to contain a pleasure that was almost as intense as pain.

They spent the summer wandering around the fringes of the Mediterranean. In the dark violet shadows cast by the curved walls of the Neolithic temples of Malta they embraced, breathing in the scent of wild thyme as they kissed. Climbing through stony paths to reach the palace of Knossos at Crete, her body fitted into the crook of his arm, and his shadow kept the sun's glare from her eyes. Wandering through the museums and art galleries of Italy, Alix recognized in the curve of a marble shoulder and the smile on a painted lip what she herself had discovered. That love transformed, that it allowed her to greet the future with optimism. Woken each morning by the bright white sunlight cut into slices by the shutters, she would turn and see Edward's head on the pillow beside her. Marrying him, she had gambled, tossing a coin in the air, picking a card from a pack. And somehow, she had chosen well.

In the autumn, they returned to the Eagle's Nest. On the strength of the finds of the previous season, Freddie had agreed to finance further excavations. The work, at first promising, became difficult and frustrating. Deep trenches revealed nothing more than a few broken potsherds; what little they found crumbled into fragments as soon as it was exposed to the sun. In the spring, Alix fell ill. Her stomach heaved at the sight of food, and the muscles in her legs cramped.

In the summer of 1921, they travelled to Florence. Alix had thought that when she was able to lie in a real bed and eat fresh food, she would be well again. Yet the nausea persisted. She lay on the bed in their hotel in the piazza Massimo D'Azeglio, her hair sticking damply to her scalp, her stomach twisting and curling, her hot limbs flung out in an attempt to catch the slightest breeze.

Lord Maycross arrived at the hotel one evening at the beginning of July. The following morning Alix consulted a doctor. As she emerged from the surgery, the midday sun blinded her. She crossed the road without looking: horns hooted, someone shouted.

She heard their raised voices as she walked down the corridor of the hotel to their room. Freddie's: Can't keep shelling out money like peas, dear old thing. Edward's: One more season. Just one more. I can *feel* that there's something marvellous out there. *Please*, Freddie.

Alix turned on her heel and went outside to the garden. She sat at a table beside a crumbling fountain. Neptune spat out olivine water, a maid brought her crushed ice. She pressed the cold glass against her forehead, and watched the cypresses make their dappled pattern on the scorched grass. After a while, looking up, she saw Edward crossing the grass to her.

'Alix. I've been looking for you everywhere. Did you see the quack? What's the verdict?'

The muscles in her legs were trembling. 'Tell me, darling,' he said gently. He took her hand. 'If it's something awful, it's better shared.'

'I'm going to have a baby.' The words came out, bald and unsoftened. She saw his expression alter, and she added bluntly, 'We weren't as careful as we thought we'd been.'

He said carefully, 'I know this wasn't what you wanted. But Alix—' He broke off, but she could see the pride and delight in his eyes. His fingers curled around hers. 'When?'

'January or February, the doctor thought.'

'It won't be so bad,' he coaxed. 'I'll see you have the best doctors . . . everything.'

I am not afraid of *that*, she wanted to say. Her mind seemed frozen with shock.

'I'll make arrangements for you to go back to England.'

'England?' She stared at him. 'Why, Edward?'

'Freddie has agreed to cough up enough cash for another three months' work. It took some arm-twisting, I can tell you.' He squeezed her hand. 'I'm sorry, darling. If I'd known . . .'

'I'm not going back to England.' She pulled away, glaring down at the table, crushing the remaining ice in the glass savagely with her spoon.

'Darling, I'm going to have to return to the site.'

'I'm coming with you. I am, Edward.'

'Alix, the Eagle's Nest is in the middle of nowhere. There are no doctors . . . no other women . . .'

83

She needed the desert, she thought. She needed its extremes of heat and cold, its empty simplicity of sand and sky. And she needed Edward. From the protection and love of his frail, damaged body she had acquired both strength and the capacity for happiness.

Their small, united band began to disintegrate. At the end of October, Robin Pennant deserted the expedition in hopes of more spectacular finds in Egypt. Duffy Hardwick had remained behind in England, at the bedside of his sick mother. The site refused to yield further finds, so that they became quarrelsome, impatient and exhausted. Too much hope and too much work, too many expectations wore them down. Copper daggers, clay drinking vessels, these were not enough to appease Freddie.

Edward insisted on lighting oil-lamps so that they could work late into the night. Time, and Freddie's ultimatum, had become a tyrant. Alix's own body had become unfamiliar and demanding. She had to unpick the side seam of her skirt and tie the waistband with a length of tape. Blue veins stood out in her breasts, and her ankles swelled in the heat. During the day, the coming child was a strange, wriggling weight in her belly, and a collection of inconvenient symptoms. But, waking in the night, she sensed change, upheavals, and the approaching weight of responsibility. Her knowledge of childbirth was limited to the lurid and terrifying stories related to her by one of the probationer nurses at Fallowfield. She knew nothing about babies; her only contact with small children had been the disastrous holiday she had spent helping to look after her Lanchbury cousins. Yet, lying in the dark, her hand resting on her stomach, feeling the child's strange, fluttering movements, she was aware of both excitement and joy, as though the happiness she had discovered with Edward had erased some of the fears that had once haunted her.

In the middle of November, Edward, working late in the evening, slipped and fell as he climbed into a trench. They carried him back to his tent and laid him carefully on the camp bed. Alix saw how white his face was as her fingers traced the small, sharp bones of his spine. 'Try and wiggle your toes,' she said, and when she saw that he was able to she felt faint with relief. 'You must rest, Edward,' she said. 'Then you'll be well again.' She gave him aspirin, and he closed his eyes and slept.

After a couple of days his lungs began to fill with fluid. Alix helped him to sit up, propping him up with cushions. For a long time, he remained still, unspeaking, his eyes tightly closed, his features rigid with pain. Then he said, 'I imagine our son at Owlscote. Playing in the rooms I used to play in . . . climbing the trees Rory and I used to climb . . .'

She took his hand. 'Don't talk, Edward. Save your strength.'

'I want to talk. Lots of things to say. Not much time to say them.'

She began to speak. 'Hush,' he said. 'I'm dying, Alix, you know that.' He touched his fist to his chest. 'Not easy to breathe now. I'm drowning. Almost happened in 1918. Was gassed, ended up in a shell-hole. When I came to, the water was up to my chin.' He smiled at her. 'I reckon I've had more than three extra years. Three wonderful years. You made me feel alive again, Alix.'

She said desperately, 'We'll take you to the hospital at Basra, Edward. You'll be all right, darling, honestly. We'll set off at first light tomorrow.'

His hand reached for hers. 'Can't face the journey, my love. Too far.' He closed his eyes.

She sat at his bedside day and night. When Edward dozed, sitting upright, the face that had become familiar and beautiful to her was creased with exhaustion. When he was awake, he talked of his boyhood at Owlscote, and his years at Oxford. Alix understood that he was giving her his memories, which one day she must pass on to their child. She understood also that to Edward their child was a solace, a living token of their love, and a symbol of hope for a better future. When Edward grew weary, she talked to him of her Suffolk childhood, and her long walks through the countryside with her father, and her work in the nursing home. Sometimes her soft voice managed to lull him into a short sleep.

One night, waking suddenly, he said, 'You must sell Owlscote, Alix. When you go home, you must sell Owlscote.' He coughed, and when he had gathered his breath he explained: 'I have . . . evaded things. Coming here allowed me to avoid difficult decisions. But you must do what I should have done years ago.'

'You mustn't worry,' she said. She threaded her fingers through his. 'I'll take care of everything.'

'I know you will. You're strong, Alix, I know that. I know you'll be all right.' He smiled. 'It's been a funny sort of marriage, hasn't it?'

'It's been a wonderful sort of marriage.' She kissed his forehead.

'And you must promise me to be happy, Alix. Look after the boy, and be happy. Marry again. Find a chap who'll be good to you . . .'

He was silent for a long time. She thought he had fallen asleep, but then he said, 'My sort of people . . .

we're finished with. I saw that in the trenches. With our old houses and our old names and our lands we can't afford to look after. I don't mind, Alix, you mustn't think that. When you're up to the waist in mud with a chap who's worked since he was fourteen in a coal pit, you can't go on believing that you're better than him. I just . . . I would have liked our boy to have known the house.' His face lightened. 'It is a boy, Alix, I'm sure of it. I thought . . .'

'What, Edward?'

'I thought you might call him Rory. After my brother. It would be a way of bringing him home, you see.'

'Yes, Edward.'

He said, 'Tired. So tired.' He lay back on the pillows, and closed his eyes.

They buried Edward the next morning, a short distance from the temple and the ancient graves. He would have wanted it, Alix said fiercely, when the others demurred. He never chose to go home.

They packed up tools and artefacts, struck camp and headed for Basra. Alix parted from Tony and Philippe at Alexandria, and took ship for Naples. As the sea changed from a smooth turquoise blue to a sullen grey, she wrapped her arms around her swollen belly. The child moved inside her, coiling like a serpent. She watched the tempest through the tiny porthole in her cabin. White forks of lightning stabbed the horizon. Clouds bubbled and spilled over: charcoal, purple, rose, yellow.

The boat bounced and lurched on the sea's uneven surface. Pain gathered, weak and pulsating at first, in the small of her back. When she rested her hand on her swollen stomach, she felt it shrink, becoming iron-hard.

She wondered whether the pain was to do with the baby. December, she thought, it is only December. The doctor had told her the baby would not be born until January. The stewardess brought her glasses of water, offered her brandy, and looked at her anxiously. Alix shook her head to the stewardess's enquiries, and longed for land. She would not let her baby be born here, drifting between continents.

She gave birth to her son in a hospital in Naples. None of the doctors or nurses spoke English, and she had forgotten all her Italian. She did not understand what was happening; her body was taken over by forces that were powerful and primitive. In labour, she cried out for Edward, and then, remembering that he had said, *You are strong, Alix*, she bit her lip and endured it all in silence. At sunrise, she was delivered of a fine healthy boy. They placed him in her arms and, just for a moment, his flickering gaze met hers. Through the grief that she endured, thinking of Edward, she was aware of an intense, almost painful, joy. She hadn't the strength to speak, but she thought, I shall keep you safe, Rory. I promise you that I shall always keep you safe.

They left Naples a fortnight later. Her breasts, full with milk, hurt. Rory rarely slept, often cried. He cried on the train, tucked in the *wagon-lit* beside her, and he cried in the dining car, curled in the crook of her arm. Italy, Switzerland, and France sped by outside the window, but Alix saw only Rory's small, angry face, and the fury in his dark blue eyes. She changed trains in Paris. Smoke clouded from the funnels of the engines, and the guards' whistles mingled with her son's howls. They boarded the steam ferry at Calais. The sea was rough, and sleet darted through the night air. Rory dozed fitfully. When he woke, Alix also woke, and put him to her breast to still his cries.

London assaulted her, a muddle of fast motor-cars and rushing, careless people. She stayed the night at an hotel, and in the morning took a cab to Waterloo Station. Rory woke frequently during the night, and howled in the cab. At the station, she was confused by the noise and hemmed in by the crowds. A porter swept up her bags and helped her onto the train. She fumbled in her purse for coins to tip him. Rory's cries had diminished into shudders of despair. His eyes sought hers, beseeching, helpless, pleading for succour. She fed him surreptitiously, hidden beneath layers of shawl and blouse and coat. The other ladies in the carriage averted their eyes; one, with a quiver of disgust, decamped for a different compartment.

At Salisbury station, Alix hired a cab to take her to Owlscote. She sat in a corner of the vehicle, dazed with exhaustion, her mind clouded with despair. She could not comfort her son. She should never have had a child. Rory hiccuped and howled, his face creased up, blotched red with anger. Streets and houses passed by, blurred by twilight. They left the city behind them, passing through villages and between fields threaded with streams. As they headed deeper into the river valley, the countryside became wooded. The branches of the beech trees to either side of the road met overhead, enclosing the cab and its passengers in a copper-coloured tunnel. Patches of sky flickered through gaps between the branches. The only sounds were the rumble of the engine, and Rory's gulping breaths. Alix sat back in the seat, her muscles, of their own volition, relaxing, and her eyelids becoming heavy.

The cab turned off the road into a driveway. She saw the house.

Built of a patchwork of stone, flint and brick, Owlscote's single gable was shadowed by trees. Stone windows looked down over a courtyard in which dandelions pushed up between the flagstones. The meadows behind the house tailed off into the bluish mist that gathered in the curve of the valley.

Alix paid the driver, and climbed the steps to the front door. She fitted Edward's key to the lock. The key turned stiffly, and she went indoors. She became aware, walking through the house, of a strange sound. No, an absence of sound. Looking down, she saw that Rory slept soundly, swaddled in his shawl. As though, she thought, they had come home.

At first she slept, curled up on a battered chintz sofa in Owlscote's drawing-room, rising only to feed and change and bath Rory. She found coal in an outhouse, and kept the fire burning day and night. She ate out of old tins she discovered in the back of the larder, and warmed Rory's bathwater on the hearth. She thought of little except her son.

She explored the house. Thick hanks of spider-web tied doors to jambs, and dust motes swayed in the winter light. In a sunny room overlooking the back garden Alix found a cot, a high chair, and an old, heavy, Edwardian perambulator. A layer of dust blanketed an upright piano; as she touched a key, she turned, thinking that she had heard a sound, as if someone had been holding their breath and had, on her first note, let slip a sigh of relief. Opening a door, she glimpsed an officer's cap, slung on a peg, and a window sill scattered with stone artefacts. She knew that she was an intruder, an interloper, that she was interrupting a still silence inhabited only by phantoms.

At dusk, as Rory slept in the perambulator, she would walk onto the terrace and watch the ragged clouds that scudded across the grey sky. The silvery remains of the sun glinted on the tips of the trees, and on the surface of the lake. Not a leaf, not a blade of grass, moved. Sometimes an owl, its great wings outspread, flew from the roof of the outhouse to the copse and, watching, she smiled.

At the end of the first week, padding through the house to fetch water, she caught sight of her reflection in a mirror. Straggling hair, pale, pinched features, grubby dress. She hardly recognized herself. You must pull yourself together, Alix North, she whispered out loud. It seemed to her that she had lived so long in tents and hotels that she had almost forgotten how to exist in a house.

She ventured into the kitchen, where cobwebs were slung between the ceiling rafters. Her stockinged feet curled at the icy touch of the kitchen tiles, and her bones seemed to jangle against each other in the frozen air. The kitchen range was a vast, daunting affair, composed of metal drawers and doors and trays. When she pulled open one of the drawers a cloud of ash tumbled onto the floor. She knelt in front of the monstrous thing for the entire morning, sweeping out ash, laying kindling, riddling coal, yet still it refused to light. Cursing, she wrapped Rory up in shawls and blankets and set off down the road to the village. The fields and woodlands resembled a charcoal drawing, grey and black and white where the frost still clung. When she marched into the public house the barroom fell silent. Often, later, Alix thought how she must have looked: foul-tempered, and her hair grey with ash, and the baby bundled like a giant caterpillar over her shoulder. 'Is there anyone here who knows how to mend stoves?' she called out, staring at each of the men at the bar in turn.

She was lucky. She found Jacob Long, whose family had worked for Edward's for years, before Owlscote had been closed up. Jacob, a large, patient man, walked back with her to the house, and fiddled and twisted and blew. After a while, the stove rewarded him by giving out heat. Alix made a cup of tea for both of them, cradling it in her hands, her fingers slowly thawing.

Ladies in tweeds and brogues called, introducing themselves. Alix did not return the calls. She needed only Rory and Owlscote. She became as familiar with Owlscote's moods – sunlit and glittering sometimes, dark and sombre at others – as one would become familiar with the moods of a lover. When the winter eased, she explored the grounds. Knot-garden, terrace and borders remained, lacy skeletons beneath their smothering blanket of weeds and fallen leaves.

She went to see Mr Battersby, Edward's solicitor in Salisbury. Rory, who was teething, wriggled and dribbled on her lap throughout the interview. Mr Battersby chucked the baby under the chin, then surreptitiously wiped his fingers on his handkerchief, and told Alix that as the estate had had to pay three death duties in close succession, there was now little money left in the bank. Mr Battersby recommended that she sell the house.

Alix tucked her son under her arm, and left the solicitor's office. Returning home, she knew that she would not sell. She needed Owlscote. It was her citadel, the place where she and Rory would be safe. Owlscote's walls protected them both from an unpredictable outside world. And besides, she had fallen in love with the house. It was a foolish, unmeasured sort of love, which the passing of time only deepened. Yet she was aware too of the mouldy plaster behind the wardrobe, and the crumbling brickwork in the outhouse. The puddles in the cellar, and the banisters one dared not lean against.

In the late summer, Rory caught measles. His skin turned pink with a thousand tiny spots, and when his temperature was at its highest he screamed, his body arching, his eyes screwed tightly shut. For two weeks Alix comforted him day and night. When he began to recover, Alix herself lay awake, staring into the darkness, haunted by the stack of bills on her desk, and the bank statements whose figures frightened her.

She had made an appointment to see the bank manager in Salisbury one morning. Martha Long, Jacob's daughter, came to the house to babysit Rory. As always, Alix had to fight the instinct to take Rory with her, to keep him constantly in her sight. But she reminded herself of his recent illness, and kissed him goodbye and walked to the bus stop.

The bank manager was polite, but unhelpful. After she had left his office, Alix walked around the Market Square, dazed with anxiety and tiredness, struggling to think clearly. Alarming sums added and subtracted themselves in her head, their answers inescapable. Six months, she thought. Apart from Edward's small army pension, I have only enough money to survive for six more months. Her shoulders hunched, her gaze fixed on the cobblestones, she walked quickly between the stalls, and thought, even if we eat only the cheapest, dullest food, and even if I never buy myself anything new to wear, I have only enough money left in the bank to keep Rory and myself for six months.

Something large and soft struck her in the face, and she teetered, wobbled, and would have fallen onto the cobbles had not a hand grabbed her, supporting her.

A voice said, 'I say, I'm most terribly sorry.'

Alix became aware of two things: that the contents of her shopping bag were scattered across the pavement, and that she, preoccupied with her financial difficulties, had cannoned straight into Jonathan Fox.

'*Jonathan*,' she said weakly.

He looked more closely at her. 'Good lord. It isn't . . . Good lord, how utterly splendid. It is you, isn't it, Alix?'

Breathless, she could only nod her head, and look at him. She thought how well, how composed, how handsome he looked. She began to tuck her hair beneath her hat, to rearrange her dishevelled clothes.

'Are you all right, Alix? My humblest apologies for barging into you like that.'

She smiled. 'You always were the perfect gentleman, Jonathan. It was my fault. I hope I didn't hurt you.'

Jonathan rubbed his midriff. 'Took me back to my rugby-playing days. A jolly good tackle. Let me pick up your things.' Alix's basket had tumbled to the ground. A pound of onions and a fillet of haddock, still wrapped in newspaper, lay on the cobbles surrounded by a snow-storm of flour.

'I'm afraid the flour's done for, old thing.'

Struggling to repack her basket, she heard Jonathan ask, 'What are you doing in Salisbury, Alix?'

'Just a bit of shopping.' She tried not to think about the dispiriting interview with the bank manager. 'I live nearby, you see, Jonathan.' She glanced at her watch. 'My bus—'

'Don't you dare dash off,' he said, linking his arm through hers. 'I shall drive you home, Alix. But first you must have lunch with me.'

They lunched in a small restaurant near the Poultry Cross. Jonathan had to stoop to avoid hitting his head on the low beams, and the table wobbled on the uneven floor.

'Tell me what you've been doing,' said Jonathan, after the waitress had taken their order. 'You never wrote.' His voice was puzzled, not accusing.

Alix felt ashamed of herself. She remembered the months after she had left Fallowfield, the tedium of living with her mother again, and her initial doubts about her engagement to Edward. She tried to explain. 'I'm sorry. Things were . . . complicated.'

He glanced at her left hand. 'You're married?'

'Widowed. I married Edward North, from the nursing home. Do you remember him?'

Jonathan frowned. 'Tall chap. Quiet.' He shook his head. 'I say, how rotten for you.'

She told him about Mesopotamia, and about the archaeological expedition. Then she said firmly, 'I miss Edward dreadfully, of course, but I have been very lucky. We were very happy, you see. And I have a lovely house, and a son, Rory, who's eight months old and utterly adorable.' She looked at him. 'What about you, Jonathan? Have you married?'

He laughed. 'Good lord, no. I'm living with my parents in Andover. I work for my father, who's a solicitor. I'm visiting clients in Salisbury just now, so I've been staying here for the last couple of days, lodging in a rather grim little place in Fisherton Street. The guest house where I usually stay was booked up – Salisbury can get so crowded on market days.' He smiled. 'No room at the inn, you see.'

After lunch, Jonathan insisted on driving her home. The clouds had thinned, and sunlight, pouring through the trees, dappled the road out of town.

Reaching Owlscote, he braked, and climbed out of the car. She heard his long, slow exhalation of breath. 'Good lord. *Alix*. It's stunning. *Huge*.'

'Rory and I do rattle around rather.'

'You could put up *thousands*.' He opened the car door for her.

'Come in, won't you, Jonathan?'

'Can't, old thing.' He glanced at his watch. 'I've an appointment, I'm afraid.'

She stood on her tiptoes, and kissed his cheek. 'Then you'll visit. You must promise.'

'Wild horses won't keep me away.'

Alix watched the motor-car speed up the drive in a cloud of dust. Unlocking the door, she walked into the house. She thought, *You could put up thousands . . . Rory and I do rattle around rather . . . No room at the inn . . .*

CHAPTER FOUR

There was a café in Fitzrovia where they all met. Roma had painted the murals: jangling, geometric shapes, executed in yellows and russets and vermilion, which took your mind off the broken-legged chairs and scuffed tabletops. The cook served (if he was in a good temper) stacks of pancakes, dripping with syrup. Roma went to the café for the pancakes and the company. The regulars were there most nights, and there were other occasional visitors, who always made Roma think of migrating birds, alighting in a flutter of glamour and then disappearing to some distant home.

Sophie and Lawrence shared a table with Roma one evening. Sophie Berkoff was a psychoanalyst, Lawrence Corcoran a dancer. They drank brandy and smoked Turkish cigarettes as Roma described to them the drawing-room she was decorating.

'Black and white, darlings. Black silk on the walls and black *devoré* velvet curtains.'

Lawrence lit a cigarette. 'Won't that be rather gloomy?'

'A white carpet and white cushions. Delightful simplicity. You know I revel in simplicity.'

Sophie gave her throaty laugh. 'You have six rooms

all to yourself, Roma. Simplicity is living in a single room, as I do.'

'You should have been a nun, Sophie. You have the inclinations of a nun.'

Sophie laughed again. 'Some of them.' She cradled her glass in her small, white fingers.

At midnight, Roma left the café and hailed a taxi. The taxi-driver was young and dark-haired. For a while she watched his long hands move on the steering-wheel, and then she struck up a conversation.

'I always think that London looks so wonderfully seedy at night. Even the expensive bits.'

They were driving through Mayfair. Gaslights flared. He said, 'The expensive bits look worst, don't you think? Too much glitter. Like a high-class whore.'

He had a pleasant voice, light and unaccented. Roma had expected dropped aitches and glottal stops from a taxi-driver. She looked at him more carefully, noting the deepset dark eyes, the twist of black curl against olive skin, and she thought, if I cared for men . . .

He said, 'Do you mind if I stop for a moment? I'm lost, and I need to look at a map.' He drew over to the kerb.

His battered map was illuminated by a street lamp. Roma waited in silence, smoking, and then they set off again.

'Don't you know London well?'

'Just bits of it.'

'How long have you lived here?'

'Two months. But the roads are confusing.'

'You are English, aren't you?' He had, she thought, a slightly foreign look about him.

But he said, 'Through and through,' and they sped along Grosvenor Place, the blackness of the gardens to one side of them, the vast bulk of Belgravia to the other.

'And before you came to London? Where did you live?' How disappointing, she thought, if he names some dreadful little suburban town.

'I've been abroad for a few years.'

'Tell me.'

'I left England with a friend in 1919. After six months we went our separate ways. I travelled a bit, and I studied at the Sorbonne for a while. And then I lived in South America for a few years.'

'And now you are driving a cab. At night? Only at night?'

'Yes.'

'Are you an artist? Or a dancer?' She imagined taking him to the café, and introducing him to Sophie. Sophie would adore him and would add him to her collection.

'Good lord, no.' He seemed amused. 'I work by day for a barrister called Mr Swinton.'

He braked as they approached Roma's house. The taxi drew to a halt. He looked back at her. 'That'll be ninepence, madam.'

'I have an engagement tomorrow evening,' said Roma. 'Could you pick me up at ten o'clock, do you think? My name's Mrs Storm.' She dropped some coins into his palm.

Roma Storm had lived in London all her life. After art school, at which she studied portraiture, she had married. Her marriage had been short-lived and disastrous, and she had not repeated the experiment.

By the end of her twenties, she had abandoned portraiture for interior design, because it paid better. Roma inherited a flat in Pimlico on her parents' death, and set up an office for herself in the spare bedroom. She dreamed of the shop she would one day own, which would sell exquisite glassware and wallcoverings and furniture. But, ten years on, for want of capital, the shop remained a dream, and Roma's spare room still housed a clutter of fabric samples, paints and brushes.

Though she had abandoned portraiture, Roma Storm retained an eye for beauty. Thus her interest in her taxi-driver – twenty years ago, she thought, as she poured herself a drink and sank into the deep embrace of the sofa, she would have wanted to paint him. She did not want to now, and neither did she want to bed him. Partly because she had discovered, in the course of her brief marriage, that men did not suit her, and partly because, noticing her driver's frayed cuffs and hollow eyes, she had been surprised to recognize in herself a long-buried, almost-atrophied flicker of maternal instinct.

Derry drove for a few more hours, and then, when all the fares had been scooped up and the streets were empty of stragglers, he parked the cab outside Bill's house. The cab belonged to Bill, whom Derry had met in a pub. Derry drove a few nights a week because the money was useful, and because there was an excitement about London at night.

He walked to his lodgings in White Street in Stepney. The room was narrow, L-shaped because a piece had been cut out from it, partitioned with tin-tacked plywood to make space for another tenant. One of the window panes had cracked, so he had stuck on brown paper to hold the glass together. But through the clear panes he could see the river and its great fringe of cranes and steelyards. When the ships blew their funnels as they headed to open sea, Derry's heart always lifted.

Usually, he grabbed a few hours' sleep between abandoning the taxi and heading for Mr Swinton's chambers. But tonight he felt wide awake and alert, his mind buzzing with ideas. He made tea on the gas ring and, wrapping himself up in coat and blankets (he had forgotten how cold England was), he began to write. *The stagnation of the England of the mid-1920s*, he scribbled, *is a direct consequence of the continuing grip of the upper classes on the sources of power. Though war has led to the death of a generation, and though death duties have eaten away at land ownership, influence remains the prerogative of a handful of families.*

After a while, pausing, he read the piece through. Didactic and dull, he said out loud, tearing the page out of his notebook, crumpling it up, and throwing it into the bin.

At half past eight he took a bus to Mr Swinton's chambers. The two small offices were dusty and cramped, heaped with documents and folders. Mr Swinton appeared at ten o'clock. He had a bruise on his forehead and purple bags under his eyes.

'Bad night, Jack?' asked Derry sympathetically.

'Bloody awful.' Jack Swinton took a bottle from the bottom drawer of a filing cabinet. 'A swine in a pub said I'd cheated him. Said I'd take him to court for slander.'

'And battery,' said Derry, looking at the bruise.

'Absolutely.' Mr Swinton turned to Derry. 'What am I doing today?'

'You're representing a trade unionist. He's supposed to have committed an unprovoked attack, but he says mounted police came at him, truncheons swinging.' Derry indicated a heap of paperwork. 'I've made some notes.'

Mr Swinton lost the case, as Derry had expected him

to, so they commiserated with each other in a pub in Liverpool Street. After he had seen Mr Swinton, swaying slightly, onto his train, Derry walked back to his rooms.

It was Friday evening. Everyone seemed to be hurrying somewhere. He, alone, had no particular place to go. He had realized that London, like many of the other great cities of the world, was composed of a vast number of little enclaves. The ones he could have joined he did not wish to belong to. The ones he wanted to be part of did not, at the moment, include him.

At ten o'clock he drove to Mrs Storm's house. The previous night she had worn purple velvet; now she was dressed in iron-grey serge, much the same colour as her hair. She asked Derry to take her to a party in Bloomsbury. As he drew up outside the house, she said, 'Would you wait for me? This may be frightful.'

He fell asleep, waiting for her. Mrs Storm had to shake his shoulder to wake him. 'Dreadful, simply dreadful. *Poetry readings.*' She shuddered. 'I had to go,' she explained. 'Duty, not pleasure. They've just moved in, and the house is a mess, and I'm hoping they'll engage me to sort it out. I'm an interior designer, you see, darling,' she added, as she climbed into the back of the cab. 'Now, take me to Fitzroy Street, won't you? The Rose Café.'

It had begun to rain, and gaslights shimmered in the drizzle. Nights like this, Derry fell in love with London. Each closed doorway, every curtained window, seemed to offer promise and mystery. He had only to twitch aside the curtain, or to turn a handle.

The Rose Café was a narrow little façade of grimy window panes and peeling Art Nouveau lettering. The wheels of the taxi cast up curls of brown water from the puddles as Derry parked. Figures, blurred and hazy, moved behind the smeared glass. He could hear laughter and music.

Mrs Storm leaned forward, placing her hand on his shoulder. 'Now, my darling, I could pay you and you could drive away, and I could engage another cab to take me home tonight. Or . . .' She paused.

'Or?' he repeated.

'Or you could come in, and I could introduce you to some people.'

Looking at the café, Derry glimpsed bright colours and laughing faces.

'The cook,' coaxed Mrs Storm, 'makes the most marvellous pancakes. Do you like pancakes?'

'Immensely,' said Derry, and got out of the cab.

Inside the room, he stood at first in a corner, watching them. He had a sense of something about to happen, doors about to open.

Mrs Storm beckoned to him. 'Come and meet some of my friends. This is Lawrence Corcoran' – a thin, pale-haired boy – 'and this is Ruth Duncan.' Ruth was pink-cheeked, and her red-gold hair was cut into a bob. 'Lawrence and Ruth, this is . . .' She looked at Derry. 'You haven't told me your name, darling.'

'Derry Fox,' he said.

'Lawrence and Ruth are studying with Madame Rambert. I occasionally design sets, but ballet isn't really my *métier*.'

'Roma is too fond of black velvet and grey gauze,' said Lawrence. 'Like dancing in a cave.'

Several others had joined the table. Plates of pancakes and jars of syrup were placed in front of them. Their chatter filled the small room.

'. . . invited to a party in Hampstead.'

'Thank God the Tutankhamun craze is over. I was so utterly weary of sand-coloured upholstery and hieroglyphs.'

'I'll go because I haven't had a decent meal for ages, and the food's always marvellous there.'

A voice whispered in Derry's ear, 'You're not eating.'

He turned to look at her. Her hair clouded in a dark tangle around her small, pale face, and her eyes were a cool, intelligent hazel. 'I'm not hungry,' he said.

'I can never eat and talk at the same time. I find the one distracts from the other.' Her voice was pleasant, slightly accented.

Derry knew he was being observed and appraised. 'That must,' he said, 'make suppers rather awkward.'

'I listen,' she said. 'I like to listen. And to watch. You learn a great deal about people that way.' She looked at him. 'You, for instance.'

'What have you learned by watching me?'

'That you're not as at ease as you pretend to be.'

He felt himself flush. 'Don't be cross,' she said. 'It's not a failing.'

'I think it is.'

She shrugged. 'What else? That you're short of money.' She touched the frayed sleeve of his jacket.

'My belongings haven't yet arrived from South America. That's why I'm living a bit hand to mouth.'

'What were you doing in South America?'

It amused Derry to meet someone as direct as himself. 'Oh,' he said, 'various things. I taught English, and I wrote for a newspaper . . . but I was very bad at it, because everything I do reads like a pastiche, even when I don't mean it to.'

'And now? What will you do now?'

'Oh, I intend to be famous.'

Her brows rose. 'How?'

'I haven't worked that out yet,' he said cheerfully. 'I'll think of something.'

Mrs Storm called, 'Sophie, you're monopolizing my taxi-driver.'

Derry was drawn into the general conversation. The woman – Sophie – began to talk to someone else. The evening lengthened, the night punctured by new faces and fragments of conversation.

After Derry had driven Mrs Storm home that night, she asked him into her flat. The rooms were an extraordinary monochrome of black, white and silver. Derry imagined the surface of the moon to resemble Mrs Storm's drawing-room. She poured him a drink as he slithered uneasily on a vast white leather sofa.

There was a silence. She said, 'I wanted to ask you . . .'

'Yes?' His nerves tingled.

She looked at him. 'Not *that*.' She smiled. Then she looked down at her glass. 'I have a friend who stays with me sometimes. Her name is Leonora, and she has the loveliest little waist. I can circle it with my fingers.'

'*Oh*,' he said. He felt rather stupid.

'What I wanted to ask you, Derry, was, can you drive me at the weekend? I need to travel to a house in Harrow.'

Derry shook his head. 'I'm going to visit my parents. Besides, I only have the cab at night. But I could ask my friend to drive you, if you like.'

Derry sent a note to Jonathan on Friday: not enough time for himself to have second thoughts, or for his family to prevaricate.

He bought a new jacket with his taxi money and the

pittance he earned from Mr Swinton. He would not have his family think that he had failed. He was returning home for the first time since he had left England in 1919.

He arrived in Andover at mid-afternoon. Tea time. He imagined them sitting in the parlour at four o'clock, waiting for the maid to bring in tea and sandwiches, just as they had done throughout the years of his childhood. Everything unchanged, everything just the same.

Yet he noticed the differences as soon as he opened the garden gate. The front of the house had been repainted, and vast new flower beds, a municipal eruption of yellow primulas and scarlet tulips, lay to either side of the path. There was a motor-car parked in the driveway.

He was about to press the front doorbell, but a voice called out his name, and he turned and saw Jonathan.

'*Derry.*' His hand was seized, and pumped vigorously up and down. 'Derry – how marvellous – you've *grown* – and so *brown* . . .'

Derry remembered the last time he had seen Jonathan, five years ago, in the café near Victoria Station. The pallor and fragility had vanished, and now Jonathan's golden hair gleamed in the spring sunshine, and he looked tanned and fit, with no trace of a limp. Derry was aware of the usual mixture of emotions, affection and envy and an indefinable sort of regret.

He said, 'You look well, Jon.' Then he threw his arms round his brother and hugged him. His throat felt oddly tight, yet through his efforts not to disgrace himself and blub like a child, he noticed with some satisfaction that he himself was now almost as tall as Jonathan.

'Have you visitors? Whose is the car?'

'This?' Jonathan patted the bonnet of the MG. 'It's mine. Well, Dad bought it for me. We thought it would be handy for taking Mother out.'

They went inside the house. The familiarity of it, as well as the alterations, assaulted Derry. He pulled at the collar of his shirt. He felt suddenly nervous. His palms were damp with sweat.

'Are you all right?'

'Of course.' Derry made himself smile. 'Are they in the parlour?' He opened a door.

They sat in the overheated room, balancing cups of tea and plates of cake on their knees. His mother's conversation initially consisted of a list of her acquaintances who had died during the years of his absence. Derry half listened, his gaze flicking from one object to another – curtains, ornaments, antimacassars – assessing what was the same, and what was different. His mother, he thought, had not changed at all. The dim light (the room had a northern aspect, and the heavy curtains subtracted from what little sun there was) shadowed her beautiful eyes and fine cheekbones. He felt as he had felt most of his life, that there was a barrier between them, that those lovely blue eyes looked at him, and saw – what? He did not know.

Eva Fox added complacently, 'And Lily Carr – I believe she's failing fast.'

'Mrs Carr?' repeated Jonathan. 'Edith's mother?' He turned to Derry. 'You remember Edith Carr. We used to climb trees together.'

'*You* used to climb trees,' said Derry, 'And *I* used to fall out of them.' Jonathan laughed.

Derry turned to his father. 'Business going well, is it, Dad?'

Nicholas Fox stirred his tea. 'Very well. Jonathan has

been such a tremendous asset. We've been able to take on a number of new clients.'

His father *had* altered, thought Derry. Greyer, older, thinner. As though success, and his struggle from humble origins up the ladder to respectability, had worn away at him, exhausting him.

There was a silence. Then Jonathan said, 'Tell us what you've been doing with yourself, Derry.'

Derry glanced at the clock. Three-quarters of an hour, he thought. Three-quarters of an hour I've been here, and that's the first time anyone's asked me. It was as though he had been absent for five hours, not five years. His mouth was dry as he focused on his father. He felt as though he was spreading out the last few years of his life in front of him, to be picked over, examined, and found wanting.

'I travelled a bit,' he said. 'France and Italy and Germany to begin with. And then I was at the Sorbonne—'

'In *Paris*?'

'The Sorbonne's generally considered to be in Paris.'

Nicholas Fox's brow creased. Derry dug his nails into his palms.

'The Sorbonne . . .' prompted Jonathan tactfully.

'And then I went to South America.'

Eva Fox's pretty face puckered. 'The *diseases*, Derry. You are well, aren't you?'

He began to reassure her, but she went on, 'No fevers . . . rashes . . . I have to be so careful . . .'

'I'm fine.' Anger coiled in the pit of his stomach, a small, hard seed, waiting to flower. 'And I did some translating, and I worked for a newspaper.' He watched his father as he spoke. Say something, damn you, he thought. A single word . . . a smile . . . a gesture . . .

Flames roared in the fireplace; the heat reminded Derry of Lima in August. He was beginning to realize just how greatly he had underestimated his father's still smouldering disapproval of his own love affair with Sara Kessel. He said quickly, desperately, 'And I worked in a gold mine for a while – in the office, of course, not actually prospecting . . .'

'You surprise me,' murmured Mr Fox. 'I had assumed, Derry, that you had debased yourself in every possible fashion.'

There was a silence. The room was much too hot. Derry said, 'And now I'm working for a barrister in London.'

'His name, Derry?'

'Mr Swinton.'

'*Jack* Swinton?'

Derry nodded. What he most regretted was having been so stupid. To have believed for one moment that he could have ceased to be the small, dark, scapegrace son, to have thought that they might now see him differently.

His father stood up and went to the window, his back to his sons. Derry heard him sigh.

'I suppose I should have anticipated that. A final touch to your disreputable and shameful career.'

'I thought you'd be *pleased* about Mr Swinton, Dad – after all, he's a lawyer, like you.'

'Jack Swinton is a scoundrel. He is notorious. He defends Bolsheviks and shirkers. He's hardly ever sober, even when he's in court.'

'Can't be as bad as all that,' said Jonathan, placatingly.

'I assure you he is, Jonathan.'

'Absolutely,' said Derry. The fire roared; the room

was stifling, and he couldn't breathe. 'Can't argue with you, Dad. But it's a tricky question, isn't it? Is it better to be a drunken sot who nevertheless tries to look out for those who really need help, or is it better to be a sycophant who concentrates on watching his own back, and feathering his nest? *I* don't know. *You* decide.'

Nicholas Fox's face was purple. Eva Fox said faintly, 'So chilly . . . Do you think, Jonathan . . . a little more coal . . . ?'

'And Mother seemed to think that I must be carrying bubonic plague,' said Derry.

It was two days later. He was in bed with Sophie Berkoff. Sophie rented a room near the Embankment. There was a fold-down bed that threatened to fold up if one moved too quickly, and a chair, and a table, piled high with books and writing paper.

'I haven't asked anything of my father in five years. And all that I've done . . . he just crushed. Like this.' Derry clenched his fist.

Sophie shrugged. 'What did you expect, having been away so long?'

He didn't know. He sat up, his gaze fixed on the grimy little window.

'I expect they felt neglected and deserted,' she said gently. 'It's always easier to be the one who goes away than the ones who are left behind.'

Derry thought back to his afternoon in Andover, and groaned. 'And of course I ended up being sarcastic. And offensive. Just as I'd promised myself not to.' He put his head in his hands. 'They are so unspeakably awful, so why do I care?'

'They're your parents, Derry.'

'I even found myself claiming that I was working for

Jack Swinton out of altruism . . . or idealism. I'm not, of course. It's just a job.' He added angrily, 'Of course bloody Jonathan tried to smooth things over, just as he always does.'

'Jonathan?'

'My brother. The perfect Jonathan.'

'Why do you call him that?'

'Because he *is* perfect.' Derry flung out his hands. 'Handsome . . . athletic . . . *nice*.'

Sophie offered him a cigarette and lit one for herself. The frayed edge of the blanket had slipped down, revealing her small, pointed breasts. She smoked for a while, and then she said, 'You wanted your father to say, "I was wrong all the time. You're the better son, Derry. Please forgive me." ' Her cool hazel eyes focused on him.

'Shut up, Sophie,' he said amiably. He began to kiss her, pressing his mouth against her hard rosy nipples.

'It's true. You know that it is. And your desire for fame and recognition is, of course, just an expression of your need for a pat on the back from your father.'

He looked up at her. She was tiny, about four foot ten, with slender, fragile limbs, and that wonderful tangle of black hair. He imagined that all her patients must fall in love with her. She would call it *transference*, or some such Freudian claptrap.

Wriggling beneath the bedclothes, Derry ran his tongue along the sole of Sophie's foot. Suddenly, he grinned. 'And they didn't even mention Mrs Kessel.'

'Who's Mrs Kessel?'

'A friend,' he said vaguely. His voice was muffled by sheet and blanket. 'I went abroad with her when I was eighteen.'

'Will you go and see them again?' Sophie squirmed luxuriously as, one by one, he sucked each of her toes.

Derry momentarily emerged from the blankets. 'Jonathan made me promise, but I shan't.' His lip curled. 'I should never have gone back.'

Most nights of the week there were half a dozen paying guests staying at Owlscote. Half a dozen breakfasts to cook in the morning: eighteen rashers of bacon, twelve eggs, six sausages, six tomatoes. Alix was up before dawn on the busiest mornings, Rory under her feet as she dashed around the kitchen, yawning as she poured boiling water into teapots and made up tables. Her mother told her to get a girl in from the village to help, but Alix, checking figures in account books, refused. When they were safe, she said. They were not safe yet.

Two years earlier, Jonathan Fox had planted the idea that had saved Owlscote. *Salisbury can get so crowded on market days*, he had told her. *No room at the inn.* Alix had remained awake the entire night after that chance meeting, thinking, calculating. The next day she had put up a notice in the village post office. *Private Guest House. Competitive Rates. Home Cooking.* Her first paying guest, a carpet salesman, had knocked at Owlscote's door three days later. Mice ran over his bed during the night; in the morning, Alix burnt the sausages and boiled his egg to a grey, rubbery mass. The carpet salesman paid his twelve shillings and she never saw him again.

She bought a cat and a cookery book. More guests arrived: farmers visiting the market, men selling sheet music or mops and brushes. Some of them returned to Owlscote the next time they were in Wiltshire, as they travelled their slow circuits around the south of England. They told her their worries – their fickle wives and sick children, their uncertain jobs and palpitating hearts. She thought of them as her Gentlemen, and became fond of some of them, and was grateful to all of them because they had allowed her to keep Owlscote.

Alix shook the dust sheets from more bedrooms, scrubbing floors on her hands and knees, polishing windows until they gleamed. She laid fires in grates that had not been used in a decade; the chimneys coughed, spluttered, and spewed soot over the furniture, so she engaged a chimney sweep, and cleaned the rooms once more. It gave her immense pride and pleasure to bring the house slowly back to life. It was as though she was waking it up from a long sleep. She did not mind that she was exhausted, and that sometimes, retiring to bed at night, she was too tired to undress fully, so that she collapsed into bed in her skirt and jersey, pausing only long enough to kick off her shoes and stockings.

In the evenings, putting Rory to bed, she told him fairy stories, and sang him songs. She remembered how, a long time ago at the nursing home, she had said to Edward, *I shall never want children*. She thought how empty her life must have been then, and how hollow her heart. The passing of time was marked by another room opened and cleaned, and by the alterations in Rory. His first step, his first word, his first sentence. His small hand in hers as they walked through the garden at dawn, the long grass wet against their legs. He was a source of endless delight and pleasure and pride, and she guarded him with a fierce, protective love from the dangers that seemed to lurk around every corner: sickness and accident, and the possibility that one day, without warning, she might just turn and find him no longer there.

After the guest house had been running for six months, Alix persuaded her mother to come and live at Owlscote. Since Aylwyn Gregory's death, Beatrice had been subsisting in two rooms in Ipswich, supporting herself by taking in dressmaking. Letters crossed the country, mother to daughter, daughter to mother, Beatrice's notes dubious, afraid of change; Alix's coaxing and persuasive.

Beatrice Gregory arrived at Owlscote one damp spring morning. She said doubtfully, 'It's a lovely house. But – *paying guests*. It doesn't seem right, Alix. Who knows what sort of people . . . ?'

Mrs Gregory promised to stay for a fortnight to help make new curtains. The curtains took longer than expected, and somehow the fortnight extended into a month, and then two. After three months, Beatrice had become so attached to her small grandson that she could not bear to leave. In the evenings, she sometimes passed the time of day with one or two of the better class of guest. An expert gardener, she spent much of her time outdoors, unearthing shrubs and perennials from the blanket of weed that choked Owlscote's flower beds. Their relationship remained, Alix thought, amiable but distant. They neither quarrelled nor confided. They talked about Rory and the garden and the guest house. Never of Bell Wood, Beatrice's childhood home. Never of Charlie Lanchbury.

At the beginning of 1924, Alix sold two water-meadows, which paid for the cost of repairs to Owlscote's roof. With Freddie Maycross's help, she sold drawings from her archaeological sketchbook, capitalizing on the craze for all things ancient that had followed the discovery of Tutankhamun's tomb. The sketches paid for a new, modern range for the kitchen.

Beatrice told her not to work so hard. 'You should go out with friends, Alix. Go dancing . . . enjoy yourself. You're still young.'

'I've Rory and you, Mother, and my Gentlemen. And there's Jonathan, of course. What more could I want?' She needed, she thought, no-one else. And besides, she did not have time for anything else. Every moment of her day was taken up with Rory, or with Owlscote, or with the paying guests.

Jonathan Fox visited every now and then, and took them out for a spin in his motor-car. The car would gather speed, racing down the hills, and Rory, clasped tightly in Alix's arms, would scream with delight.

The part of the day Jonathan most enjoyed was walking home from work. He would go down the High Street, then past the Guildhall, turning towards the railway station. Then he headed up Weyhill Road, into the suburbs, passing familiar landmarks – the Faulkner-Greenes' house, with its octagonal turret dabbed on top like a cherry on a cake, and the Wicklows' rose garden, each bloom a triumphant twirl of brightly coloured perfection. There was a sameness, an unsurprisingness about his route home which Jonathan found deeply reassuring. He could, Jonathan sometimes thought, have walked back to the Avenue blindfolded.

At dinner one evening, Nicholas Fox said, 'I took tea with Mrs Winstanley this afternoon. The Misses Carr are staying there.'

Jonathan looked up. 'Edie's in Andover?'

'She asked after you, Jonathan.'

'How splendid. I haven't seen Edie for . . .' he thought back '. . . seven or eight years. How is she?'

'Very well, I believe, very well. Though Mrs Carr died recently.'

'London air,' murmured Eva Fox. 'So unhealthy. Poor Lily. She was a great reader, like myself. George

Carr came from a good family, but he was hopeless with money, of course. He left Lily and the girls very poorly provided for when he died.'

'She had a younger sister.' Jonathan's brow creased. 'Minnie . . .'

'Mina,' said Mrs Fox. 'A plain little thing. I always notice how beauty tends to concentrate itself in only one member of a family.'

Jonathan smiled. 'I'd love to see Edith again. She was such a good sport.'

He remembered Edith coxing the boat as he rowed along the river, Edith climbing the horse chestnut tree, her skirt tucked into the legs of her knickers, her knees scuffed and scabbed, Edith playing cricket on the Winstanleys' back lawn. She had bowled overarm; Jonathan recalled the crack of the ball against the stumps and Edith jumping up and down, her messy, tow-coloured plaits beating against her shoulders as she shouted, 'Bowled, Jon! You're bowled!'

'I suppose they could come to tea,' Eva said faintly. 'If I'm feeling better . . .'

Jonathan noticed that his mother had eaten hardly anything. The boiled mutton, potatoes and peas remained on her plate, untouched. She wore a dove-grey dress with a lace collar and a string of pearls. The pale, shimmering colours emphasized her fragile frame and delicate features. He felt a rush of anxiety for her. He wanted – *needed* – everything to stay just the same.

'If it'll be too much for you, Mother,' he said, 'then I could call on the Winstanleys myself. I'm sure Edith will understand.'

Eva Fox began to say bravely, 'You mustn't worry about me, dear—' but Jonathan's father interrupted.

'We should renew the acquaintance. As Miss Carr is Mrs Winstanley's goddaughter—'

'If Mother doesn't feel up to it—'

'Sadie can make the sandwiches and whatnot. You won't need to exert yourself, Eva.'

'I'll write a note, expressing my condolences.'

'. . . our duty. We must fulfil our obligations to society.'

Eva Fox said, 'I shall invite the Carr girls to tea next week. Thursday. Yes, Thursday.'

Jonathan came home early from the office the following Thursday, having looked forward all day to seeing Edith Carr again. Yet, when he opened the door of the drawing-room, there was only his mother and an unfamiliar woman.

It took him a second or two to realize that the woman was Edith. She was wearing a pink and white striped dress, white gloves, white shoes and stockings. Her hair was no longer two tangled, tow-coloured plaits, but a gleaming knot of gold tucked beneath a little pink hat.

'Edie,' he said, dazed. Then, 'I'm sorry . . . Miss Carr . . .'

She laughed. 'Edie will do, Jonathan. I always liked Edie.'

'You look . . . different.'

She laughed again. 'So do you.'

Jonathan kissed his mother on the cheek and, turning back to Edith, said, 'Your sister . . . ?'

'Mina isn't well, I'm afraid. It may be measles.'

Jonathan could see nothing of the tomboy in this elegant young woman. Only her eyes, a light, sparkling aquamarine, were familiar.

'I was so sorry to hear about your mother, Edith,' he said. 'You must miss her terribly.'

Edith murmured thanks. 'Auntie Marion was kind enough to invite Mina and me to stay with her, and we're having such a lovely time.'

'How old is Mina now?'

'She's fifteen.'

Jonathan shook his head. 'You're making me feel terribly ancient. To me, Mina's still a plump little girl in a pinafore dress.'

Edith glanced sideways at Jonathan. 'And Derry . . . how's Derry?'

'Oh, very well, I think,' said Jonathan vaguely.

'Aunt Marion told me he was abroad.'

'He's back in England now. Living in London. Having the time of his life, I don't doubt.' The Foxes had neither heard from nor seen Derry since he had visited in April.

After tea, Jonathan suggested to Edith that they walk in the garden. Her white-kid-shod feet trod carefully through the narrow gravel paths. The fast strides of the girl he remembered had diminished into neat, swaying little steps.

Jonathan smiled at her. 'Tell me what you've been doing, Edie.'

'Not much. I was engaged, but he was killed in the war.'

'I'm sorry.'

'And then we rented a house in Brighton – Mother thought the sea air might do her good – and after that we were in Scotland – the mountains, you see. But nothing worked, so we came back to London. Mother became bedridden, so I looked after her, and then she died. And one has a great deal to sort out after a death.' Edith's face had become closed and still.

He said, to cheer her up, 'We should play tennis. You always had a terrific forehand.'

She smiled. 'Aunt Marion's court isn't bad at all. What about Sunday, Jon?'

The noise woke Alix. A loud *boom*. She sat bolt upright in bed, her heart pounding. The boom was followed by a tearing, grinding noise, and then a loud, discordant clatter that seemed to fill her bedroom. She expected cracks to snake through the plasterwork, and Owlscote's old walls to crumble and decay. She grabbed her torch and coat and ran downstairs and out into the night.

Broken branches and dead leaves littered the ground. The storm had set in that evening, the first of the autumn gales. The heavy rain battered trees and gravel court-yard alike, so that fragments of twig and bark floated through rivulets of yellow water. Alix hoicked the long skirts of her nightdress out of the mud, and ran towards the copse. Conkers, expelled from their spiky green cases, lay scattered like marbles among the debris. The rain plastered her hair to her scalp.

Shining the torch, looking up, she saw that the horse chestnut at the edge of the copse had been felled by the wind. Half the great trunk, which the force of the gale had riven in two, listed against the furthermost corner of the house. The single-storey outhouse beneath was an unrecognizable heap of bricks and plaster. Lengths of guttering, caught up in the broken branches, protruded at acute angles from the side of the building. Tiles, sliding slowly from the apex of the roof, lay like scattered jigsaw pieces on the grass, their lichened surfaces smeared with mud. Huddled in her coat, Alix stepped between the broken branches and fragments of tile. Twigs and dead leaves, golden in the light of the torch, whirled in eddies around her head. The split halves of the tree trunk shivered and groaned as the wind blew harder.

The torchlight delineated the branches of the tree, and their close embrace of the house. The light swayed, a second moon sliding up the walls towards the roof. A sudden violent gust of wind dislodged another tile, sending it snaking towards the ground only a few feet away from her, smashing it to smithereens. Alix saw that the fallen tree was lodged against Owlscote's eaves. She thought, *Rory*, and ran back indoors.

Yet he slept undisturbed, thumb in mouth, his knees drawn up to his chin. Alix tucked the blankets around him, and climbed the stairs to the attics. There was no electric light in these rooms, and the gleam from her torch cast up from the darkness the shadowed swirl of an ammonite, and the curve of a white bone, dug up from some ancient tumulus. When she reached the furthermost attic, she saw the broken glass, and the litter of leaf and twig and rafter. Her knuckles pressed against her teeth as she stared up at the rain that drummed through the gaping hole in the ceiling.

There wasn't enough money in the bank to repair the roof. Tarpaulins flapped at Owlscote's gable end. No-one dared walk round the side of the house for fear of being decapitated by falling tiles. Some of Alix's regulars, alarmed by Owlscote's rackety appearance, decamped to the White Hart in Salisbury. Rory's toes were touching the ends of his boots, and he had grown out of his winter coat. The fires gobbled up coal.

Alix pinned up another advertisement in the village

pub. Two men in boots and overalls knocked at the door, asking to be put up for the night. After they had been shown into the house, Beatrice Gregory whispered, 'Alix, it won't do. People will think Owlscote is a working-men's hostel!' to which Alix hissed furiously, 'I don't care what people think. Those men have *money*. *That's* what matters.'

Jonathan Fox called one afternoon. They were drinking tea in the kitchen when he suggested Alix accompany him for a day out in London. She snapped, 'The rail fare, Jonathan. How could I possibly afford the rail fare?'

'I meant . . . as a treat. You look tired. I thought you might like a day out. And besides—'

'I won't accept charity.'

He turned away then, but she glimpsed the expression in his eyes. She saw what she was becoming, and what worry and responsibility were turning her into, and she touched his hand. 'Jonathan, I'm so sorry . . .'

'I thought I'd drive, actually, Alix. It would mean an early start, but I'm going to call on an old friend – Edith Carr – who works in London, and then I'm going to see if I can find my brother.' He frowned. 'Derry. Do you remember him?'

In a sudden sharp recollection, Alix recalled the nursing home, and the impatience and anger in Derry Fox's dark eyes when, all those years ago, he had said to her, *our generation – yours and mine – will probably never come to anything much.*

'Derry hasn't visited or written since April,' explained Jonathan. 'He came home just the once. The visit wasn't a success, I'm afraid – Derry and Dad argued. He was abroad for years, and I thought that once he came back to England we'd see each other, and that everything would be like it used to be. He promised to write, but he hasn't. I'm worried that something may have happened to him, or that he may be unwell.'

'Do you know where he's living?'

'He didn't leave an address, but he told us that he was working for a barrister in London.' Jonathan smiled. 'What do you say, Alix? How about a day's holiday?'

Suddenly she thought of Freddie Maycross. An idea – the answer to her financial worries – began to form in the back of her head.

'I'd love to, Jonathan.'

CHAPTER FIVE

In London they parted, Jonathan heading for Edith Carr's offices in Golden Square, and Alix travelling by Tube to the Embankment, and then to the Savoy Hotel, where she met Lord Maycross.

After she and Freddie Maycross had dined, Alix slid her portfolio across the table towards him. 'I brought these on the off chance. I wondered whether you might be able to place them for me, Freddie. There are some drawings and a series of articles I've written for a magazine. I've called them "Married Life in Mesopotamia".'

Beneath the table, she knotted her fingers together. Freddie put on his reading glasses and peered at the handwritten pages.

'Terrific stuff,' he said at last. 'Terrific. Don't know how you do it, Alix. Hellishly clever.'

'Do you think you can find me a publisher?'

Freddie took off his spectacles and polished the glass with a linen handkerchief. 'Might take a while – Billy Beresford's in Egypt. Three or four months.' He looked at her. 'No rush, is there, dear girl?'

Alix made an effort to rearrange her features. 'Of course not, Freddie. No rush at all.' She replaced the written sheets and drawings in the folder.

'How's things, then? How's the boy?'

'Rory's splendid. My mother's looking after him. He can count up to five.' Alix marvelled at how she could talk so easily when panic had begun to flutter once more in the pit of her stomach. When she thought of Owlscote she felt angry, angry that after all her hard work, all her ingenuity, she might yet lose her home.

Later, parting from Freddie, her low spirits seemed to reflect the bleakness of the December weather. Iron-grey clouds swelled on the horizon. Another storm, she thought furiously, and Owlscote's attics would be awash.

Jonathan picked her up outside the hotel, and they headed east. The offices of Jack Swinton, Derry Fox's employer, were above a grocery shop in Cheapside. Jonathan and Alix climbed two flights of stairs which were perfumed with nutmeg and molasses. Peeling gilt paint announced Mr Swinton's name. There was no answer to Jonathan's knock, so, after a few moments, he pushed the door open.

The rooms seemed at first to be empty. Towers of paperwork sprouted from floors and chests of drawers, and every ashtray overflowed with dog ends. An inefficient coal fire belched out smoke. There were avalanches of box-files and notebooks, and cardboard boxes full of empty bottles. Crusts curled on crumb-ridden plates. Jonathan coughed loudly.

An inner door opened. A voice said, 'Thank goodness. I thought you were the bailiffs.'

Alix could hardly remember Derry Fox. Only his dark, unsettling eyes remained fixed in her memory. She did not think, though, that this plump, shambling, untidy man could be Jonathan Fox's brother.

'Mr Swinton?' asked Jonathan.

'Jack Swinton.' He was eating a Chelsea bun. He wiped icing sugar from his fingers and held out his hand.

'Can I help you, Mr . . . ?'

'Fox. Jonathan Fox. And this is Mrs North.'

'*Ah*.' A sticky handshake. Mr Swinton looked disappointed. 'Not a customer then.' He looked at Jonathan. 'Some relation of the elusive Derry?'

'His brother.'

'Ah,' said Mr Swinton again. '*Brother* . . . I hadn't expected . . . somehow one always imagines Derry to be cast adrift, like an orphan in a storm . . .' He swallowed the last piece of Chelsea bun, and said, through a mouthful of crumbs, 'His lost look, I suppose, which makes one feel sorry for him even when one wants to throttle him.'

'Isn't he here, Mr Swinton?'

'I'm afraid not. Haven't seen him all week.'

'Do you know where I might find him? Have you his home address?'

'I may have a note of it . . .' Mr Swinton, opening a drawer, rifled through its overflowing contents. 'Accounts . . . bills . . . it's in the cabinet, perhaps . . .' Crossing the room, he opened a door. Letters and folders waterfalled to the floor. 'Oh dear. How long do you have? This could take a while . . .'

Jonathan picked up his hat. 'If you could tell Derry I called.'

'My pleasure.' As Jonathan opened the door, Mr Swinton added, 'He frequents a café in Fitzroy Street, I believe.'

'A café?'

'The Rose Café. You may find him there.'

Outside, Jonathan said, 'Do you mind, Alix? If you have to get back . . . It shouldn't take long, though.'

Alix murmured reassurances. The night was drawing in, and it had begun to rain. As they drove to Fitzroy Street, raindrops made dark circles on the pavement. Outside the narrow, shabby facia of a café, Jonathan paused.

'This must be it.' He sounded doubtful.

Alix could hear music, only slightly muffled by the fragile barrier of glass and wood. The window panes seemed to vibrate with the noise. Bodies pressed against the glass, and she glimpsed an outflung arm, a lock of fair hair, and a leg encased in a scarlet stocking. She pushed open the door.

It was as though she had been hit by a tidal wave. The heat and noise and the gaudy colours of the place assaulted her. Behind her, she heard Jonathan shout, 'Is Derry Fox here?' and a woman's voice called back: 'I think I've seen him. Somewhere, darling . . .'

Alix pressed further into the crowd. When she looked back, she saw that Jonathan was talking to a woman wearing a pink feather boa. People moved and jostled, and he was gone. A man touched Alix's arm, and said enquiringly, 'Betty? No, *much* prettier than Betty . . .' and she pulled away, threading through tables and chairs, almost tripping over an overturned orange box with an ouija board on top of it. Someone pushed a glass into her hand, and, thirsty, Alix gulped down its contents. She was unable to identify what she was drinking; it tasted of humbugs, perhaps, or furniture polish. On a tiny dance floor, not more than six foot square, a dozen couples were dancing, their bodies folded against each other, writhing in time to the music, their feet hardly moving at all. Alix drained her glass.

A voice in her ear said, 'Even the decadent French poets didn't knock back their absinthe as fast as you drink our rather dreadful punch, Miss Gregory.'

She spun round. Derry Fox added, 'How marvellous to see you, and how clever of Fate, to bring us together again. Have you forgotten me, Miss Gregory? We met years ago, in a nursing home, over a great many chamber pots.'

Alix said sharply, 'Your brother's looking for you, Mr Fox. And I'm Mrs North now, not Miss Gregory.'

'Jonathan?' Derry Fox peered into the crowds. 'Jonathan's here?'

Alix felt peculiarly blurred. 'Jonathan was worried about you, Mr Fox, so he came to find you. And the sooner you've introduced yourself to him, and reassured him that you're alive and well, the sooner I'll be able to go home.'

He did not go, but said, 'Don't you like parties?'

'I haven't been to many. I can't really see the point of them.' She undid the buttons of her coat; the room was much too hot.

'They're for mixing people up, Mrs North. Actually, they are for giving people an excuse to go to bed with each other.'

She thought he was trying to shock her, so she ignored him and looked through the crowds, trying to find Jonathan.

'I've always rather liked parties,' said Derry. 'You set things up, and then you sit back and watch what happens. It's so unpredictable. Like writing a story without having to work out the ending. Endings are the most difficult bit, don't you think? I'm writing something at the moment, and I'm hellishly stuck for an ending.'

She looked sharply at him. 'I thought you worked for a barrister.'

'Some of the time. And sometimes I drive a taxi, which is great fun, and sometimes I write my memoirs. Well, not *mine*, obviously – I haven't done enough yet. No, I'm an anonymous aristocrat, telling all. It's splendidly salacious.' He paused. 'What about you, Mrs North? Do you do anything, or is Mr North so fabulously rich you'll never have to wash another chamber pot again?'

She said, 'I run a guest house. And Captain North is dead,' and one of the couples on the dance floor stumbled and fell against them, dividing her from Derry Fox.

Pinioned against the wall, Alix struggled to recover her breath. The dregs of her glass had spilt over her dress. Her hair had come down from the neat bun she had pinned it in that morning, falling over her shoulders in a straggling dark knot. Disentangling herself, she heard Derry say, 'My father always used to point out to me how *damnably* crass I can be. I'm sorry.'

'It doesn't matter.'

'Was he nice?'

She was silent for a moment, and then she said, 'Edward? Yes. Very. He was kind and gentle and intelligent. Not clever – intelligent. There's a difference.'

'Of course.'

She could not think why she was telling Derry Fox about Edward. She never talked much about Edward. Talking about him reminded her how much she missed him.

'Did you love him?'

'That's an impertinent question, don't you think, Mr Fox?'

'I only ask,' said Derry, 'because I'm never sure how one knows. I mean, desire is easy, isn't it? But love . . . I only tend to know when I *don't* love someone.'

'I didn't love Edward at first, I suppose, but then I did.

Or I thought I did.' Her voice was harsh. 'But now . . . sometimes I can't remember what he looked like. Is that love, d'you think, Mr Fox, if, when someone's been dead for three years, you can't remember what they looked like?'

She broke away from him, pushing her way through the crowds towards the door. Outside, she leaned against the peeling facia, breathing in the cool late afternoon air. Her anger had died, leaving her drained and weary, and still faced with insoluble financial problems. The alcohol, she thought: she must have drunk too much, or she would never have voiced to a stranger some of the doubts that had come to haunt her over the past months. Mist swirled around the gaslamps and the headlights of the cars; perched on the narrow window sill, she raised her head and let the tiny droplets of water cool her face.

A voice said, 'I thought you might like this.' Derry Fox held out a cup to her.

Alix shook her head.

'It's tea.'

'*Oh.*' She took the cup, warming her hands.

'And I've seen Jon. We've kissed and made up, in fact.'

She drank her tea. Then she put down the cup, and said, 'In there . . . I'm afraid I'd had too much to drink.'

'I prefer you angry to embarrassed, Mrs North,' he said. 'Your eyes look marvellously green when you're angry, did you know that? Like pea pods.' He gave her his hand to help her up. 'And now, won't you let me introduce you to my friends?'

She met Lawrence and Sophie and Eric and Poppet. They all wore either funereal black or startling, outlandish colours, and beside them Alix felt drab and old-fashioned. Then Derry said, 'I particularly wanted *you* to meet Mrs North, Roma.'

Roma was in her mid-forties, Alix guessed, and tall and thin. Her hair was cut in a severe bob, her grey eyes rimmed with kohl. She shook Alix's hand.

'My brother tells me,' Derry explained to Roma, 'that Mrs North lives in a wonderful old house which is falling to bits and is terribly expensive to repair.'

'*Jonathan*,' said Alix, furiously.

'I'm sorry, Alix.' Jonathan, red-faced, ran his hands through his hair. 'It just slipped out.'

They were crushed around a table in the centre of the café. The room had emptied, and the pianist's music had become gentle and seductive. A single couple remained on the dance floor, two bodies melting into one, swaying slowly.

Mrs Storm sat down next to Alix. 'I adore old houses. Tell me about your home.'

'Owlscote?'

'Marvellous name,' interrupted Derry. 'Makes one think of darkened windows and crumbling archways and simply *festoons* of cobwebs.'

'That's just about it,' Alix admitted. 'Especially the crumbling and the cobwebs.'

'Wonderful place for a party.'

Roma's eyes had narrowed. 'You are plotting again, my darling Derry.'

'I'm thinking of Peggy Gordon.'

'A finger in every pie, my dear. Our Derry has a finger in every pie.'

'We'd like to borrow your house, you see, Mrs North. For a suitable fee, of course.'

'Borrow Owlscote?' Jonathan looked startled. '*Derry . . .*'

Alix's gaze had focused on her gloves, which were lying on the table. The darns at each fingertip, the small pearl button hanging by a thread. 'Please explain.'

'A friend of mine, Peggy Gordon, wants to give a really wonderful Christmas party. But she lives with a miserable old guardian whose idea of fun is a glass of lukewarm sherry and a round of canasta.'

Roma Storm offered her cigarette case to Alix. 'I've only Virginian, I'm afraid – autumn's always a thin time for me. People will insist on having their houses decorated in the spring.' She fitted a cigarette into an ebony holder. 'Fancy dress parties are all the rage just now,' she explained. 'And not everyone has the space. Or wants their home transformed into the Temple of Nefertiti.'

'Owlscote could be a marvellous backdrop.' Derry's voice coaxed. 'And financially rewarding for you, of course.'

Roma Storm said, '*Possibly* one of your more sensible notions, Derry.'

'Peggy's wouldn't be too big an affair. A sort of trial run, if you like.'

Alix thought of the tarpaulin over Owlscote's roof. She remembered Freddie Maycross saying, *It might take a while . . . three or four months*. In only a few years' time, she would have to find money to pay Rory's school fees. How foolish, she thought, to let her pride, her enjoyment of her privacy, jeopardize both Owlscote and Rory.

'I'm not sure . . .'

'Just an evening . . .'

'We'd clear up all the mess afterwards.'

'I'd organize the decorations.'

'And I do so adore parties . . .'

There was a silence. She felt them looking at her. She said doubtfully, 'Would it work?'

'Of course it would. I always find that one can do anything one wants as long as one wants it enough.'

'But then you, Derry,' said Mrs Storm crushingly, 'have no shame.' She looked at Alix. 'Would you mind letting strangers into your beautiful home? Have you reservations?'

'I can't afford to have reservations, Mrs Storm,' Alix said bluntly. 'I need to earn money.' Out of the blue, she had been offered a solution to her problems. A weight seemed to be lifting from her shoulders.

'It would mean a lot of work for you.'

'I don't mind work. And the paying guests don't tend to stay at weekends. But some of the rooms are rather dreadful, I'm afraid. There's damp, and the plaster's falling away.'

'Character,' said Derry firmly.

'Absolutely. Part of the charm of the place.'

'And there's only electricity in some of the rooms, and no running hot water.'

'Dear me.' Mrs Storm shook her head. 'How people *survive* in the country . . . And not much in the way of heating, I assume? We shall just have to give our guests such a splendid time that they shan't notice such inconveniences.' Mrs Storm smiled. 'I think it's a splendid idea, don't you?'

Returning to Owlscote, Alix thought, fancy dress parties . . . *ridiculous*, and put to the back of her mind her conversation with Derry Fox and Roma Storm. Then the wind got up again, sweeping one of the tarpaulins from the roof, and she spent a morning perched precariously on a ladder, helping Jacob Long reinstate it. The following morning, a postcard arrived from Derry. It said, 'Peggy says *yes*. What about the 23rd?' That evening, she wrote a letter, inviting both Derry Fox and Roma Storm to Owlscote.

They arrived one afternoon the following week. Alix showed them into the house. In the hall, Derry paused, looking round, and whistled.

'So terribly dramatic,' said Roma Storm, eyeing the high ceiling. 'So many *possibilities*.' She consulted a notebook. 'We'll need a room for dining, and a room for dancing, of course.'

Alix opened the door to the Great Hall. 'I thought they could dance in here.'

'Yes. Such a marvellous floor . . . and that stunning fireplace. It's perfect, my dear.' Then Roma frowned. 'We'll have to hire musicians. Derry . . . ?'

'I know some people. Friends of Lawrence's.'

Roma turned to Alix. 'What about chairs . . . tables . . . or shall we have a buffet?'

'How many guests will there be?'

'Sixty,' said Derry. 'Maybe sixty-five.'

'*Sixty!*' Alix stared at Derry. 'But you said it would be a *small* affair . . . I imagined twenty – thirty at the most . . .'

'If you're having second thoughts, Mrs North . . .'

'Five pounds a head,' said Derry.

'. . . only you'd better let us know, because we'll have to make other arrangements.'

Sixty-five times five pounds. Alix made quick calculations. She took a deep breath. 'Of course I'm not having second thoughts. And there's plenty of chairs and tables. We'll have a sit-down dinner, not a buffet. Less messy.'

Derry said, 'We thought a three-way division of profits—' but Alix interrupted him.

'No. A half for me, the other half to be split between Mrs Storm and yourself. I'll be providing the house, after all. And the food.' She swallowed. 'But there's one thing I must insist on. I want to see the guest list before the party. And I want it to be understood that I may refuse to admit any guest I choose, without explanation.'

'How extraordinary.' In the cobwebby shadows of the hall, Derry Fox stared back at her, dark eyes wide. 'Why? Are you trying to avoid someone? Have you a guilty secret? Do you—'

She said coldly, 'If I choose not to admit a guest because I dislike the colour of his hair, or because I take offence at the initials of his Christian names, then so be it.'

Alix had noticed that Roma Storm, in her elegant velvet coat, was shivering, so she offered them both a cup of tea. In the kitchen, Roma checked her list once more.

'Dinner – we'll leave that to you, if we may, Mrs North – but my advice is to keep it simple. People never eat a great deal at these affairs – too keen to get back to the dancing.'

'Decorations?'

'Again, we'll keep it simple this time. Something Christmassy. I'll send down some streamers and lanterns. And perhaps you can supply the greenery . . .' Roma glanced out of the window. Sleet slithered down the pane. She shivered again.

'There's masses of holly and ivy in the woods.' Rory, Alix thought, would enjoy helping her to gather it.

'And champagne. We'll need plenty of champagne.'

'I'll organize that,' said Derry. 'I know a chap with a van who'll drive it down.'

Roma lit a cigarette. 'I won't come to the party, of course.'

'Roma hardly ever leaves London,' explained Derry. 'She thinks that the world ends at Ealing.'

'Ridiculous boy,' said Roma fondly. She had put her fur collar up around her face. 'Such a wonderful house . . . But the *cold* . . .'

Roma and Derry caught a bus back to Salisbury, and then took the London train. Roma sat in the corner of the carriage and smoked, and Derry watched the first dusting of snow bleach the ploughed fields and the roofs of the houses. He thought that the party idea would be useful, because then he would meet people. He had known for a long time that you didn't get anywhere unless you knew the right people.

The train paused for a while at Andover station, but Derry remained in the carriage. He would not visit his parents until he had something to show for his efforts: his name on the spine of a book, perhaps, or on the lease of a house. It had been a mistake to go home in April. He'd keep in touch with Jonathan, though, because otherwise Jon would look at him with wounded eyes, and make him feel a heel. Or worse, Jon might turn up again at Jack Swinton's, and witness the empty Scotch bottles and the unpaid bills. Derry himself had not been paid by Mr Swinton in three weeks. He still sometimes went to the office, though, because it was quiet there, and he could write his memoirs in peace. His White Street rooms were impossible just now because the next door tenant gave frequent piano lessons to children startlingly lacking in talent.

As the train drew out of the station, Derry settled back in a corner of the carriage and closed his eyes. He thought about Alix North. Beautiful, reserved Alix North. There was a solidity about her that belied her fragile, willowy appearance. Her house, and her child, gave her a permanence that contrasted sharply with the transient, capricious people with whom he spent much of his time. He had been intrigued by her insistence on checking the guest list – secrets there, he suspected. He thought of the house, Owlscote. How much easier it was, in some ways, if you were a woman, and beautiful, and could marry into that sort of thing. Only it wasn't exactly the house, or the money, or the status that he wanted. He remembered Sophie Berkoff saying, *You want your father to say, 'You're the better son, Derry.'* Reluctantly, he acknowledged the grain of truth in her words, but he knew that he wanted more than that. Yet fame and recognition, he reflected, were proving rather more elusive than he had anticipated when he had left England in 1919.

It didn't seem much to ask, the chance to make his mark. To say, look at that, I was there, I did that. He needed to prove he existed; he needed to show that he had sloughed off for ever the stifled, narrow world that was his birthright. How dreadful, Derry thought, as he dozed off, to drift through life leaving no evidence of your passing, like the gobbets of snow that slid ever so slowly down the smoky windows of the carriage.

At eight o'clock, just before the guests were due to arrive, Alix took from the cupboard the bottle of Scotch she kept for colds and influenza, and poured herself a large measure. Then she walked out of the room, the glass clutched in her hand. She moved quickly round Owlscote, glancing into the dining-hall, where plates and cutlery were set out on the long oak table, pausing in the Great Hall to throw more logs on the fire. At the top of the stairs, she looked out of the window. The moon silvered the lawn and the naked branches of the trees in the copse. She could just see the splintered stump of the fallen horse chestnut.

The past fortnight had been a marathon of organization and hard work. Alix had mopped floors, polished furniture, cleaned windows. She had prepared and cooked, with the help of Martha Long, a dinner for sixty. She had wandered through the woods and the orchard, Rory at her side, cutting armfuls of holly, ivy and mistletoe. She had tried to reassure her mother that the party was not another downward plunge in Owlscote's and her own slow but steady loss of reputation. She had scanned the guest list, running her finger down the column of names until, shaky with relief, she had reassured herself that the name she dreaded seeing was not there.

Now, all her doubts flooded back, tenfold. Alix swallowed the whisky quickly, struggling to damp down her sudden nervousness. Hearing a footstep on the stairs behind her, she spun round.

Derry said, 'It'll be all right. I promise.'

'It's just . . . all those *strangers*.'

'They're nice people. Really.'

'What if it just doesn't *work*?'

'It will do.'

'And Rory . . .' Alix glanced at the nursery door.

'A friend of mine will sit here and shoo the stragglers downstairs. Bill is enormously large, and no-one will argue with him. Rory won't hear a thing.' Derry held out his hand to her. 'Come down now. There's something we have to do.'

They went into the Great Hall. Alix thought how marvellous the room looked, dripping with greenery and candles. And how right it was that music and laughter would echo here again. Her anxieties receded.

'The jazz band's not quite ready,' said Derry. 'But I have a gramophone.'

He fitted a needle to the arm. The small, tinny notes of the foxtrot were almost lost in the cavernous acreage of the Hall.

'Will you dance, Mrs North?'

She found herself in his arms. She could not remember when she had last danced – in the desert, with Edward, perhaps – but her feet, rusty at first, seemed after a little while to recall the steps. Swept up by music and movement, she forgot her nervousness. Alix and Derry whirled round the perimeter of the room, she tripping over her toes and collapsing into giggles as the first motor-cars headed down the driveway.

Alix handed round champagne and wine as the guests poured into the house. Later, she helped Martha and a girl from the village serve dinner. In the kitchen, they scraped plates and hurled dirty cutlery into scalding water, and washed and polished more glasses, and uncorked another dozen bottles of champagne. Opening the door to the Great Hall, Alix paused, momentarily dazed, hardly able to recognize the room. Sixty guests, the women's beaded dresses and jewelled headbands sparkling, danced to the music of the jazz band. Alix checked that no hot cinders had escaped from the log fire, and that the candles were a safe distance from embroidered muslin skirts and long, fringed silk scarves. In the bedroom set aside as a ladies' cloakroom, she offered a needle and thread to a girl whose hem had come down, and a handkerchief to another who had been crossed in love. She found aspirins and water for a green-hued young man who had drunk too much, and a sticking plaster for another who had stabbed himself on a holly branch. On the upstairs landing she nodded to Derry Fox's friend, Bill, who stood, arms folded and silent, guarding the nursery door. Inside the nursery, she lingered for a moment, treasuring the silence, looking down at her sleeping son. Then she trailed the back of her fingers very gently against the pink, velvety cushion of Rory's cheek, and returned to the party.

At midnight, they toasted Miss Gordon. All the guests roared 'For she's a jolly good fellow'. Balloons billowed from the ceiling, and streamers zigzagged through the air. When a solo voice fluted out the opening phrases of 'The First Nowell', a shiver ran the length of Alix's spine. Then everyone in the room joined in. She thought that the chorus might raise the roof.

At around two in the morning, the guests began to drift away. After the last straggler had left the house, Alix returned to the kitchen. Pots and pans and trays of glasses were piled high on the table.

Derry was feeding tangled paper streamers to the stove. 'Have they all gone? None asleep in a cupboard upstairs?'

'I've checked. They've all left. And I've sent Martha and Sally home. They looked exhausted.' Alix piled some of the better leftovers onto a plate and curled up on the sofa.

'I can never sleep after parties,' said Derry. 'I usually write my memoirs or go for a walk.' He glanced at her. 'Did you enjoy it?'

She realized that she had enjoyed it immensely. 'Very

much. I've never given a party before, you know.' Every muscle in her body ached. Alix knew that she should go to bed, that in a few short hours she must be up to attend to Rory, yet she felt elated and wakeful.

Derry used the poker to shove the last of the streamers into the stove. 'Not even when you were a little girl?'

'My parents were both quite old when they married, and my father was often unwell, so we lived very quietly. What about you?'

'Parties? No, not when I was a child. I've always thought that's why I like them so much now.' He lit a cigarette. 'Jonathan had birthday parties, though.'

'Why Jonathan and not you?'

He grinned. 'Because I could always be relied on to do something inconvenient – get over-excited and run a temperature – fuss if I didn't win Oranges and Lemons.'

'And Jonathan?'

'Oh, Jon tried to please. To play happy families. As he does now.' Derry propped himself against the wall. 'Rather a challenge, even for Jon.'

His tone of voice annoyed her. 'I'm very fond of Jonathan,' she said. 'He's kind, honest, straight-forward—'

'Of course he is. A source of utter torment to me at prep school and beyond.'

'What do you mean?'

'You haven't any brothers or sisters, have you? Of course not, or you'd know *exactly* what I mean. When I first went to school, I longed to be like Jonathan. I used to fantasize that he might break his leg, and then I'd have to take his place in the team, and everyone would see how wonderful I was. Of course' – Derry raised his shoulders – 'the truth is that my life would have been hell if it hadn't been for Jonathan. He protected me.'

'Which you resented.'

He smiled. After a while he went on, 'I was still at school, of course, when they started adding the dates to the notice board. You know – "So-and-So Minor 1897–1916". The old boys who'd died in France. It always seemed to be the most glorious ones who were killed – the rowing blues, the captains of the first fifteen or whatever. I'd have *prayed* for Jon if I hadn't been a convinced atheist by then.' His dark eyes narrowed. 'Anyway, he came back, as you know. You helped put him together. Only he isn't quite as all right as he pretends to be, is he? No-one would be after *that*.'

'It's an understandable sort of self-deception.'

'Of course it is. And we all do it.'

'Even you?' She put aside her plate.

'Most certainly me.' Derry closed his eyes. Alix thought for a moment that he had fallen asleep, but then he said slowly, 'I deceived myself into thinking that my father would have forgiven me for something that happened six years ago. That he would welcome me back into the family with open arms. The prodigal son . . . When I think how stupid I was . . . it *embarrasses* me.'

She thought that embarrass was not the right word. *Hurt*, perhaps. But she was too tired to argue.

'What did you do?'

'Oh, my father's best client's sister-in-law took me for her lover. She was forty-one, which people thought very shocking, for some reason. Here – have my jacket – you look cold.'

Alix tucked Derry's jacket around her shoulders. Of their own volition, her lids were closing. 'Perhaps your father thought,' she said, 'that you'd done it deliberately.'

'Well, one doesn't do that sort of thing accidentally. Oh. You mean, chosen *her* deliberately. To spite him.'

'Yes.'

'You sound like Sophie. People will persist in trying to psychoanalyse me.'

'Had you?'

'Intended to annoy?' Another silence. 'I don't know. Perhaps. Probably.'

Alix's eyes had closed. Fleeting images from the evening fluttered in her mind's eye. Twins, identical in eau de Nil chiffon, sliding down the banisters. Miss Gordon, clapping her hands together and proclaiming it the best party ever. A red-haired young man, smiling widely, walking towards her and shaking her hand, thanking her for letting them borrow Owlscote. She saw his face so clearly now. She whispered, 'It's so lovely to see you again, Charlie,' and then she fell asleep.

Much later, the sun, filtering through the curtains, woke her. Alix struggled to open her eyes. The room seemed unfamiliar. It took a moment or two to recall that she had not gone to her bedroom, but had slept the night on the sofa in the kitchen. There was a blanket tucked over her shoulders and something heavy against her feet. Wriggling upright, she opened her eyes properly, and saw Derry Fox.

He was curled up on the other end of the sofa, his head resting on its upholstered arm. His eyes were shut. She shook his shoulder.

'You have to wake up. My *mother* . . .' she hissed. She stood up. The blanket slithered to the floor. She couldn't find her shoes. Derry didn't move, but remained where he was, his clothes dishevelled, his hair a dark bird's nest, rubbing his eyes.

'Mr Fox!' she cried. 'You have to go home!'

'I do feel' – and he stared at her – 'that having spent the night together, we could dispense with formalities.'

Alix's face burned. Turning her back to him, she filled the kettle and plonked it loudly on the stove. 'Derry, then. You have to go, Derry.'

'Of course. Or your mother will drive me out with a pitchfork.'

She found herself torn between exasperation and laughter. Derry headed for the door, laces trailing from his shoes. Then he turned and looked back at her.

'It was a good party, wasn't it, Alix?'

She smiled. 'It was a wonderful party.'

The success of Peggy Gordon's party allowed Alix to repair Owlscote's roof. As soon as the weather improved, the tarpaulins were stripped off, the eaves mended, and the tiles replaced. Alix bought Rory a new pair of shoes, and put aside a portion of her earnings in the bank for rainy days to come.

They gave another party. A Scottish party, for a hundred guests. Derry Fox decorated the Great Hall with tartans, and painted papier mâché shields and claymores, sent by Roma. Alix cooked mounds of haggis, tatties and neeps. Before the party, she ran her fingertip down the guest list, checking that the name she dreaded seeing was not there. At Owlscote's front door, a piper welcomed the guests, and a fiddler played jigs and reels. Once more, the party was a resounding success; once more, Alix found herself swept up in the music and conversation and laughter. Afterwards, she bought a new coat for Rory, and had a hundredweight of coal delivered to the outhouse.

She kept the paying guests and the party guests separate. Paying guests from Monday to Friday, parties on Saturday night. She ignored the curious stares of the villagers and her mother's sniffs and disapproving comments. She engaged a plasterer to repair the chimney piece in the drawing-room. She helped Derry pin up decorations, and she cooked tureen-loads of food. Together they welcomed armies of celebrants and hustled them out of the house when the evening was over.

During the clearing up Alix found herself embroiled with Derry Fox in long, complicated conversations. It seemed to her that Derry took nothing seriously. His frivolity infected her, so that she found herself becoming more light-hearted, and forgetting the weight of her responsibilities.

Rory adored Derry, Beatrice distrusted him. 'He isn't the gentleman his brother is. And his hair needs cutting.' Sometimes Derry charmed; sometimes he infuriated. Sometimes their arguments echoed against the ceiling of Owlscote's cavernous kitchen. Sometimes Alix bundled him out of the front door, slamming it behind him, regardless of the time of night. But he had always forgotten their quarrel by the next time they met.

In April, they gave a Chinese party, hanging paper lanterns around the garden, topping the stone terrace with pagoda shapes. Candles flickered in the gentle breeze. Roma made an arched Chinese bridge out of cardboard, and sent to Owlscote lengths of coloured silks to drape over the dining-table. Derry, watching Fu Man Chus and mandarins assemble on the terrace, murmured, 'I feel we should be offering them opium and clay pipes,' but Alix, looking down across the broad sweep of the lawn to the distant meadow, thought only how beautiful it all was, the thousand tiny lights reflected in the still waters of the lake, the drifts of blossom smeared pale pink across the grass in the orchard.

Derry had completed his memoirs. Sophie Berkoff read them one night, howling with laughter as she turned the pages. When she caught her breath, she promised to show the book to a publisher friend of hers. Derry promptly forgot about it. What he had intended as an indictment of the British class system had somehow transformed itself into a series of belly-laughs. He was thankful for the Owlscote parties and the language lessons – without them he would not have eaten. But he seemed little nearer to doing something, or being someone, than he had been a year and a half ago, when he had returned to England.

Jonathan, as Derry had predicted, had taken it upon himself to keep an eye on him. Jon turned up at the Rose Café once a month or so, his sober tweeds and neatly cut hair standing out among the more exotically dressed denizens of the café like a dog rose in an orchid-house. Derry avoided giving Jonathan his home address because he knew that if he did, Jon would turn up unexpectedly one day and see the rickety furniture, the bloom of black mould on the wallpaper, the dreadful shared lavatory. And he could not have borne that.

In June, Jonathan called at the café and said, 'It's Edith's birthday tomorrow. She's asked me to tea and she wondered if you'd like to come too, Derry.' There was a studied nonchalance about the suggestion that Derry immediately saw through. Derry knew that Edith Carr (who was, after all, Mrs Winstanley's god-daughter) would never of her own volition have invited him to her house, and that the invitation was part of Jonathan's doomed campaign to build bridges, to hold the family together.

Nevertheless, he accepted. He had run out of money that week, and he was, from time to time, hungry. In the mould-ridden airlessness of his lodging house, he had acquired a persistent cough. It would be nice to breathe fresh air, and see the more salubrious parts of the river. And besides, he had not seen Edith Carr for *decades*, and he was curious.

Edith said, 'For me? Jon, how *sweet*.'

Derry watched her open the box, and unwrap the pendant. They were in the hall of the Carrs' Richmond villa.

'Aquamarines.' Edith smiled. 'Jon, how clever of you – they're my favourite.'

'They're the same colour as your eyes.' Jonathan fastened the pendant round Edith's neck.

On the whole, Derry thought, people handed out such compliments with wild inaccuracy. But in Edith Carr's instance it was true. Her eyes were a light turquoise, a similar colour to the stones. Her face had a symmetry that one generally saw only in Greek statues or Renaissance paintings. Her beauty took him by surprise; he had expected only prettiness.

Derry picked up the birdcage, and presented it to Edith. 'Happy birthday.'

'*Oh*,' said Edith, and stared at the canary as though unsure what to do with it.

'A friend of mine gave her to me because she couldn't bear the chirping, but she gives me asthma, so I thought you might like her. She's called Dame Nellie Melba.'

'Thank you, Mr Fox.' Edith put the birdcage on a sideboard.

'Derry.'

'Of course. Derry.' There was the sound of footsteps on the stairs. 'Mina,' said Edith. 'Come and see the lovely necklace Jon has given to me.'

Mina admired the necklace, cooed at the canary, and kissed Jonathan on the cheek.

She offered her hand to Derry. 'It's always funny to meet someone you've heard masses about, but have never actually seen.'

Mina's features were clumsy, her large, brown, myopic eyes half hidden by heavy spectacles. Her hair was scraped back in a thin, mousy plait, and she wore a hideous bottle-green striped dress – her school uniform, Derry supposed.

'We have met, actually. Years ago, when you were a baby. Do I come up to your expectations?'

Mina stared at him with a directness he found slightly chilling. 'I thought you'd look more *wicked*.'

Edith led them through the house. The rooms were small and cottagey, the ceilings low. Little frilled footstools stood beside bowed chests of drawers, and tiny tables with spindly legs spilled from alcoves. Curtains fussed and furbelowed at the windows, and the sofas were upholstered in a complicated floral chintz that had begun to fray around the arms.

They had tea in the garden, which was small and pretty and overcrowded, like the house. The breeze extinguished the candles on the cake before Edith could blow them out. Earwigs, falling from the horse chestnut tree, plopped onto the sandwiches. Though it was midsummer, there was a cold edge to the air.

Jonathan and Edith talked about their mutual acquaintances and about the advertising agency where Edith worked. Derry ate, and drank tea, and glanced every now and then at Edith, because it was nice just to look at Edith. Once or twice he caught the younger sister staring at him with her baleful, glassy glare, and he almost said something, and then didn't, because he was on his best behaviour. The sun went behind a cloud, and the tea became tepid. Mina cleared away the tea things, and Edith found racquets and suggested to Jon that they knock a tennis ball about. Derry, shivering in his thin jacket, went back into the house.

There was a small sun-room that trapped the heat. The chill slid off him as he dawdled among withered pot plants and dusty wicker furniture. A huge bunch of dead-white lilies stood on a small circular table. Derry breathed in their scent, and sneezed.

Mina Carr, coming into the room, said, 'They're horrible, aren't they?'

'A touch funereal.'

'Edith's friend sent them. They arrived this morning, in a Bentley.'

He saw that he was supposed to be impressed and curious, so he obliged. 'Which friend?'

'He's called Marcus Wenlock.' Mina brushed her fingertip against the stamens of the lilies, showering the tabletop with ochre powder. 'He's terribly rich. He owns a bank. And he has a place in London and a country house called Marblehurst. He's madly in love with Edith. I think she might marry him.'

'Do you?'

'Jonathan would be devastated, of course.'

'Would he?'

'He's desperately in love with her, isn't he?'

Derry shrugged. 'I wouldn't know.'

'I thought you were an *expert* in things like that.'

He turned to look at her. She had taken off her glasses, and without them her features seemed naked and defenceless. He felt suddenly sorry for her, understanding the removal of her spectacles to be an attempt at self-improvement.

She said, 'Did you love Mrs Kessel?'

His sympathy vanished. 'That's none of your business, is it?'

'What a conventional answer.'

'Perhaps I'm a conventional man.' Looking outside, Derry saw that it had begun to drizzle. Edith was collecting racquets and balls, Jonathan was upending the garden chairs on top of the table. 'But no, if you must know, I didn't love Sara. I liked her a great deal, though.'

'Even though she was wicked?'

'She wasn't wicked. She was nice. Very nice to me.' Derry saw, with a certain relief, that Jonathan and Edith were coming back into the house. Rain beat against the window panes, and seeped through the gaps where the frames had rotted.

Alix was cleaning out the gutters by the front entrance when she heard footsteps crunching the gravel. Looking up, she said, '*Derry*—' and he said: 'Other people have handymen. And housemaids. It wouldn't surprise me to find you sweeping the chimney, Alix, or retiling the roof.'

'It's cheaper to do it myself.' She glanced at him. She thought he looked cheerful. 'I wasn't expecting you, Derry.'

'Another party,' he said. 'This Saturday.'

It was Tuesday. She stared at him. 'There isn't time—'

'Twice the usual rate.'

'*Oh.*' Alix brushed the earth from her hands, and went into the house. Derry's voice followed her down the passageway.

'For a friend of mine, called Dinah Mason. I met her through Jack Swinton. Someone's just died and left her a fortune and she wants to celebrate as soon as possible. A fancy dress party. I told her about Owlscote. Roma can't help, though, she has too many commissions just now. I said we could manage. We could keep the theme simple . . . ghosts and ghouls . . . or a masked ball . . . Nothing too *literary*. There must be masses of stuff here. Props, I mean. We don't have to *make* things.'

'There are the attic rooms. There's plenty of bric-a-brac up there.'

Alix fetched keys and an oil-lamp from the kitchen, and they went upstairs. The lock creaked as she turned the key. 'I use these rooms for storage,' she explained. 'I hardly ever go into them. I keep them locked because of Rory.'

She pushed open the door. The attics smelled of spider-webs and damp. Grey dust smeared the window. Alix lit the oil-lamp and looked around.

'I put Edward's things in here – his archaeological things.' His trowel, and his theodolite, wrapped in tissue paper, stood on a shelf. 'His maps and his books are in the library, of course. I thought that if Rory follows in his father's footsteps, he might be able to use some of these.' Her fingertips touched the handle of the trowel, and then drew away. She swung the lamp around the room. The battered trunks, the broken armchairs and Rory's perambulator cast dark shadows.

'There's nothing much for us here.' Her voice echoed.

She fitted the key to the inner door. The lock was stiff to turn, so she passed the lamp to Derry, and used both hands. The second room was dark. Derry drew the curtains aside as the lamplight slid slowly from umbrella stand to epergne, from marble-topped table to broken-legged writing desk.

'It looks like a pawnbroker's, I'm afraid.'

'It's wonderful. Miss Havisham's bridal chamber . . .' Derry picked up a pith helmet. 'Owlscote's colonial past, I suppose.'

'Edward's grandfather was an aide to a Viceroy of India. He bought the house.'

'Not in the family since the Conquest, then?'

Alix shook her head. 'In the last century, Owlscote was entailed to a family called Gardiner. But the line died out – there were no male heirs – and it was sold.' Kneeling, she opened a chest. Candlesticks, lanterns and jardinières gleamed. She ran her finger along the cold metal. 'When the Gardiners owned the house, there was almost a thousand acres of land with it. Most of the cottages in the village belonged to Owlscote. It's all been sold off since. There's only a few acres left.'

There were no corridors; each room opened into the adjacent one. 'Like Chinese boxes,' said Derry, coughing. 'The dust,' he explained.

They went into the next attic. The small stone-framed window permitted little light to illuminate the rows of fossils arranged on shelves, and the flint axes and scrapers, all the mementoes of Edward's fascination with the distant past. When Alix wiped away the felting of dust from a shard of pottery, she saw the black chevrons engraved on the terracotta.

Derry, struggling to stifle his coughs, upended a

sandglass. Grains trailed slowly through its narrow waist. 'Do you think,' he said, 'that in the furthest room we'll come across a pair of Elizabethan gentlemen, still wearing their ruffs, desiccated over their game of dice? Or one of those brides who are forever getting lost on their wedding night. You know – there's a game of hide and seek and the daughter of the house disappears, and *aeons* later some poor sod unlocks a casket and—' He broke off, seeing her face.

'It's unsettling enough, isn't it, all this, without me telling ghost stories.'

'It's not that. It's just the dust. And the dark.' And the memories, she thought, her gaze focused on the shards of pottery.

He crossed the room to her. 'If you take my hand I'll show you a way through the clutter. And Sophie Berkoff would say that story's just about fear of sex. The poor girl didn't want to lose her virginity. Unopened caskets, you see.' He looked at her again. 'We can go back downstairs, if you like.'

'I told you. I'm fine.' She threw open the final door.

The last room was empty. This was the room that the fallen tree had struck: Alix remembered that she had instructed the builders to throw away the room's soaking, plaster-whitened contents. The regrown branches of the tree, newly leaved in acid-green, tapped at the window pane. She flung open the window, in an attempt to erase the dank smell of the plaster and the staleness of the dust that clung to their clothes. She saw Derry lean out over the sill, taking in lungfuls of fresh air.

'Ages ago,' she said slowly, 'before we had the parties, I wrote a series of articles for a magazine. They were called "Married Life in Mesopotamia" – they were based on my years digging with Edward. Anyway, I forgot all about them, but a fortnight ago an editor of a magazine sent me a cheque and a letter asking me to write more. So I've been lying awake at night, trying to think of something. But all I seem to do is to chew my pencil and cross things out. It's over with, that part of my life – my marriage, and the archaeological dig – I can't seem to think of anything more to say about it. But I thought just now – why not write about the house? Why not write about Owlscote?'

He glanced over his shoulder at her. 'Its history?'

'Yes. Going back through the ages, like you said.'

'Won't you hate it? More strangers peering at Owlscote, if only in the pages of historical journals? And you might get sightseers, perhaps, people tramping round the house. That's what you most loathe, isn't it?'

She resented that he understood so well her need for privacy. 'I need the money,' she said stubbornly.

'There's the parties. Though Saturday's will be the last one for a while.'

'Why?'

'Everyone's going abroad for the summer. The Riviera, my dear.'

She felt unexpectedly disappointed. 'Will you?'

Derry shook his head. She saw the way he looked at her, and she repeated fiercely, 'I need the money, Derry. I need to be safe.'

'One can't ever be safe.' He had perched on the sill, his back against the wall.

'Oh, you can. You can be safe if you have money in the bank . . . and a secure home . . . and you are careful whom you trust.'

'Ah,' he said. He looked out of the window, down to the emerald-green lawn. 'That's not *safety*, Alix. That's self-immolation.'

*　　*　　*

In August, there was a heatwave. Owlscote's lawns were sun-bleached to the colour of hessian, and the level of the lake sank as the water became an emerald-green soup. The cool, stone walls of the house provided the only sanctuary from the heat. There was first an invasion of ants, then a plague of houseflies, and towards the end of the month swarms of wasps made their way from the orchard to the kitchen. Rory was fractious, refusing his food and sleeping badly. Attempting to shoo a fly from Rory's apple, Beatrice slipped and sprained her ankle, and limped around the house, her mouth set in weary stoicism. Alix swatted wasps, and wondered whether the well would dry up.

Jonathan Fox turned up one morning and suggested a day at the seaside. They drove to Bournemouth, where the cooler air from the sea soothed them, and their bad temper eased. Beatrice dozed in a deckchair. Jonathan glanced at Alix. 'I'll take the little chap for a paddle. You'd like to paddle, wouldn't you, Rory?'

Jonathan and Rory walked towards the sea. The beach was crowded and the tide was out. Alix watched them weave through the crowds. Rory's hand was in Jonathan's; both were barefoot. Their figures became smaller and smaller. There were only a handful of people in the world, Alix thought, whom she would have trusted to take Rory out of her sight. Her mother, of course, and Martha, Jacob Long's daughter. And Jonathan, and Derry. She would, she thought, have let no-one other than those four people lead her son through ranks of milling, anonymous strangers, and introduce him to the dangerous embrace of the sea.

Jonathan and Rory had reached the place where the waves licked the rippled sand. Standing up, shading her eyes with her hand, Alix watched Rory tentatively dip his toes in the water. She saw the way he flung back his head in sudden laughter. And how he took a step forward, becoming braver. How, full of confidence, he jumped into the water, and was surprised by the powerful suck of the waves beneath his feet, so that without Jonathan's protecting hand he would have overbalanced. Sometimes she lost sight of them, leaping and laughing amid the crowds. But then she would catch a glimpse of Jonathan's golden head, and the small, dark child at his side.

Beatrice woke, and stared sleepily around. 'Where are they?'

Alix pointed towards the sea. 'There they are. They've been paddling.'

She took off her own shoes and stockings and threaded through the crowd to join them. Together they walked along the sea shore, wavelets milling round their ankles, until they were far from the pier and the candyfloss stalls. Only a few people, with hats or knotted handkerchieves to protect their heads from the sun, clustered in small groups on the more distant beaches. Rory gathered shells from the shallow water. Jonathan, his trousers rolled up to his knees, waded deeper into the sea. Gazing towards the horizon, he squinted.

'Funny to think that France is just over there.'

'Will you ever go back?'

He shook his head.

'Do you think about it much?'

Jonathan was silent, and then he said, 'I try not to. But I dream. One can't stop oneself dreaming.' He looked back along the beach. The pier, and the crowds of people that clustered around it, had become very small, very distant. 'I often think,' he said slowly 'that if I don't ask for too much . . . if there are just a few people who are important to me, and I do my best by them . . . if I don't raise my head over the parapet, as it were, then I'll be all right.' He looked back at her. 'I'm not making sense, am I, Alix? Never much good with words.'

The sand, stirred up by the incoming waves, moved and swirled beneath their feet. Strands of seaweed wound around their ankles, as slippery as rubber. She remembered Derry saying, *That's not safety, Alix, that's self-immolation*, and she tucked her hand round Jonathan's arm, and smiled up at him, and said, 'I know just what you mean,' and then, with Rory's small wet paw in hers, they walked slowly back along the beach.

CHAPTER SIX

Derry did some translation work, and taught Spanish, but was seized every now and then by an untypical and rather frightening sort of lassitude. He had caught a summer cold which he seemed unable to shake off. At night, in the hot, confined space of his room, he struggled for air. The streets and parks of London offered little respite; the heat seemed trapped by the tall buildings and the dusty foliage. When he coughed, his ribs hurt.

But he continued to go out a lot, and to talk to a great many people, and to sleep, or not sleep, in various beds. As the summer went on, many of his friends drifted away from the city, Ruth and Lawrence to the Riviera, Sophie to her lover's cottage in the country. Roma remained in London; Roma never took holidays. Roma's Augusts were busy because her clients had their houses decorated while they were on holiday. Derry worked for Roma, scouring shops for eighteenth-century bureaux, or carrying Lalique lamps and Chinese cabinets into houses in Bloomsbury and Chelsea.

The heat became unbearable. It gathered and multiplied in the crowded streets of the East End. It seemed to Derry that it was an effort just to extract oxygen from the hot, clammy air. Sometimes the city felt empty and unreal; those who could not escape it were languid or short-tempered. The wealthy had deserted the town, leaving it to the ragged men who hung around street corners, and the barefoot children who squabbled in gutters, searching for pennies. Derry slept badly, kept awake by his persistent cough. It occurred to him that he should visit a doctor, but he could not afford to. He avoided Jonathan, preferring to be spared his concern and offers of help.

Towards the end of August, returning to his White Street rooms late one afternoon, Derry found a letter waiting for him. The envelope was long and white, with a foreign stamp. He slit it open with his thumbnail, and drew out the typed letter. He read, 'Dear Mr Fox, As the solicitors acting as executors for the estate of the late Mrs Sarah Elizabeth Kessel . . .' and then, unable to read any more, he crushed the letter into his jacket pocket and left the building.

The sun blinded him. He walked to the river. The smell that rose from the stagnant water was suffocating. The foul air made him cough. His own voice echoed in his ears, telling Mina Carr that he had not loved Sara Kessel. Now, he remembered seeing Paris and Rome for the first time with Sara. He remembered the beds they had shared, and the threads of grey in her long chestnut hair. He remembered that she had taught him carefully and patiently, and that she had not expected love – only companionship – in return. And that when he, inevitably, had met someone else, she had let him go with a kiss and a smile. He had never quite understood why what they had done had offended people so much. They had not, after all, harmed anyone.

He began to walk again, choosing his direction at

random. He was heading along the Embankment when he heard a voice call out his name. Turning, he saw Ruth Duncan.

He said, 'I thought you were abroad.'

'I came back from France a couple of days ago. No-one was at the café. I went there, but it was empty. I didn't know what to do.'

'Roma has a new lover. She sells stockings in a department store. And Sophie is in the country. And I thought Lawrence was with you, Ruth.'

'He's gone to stay in a castle in Austria. So have Bernard and Tiggy. They didn't ask me.' Ruth looked at him. She was very young, and she had soft red-gold hair and pink and white skin and trusting blue eyes surrounded by skin so fine it always looked bruised. Her snub nose had peeled a little: the Mediterranean sun, he supposed.

'I've been looking for you, Derry. Are you busy? Only I'm not.' Ruth tugged at his sleeve. '*Please*, Derry. Let's spend the evening together. Please. I'll love you for ever, darling Derry.'

They went to dinner at the Café Royal. Ruth paid; he could not eat. Then to a pub in Leicester Square. Then her rooms where, naked in his arms, she was pink and gold and white, like a china figurine.

Afterwards, Ruth suggested a party. 'It's at my sister's house. Laura's come back to London early because she quarrelled with my brother-in-law.'

Ruth introduced Derry to her elder sister, who was Lady Something or other. 'No-one's in London yet, so I'm calling it my leftovers party,' said her ladyship, peering at Derry through a lorgnette, sizing him up and making her opinion of him plain. 'Scraping together all the odds and ends I can find.'

The house was in Mayfair. There was an enormous aviary full of hot, drooping, colourful birds. And a pool and a fountain and a pavilion in which an Indian butler, swathed in a turban, was serving cocktails. Derry wandered around house and gardens, running his fingertips along the spines of the leather-covered books, breathing in the scent of the jasmine that trailed from the pergola. People clustered round him. He told them about driving Bill's taxi. 'Fell asleep at the wheel. Five in the morning. Ran off the road into a florist's shop. *Buckets* of flowers over the bonnet. Positively *bridal*.' They roared with laughter, and brought him more champagne. He saw that he could make them laugh when he chose, and that he could make them listen to him. He knew their adoration would only last until he was out of sight, and then they would forget him and find someone else, but just now he needed their indiscriminate love. He continued to entertain them, telling them about Jack Swinton. 'Neglected his clients. *Not* a good idea. Jack was representing an arsonist. Frightfully polite chap until provoked, and then – I came to work one morning, and it was like Guy Fawkes' Night. Firemen rushing all over the place. Filing cabinets swimming with water.' He was, he thought, serving up his own failure for their amusement.

A tall, slope-shouldered woman with a narrow face suggested he write for her magazine. '*Chrome* is satirical, darling. Frightfully daring. Pokes fun at people in the highest places.'

A mournful young man latched onto him, trailing him from garden to drawing-room to library (to bedroom, too, Derry suspected, given the encouragement), reciting his troubles. 'On my uppers – estate's mortgaged to the hilt. Rents and income from the farm don't cover the cost of the mortgage. Damned bank say they'll sell my little place in Chelsea. Nice little house. Shame.'

People were dancing in the pool, standing beneath the fountain, hair like dark riverweed plastered to wet scalps, sparkling drops of water, diamonds, and beaded dresses streaming from the fringes. The marble paving was wet and glazed and cold. Voices called his name. *I have the most marvellous idea, Derry . . . You must dance with me, Derry . . . Tell me that story again. The one about the boa constrictor. So amusing . . .*

He juddered with exhaustion, chilled by the water from the fountain. In his pocket, the handwritten signature on Sara's solicitor's letter blurred and ran. The feeling of desperation, that there was no place for him, became unbearable. He escaped into the dark, lush sanctuary of the aviary.

Palms dipped graceful fronds to the seed-scattered ground. Purple bougainvillaea snaked up the bars. There was a hot, acrid scent of feathers and vegetation. It reminded him of the Winstanleys' conservatory. *Pick me a peach, won't you, Derry?* Bright wings flickered overhead. A squawk, a chirp: he hushed them. There was a sensation in his chest which was at first merely unpleasant, and then, as he began to cough, to fight for breath, both frightening and painful. As though the bones in his ribs were turning to iron. He stooped, breathing in small, downy feathers and the heavy, sweet scent of the hoya. He heard the wheezing, tortuous sound of his struggle to draw oxygen into his lungs.

He stumbled out of the cage, leaving the door wide open. He imagined them following behind him, trailing him through the streets of London, a bright, glittering, gorgeous banner. He wanted to curl up in the darkness and sleep, for a week, perhaps, so he slipped out of a side gate and headed home.

Jonathan hated the hot weather. It reminded him of France. He remembered insisting his men wore their tin hats in the midday sun. And Gunner Harris complaining, 'Makes me head feel like a tin of bully beef, Lieutenant Fox.' When he pressed Edith's door-bell, the shrill sound made him wince, and he saw Gunner Harris, without the tin hat, a small, round, red hole in the centre of his forehead. The door opened. Jonathan blinked, and Gunner Harris disappeared.

'Jon? What a lovely surprise. Are those for me?'

He couldn't at first think what Edith was talking about; then he saw the bunch of cornflowers and poppies clutched in his hand.

'Rather wilted, I'm afraid.'

He followed Edith into the house. He watched her fill a jug with water and arrange the flowers. The simple, repetitive actions soothed him. He thought how just to be with certain people made him feel better. A few people, so few. Edith and Alix and his mother, when she was well. Not Derry: Derry was for making him laugh, which was different.

'Are you all right, Jon? You look pale.'

'Bit of a headache.' He pressed his fingers against the throbbing vein to the side of his head.

'Poor Jon. Go and sit outside. It'll be cool there. I'll make us some lemonade.'

He went into the garden. The sun had burnt the lawn to the colour of old straw, but the gnarled trees and the vast, rambling roses made restful patches of green. He focused on the plants and shrubs, trying to remember their names. Delphinium, pelargonium, lavender. The medlar's curious fruit had not yet ripened, but the leaves formed a heavy canopy, shutting out the blinding glare of the sun.

Edith came out of the house, tray in hand. 'Drink this.' She handed Jonathan a large glass of lemonade. 'Now, sit down on the grass, and I'll rub your temples. You can rest against my knees.'

He sat on the papery remains of the lawn, and she perched on the bench behind him. Her fingertips made circular movements, coaxing the pain from his aching head. 'I used to do this for my mother, when she was ill,' she said. 'Just relax, Jon. Close your eyes and lean against me.'

He did as he was told, shutting his eyes. The movement of her fingers was slow and rhythmic. He could feel her knees and shins, pressing against his back. He had noticed that she was not wearing stockings; he thought he could smell the warm, salty scent of her bare skin. He let himself drift away, into a dark, empty space into which his worst memories could not intrude. Her fingertips moved away from his temples, and travelled slowly and gently to the back of his neck, where they continued to knead and release the tense muscles. He felt her lean forward, and kiss the top of his head.

'Edith.'

'I'm sorry. I couldn't stop myself. Do you mind?'

Jonathan's heart was beating very fast. He stood up, walked away a few paces, and paused, his back to Edith.

'I'm sorry, Jon.' She sounded upset.

He turned to face her. 'It doesn't matter.'

Her face crumpled. 'Doesn't it?'

'I mean,' he said, confused, 'there's no need to apologize . . . to be sorry.'

She looked up at him. Then she said slowly,

'You know that I love you, don't you, Jon?'

His heart, beating fast because of the heat and her touch, doubled its rate. He whispered, 'I thought we were *friends* . . .'

'If that's all you want.'

'No.' He shook his head. 'That's not all I want. Only I didn't think . . . I didn't dare hope . . .'

'And I,' she whispered, and suddenly smiled. 'Dear Jon – is it possible that we've both been so foolish . . . both so pessimistic . . . you do love me, don't you, Jon?'

He went to her then, and took her hand in his, kissing her fingertips slowly, one by one, almost drunk with the press of her soft flesh against his lips. He had imagined this moment so often that now he could hardly persuade himself that it was actually happening. Accustomed to dreams that took form and substance, he struggled to convince himself that this was not just some more pleasant, but equally false, manifestation.

So he drew her to him, so that he could feel the solidity and warmth of her body against his own. Her golden head was tucked beneath his chin, her full breasts pressed against his ribcage. Then he asked her to marry him.

There was a sequence one did with starting-handle and clutch and accelerator, but he could not at first remember it. Jonathan sat in the front seat of the motorcar, his hands hovering over the controls, his mind empty of everything except a glorious, unquenchable delight.

At last he put the car into gear, and headed up the road. He drove fast, turning corners, taking unfamiliar roads at random, the speed of his journey reflecting his exhilaration, but then, knowing that if he was not careful he would simply lean over the door and shout the cause of his joy to passers-by, he headed into the centre of Town, to the Rose Café, and Derry. He needed to tell someone. Telling someone would make it real. He imagined walking into that funny little café, and seeing Derry, who would be sitting in a corner with a drink and a cigarette. And Derry would smile his crooked smile and say, '*Jon. My chaperon*,' and they would have a drink together, and he would tell Derry about Edie. Swearing him to secrecy, of course, because Mother would have to be told gently, carefully.

It was late afternoon by the time he reached Fitzroy Street. Jonathan parked, wiped the perspiration from his forehead with his handkerchief, and went into the café. He looked round, scanning face after face, but could not see Derry.

He made enquiries at the counter. The proprietor shrugged and shook his head. 'Haven't seen him for a while. Owes me for last week,' he added meaningfully, eyeing Jonathan's well-cut suit and silk tie.

Jonathan took his wallet from his pocket. 'Let me.'

He paid Derry's bill, and was offered tea. He was sitting at a table, stirring sugar into his cup, when a voice said, 'Excuse me – you are Derry Fox's brother, aren't you?'

Jonathan looked up. She was tiny, dark and elegant.

'Jonathan Fox,' he said, and held out his hand.

'I'm Sophie Berkoff. Are you looking for Derry?'

'I hoped he might be here.'

'And I. I've a message for him. No-one's seen him for days. Ruth Duncan seems to have been the last person to have spoken to him. She told me a peculiar story about Derry releasing birds from an aviary – it all sounded rather improbable. She's an odd child. Sexually repressed, of course.'

'I thought I'd try his employer. Jack Swinton.'

'May I come? Only it's an important message.'

They left the café, and drove to Jack Swinton's offices in Cheapside. As they drew up by the grocer's shop, Miss Berkoff said, '*Oh,*' and Jonathan, looking up, saw the smears of soot on the walls, and the black, distorted window frames.

He made enquiries at the shop. When he came back to the car, Sophie Berkoff said, 'Any news?'

'Not of Derry. Apparently Mr Swinton's offices were burnt down three weeks ago.' Jonathan drummed his fingers against the steering-wheel. 'Where now?'

'His lodgings, I suppose. Though I tried before, and there was no reply.'

'You'll have to direct me. I don't know where he lives.'

Miss Berkoff glanced at him, but said nothing, and began to direct him to the East End. Jonathan had not visited this part of London before. The rows of cramped houses, the blackened, smoky air and ragged children playing on the pavements, all shocked him. He had seen poverty before, but that had been in France. He remembered blasted villages and exhausted, bewildered refugees wandering among the ruins. A memory, long buried, surfaced. It had been during his first few weeks in France. His battalion had been marching; he could recall neither his starting point nor his destination. They had passed what had once been a village – stumps of wall, hardly recognizable as houses – and he had caught sight of a small child, two or three years old perhaps, naked and weeping among the rubble. He had wanted to do something – he had not known what – but they had marched on, and he had had to force himself not to look back. As time went on, he had seen many such children, so that he no longer even turned to look.

He heard her say, 'The East End always makes me think of Berlin, after the war. People tease me for living where I do – a friend of mine wants to buy me a nice little house' – her voice was mocking – 'but I prefer my single room. What you don't have, you can't lose.'

Jonathan shivered. He wondered whether he had wanted too much. Whether in finding Edith – in sticking his head over the parapet – he might somehow have lost Derry. He continued to follow Sophie Berkoff's directions. At length, she instructed him to draw up outside a tenement block. The bricks were stained black by smoke; not far away, beyond the dark silhouettes of warehouses and factories, he could see the tall spikes of the cranes at the docks. Half a dozen small boys, grubby-faced and ragged, swarmed around the car like ants. Sophie pressed a doorbell. There was no answer. When she pushed the door, it swung open.

Climbing the stairs, the joy that Jonathan had experienced that afternoon began to be replaced by anger. The stairwell was ill-lit and uncarpeted. Balls of dust gathered in the corners of treads. The air was hot and suffocating. He muttered, 'If I'd known – dear God, if I'd known he was living in a place like this . . .'

Sophie glanced back at him briefly. 'If you didn't know, Mr Fox, then I'm sure it was because Derry didn't want you to know.'

Pausing, she knocked at a door. When there was no reply, she rattled the handle and called out, 'Derry? Are you in there? It's me, Sophie. You must open the door. I have something to tell you.'

Jonathan said, 'Let me,' and put his shoulder to the

door. It was flimsily built and opened easily.

The blinds were pulled down. He thought at first that the room was untenanted. Searching in the dark, he began to make out form, shape, possibility. A tangle of dark hair, a hunched shape in the bed. When Miss Berkoff pulled back the blind and sunlight picked out the corners of the cramped, dilapidated little room, Jonathan had to bite his lip to stop himself giving vent to his anger.

Then, going to the bed, murmuring Derry's name, shaking his shoulder in a futile effort to rouse him, Jonathan's anger was replaced by fear. He heard Miss Berkoff say, 'I'll fetch a doctor—' but he swung round, halting her.

'No.' His voice was sharp. 'He's not staying a moment longer in this place. I'm taking him home. Now.'

Clouds, billowing upwards in tall anvil-shapes, signalled the thunderstorm that brought the heatwave to an end. Alix stood on the terrace, her eyes closed, letting the rain drum against her face and soak through her clothes. Overnight, the season had shifted. The summer, that had gone on too long, had been replaced by a damp, blowy autumn.

The paying guests, refreshed by their holidays in Blackpool or Bournemouth, returned to Owlscote. Alix made up beds, cooked breakfasts, wrote accounts. She told herself that she was glad to be back at work again, that everything was exactly as she would have chosen. Rory was happy and healthy, and her mother was comfortable and wanted for nothing. And the house that she loved was sloughing off the years of its neglect, and emerging, like some crumpled, beautiful butterfly, from its chrysalis of dust and cobweb.

Yet she found herself noticing the empty evenings, and the long, lonely hours between Rory's bedtime and her own. Beatrice sewed and dozed over a novel; Alix, restless, wandered between kitchen and drawing-room and library, always busy, but unable to settle to anything. Sometimes she found herself listening for a footstep on the gravel, or for the fall of a letter through the door. But all the letters were bills and circulars, and only tradesmen and paying guests came down the long, winding path from the road to the house.

She began work on her history of Owlscote. She unearthed books and papers from drawers and chests, and took the bus into Salisbury to pore over old maps in the public library. In one of the little boxrooms, beneath discarded fishing rods and tins of hardened, darkened watercolours, she discovered Edward's note-books. She put aside the volumes that detailed his expeditions to Egypt and Mesopotamia, and took to bed with her those that described his research into the history of the house. She stayed awake into the small hours, propped on pillows, wrapped in blankets, reading the handwriting that was still familiar to her. She knew that she had not, as she had once feared, forgotten Edward, or not loved him enough. It was just that one could only bear so much, and that sometimes one had to concentrate on the business of survival. During the last four years all her energies had gone into caring for Edward's son, and saving his house. That had been her way of showing how much she had loved him.

In mid-September, a letter arrived. Purple ink on expensive white paper; Alix did not recognize the signature. A Miss Madeline Ferraby asked – no, *pleaded* – to stay at Owlscote one weekend in September. 'It's my birthday, and I don't want a big celebration because

169

my father died a couple of months ago. Just something quiet with a few friends. I fell in love with your house when I was a guest at Peggy Gordon's party last year. I tried to find Derry Fox to ask him whether you are still giving parties, but no-one seems to know where he is. So I am writing to you, Mrs North, in the hope that you will take pity on me, and that you will be so kind as to let myself and a few friends stay in your beautiful home.'

Derry was walking through Owlscote. He opened door after door, entered room after room. There were tens, hundreds, thousands of rooms. Some of the rooms seemed to be empty, though there was often the feeling that something was just round the corner, hidden, out of sight. Other rooms were cluttered with objects. He saw the trunk that he had used as a schoolboy, and a brass theodolite, and a gilt and painted Madonna that he remembered from a procession in Lima. Many of the rooms were huge, vast, gaping caverns. Great heaps of objects were piled to the lofty ceilings, like treasure in a dragon's cave. There was a thick layer of dust over everything, and the patches of mould on the walls had rotted into gaping holes. The cornices of the rooms were thick with cobwebs, and many of the doors and window frames had crumbled and distorted.

Some time later – he could not tell how much time had elapsed – he was in a forest. Overhead, a glaring sun flickered intermittently through the canopy of leaves. Thick creepers trailed from high branches to the under-growth, knotting themselves round tree trunks, twisting round the stems of brightly coloured flowers. Birds, their long tail feathers streaming behind them, flitted between the branches. Their cries filled his head. He put his hands over his ears to shut out the noise. But the birds swooped lower, so that he could feel the rush of air from their flapping wings. He crouched, kneeling in the tangle of weeds and vines that covered the forest floor. A feather brushed his cheek. He was about to cry out when he heard Jonathan say, 'It doesn't matter if we're a bit late.' For some reason this comforted him, and the birds, creepers and flowers dissolved.

He was at Owlscote again. The house had retreated to its accustomed size, and the rooms were cool, calm, ordered. He went into the kitchen. Alix was asleep on the sofa. Her long, dark hair curtained her face, and her skin looked pale and chilled. He wanted to kiss her smooth forehead, but instead he arranged a blanket around her shoulders. Sitting down beside her, he closed his eyes.

Derry awoke. Though he guessed that he had been asleep for a very long time, he was nevertheless still too tired to raise his head. He let his gaze drift slowly from one object to another, trying to work out where he was. Curtains (closed), armchair (floral), desk with inkstand and blotter. He remembered writing his homework at that desk. He focused, at last, on Jonathan, who was sitting beside the bed.

'Jon?' He tried to speak, but what came out was only a croak.

'Derry? You're awake.'

He said, puzzled, 'I'm home, aren't I?'

'You have been for a week.'

Derry closed his eyes again and concentrated very hard. He could remember Ruth Duncan, and letting the birds out of the aviary, and going back to White Street, and feeling rotten. Flinging open the window and still not being able to breathe.

'Have I been ill?'

'I'm afraid so. That's why I brought you here. So you could get better.'

That's why I brought you here. He tried to work that out, and failed.

Jonathan, seeing his confusion, said, 'I was in London, and I tried to find you. A friend of yours, Miss Berkoff, took me to your lodgings. Good thing she did – I doubt if you'd have survived another couple of days in that frightful slum. Why didn't you tell me you were short of cash, Derry? I could have given you something to tide you over. Anyway, you're safe now. Do you want anything . . . a drink of water . . . anything?'

Derry shook his head. 'I just want to sleep.' He glanced at the drawn curtains. 'It's late, isn't it?'

'Almost midnight.'

'You go to bed.'

Jonathan frowned. 'I'm not sure—'

'I'll be all right, honestly, Jon.'

'I'll look in in a few hours.' Jonathan rose. 'If you want anything, then, Derry,' he added kindly, 'just give me a shout.'

When he was alone, Derry shuffled upright on the pillows and took the glass of water from the bedside table. His hand shook ridiculously, threatening to spill water over the bedspread. Just the action of drinking exhausted him, so after a few mouthfuls he put the glass aside and lay back, his eyes closed.

He must have fallen ill in London, after the party. He remembered stooping bent double in the aviary, his ribs like iron. He had gone back to his White Street rooms. He had a vague memory of Sophie knocking on the door and calling out his name, and not answering her because he felt too ill. He had heard her high heels clacking on the stairs, fading away. Try as he might, he could not remember what had happened after that.

But now he began to fill in the missing bits. Jonathan had met Sophie in the Rose. Sophie had taken Jonathan to his rooms. Which meant that Jonathan had seen the black mould on the walls and the dripping communal tap in the hallway. Jonathan had smelt the foul air from the docks, and the dreadful, indefinable stench from the tripe shop across the road. And Jonathan – and the humiliation made Derry shiver, as though the fever had returned – had seen him at his most helpless, abject worst.

Alix considered the letter written in purple ink. Miss Ferraby had asked to stay at Owlscote for a whole weekend; Alix enjoyed having the house to herself on Sundays. And she had not previously organized a party on her own; there had always been Derry. Glancing through her diary, she tried to remember when she had last seen either Jonathan or Derry. She recalled the day she had spent at the seaside with Jonathan at the end of August, but, counting back through the weeks, she calculated that it was more than two months since she had seen or heard from Derry.

She wrote letters to his lodgings in Stepney, and to the Rose Café. She received no reply to either. She felt abandoned and let down. Then angry. They had gone into business together, and now, when she needed him, he was nowhere to be found. She remembered Derry saying, *People tramping round the house. That's what you most loathe*, so she wrote back to Miss Ferraby, agreeing that she and her party could stay at Owlscote. She wanted to prove him wrong. Even if she never saw him again. Thinking of Derry Fox, Alix heaved saucepans down from the shelf and slammed them noisily on the stove.

On a blowy Friday evening two cream-coloured open-topped motor-cars, both mud-spattered and heaped with luggage, arrived at Owlscote. Miss Ferraby introduced herself to Alix – 'My name's Madeline, but call me Maddy, everyone else does.' There were three young men and three girls, and a short, square, ancient person whom Maddy announced to be her nanny. All the young people were noisy and high-spirited and care-free, and Alix did her best to make them comfortable, lighting fires and cooking meals, offering drinks, and suggesting walks and drives. Whenever she could, she escaped to the nursery and Rory, or to the library, and her History.

On Sunday evening, she was washing up when the kitchen door opened. Maddy, dressed in red chiffon, with a glass and shaker in hand, said, 'I've made you a cocktail, Mrs North, to say thank you for such a marvellous weekend.' A glass was placed in Alix's soapy hand. 'I'll do the drying up, so you can drink in peace.'

Alix sat against the edge of the table and drank. Maddy, dabbing ineffectually at crockery with a tea towel, talked.

'It's been absolutely top-hole. So terrific to escape from dreary old London. I shall tell all my friends about it. It must be great fun living here, though jolly hard work. Did you always want to run an hotel, Mrs North?'

Alix shook her head. The cocktail was, as Maddy had said, delicious. 'It just – happened.'

'Derry told me about Captain North. So sad. You must have married very young.'

'Nineteen,' Alix said. 'I was nineteen.'

'Goodness.' Round blue eyes stared at her. 'I was twenty-three this birthday. I've never even been *engaged*.'

Alix took a large gulp of her drink. 'Is Derry Fox a friend of yours?'

'We've been friends for simply ages. I met him . . . I can't remember where. At the Gibsons', perhaps . . . or at Sally Redmayne's. But simply *everyone* knows Derry.'

When Maddy left the room Alix did not immediately go back to the dishes. She remembered dancing with Derry in the Great Hall before the first party at Owlscote, and she remembered the long conversations they had had over the washing up. When Derry had been there, the parties had been fun, rather than a duty. He had become a friend. Yet she now realized that for him she must always have been one of many. The thought occurred to her, and could not quite be brushed away, that for Derry their acquaintance must always have been to do with money, rather than affection.

Alix pictured Maddy in her red chiffon dress. There were only two years between Madeline Ferraby and herself, she realized, but an acre of experience. She had been married and widowed and had nursed sick soldiers and a tiny baby. Recalling Maddy's manicured nails and coiffured hair, Alix looked down at her own workworn hands, and thought, and why should Derry Fox seek *my* company? Why should he not choose to spend his time elsewhere?

She unscrewed the cocktail shaker, and refilled her glass. She needed to blur the sudden feeling of loneliness. She thought of writing to Jonathan, and almost went to the library to fetch pen and paper, but in the end remained where she was, drinking until her thoughts had slowed and the heartache had lessened.

Derry was at the bored, aimless stage of convalescence when his father spoke to him. Jon was away on business, and his mother had gone shopping, and he had tried to read a book but was unable to concentrate, and was reduced to playing chess against himself, very badly.

His father always came home to lunch; the maid served the mushroom soup and lamb chops. When they reached the steamed pudding, Nicholas Fox said: 'I've been meaning to talk to you, Derry, and now that you're so much better . . .' He poured custard on his pudding. 'Mrs Winstanley told me last week that her sister-in-law had passed away. You had heard, I assume?'

'I had a letter.' *The solicitors acting as executors for the estate of the late Mrs Sarah Elizabeth Kessel.* Derry had mislaid the letter, and could not remember the rest of it. He could not remember whether he had read the rest of it.

'I think, therefore, that we can draw a line beneath that sorry episode.'

Once he would have pointed out that one couldn't draw a line under people, that they, or their memory, persisted. Now, aware only of failure and futility, he held his tongue.

'We'll agree to say no more about it, then. Water under the bridge. The question is, Derry – what do you intend to do now?'

He began to speak, but his father raised his spoon, silencing him. 'Jonathan told me about your way of life in London. Taxi-driving . . . story-writing . . . and some nonsense about parties. Hardly suitable occupations for a man of your eduction, Derry. Jonathan also told me about the place where you were living. How you could let yourself sink to such degradation . . .'

Again, Derry said nothing. He imagined, once again, Jonathan looking round the White Street rooms, and the curl of Jonathan's lip, and the disgust in his blue eyes.

'You are twenty-five, Derry. A brief sowing of wild oats is understandable in a young man, but we all have to accept our responsibilities.' Placing his spoon in his empty bowl, Nicholas Fox dabbed at his moustache with his napkin, and gave a small cough. 'I have made enquiries at the office. A position for a junior clerk should fall vacant within the next month.'

Derry abandoned all pretence of eating. He looked at his father.

'The post is yours, if you choose to take it. I hope you'll be sensible. It would be the bottom rung of the ladder, but then, we all have to start somewhere.'

His father talked, Derry thought savagely, in a succession of clichés. As though a not quite English enough background, and the effort of climbing from one class to the next, had denied him the ability to put words together in an original fashion.

'You're suggesting that I come and work for you?'

Mr Fox leaned forward, imparting secrets. 'There is talk of an . . . association . . . with Campkins. Between you and me, Derry, Reginald Campkin has struggled since Ronald's death. Whereas Jonathan, of course, has been such an asset to the firm. He has done the work of two.'

The maid came into the room to serve coffee. When she had gone, Nicholas Fox offered the brandy decanter to Derry, who shook his head. He watched his father pour himself a measure and light a cigar.

'Exciting times, you see. Fox and Broughton may become the foremost solicitors in Andover.'

Derry's head had begun to ache. 'That's terrific, Dad.'

'Of course, I would not expect you, Derry, to match up to Jonathan.' Blue smoke clouded the room. 'Just to do your best.' Nicholas Fox looked critically at his younger son. 'A second chance, you might say. I'm offering you a second chance.'

'Generous of you, Dad.'

His father looked again, suspicious of sarcasm. After few moments he added, 'You may start work at the end of next month. You must get a haircut, of course, and buy yourself a decent suit. If your financial situation will not extend to that, you may have an advance on your first week's wages.'

Soon afterwards, his father returned to the office. In the drawing-room, Derry stood at the window. Outside, the clouds were thick and grey and oppressive, and through the pane of glass he sensed the chill in the air. Large, dark blots of rain had begun to mark the driveway and paths. He imagined living here and working here, looking out of this window, and seeing this scene every day of his life. He imagined going to dances at the tennis club, or having a drink or two at the Conservative Association, perhaps. The occasional excitement of a day in London or a trip to the seaside. The routine of office life, with its small triumphs, its petty squabbles and rivalries.

He imagined working for Jonathan. *Jonathan has been such an asset to the firm. Of course, I would not expect you, Derry, to match up to Jonathan.* His fists clenched.

Yet what alternative had he but to accept his father's offer? He had left this house, penniless but full of ambition, six years before. He had since returned equally penniless, having fulfilled none of his ambitions. All his schemes had come to nothing. Everything his father had accused him of was true. He had succeeded only in degrading himself. He could not afford a new suit; he doubted if he could afford a haircut. Whereas Jonathan had everything – career, money, motor-car. And it had always been so. There had always been Jonathan, the golden, first-born son, for ever at the head of the race, while he himself trailed miserably in the rearguard.

The maid knocked at the door. 'Miss Carr is here, Mr Derry.'

He looked round, and there was Edith Carr, in a cream-coloured coat and a close-fitting hat. Her eyes – those extraordinary eyes – were shaded by the hat's small brim. Derry remembered that Jonathan had mentioned Edith was staying with the Winstanleys.

He said, 'Jonathan's away on business, I'm afraid. He should be back in a couple of days.'

'I've come to see you.'

'Why?'

'Jonathan suggested I might.'

Derry imagined their conversation. Jonathan: *It's a bore, Edie, but do you think you could bear to call on Derry? I know he's a bit of a lame duck, but . . .* And Edith, reluctantly: *Of course, if you think it'll help . . .*

He said slowly, 'Charity visiting.'

'Jon thought you might need cheering up.'

He swung round. 'And how do you propose to cheer me up, Miss Carr?'

'I don't know. I hadn't thought. Anything you like.'

'Really? I mean . . . anything?'

179

'I meant – conversation . . . or are you up to a walk . . . or tennis . . .'

He saw the indifference in her eyes. 'Can't hit a ball.' He glanced out of the window again. 'And the weather's not exactly conducive to walking.'

'I suppose not. And if you've been unwell . . .'

She yawned. Just a small opening of her sculptured lips, quickly disguised beneath her outstretched fingers. He had a sudden vengeful need to provoke some sort of response in her, to make her notice him, to jolt her out of her dutiful complacency.

He said, 'People play chess or cards, I suppose, in circumstances like this. To pass the time.'

'I loathe chess. And cards.'

He wondered whether, alone with Jonathan, those bored, beautiful eyes acquired animation. 'It's a problem, isn't it?' he said lightly. 'I detest ball games, and you detest board games. What shall we do?'

Edith raised her shoulders. 'I could read to you, if you want.'

'What a delightful idea. What would you like to read?'

Her lips pursed into a small, unconcerned moue. 'I don't mind. Whatever you choose, Mr Fox.'

'Derry,' he said. 'Don't you remember, Edith, that you agreed to call me Derry?'

A flicker of irritation, and he was aware of a fleeting sense of triumph. 'Of course. Derry.' She looked around, and glimpsed the *Financial Times*, folded on the sideboard. 'I could read you the newspaper, I suppose.'

'Very dull. Stocks and shares, of which I don't possess a single one, and some monologue about the gold standard. And I don't suppose, Edith, that you lie awake at night worrying about the gold standard, do you?'

'I don't worry about anything.' There was now an edge to her voice. 'I sleep very well, thank you.'

'How nice for you. Whereas I sleep appallingly.'

She said sharply, 'A guilty conscience, perhaps,' and then flushed, and pressed her lips together tightly.

'My sins are catching up with me, do you think?'

'I'm sorry. I didn't mean—'

'I'm not offended. Perhaps you believe that one reaps what one sows.' He sounded, he thought, like his father. Any moment, and he'd catch himself saying, *Look after the pennies and the pounds will take care of themselves*, or *Better late than never*.

But she was looking at him properly for the first time. 'Not at all,' she said. 'To me everything seems rather . . . random.' She stood up and went to the bookshelves. Her back was to him.

'Why do you think that?'

She did not answer at first, but then she said, 'Because of my mother, I suppose.'

'Your mother?'

'It doesn't matter.'

'It does, or you wouldn't have mentioned it.'

'She was a good, kind person, and she died horribly. That's all.' Edith took a book from the shelf and opened it, but did not look at the pages.

'Whereas the most frightful brutes often survive into peaceful old age.'

'Precisely.' The book snapped shut, and she replaced it on the shelf. There was a silence. She stared at him. 'You're supposed to say something, Derry.' Her voice was cold and hard. 'You're supposed to express sympathy or tell me that I must miss her terribly or—'

'Do you?' he said, looking at her. 'Miss her, I mean?'

Her gaze dropped. 'Hardly at all.' The whispered

words shook slightly. 'I'm glad that she's gone.' She pulled from the shelves another book at random, and stood still, flicking through the pages without looking at them.

'Because it was so awful?'

'Yes. But not just because she isn't suffering any more. Because of me, too.' She stared at him defiantly. 'Are you shocked?'

'Should I be?'

'A daughter isn't supposed to resent caring for her sick mother.'

He shrugged. 'You can't help how you feel.'

'I felt so trapped. For years and years and years. And besides—' She broke off.

'And besides . . . ?' he repeated gently.

'I can't bear ill people.'

'*Not* a Florence Nightingale . . .'

'Certainly not. It made me feel so guilty. After my mother died, everyone was very kind to me, and I hated it.' Edith's phrases were low and rushed. 'I just wanted to be on my own. Not to have to bother with anyone. And I detested the house.'

'Too many memories.'

'Yes.' Again, that sharp blue stare.

'If you hate it,' he said curiously, 'then why don't you leave?'

'Because I can't afford to, and because of Mina. Though she intends to move out.' Edith gave a humourless laugh. 'All this time I've worked at my dreary job and lived in that beastly house, so that Mina could stay at her school. And now she tells me that she means to leave at the end of term and become a *novelist*.' Another croak of unamused laughter. 'And just think of all the effort that moving house would involve! I couldn't bear it.' Her eyes narrowed, looking at him. 'You – why did *you* come back?'

'Because Jon rescued me.' He smiled at her. 'And because I'd run out of other options.'

'I assumed people like you always had plenty of other options.'

'People like me?'

'People who enjoy flouting convention.'

'You don't?'

'No.' A quick shake of the head. 'I think conventions are there to make life easier. So that we know the rules, and don't have to think all the time.'

'Don't you like thinking?'

'I like to know what I'm supposed to do. I dislike – fuss. Messiness. Complications.'

The corners of his mouth curled. 'And I was beginning to believe we had something in common. Now, I adore fuss. And complications. In fact, I like things to be as complicated as possible.' His gaze held hers. 'Like a cat's cradle,' he said softly.

A moment of stillness, and then she looked away, and sat down. She began to read where the pages of the book fell open. '"The expense of spirit in a waste of shame, Is lust in action—"' She stopped suddenly, and then slammed the book shut.

'Don't you like that sonnet? Rather *brooding*, I've always thought. If one's going to sin, one should just do it, and have the courage of one's convictions.'

He went to stand behind her, leaning over her shoulder, one arm along the back of the sofa, his fingers flicking through the pages of the book that she still held loosely in her hand.

'Another one, then. There must be something more appropriate.' He could smell the lily-of-the-valley scent that she wore, and he could see where the tiny tendrils of golden hair clustered at the nape of her neck.

'Ah, here we are. What do you think of this one, Edith?' He quoted, '"When, in disgrace with fortune and men's eyes, I all alone beweep my outcast state . . ."'

Jonathan, coming home at the end of the week, drew Derry aside. 'There's something I want to tell you, Derry. Well, two things, actually. Do you mind if I'm frightfully selfish and begin with the one that concerns me?'

'Spit it out, Jon.'

Jonathan glanced out of the window. It was afternoon, and a watery sun lit up the garden. Mrs Fox had fallen asleep on the drawing-room sofa, and the maid was clearing away the tea things.

'Do you mind if we talk outside? It would be more private. It's stopped raining, and the weather's quite mild.'

There was a brief fuss while Jonathan insisted Derry borrow his coat, and Derry, smothered in thick grey wool, tried to summon up enthusiasm for the role of confidant.

They walked through the garden. 'It's about Edith,' said Jonathan. 'She said that I could tell you. We're going to be married.'

Later, looking back, Derry did not know why Jonathan's announcement shocked him so much. Or why, with untypical clumsiness, he began to say, 'But she doesn't—' and then, seeing suddenly the happiness in Jonathan's eyes, had to change it to: 'She didn't say anything. She visited me, and . . .' He looked at Jonathan. 'How long? Just now?'

'We've been engaged since the end of last month. I

asked Edie to marry me the day I took you home. We didn't tell anyone else because you were so ill. I didn't want to give Mother too many shocks at once. But I had to tell you, Derry, I just couldn't wait any longer.'

'That's wonderful, Jon. Congratulations.' His voice sounded hollow. A succession of thoughts, most of them unpalatable, flickered through his head.

Jonathan was still talking. 'We won't get married for six months, maybe a year. I'd like it to be sooner, of course, but there's the partnership to be sorted out, and we'd have to find a house, and there's Mina to think of, of course.'

Derry tried again. 'It's terrific news, Jon. I'm so pleased for you. She's a beautiful girl.'

'Isn't she? I just can't believe my luck. I never thought she'd say yes. And when she did . . . it seemed too good to be true.' Jonathan's expression altered. 'You see, there have been times when I've felt like giving up. Giving up on everything, I mean. When I was in France . . . and in hospital, when I thought I'd end up a cripple . . . only now I can forget all that, can't I?'

Derry had to suppress a shiver. 'Of course you can, Jon. I'm glad everything's worked out for you.'

'As it will for you, Derry, soon, I'm sure of it.' Jonathan delved in his pocket and drew out an envelope. 'This is for you.' He placed it in Derry's hands.

'What is it?'

'Miss Berkoff found a letter in your jacket pocket, when you were ill, Derry. I'm afraid I had to open it – I'm sorry, but I thought it might be important. But the paper had got wet somehow, and the ink had run, and I couldn't make out much more than the address. So I wrote back, asking for a copy. And they sent this to me.'

Derry took the letter out of the envelope. He read, for

a second time, *The solicitors acting as executors for the estate of the late Mrs Sarah Elizabeth Kessel*, and then he let drop his hand, and said: 'I've seen this before.'

'Did you read it? All of it?'

He shook his head. Jonathan said gently, 'You must read it, Derry. She was your friend, wasn't she? Then read it. I'll go. Leave you in peace.' Fleetingly Jonathan's hand touched Derry's shoulder, and then he was alone.

He sat on a wrought-iron bench, and read the letter through. Twice. Then he folded the single piece of paper, and closed his eyes tightly, remembering.

Alix thought, if Derry doesn't visit by the end of September, I'll never see him again. And I'll know that I was right, we were just business acquaintances.

She kept very busy. She hung the new curtains her mother had made in the library, and turned out the cellar, untouched since her arrival at Owlscote. Treasures – a rusty bicycle and cases of wine, encrusted with cobwebs – lay discarded among the detritus. She made a huge bonfire out of the broken packing cases and heaps of yellowing newspapers. With Rory's hand clutched in hers she watched the sparks dance in the inky sky.

Jacob Long cleaned up the old bicycle and made a seat for Rory out of a wicker basket. With Rory perched behind her, Alix cycled to the village shops. The villagers stared at her, and a motor-car drove slowly by, its fur-clad passenger not giving so much as a nod of greeting. Alix remembered how, when she had first arrived at Owlscote, she had shut herself off from the world. Her friendship with Derry Fox had broken through that isolation, bringing the rest of the world to her. She freewheeled down the hill. The bicycle gathered momentum, and Rory screamed with delight. Alix thought, I'm glad that I shan't see Derry any more. There'll be just me and Rory and Mother again. I won't miss him at all.

Yet the next day, the last day of September, as she and Rory searched for conkers in the wood, she found herself glancing continually back to the drive that led from the house to the road. They walked along paths scattered with fallen leaves and broken twigs, moving aside fronds of bracken to discover the spiked green cases that lay hidden in the undergrowth. The boughs of the trees, heavy with dried copper-coloured leaves, dipped across her view, and the wind called up vortices of leaves, drawing them into small, whirling columns, fleetingly giving them movement and half-human shape, so that every now and then her heart beat faster.

In the early evening of the following day, before it became dark, Alix went outside, back to the woods to search for a mitten that Rory had lost during their conker-hunt. It had rained overnight, and black puddles pooled in the mossy hollows of trees and in the muddy shallows that their feet had made the previous day. She had forgotten her own gloves, and her fingers, moving aside brambles and clumps of nettle, became damp and cold. The silence was punctuated by the beat of an owl's wings, and the soughing of the dead leaves on the branches. And then, by a voice calling out her name.

She saw the scarlet mitten, caught high up on a thorn; and she saw him, standing in the shadow of the trees.

'Derry,' she whispered.

'I saw you from the path. What are you doing? Mushroom-hunting?'

'Rory lost his glove.' Alix stood on tiptoe, but could

not reach it. 'The wind must have caught it.'

Derry rescued the mitten, and pressed it into her hand. 'There.' He did not immediately let go of her. 'You're frozen – and cut to pieces . . .'

'The brambles,' she said, and pulled away from him. She walked to the house, not looking back at him. At the front door she paused and said, with an effort, 'Have you time for tea? I was just going to make some.'

They went into the house. In the kitchen she warmed the pot, spooned tea, found milk and sugar. When she put the cup in front of him she saw that he was thin and pale, and that there was a bruised, tired look to his eyes. She had seen him like that before: after one of their better parties, after several nights without sleep.

She said, 'I held a party for a Madeline Ferraby a fortnight ago. She's a friend of yours, isn't she, Derry? It wasn't a big affair – just half a dozen people for a weekend. It went well, I think – two of Maddy's friends have written since, asking to stay at Owlscote next month.' She took the biscuit barrel out of a cupboard. 'I'm going to have the drawing-room repapered. And I'm thinking of putting in another bathroom. It must put guests off, don't you agree, queuing up for the bathroom.' She pushed the barrel towards him.

He put down his cup. 'Why are you cross with me, Alix?'

She was silent for a moment, and then she whispered, 'Because you didn't visit. And you didn't write.'

He looked down. 'I was – otherwise engaged.'

'Of course.' She stood up and, sweeping up her unfinished tea, poured it down the sink. She said coldly, 'I don't see how we can run a business together when you just *disappear*. It's so inconvenient.' Her back to him, she turned on the tap. 'Perhaps it would be better if we agreed to part. I don't need you any more, Derry. I can manage the parties without you. I could pay you and Roma some sort of severance fee, I suppose.'

He said, 'I was ill,' and she stood still, watching the water billow in the ceramic bowl.

'Ill?'

'Asthma and bronchitis. I've been at home for a month. My parents' home.'

She turned to face him. 'You could have written.'

'I lost a week. Can't remember a thing about it. Just . . . dreams. And then, when I began to get better, I saw what a mess I'd made of it all. I was ashamed of myself, actually. And I tried to write, but I couldn't. *Dear Alix, everything I've tried to do has fouled up.* What would have been the point?' He looked up at her. 'The sink's overflowing, Alix.'

She spun round and pulled out the plug. Water gurgled, swimming round her ankles. As she mopped up the mess, she heard him say: 'And then something happened. Do you remember that I told you that six years ago I had an affair?'

'Your father's best client's sister-in-law?'

'Yes. She died a few months ago.'

'I'm sorry.'

'Thank you. A great many other people seem to be delighted. A convenient sort of tidying up. Anyway, Sara left me a legacy. A small amount of money and some shares in a South American mine. It'll give me a second chance, you see, Alix. When I was at home . . . when I was at home I thought that's it, I've had my shot at independence – at making something of my life – and I've wasted it.' He looked at her. 'I missed you, though.'

She snorted, and squeezed the floorcloth into the sink.

'It's true. When I was ill, I dreamed of Owlscote. And

I dreamed of you. You were in this room, sleeping on the sofa. Honestly, I missed you. It's not the same arguing with Jon. He's too polite. He hasn't your—'

She threw the floorcloth at him. '—hasn't your *aim*,' he said, and caught it, and rose from his seat, crossing the room to her. 'Your cloth, madam.'

'You are—'

'Infuriating? So everyone tells me.' He hugged her tightly.

'I was going to say, you are skin and bone. Put me down, Derry, I can't breathe.'

'Forgive me?'

'I suppose.' He kissed her forehead, then let her go. 'Are you well now?'

'Perfectly. And will continue to be as long as I avoid feather beds and bolsters, plumed hats, quill pens . . . Feathers give me asthma, apparently.' He added pleadingly, 'So we can have more parties, can't we, please, Alix?'

'I shall tell our guests not to wear feather boas.' She sat down at the table. Her heart was beating much too fast.

'What will you do, Derry? Will you go back to London?'

'Tonight, I think. I had to tell my father I couldn't take up his offer to work for the family firm. More gnashing of teeth. And I tried so hard to be tactful.'

'How's Jonathan?'

'Jonathan's very happy.'

She could not make out his expression. Derry explained, 'Jonathan's engaged to be married.'

Alix stared at him. '*Engaged*?'

'To Edith Carr.'

She looked at him narrowly. 'You don't seem pleased.'

'On the contrary, I'm delighted. If it makes Jon happy.'

'*Derry*. What's she like? Is she pretty?'

'Not *pretty*. Edith is beautiful. Undeniably beautiful. She has long golden hair, and the most extraordinary blue eyes, and it's a pleasure just to look at her. And she has a sister who's very plain and has a tongue like a cat's. It must be awful,' he said meditatively, 'to be Mina Carr. Such a *shadow*.' He crumbled fragments of biscuit between forefinger and thumb. 'The thing is, Alix . . .'

'What?'

'The thing is that she doesn't love him.' His voice was flat.

'You can't know that, Derry.'

'I've seen them together. She has a sort of *indolence*. It's quite attractive at first, actually. But then it makes you want to provoke. You think, such a lovely face – there must be something – passion, I suppose – beneath. Then you realize that she just wants things to be *easy*. I suspect that if you look like Edith things often *are* easy, and when they're not, it's probably a bit of a shock.' His eyes were dark and unreadable. 'You see, it seems to me quite possible that Edith agreed to marry Jon because that was the simplest thing to do.'

Alix remembered walking across the South Downs with Edward. The cold, still, circular pond. Edward had asked her to marry him, and she, who had been able to see no future for herself, had, in a mood of resignation and hopelessness, accepted him.

'Even if what you say is true, Derry, it doesn't necessarily mean the marriage won't be happy. Does Jonathan love Edith?'

'Yes. I wasn't sure before, but – yes, he does.'

'Then she may grow to love him.'

'Do you think so? I'm not sure it works like that. And besides . . .'

'What is it?'

Derry shook his head. 'Nothing. Nothing at all.' He changed the subject. 'Tell me about you, Alix. How was Maddy? Did she bring her fearsome old nanny?'

Alix insisted on cooking Derry supper. She sat next to him as he ate it. Later, rummaging through trunks in the boxroom, she found a cashmere scarf that had once belonged to Edward, and made him wrap it round his throat. She took a book of short stories from the library and tucked it into his jacket pocket – 'to read on the train' – and put a bar of chocolate and an apple in his other pocket. He did not protest, and she knew, at last, why she did these things.

It was almost dark. She walked with him to the road. Their feet crunched on the gravel. At the end of the path, they embraced and she watched him disappear into the night. She waited until she could no longer hear his footsteps, and then she walked back to the house. She thought how unexpected love was, how it waited, hidden in the darkness, coming upon you, a shocking delight, without warning.

She acknowledged that she, who had been content to love only Rory and Owlscote, also loved Derry Fox. And that she had loved him for many months, but had not admitted it even to herself.

She suspected also that she had a place in Derry Fox's patched, unpredictable heart. She did not need to be the only one, or even the most loved one. She, who had for years struggled through thorn and briars, had recently found an equilibrium, a balance. She did not intend to disrupt that balance.

As for the rest of it . . . as for the business of love . . . the kisses, the caresses, the sharing of a bed. Alix paused on the path, her arms clasped around herself, her eyes closed. She had believed herself immune to all that; she had assumed that part of herself had died with Edward. Now she knew that was not so. Had Derry, in the kitchen, embracing her, gone on to touch her as Edward had once touched her, she would not have stopped him. No, she would have stripped naked for him, on the cold flags, with her mother two rooms away, and her small son asleep upstairs in his cot.

She walked back to the house. Lights flared in the windows. She smiled to herself. She thought, I have danced in the desert, and now I dance through different rooms, and I will follow to wherever the music takes me.

PART THREE

1926–1927

A Fancy Dress Party

CHAPTER SEVEN

'Gently round the corner . . . Are you all right, Mina old thing? Just a few more steps . . . here we are. I'll take the weight, and you open the door.'

Jonathan had volunteered to help Mina Carr move into the room she had rented in Shepherd's Bush. They had hauled boxes of books and cases of linen and clothes up three flights of stairs. The room was furnished, but Mina had brought with her the writing-desk from the Richmond house.

Mina opened the door, and together they lifted in the desk. 'Over there,' she said, pointing to the window.

Sunlight gleamed on the polished walnut top. Mina, placing a chair at the desk, smiled. Jonathan looked around the room. There was a bed which by day Mina could use as a sofa, and an armchair and a bookcase and a wardrobe. Along the corridor was a kitchen and a bathroom, shared with other inhabitants of the lodging house. Mina drew aside the lace curtain. Looking down, Jonathan saw a small square, with swings and a pond and dusty privet bushes. The distant rumble of the motor-cars and lorries and vans that plied the Goldhawk Road rose to a roar when Mina opened the window. The air smelt of soot and new grass and vegetable peelings.

'Have you time for a cup of tea, Jonathan?'

'I'd better get back to Edith.' After eight months of engagement, Jonathan and Edith had still not set the date of the wedding. He had put Edith's reluctance to begin her new life down to her anxiety about Mina. But with Mina now moved into her lodgings, Jonathan had resolved that today they should name the day.

Yet, looking at Mina, Jonathan was suddenly concerned. She seemed so horribly young. Her short hair was pushed back into an Alice band, and she was wearing her green and white school dress.

'What about you, Mina? Will you be all right?' The small room was cluttered with suitcases and boxes. 'I could give you a hand unpacking all this.'

'I'll be fine, Jon.' Two-handedly, she was hauling the heavy typewriter across the floor.

'Let me help.' He took the typewriter from her, and placed it on the desk. He watched her take off the cover, and fleetingly her fingertips brushed across the rows of keys. Mina's eyes gleamed and, just for a moment, released from the shadow of her sister and transformed by happiness, she was beautiful.

Edith said, 'I thought she'd take more . . . an armchair or two . . . or an occasional table . . .'

'She's just the one room,' Jonathan reminded her.

'Of course.' The drawing-room of the Richmond house looked, Jonathan thought, peculiarly empty without the writing-desk. The dark patch on the wall showed where it had once stood: the sun had bleached the surrounding wallpaper.

Edith's hands were knotted, and she was biting her

lip. 'Mina'll be fine, Edie,' said Jonathan gently. 'Honestly, she'll be fine.'

'She's only seventeen, Jon.'

'She's a tough little thing, though. Hauled all those boxes and bits and bobs up the stairs like a navvy.'

'And that awful lodging house . . .'

'It's pretty grim, but Mina adores it. I've never seen her so happy.' He thought that Edith looked white and strained, so he squeezed her hand comfortingly. 'I wouldn't worry about Mina at all. I worry far more about you.'

'Worry about me, Jon? What on earth for?' Pulling away from him, she went into the kitchen. He heard her filling the kettle.

'I don't like to think of you living here on your own.'

'Oh, I'm used to being by myself. You know that.' She spooned tea into the pot and poured boiling water. 'Shall we have tea outside, Jon? I know it's only April, but it's so lovely and warm.' There was an artificial cheerfulness about her tone that he immediately saw through.

He wanted to hug her, to comfort her, but she was bustling around with biscuit barrel and teaspoons. He took a deep breath and said, 'I know you're feeling sad about Mina, but I can't help being rather glad, Edie. Now that she's settled, we can fix a date for the wedding.'

'Settled?' Edith busied herself with trays and cups and sugar bowl. 'Don't you think it's rather early to talk of Mina being settled, Jon? After all, she only left home today.'

'I can't imagine Mina changing her mind.'

Edith's smile was brittle. 'Mina's never been very domesticated. Having to do her own cooking and washing and cleaning . . . I shouldn't be surprised if she's tired of living by herself in a week.'

It had begun to drizzle, so Edith put the tea things down on the wrought-iron table in the sun-room.

'You've got to start thinking about yourself, Edie,' said Jonathan. 'I know it must be hard – first your mother to look after, then Mina. You're so used to having to bother about everyone else, you've never had time for yourself. But things are different now. You must think about *us*. I don't like to think of you struggling on by yourself. And having to slave away at that job, running around at everyone's beck and call. It's time someone looked after *you*.'

Sitting beside her, he took her fist in his hand and stroked her clenched fingers. Then he pressed his lips against her knuckles. Edith closed her eyes for a moment, and put up her fingertips to her creased brow. And at last some of the tension seem to slip from her and her shoulders relaxed, and she sat back in her chair.

'The wedding . . .' he said softly.

'Not now, Jon, please.' Her voice was suddenly sharp. Her eyes, now wide open, caught him in their pleading turquoise gaze.

He capitulated immediately, just as he always did. 'Whatever you like, Edie.' He kissed her again, and then he smiled. 'You know I'd wait to doomsday, if that's what it takes.'

'. . . and I am accustomed to cooking for the most *refined* families.' Miss Barton coughed genteelly.

Alix struggled to suppress a yawn. 'We put up paying guests during the week, Miss Barton, and hire rooms out for house parties at the weekend. The cook I engage would be expected to cater for both.'

It was late afternoon. A fortnight earlier Alix had placed an advertisement for a cook in the Salisbury newspaper. A succession of unsuitable females – nervous, whispering debutantes who had gone down in the world, beefy farm girls with grubby fingernails, cordon bleu chefs who knew how to make lobster mayonnaise but could not boil a potato – had sat on the other side of the library desk from Alix as she interviewed them for the post. Two and a half hours had passed, and she had begun to despair of ever finding Owlscote a cook.

Alix looked Miss Barton in the eye. 'The paying guests are working men. Obviously they would require a different type of cuisine from the weekend guests. Do you think you could cope with that?'

Miss Barton looked outraged. '*Working men . . .*'

'Travelling salesmen, mostly.'

'I am not accustomed . . .'

Alix finished the interview soon afterwards. She glanced at her list. There was only one name left, a Miss Polly Daniels. She had no great hopes of Miss Daniels; the letter of application said that she was a vicar's daughter, twenty-three years old, and that this was her first job application. Alix thought, she will faint at the thought of stringing beans for fifty, she will be a naturist and insist on prancing naked on the lawn first thing every morning. Sighing, she went to the window.

It had rained on and off for the last fortnight. The cowslips and narcissi dotted through the lawn struggled to survive the downpour. Puddles smeared the stone terrace, and fat raindrops slid from the unfurled leaves on the trees. But on the horizon, the sky seemed to be lightening. She thought that it might be dry enough to take Rory for a walk that evening; the prospect helped dispel some of the frustration and boredom of the afternoon.

There was a knock at the door. Alix turned round.

'Miss Daniels?'

'Mrs North.' Polly Daniels held out her hand. She did not, Alix acknowledged, look the fainting sort. Her brown hair was cut in a short, fringed bob, and her blue eyes crinkled at the corners when she smiled. She was wearing a well-ironed cotton dress with a navy-blue jacket and beret, rather than the homespun pinafore or eccentric velvets of Alix's imagination. In fact, Polly Daniels looked thoroughly pleasant and sensible.

'Do sit down, Miss Daniels. Perhaps you could tell me a little bit about yourself.'

Beatrice and Rory were in the sewing-room; Alix, peering in, immediately sensed disaster.

Beatrice, pale-faced and exhausted, was scrabbling about the floor; Rory was nowhere to be seen. Beatrice gasped, 'All my bobbins . . . and the *wool* . . .'

The room was strewn with a cat's cradle of brightly coloured cottons. Alix looked around.

'The wool . . . ?'

'Out of the *window*.' Beatrice was almost in tears.

The window was wide open. Her heart in her mouth, Alix looked out. She saw that the terrace was splashed with colour, like vast fragments of confetti. But there was no sign, thank God, of a small boy, motionless on the stones.

'I'll clear this up, Mother. You sit down.'

'The men's dinners . . . you'll be late . . .'

'That won't matter for once.' Alix helped her mother into a chair. Looking at Beatrice's greyish complexion, her alarm returned. She knelt on the floor and began quickly to gather up the tangled spools. 'You have a rest, Mother. It's been a long afternoon. I'll find Rory, and then I'll fetch you a cup of tea.'

Beatrice looked severely at Alix. 'You must send him to school.'

'Rory's much too young.' They had had this conversation before. 'He's only four and a half.'

'The flour, all over the kitchen floor, yesterday . . .'

'He was trying to make a snowman.'

'Throwing his teddies down the well . . .'

'He wanted to give them a bath.'

'Rory should go to school. He needs discipline.'

'*I* give him discipline.'

'A *man's* discipline, I meant, Alix. It's not good for a boy to be brought up only by women.'

'Rory sees Jonathan . . . and Derry . . . and Jacob . . .'

'He runs rings around Jacob, and you know it, Alix. And we've seen less of Jonathan since his engagement. And as for Derry . . .' Beatrice sniffed. 'He is hardly a suitable example for a small child. In fact, they are almost as bad as each other.' She looked Alix in the eye. 'If Rory took after Edward, then I would say yes, he might wait until he was six or so before going to school. But he takes after you, Alix. You were just the same, forever up to mischief. Only your father could make you behave. But poor little Rory doesn't have a father.'

'Things'll get better soon, Mother. I've found a cook. A lovely, sensible girl called Polly Daniels. She loves cooking, and thinks the house is wonderful, and is longing to start. And when she does, I'll be able to spend more time with Rory, won't I?'

Beatrice repeated, 'He needs to go to school.' And then she sat back in the chair, her eyes closed.

Alix went to look for Rory. She found him, as she had expected, hiding in his toy cupboard. Opening the door, spying him curled among the toy trains and jack-in-a-boxes and rubber balls, she held out her arms to him, and said softly, 'Oh, Rory, Rory. What am I going to do with you?'

Rory clasped his arms round her neck. Alix kissed the top of his head. His eyes, Edward's dark, serious grey, focused on her.

'I wanted to watch the balls of wool bounce. Very, very high.'

'Yes, darling, but you mustn't open the window, must you? I've told you that lots and lots of times.' Tomorrow morning, Alix thought, she must ask Jacob to nail shut all the accessible windows.

'We'll go and collect the wool from the terrace, and then we'll make Grandma a cup of tea, and you'll say sorry to her for throwing her knitting wool out of the window.'

Rory nodded solemnly. On the terrace, disentangling damp wool from rose bushes, Alix thought that Beatrice was right: because Rory lacked a father to play boisterous games with him his abundant energy was channelled into mischief. Too much of Alix's own time was taken up running the guest house. Rory had no brothers or sisters. Beatrice was becoming too frail to be expected to look after a demanding four-year-old.

The rain had stopped, and a watery sunshine made the damp leaves and flower petals glisten. Alix straightened, her arms full of balls of wool. It was only, she thought, that she would hate to part with him. But she could put off the moment no longer. She would, she resolved, go to Salisbury the very next day and look for a school.

*　　*　　*

A month later, Alix travelled to London. Ringing the doorbell of Derry Fox's Chelsea flat, she heard footsteps through the frosted glass, and then a clinking of chains and a clattering of bolts. The door opened.

'Alix. How *splendid*.' Derry hugged her. He looked, she thought, as though he had just got out of bed. White shirt, lacking a collar, and no tie. His feet were bare. 'What an *honour*,' he added. 'But you never come to London . . .'

'I wanted to see your new flat.' She followed him indoors. 'And Rory has started school.'

Derry glanced back at her. '*Oh*,' he said. 'Poor Alix.'

'It's good for him,' she said quickly. 'He'll love it. I don't mind.'

'Of course you do. I shall have to distract you.'

He opened a door. She looked round, open-mouthed. 'Good heavens.'

'Extraordinary, isn't it? Roma insisted on being given carte blanche. She said she'd decorate the place for free, so long as I recommend her to all my friends.'

The room, whose wide windows had a view of the distant Thames, was decorated in crimson and black. There were black leather sofas, crimson silk on the walls, and lamps and occasional tables made of sinuous dark metal.

'There's something horribly *organic* about it, isn't there? The bedroom's calmer. Tasteful cream and green. Would you like to see it?'

'Not just now, thank you.'

'How dull of you, Alix,' he said equably, and led her into the kitchen.

'Coffee?'

'Please.' She watched him grind beans. 'How's the magazine, Derry?'

'Surviving. Just. I've realized I'm not a writer, though. Not *contemplative* enough.'

'If you're not a writer, then what are you?'

'I don't know. A buyer and seller, perhaps.'

'Of what?'

'Oh,' he said vaguely, 'this and that.' He poured boiling water over the beans. 'Tell me about Rory. Is it a frightful school? Chalk and canes and mortar boards and . . .'

'It's called Mrs Waldegrave's Nursery School, and Mrs Waldegrave is very nice and motherly.'

'An enormous bosom, I expect. And a piercing glare.'

Alix had to acknowledge the accuracy of this description. She said, 'Rory took to Mrs Waldegrave immediately,' and then fell silent, feeling suddenly utterly forlorn. When she thought of Rory in his tiny maroon blazer and cap, she bit her lip.

'The extraordinary thing about you, Alix,' said Derry, watching her, 'is that you never actually *howl*. Things that would reduce lesser women to a quivering jelly, you somehow surmount. I don't mind if you cry, you know. I'm sure there's a clean handkerchief somewhere.'

'Do shut up, Derry, and pour me a cup of coffee.'

He handed her a cup. She said, 'The party on the fifteenth of May . . .'

He frowned. 'Might be difficult. I know that some of the guests intend to travel by train.'

'So?'

'So,' he said, 'there may not be any trains.'

She stared at him. 'Why on earth not?'

'Don't you read the newspapers?'

'Not much, no.'

'There may be a strike. Almost certainly, in fact.'

'The railwaymen?'

'And the dockers . . . and the printers if the General Council makes the mistake of calling them out. An awful lot of things may grind to a halt, Alix. Because of the miners, you see. But as you live in the back of beyond,' added Derry, 'and don't read newspapers and don't possess a wireless, I doubt if you'll notice much difference. Sometimes it must be quite useful to be a hermit.'

She said crossly, 'I'm not a hermit.'

'Then come with me to a party tonight. Grosvenor Square. See how the other half lives.'

Alix shook her head. 'I have to get back for Rory.'

'Another time, then?'

'Perhaps,' she said, preoccupied. 'My Gentlemen . . . some of them travel by train . . . How long do you think the strike will last, Derry?'

'Oh, ages, I hope,' he said cheerfully. 'It should all be *fascinating*.' His dark eyes glittered.

Derry took Alix to lunch at a tiny restaurant that the girls from the ballet frequented, and then they walked along the Embankment for a while, and later took the Tube back to Waterloo. Waving Alix off on the train he thought how unaccustomed he was to seeing her anywhere other than at Owlscote, and how nice it had been to have the unexpected treat of her company.

Back at the flat, Derry worked on his piece for *Chrome*. As he wrote, he reflected on his change of fortune over the last six months. At the end of September, Jonathan had given him the letter telling him of Sara Kessel's legacy. A few days after his return to London, Sophie Berkoff had knocked on the door of his rooms. 'So, my dear Derry,' she had said, 'you are back from the dead.' She had added, 'I have some news for you,' and had proceeded to tell him that her publisher friend had made an offer for his book. 'David thought it was *sooooo* funny,' she had said, drawing out the word as she had a habit of doing. Listening to her, he had thought, it's happening. At last it's happening. Then she had eyed him, and had said, 'I suppose you'll move out of this place,' to which he had replied, 'I suppose I shall.' And then, for old times' sake, they had made love, and he had lain awake for the remainder of the night, staring at the ceiling, seeing the cracks in the plaster as new roads, dividing and extending, taking him where he had always intended to travel.

Two weeks later he had met for a second time the woman he had encountered at Ruth Duncan's sister's party. Her name was Andrée Garland. He wrote articles for Andrée's magazine, *Chrome*, which were featured beside woodcuts by Wyndham Lewis or pen and ink drawings by Paul Nash. He had been living in the flat in Chelsea for some months now. The flat belonged to the younger son of an earl. Down on his luck, he had confided his difficulties to Derry over a great deal of gin, and Derry had offered to rent the place from him. He would, he promised himself, never again live in a room held together with tin tacks and brown paper.

He had discovered that he had, after all, something to sell. He had neither birth, nor money, nor any particular talent. And yet, if he put his mind to it, people listened to him, and they sought his company. He thought of it like Dante's Hell, a series of concentric circles through which he had to travel. Sara Kessel's money had allowed him to buy the address and the clothes that had permitted him to set off on his journey. His first night in the flat, he had bought a bottle of the best champagne and had toasted her memory.

The reception hall of the Grosvenor Square house gleamed. There seemed to be marble everywhere. Like a very splendid and very large public convenience, Derry thought.

He wandered through the rooms, looking for Andrée. Everything glittered, the women's beaded headdresses, the men's diamond tiepins, the lead-crystal goblets, the jazz band's saxophones. Catching sight of Andrée he threaded across the room towards her.

'Derry *darling*.'

'A present for you.' He handed her his article.

She read the first lines, and giggled, and folded up the piece of paper until it fitted in her tiny, tasselled evening bag. 'I shall save the rest for later.' She looked at him. 'I didn't know that you knew the Baddeleys.'

'I don't. Not at all.'

'Gatecrashing?'

'I'm a friend of a friend of a friend.'

Andrée stared through her lorgnette to where their hosts were greeting new arrivals. 'Hubert Baddeley is American, of course. He sells motor-cars. Lavender sees herself as a society hostess. It's her birthday. Thus the party.' She looked around the room. '*Lots* of people,' she said contentedly. 'Can I introduce you to anyone, Derry?'

'I'll manage, thank you, Andrée.'

'I believe Oriana is here.'

'Oriana?'

'The gossip columnist. Hostesses fight to have their names mentioned by Oriana. If I see her, I shall mention you.' Andrée disappeared into the crowd. Derry waited for a moment, and then plunged into the fray.

He talked to a German financier, and to a manufacturer of electric light bulbs, and to a gentleman who owned a great deal of Norfolk as well as several mines in Derbyshire. He danced with the light bulb manufacturer's elegant wife, and with a viscount's youngest daughter, who was extremely drunk. He watched Mrs Baddeley blow out the candles on an immense pink cake: when she cut the cake with a knife, a flock of canaries, their feathers dyed pink, flew out. He leaned on a balcony that looked down over the marble hall, and watched the comings and goings of London's *beau monde*. From that height, the well-bred conversation, the laughter and the music blurred into a distant buzz, like the humming of a great many industrious bees.

Some time in the early hours of the morning, a voice said, 'Mr Fox? Mrs Garland insisted I introduce myself to you.'

Derry turned round. She was young and pink-cheeked and plump, with bobbed fair hair. 'Oriana?'

She held out her hand. 'I've been hoping to meet you, Mr Fox. I was at a particularly dull reception recently, and your wonderful novel saved me from falling asleep.' She was wearing a dress of mushroom-brown satin. The unrelieved shade, and the bands of sequins, emphasized her height and girth. In spite of her youth, there was something confident and stately about her, Derry thought, that justified the regal nom-de-plume.

'Are you here in your professional capacity, or do you merely enjoy birthday parties?'

'My editor insisted I come.' She looked at him. Her very pale blue eyes were set in a pleasant, ordinary face. 'And you?'

'At my next birthday, I intend to have a huge pink cake, just like the Baddeleys'.'

She murmured, 'So supremely vulgar . . .'

The band had begun to play again; taking her elbow

he walked with her into a quieter side room. 'Come now,' he said, 'aren't you tempted? Just a little?'

She shook her head. 'I don't celebrate my birthday.'

He looked at her curiously. 'Not at all?'

'Not at all.'

'Why not?'

He thought at first that she was not going to reply, but then she said, 'Because . . . because a very long time ago, when I was a little girl, something dreadful happened on my birthday.'

There was a tray of champagne abandoned on the mantelpiece, so he fetched her a glass, and changed the subject.

'Why did you become a gossip columnist?'

'Because I needed the money. And because it's easy for me, I know the right people.'

'It wasn't a childhood ambition?'

She laughed. 'Certainly not. I always wanted to be a ballerina. But a lesson a week from a woman who had once danced in the back row of the *coryphées* at the Alhambra isn't enough. And besides, I grew too much.' She put down her glass. 'I write about the ballet, though. Under a different name, of course. But it doesn't pay as well as gossip.'

'It's all watching the choreography, isn't it?'

She laughed again. 'I suppose so. And following the plot. I suppose you enjoy following the plot, Mr Fox?'

'Absolutely.' He smiled.

'Maddy Ferraby told me about your parties at a wonderful house in Wiltshire.'

'They're not *my* parties. I just helped start them off. A friend of mine, Mrs North, does most of the work.'

She offered her cigarette case to him; Derry shook his head. 'You should invite me,' she said. 'Though parties might be rather scarce on the ground, I suppose, over the next few weeks.' Oriana fitted a cigarette in a long, ebony holder and glanced at her watch. 'I have to go. It's been lovely meeting you, Mr Fox.'

'Derry,' he said. He watched her cross the room. She walked gracefully, like a dancer. He called out, 'What's your name? Your real name, I mean.'

Reaching the door, she looked back briefly. 'May,' she said. 'May Lanchbury.'

On the morning of the fourth of May, Alix and Rory waited for the Salisbury bus. When, after half an hour, the bus had not appeared, they walked back to Owlscote, where Alix put Rory in the seat on the back of her bicycle. She then cycled the three miles to Salisbury. After she had left Rory at Mrs Waldegrave's school, she walked around the town for a while. The roads were jammed with lorries and motor-cars, but the railway line was silent. The hoardings by the newspaper stands said, *No papers due to General Strike*.

Alix bought ink and writing-paper from the stationers, and then returned to Owlscote. Only two paying guests, both of whom owned motor-cars, booked to stay, and one of them, who sold penny novelettes to bus and railway-station kiosks, trailed disconsolately home after a few days. Mrs Waldegrave's school remained open. Polly Daniels did what little shopping and cooking was necessary. Alix often found herself wondering how she had managed before Polly had come to Owlscote. Polly was not only a good cook, but good company as well. Beatrice was busy in the garden. For the first time in her adult life, Alix discovered that she was having a holiday.

In the mornings she worked in the library on her

history of Owlscote. Yet towards midday she would find herself drawn outdoors by the fine weather. She would drift around Owlscote's grounds, wandering from the gardens to the lake, from the lake to the woods. Every now and then she would think, I really ought to use the good drying weather to wash the curtains, or, such an opportunity to tidy up the accounts. But the accounts remained untidy, and the curtains unwashed. Instead, she dragged the old rowing boat from the shed. Rowing around the lake in the mid-afternoon heat, she watched the mayflies alight on the water-buttercups, and saw the glimmering blue swoop that marked the kingfisher's flight from woodland to water. Sometimes she shelved the oars, and just lay back in the boat, her eyes closed, the sun on her bare limbs, gliding slowly over the cool, green water.

When it was too hot for the lake, she walked through the sun-dappled, twisting paths that led through the woods. A long time ago, looking through the dipping branches and tangled undergrowth, she had imagined sometimes that she had glimpsed a small boy's disappearing form. Now, only the pungent scent of wild garlic recalled to her faintly that distant day in northern France: the picnic, the walk through the woods, the fair. Her marriage to Edward, and her life at Owlscote with her own small son, had made those nightmares a thing of the past. Of the scars that the loss of little Charlie Lanchbury had inflicted, there remained only the divisions that persisted within her family, cutting off Beatrice from her only brother, and the lingering apprehension that still led Alix to check the list of the guests at every party, searching for the name of Lanchbury.

The sun, and the indolence enforced by the strike, worked its magic on all of them. Polly made picnics, which they ate on the lawn. Mr Thompson, Owlscote's only paying guest, dined with them. 'I am a magician,' he said. 'A tuner of pianos by day, and a magician by night.' He plucked coins from Polly's ear, and silk handkerchieves from flowerpots. Watching him, Rory's mouth rounded into a wide O of astonishment.

The strike went on into a second week. Derry, returning to his flat at midday, discovered Jonathan waiting on the doorstep.

'Jon. How unexpected. I thought you'd be hard at work at home, fending off the forces of Bolshevism.'

'I wanted to talk to you about Edith.'

Derry said, 'Shall we walk?' The weather was hot and oppressive; he did not want to be indoors.

They walked along the Embankment. Jonathan, looking out at the river, said, 'It all seems so peaceful. I didn't think it would be like this. The *British Gazette* said there were riots.'

'Not in *Chelsea*, Jon. In Stepney, and in Poplar.' Derry smiled. 'How are things at home? Is Father apoplectic about the Red Menace bringing the country to a standstill? Are his worst fears realized at last?'

'He loathes,' said Jonathan, 'not having his *Telegraph*. No crossword, you see.'

'And Mother?'

'Rather put out by the absence of any post. Apparently Cousin Dolly was due to have an operation, and Mother's being denied the details.'

The air seemed fresher, cooled by the river. There had fleetingly been, Derry realized, some sort of unconscious acknowledgement of affinity between himself and Jonathan; an unspoken admission that they had, after all, something in common, even if it was only a mutual exasperation with their parents. It occurred to Derry – an uncomfortable thought – that his envy of Jonathan had always been ill-founded, born of his own fear of failure.

Jonathan said, 'I hoped Edith would come and stay with the Winstanleys.'

'I shouldn't worry – Richmond's hardly a hotbed of revolution.'

'She insists on going to work. That wretched advertising agency. There are pickets on some of the roads – I saw them, driving in.' Jonathan, who looked hot and tired, rubbed his forehead.

'Edith'll be fine.' Derry glanced at his brother. 'You look as though you're about to melt, Jon. It's too early for a drink, but I know a nice little café.'

Over black coffee, Derry described to Jonathan the morning's events. 'There were a hundred lorries in Hyde Park. At dawn, of course – terribly dramatic. The Grenadier Guards escorted them to the docks. There were public schoolboys and students loading up the lorries. *In Fair Isle sweaters and university scarves*, Jon. And they all seemed to be enjoying themselves. Having the most terrific time. I suppose it's because they're doing something useful at last.' He looked up at his brother. 'Have you . . . ? I just wondered . . . with the car . . .'

Jonathan said drily, 'I haven't volunteered my services as a strike-breaker, if that's what you're asking, Derry.' He looked down at his cup. 'In the war, some of the men in my battalion were Welsh miners. I mean, I worry that it all may get out of hand – but I couldn't—' He broke off.

'The *British Gazette* has implored all right-thinking people – by which they mean the middle classes, of course – to *do their bit*. A phrase which I seem to have heard before.'

Derry saw that, in spite of the heat, Jonathan shuddered. So he launched into a long anecdote about the prints he had bought earlier in the week at the sale of an estate. 'By auction. In *Norfolk*, Jon. And no trains. I had to hitch lifts. Just imagine – me, clasping a portfolio of extremely dubious French prints, thumbing a ride on a cartload of manure. My *shoes*. No-one would have anything to do with me for days.'

Jonathan smiled. 'What will you do with them?'

'Oh, sell them. For a great deal more than I paid for them.'

They walked back to the motor-car. Then Jonathan said, 'Do you mind if I ask you a favour, Derry? Keep an eye on Edith for me, won't you?' Climbing into the car, Jonathan took a pen and paper from the glovebox. 'She hasn't a telephone, you see, and with no post . . . And she's been a bit' – he frowned – 'a bit *nervy* recently.' He scribbled on a scrap of paper. 'This is the address of the advertising agency. Take her out to lunch or something – she stops work at one. Please, Derry. I do worry, you see.'

Derry thought of offering his services to the strikers but could not see what use he could be. He hadn't a car or a motor-bicycle, so he could not be a dispatch rider. On some of the roads into London, burly men halted lorries driven by blacklegs. He was unable to imagine himself among their number. He knew that in the past he would have done something – anything – just to annoy his father. But that no longer seemed sufficient motive. He resigned himself to once more standing back and watching. Events of history that would echo through the century took place, he thought wryly, and Derry Fox told amusing anecdotes and wrote funny stories. He knew that the strikers could not possibly win, that their intentions were at the same time too radical and too modest, and that it would end at worst with bloodshed, and at best with humiliation.

As the strike moved into its second week, he sensed an alteration in mood. The heat persisted, bringing people onto the streets. Walking to Sophie's lodgings on Tuesday afternoon, Derry saw an overturned lorry, and heard the smash of breaking glass. Turning a corner, he glimpsed a man sitting on a doorstep, his head clutched in his hands. The thin greying hair was dyed scarlet. That evening, heavy clouds bubbled on the horizon, and when at last the sun died, its fading light daubed the London skyline blood-red and greenish-bronze: the colours of the apocalypse, he thought.

At one o'clock the next day, remembering his promise to Jonathan, Derry waited outside the doors of Edith Carr's Golden Square offices. He had seen Edith less than half a dozen times since the engagement had been made public. Always with Jonathan present, of course. On those occasions, he had concentrated on being everything a prospective brother-in-law should be – pleasant, friendly, unprovoking. Yet his former uneasiness lingered, and sometimes he was aware of those cold, turquoise eyes watching him, judging him; and once or twice Edith had seized on some casual remark he had made, poking and prodding it, pulling it to pieces with an almost febrile, triumphant glee. He guessed that she remembered too well, and resented, their tête-à-tête during his convalescence.

When the doors opened and people spilled out, he

glimpsed her, surrounded by half a dozen colleagues. He crossed the steps to her.

'I was going to suggest lunch, Edith – but perhaps you're spoken for.'

She had paused, seeing him. 'No. No, I'm not.'

They walked down the pavement. 'Is there anywhere in particular you'd like to go?'

'I don't know. I usually buy a bun.'

Derry found a place in Piccadilly. The crimson chenille curtains were fringed with bobbles, and a wasp, searching for escape, whined at the window pane.

He glanced at the menu. 'What would you like?'

'Whatever. You choose.' She lit a cigarette. He couldn't recall her smoking before. 'Why were you waiting for me, Derry?'

'Can't I ask my prospective sister-in-law to lunch?'

She looked at him. He admitted, 'Jonathan asked me to.'

'Jonathan?' She laughed. 'How amusing.'

He remembered how, months ago, looking at her perfect and impassive face, he had wanted to provoke reaction, feeling. Yet he saw that repose had now vanished, replaced by an edgy vindictiveness.

He ordered something at random from the menu. 'Are you managing? I mean – getting to work, that sort of thing.'

'A friend gives me a lift to work. And Richmond is the same as it always is.'

'It's odd, isn't it, how quite small things disrupt. Not being able to send a letter . . . and the telephone exchanges are so chaotic.'

She looked up at him. 'I thought you'd enjoy all this.'

'I did, to begin with. It was like a cross between a bank holiday and one of those wonderful saint's day processions they have in South America. A rather British version of anarchy.'

The waiter put plates in front of them, and flicked napkins onto their laps. Edith said, 'But you're not enjoying it now?'

Derry shook his head. 'One senses tragedy, don't you agree? Though tragedy's the wrong word, perhaps.' He cut up his steak, not because he wanted to eat it, but because he wanted to avoid those fierce blue eyes. 'I suppose it'll all end in a series of banal surrenders. And I'm not sure that tragedy can be banal.'

'Can't it?'

'Doesn't tragedy,' he said, 'imply a certain grandeur?'

'I would say that most tragedies are utterly banal. Death is banal, and so is illness, and so is love. Most tragedies – real tragedies, I mean, not the sorts of things people write about in books – are just a collection of banal, dull little incidents.'

Edith fell silent. Derry cast around for a change of subject. 'How's Mina?'

'Mina's very well. She's almost finished her novel.'

'I could write down a few names, if you like – people who might be able to help her get it published.'

'How *considerate* of you, Derry.'

He put down his knife and fork, and said, 'You can go if you like, Edith. You don't have to endure pudding.'

'You're not hungry?'

'Hatred gives me indigestion.'

'*Hatred*!' Her smile was bitter; she lit another cigarette and sat looking out of the window at the rush of passers-by.

He was aware of a fast uncoiling unease, but he said, 'I don't know why you're angry with me, but you've made it obvious that you're not enjoying my company.

I had to go through the motions, or Jonathan would have plagued me. I know you don't think much of me, but—'

Her high peal of laughter interrupted him. 'Don't think much of you! Good God! And you so clever, so good at reading people! Derry, I think of little else—'

Edith clamped her hand over her mouth, as if to stop herself speaking. Then she whispered, 'I hadn't meant to say that – I hadn't meant to say anything . . .' and in the long, appalled silence that followed he thought *The expense of spirit in a waste of shame* and he recalled leaning over her shoulder as she had read to him, and turning the pages of her book, and his fingers brushing against her funny, square, practical hands, hands that had suddenly made him like her better, because they had seemed so at odds with the inhuman perfection of the rest of her.

She had turned away, her lips pressed tightly together. He knew that she was waiting for him to speak. Yet he could not remember ever having felt at quite such a loss for words. Her cigarette had burned almost to her tightly clenched fingers.

She opened her eyes. She whispered, 'I'm sorry.'

'It doesn't matter.' Though it did.

'Do you think that I should break off my engagement?'

His heart pounded. 'I don't know.'

'I meant,' and she looked down at the table, 'would things alter for me if I broke off my engagement?'

He could not speak. He shook his head.

'Why not?'

His mouth was dry. 'I'm not the marrying sort.'

'I didn't say anything,' she said, 'about *marriage*.' She

closed her eyes tightly. 'I'm sorry. I didn't mean that. Please forget I said it.'

'Jonathan . . .'

'Ah, Jonathan. I would have thought that might appeal to you.'

He became very still. 'What do you mean?'

'*Derry*. That your brother's fiancée should find herself in love with you—' Breaking off, Edith giggled, a peculiar high-pitched sound. 'And you so unconventional, so keen to shock! Isn't it all part of the fun?'

Isn't it all part of the fun? He remembered being at home, and feeling sick and stifled and angry. Hating home, and hating his father, and most of all hating Jonathan, perfect Jonathan, who had everything. He was appalled again: at himself, this time.

He felt as though he had without warning found himself tiptoeing around the rim of a volcano. He had to ask, though.

'Will you break it off, Edith?'

'Do you think I should?'

'Do you love Jon?'

At last, her eyes lowered. 'In my way,' she whispered. 'In my way.' He saw that her nails were short and bitten, and that she had pulled at the torn skin around them.

Then she smiled. 'There are different sorts of love, aren't there? I have discovered, you see, Derry, that there's a sort of love that is . . . unwelcome. Destructive, perhaps.'

There were tears in her eyes. He said desperately, 'That's not love. That's desire. And it *goes*.'

'Does it? I wouldn't know. It's never happened to me before.' She stood up. 'I have to go back to work now.'

He had to know. 'What will you do?'

Edith bit her lip. 'Nothing.' Her face was white, her voice full of contempt. 'I always do nothing.' Then she left the restaurant.

Jonathan was at home when Edith telephoned. 'Jon?' she said. 'Jon? I thought we should talk.'

Her voice sounded distant and tremulous. He was aware of a stab of anxiety, but before he could speak he heard her say, 'I think we should set a date for the wedding, Jon,' and then the fear in his heart turned to joy.

CHAPTER EIGHT

On 13 May the TUC called off the General Strike. The transport workers, printers and dockers stayed out for a few more days, and then they, too, returned to work. By September only the miners, their grievances disregarded and unresolved, remained on strike, until a simple need for survival forced them also to sue for peace.

In the autumn, the parties began again. Formal soirées in the great houses in the West End, wild gatherings in terraces in Bloomsbury, and lazy weekends in draughty country mansions in the home counties.

Derry went to a party in Chelsea. The house was tiny: two rooms and a kitchen downstairs, another two rooms and a bathroom upstairs. The rooms were so densely packed he had to make his way sideways, shouldering his way through the crowd. Some of the guests wore fancy dress, others were in evening dress. Someone was playing the piano, and people were dancing, their high-heeled shoes shuffling minutely from side to side. Upstairs, because there were no chairs, guests were collapsed in heaps on the floor. Derry, stepping over outflung limbs, found himself face to face with May Lanchbury.

She said, 'You look like a vulture. Dark and hungry, searching for carrion.'

He kissed her cheek. 'Actually, I was looking for a drink. Or an inch or two of air.'

'The drinks are laced with absinthe, so I wouldn't recommend them.' She glanced at him. 'A friend of mine saw you in Scotland, at a house sale.'

'Sweeping up crumbs from the tables of the rich . . .'

May snorted. 'A Jacobean table. Rather a large crumb.'

He smiled and, taking her hand, stepped carefully across the landing. He opened a door: a couple were making love on the bed, so he closed it again, and tried the adjacent one.

'Here,' he said.

The room was occupied by only one person, a girl wearing a Chinese mask. She had collapsed on the eiderdown. May, poking her experimentally, said, 'Dead to the world,' and sat down on the edge of the bed and kicked off her shoes. 'Thank goodness. I loathe these affairs. No food, no seats, and one has to queue for the lavatory.'

'I wouldn't have thought evenings like this were gossip column fodder.'

'Then you'd be wrong. Olivia Wyndham is downstairs. And Stephen Tennant is expected later.' She looked at him. 'Why are you here, Derry? What crumbs are you gathering tonight?'

He shrugged and smiled, but said nothing.

'What have you done with your Jacobean table?'

'I've sold it to a very rich American. Who will ship it to California, and give it pride of place in his imitation Jacobean dining-room, in his imitation Spanish villa.'

May took a cigarette case from her evening bag, and

offered it to Derry, who shook his head. 'What amuses me is that you have gained entrée to society by charming your patrician hosts – by deluding them that you are their *pet* – and all the time you are nibbling away at them, making them weaker.'

'A death-watch beetle . . . a vulture . . . you're muddling your metaphors, my darling May.' Derry went to the window and looked out. Though it was raining, couples had spilled into the garden. He asked, 'Do you disapprove?'

'Not at all. You're only profiting from an inevitable decline. As I am. We both have to make a living.' She fitted a cigarette into her holder. 'Consider my family, for instance. Our London house was sold just after the war. Because the rents don't cover the mortgage on our country estate, my father has had to sell land and paintings. And because I work for my living, he despises me – we don't talk to each other now. But I'd much rather write nonsense than remain immured at Bell Wood, waiting for someone to propose to me.'

'You don't intend to marry?'

She lit her cigarette. 'I'm the middle one of three daughters. None of us will have a dowry of more than fifty pounds a year. For Daisy, my younger sister, that won't matter, because she's pretty. Eligible men tend to want money or beauty, you see. Birth is no longer enough.'

'And your elder sister?'

'Ella will never marry.' May exhaled a cloud of blue smoke. 'Ella's entire existence is devoted to pleasing one man – my father. She simply isn't interested in any others. The irony is, of course, that she can never please him.'

'Why not?'

'Because she wasn't born a boy.'

Derry felt a fleeting sympathy with the unknown, unloved Ella. 'Have you brothers, May?'

'I had a brother who died.'

'In the war?'

May shook her head. 'Before.'

'Do you really not speak to your father? Not at all?'

She was sitting up on the bed, her feet tucked beneath her. 'Oh, Christmas and birthdays. You know.'

'I do,' he said fervently. He thought of Jonathan and Edith, the unmitigated disaster of his own family life. He looked at her. 'Your mother . . . ?'

'Died when I was ten. I had a stepmother, but she left years ago. Couldn't bear Bell Wood, I suspect – all cold, endless corridors and no plumbing.'

'Mrs North's house is like that. I adore houses like that.'

'Then you are a romantic.'

'Perhaps.' He looked at her curiously. 'Do you *mind*? I mean, your sort of people . . . you must have expected a different kind of life.'

'No.' May shook her head emphatically. 'Not me. I learned quite early on that you should never take anything for granted. And besides, I like what I do. I enjoy the gossip, and I love the ballet. But some people mind. A great many of *my sort of people* have lost a great deal, and they mind. They mind very much.'

'Your father?'

Her pale blue eyes narrowed: 'My father despises the new rich, and he despises people like me who have betrayed our class in order to survive. He believes – has always believed, Derry – that the great landed families have a God-given right to govern. My father believes that society is disintegrating.'

Sitting up, May stubbed out her cigarette in a plant pot on the window sill. Then she turned to Derry and smiled.

'Dance with me, won't you, Derry? Even if we've only an inch of space to shuffle in. I do so love to dance.'

In August, during the fortnight in which the guest house was closed, Alix repainted the kitchen, and scrubbed and lined with fresh paper all the shelves in the larder. The following month, the paying guests returned, many of them by now familiar faces, appreciative of Owlscote's good food and comfortable beds.

In the morning the dining-room was full, and the kitchen noisy with the sizzling of bacon and sausages and the clatter of Polly's footsteps as she darted from stove to plate. There was now hot and cold water in the kitchen and bathrooms. Rory's school fees were paid up a term in advance. Next year, Alix thought, if she worked very hard, if she kept the guest-rooms full and booked as many parties as possible during the winter, she might be able to install central heating. She imagined scorching hot radiators in every room, and a coal boiler thundering in the cellar. Never again having to haul scuttles of coal up the stairs. Never again having to sweep out grates clogged with grey, choking ash.

One Saturday afternoon in the middle of September, Jonathan brought his fiancée to Owlscote for tea. Alix, greeting Edith Carr, remembered Derry saying, *Edith is beautiful. Undeniably beautiful*, and found herself tucking a stray strand of hair behind her ear, and wishing she had put on a smarter dress. They had tea in the drawing-room, with a fire roaring in the grate because the weather had turned cold. The afternoon was oddly constrained, their voices swallowed by the library's high ceiling. Conversation, born in fits and starts, soon drifted into silence. Rory threw sugar cubes into the flames; Beatrice scolded him and complained about the draughts. Jonathan asked when Alix had last seen Derry – 'Haven't seen him for months. I'm beginning to think he's avoiding me' – and Alix was about to tell Jonathan about the postcards that Derry had sent throughout the summer (one each week, most of them scurrilous, to be snatched off the doormat before her mother caught sight of them) when Edith said, 'Oh, Derry will be busy. You know that, darling. Derry's always busy. A busy little bee.' The acid tone of her voice took Alix by surprise. Then Beatrice asked Edith about the wedding, and the conversation changed to bridesmaids and dresses and honeymoons.

Towards the end of the month, she received a letter from Derry. 'Darling Alix, a few friends of mine would like to hire Owlscote for a party. They are rather a wild set, so you may want to turn this one down. Though they would pay well. It's up to you. Let me know. I would help you hold the fort, of course. If you agree, they would like something original, so I thought a Come As Your Best Friend party.'

In the library, huddled in cardigans and scarves as she wrote the weekly accounts, Alix inspected columns of figures, and glanced once more at the brochure left by the heating company. She wrote back to Derry, agreeing a date.

The guests arrived one dark, damp, blowy evening on the cusp between autumn and winter. Driving into the courtyard, the chrome and glass of their motor-cars glittered in the fitful light of the moon. Indoors, Alix thought, they do not suit the house. It seemed to her that, in previous parties, Owlscote had absorbed their guests, making them a part of its fabric. She sensed that these people would have walked with equal confidence and equal lack of interest into a Mayfair hotel, a Roman palazzo, a Fifth Avenue apartment. They greeted Alix herself with polite disinterest; her purpose was to ensure their comfort, nothing more. She could not imagine a single one of these bright, self-assured young men and women bringing her a cocktail in the kitchen, as Maddy Ferraby had done. They shook her hand, or nodded a greeting, but their eyes sought out Derry. 'Darling Derry, I've come as my old governess, because she was my best friend.' 'Do you like my frock, Derry? Isn't it just too dreadful?'

Some of the girls were dressed as men – short, slicked-back hair, a monocle, tweeds. A fair-haired man wore silk and chiffon, and from his neck trailed floating scarves and long strings of beads. Two women, hand in hand, were identically dressed: 'We are each other's best friends.' Derry greeted them all with a kiss. They flung their arms round his neck and cried, 'Dearest Derry, where have you *been*? We haven't seen you for *weeks*. We've *missed* you.'

Alix served drinks, and passed round canapés. People spilled from the Great Hall into the dining-room, and onto the stairs. There was a man wearing a fur coat and a wolf's head mask: 'I've come as my German Shepherd dog. He's my best friend.' Peals of laughter. More motor-cars drew up in the courtyard. They were dancing on the terrace, and on the damp grass of the lawn. Some of them meandered into the kitchen, stealing titbits from plates; a girl wearing a dress that shimmered like a snakeskin shut herself in the pantry and would not come out until Alix rapped on the door and told her the house was on fire.

In the early hours of the morning, she searched for Derry. He was not in the Great Hall, nor in the library, nor lounging, with dozens of others, on the stairs. Alix walked out through the French doors onto the terrace. The night air cooled her hot face, and assuaged her exhaustion. She wandered along the terrace, away from the gramophone playing on the stone balcony, away from the laughter and the fast-moving footsteps. A voice drifted up from a rose bed.

'. . . so glad that you're your usual divine self, Miranda. So much nicer.'

Alix stood still. She could just make out Derry, leaning against a pilaster.

The moonlight caught the fair hair and scarlet dress of the woman beside him. 'I'm dressed as myself, Derry. I'm my best friend.'

'Not me?'

'I'm never sure.' The voice was low, coquettish. 'You can be – elusive.'

'I'm here now. Not elusive at all now.'

The pale head moved closer to the dark one. Alix turned on her heel and went back into the house. Glancing up to the landing, she saw that Bill, Derry's muscular friend, was no longer sitting in his usual place, where the passageway turned off towards Beatrice's and Rory's rooms. Alix ran up the stairs, weaving in and out of the guests who were slumped against the banisters. She struggled to catch hold of herself, quietening her footsteps and pausing outside the door to the nursery. Rory would be fast asleep; she must not wake him up. She forced her heart to stop pounding. Then she heard voices coming from inside the nursery.

She flung open the door. She saw the couple, bodies intertwined, mouths murmuring, standing silhouetted in front of the moonlit window. She hissed, 'What the *hell* are you doing in here?'

The woman looked startled, but the man said insolently, 'What do you think we're doing?' His arm slid further around the woman's waist.

'This is my son's bedroom.'

The woman's hand went to her mouth, and her gaze darted round the room, pausing when she reached the small humped form in the bed. The man looked blank. They were both, Alix realized, very drunk.

Then the man smiled. 'Teach him a thing or two, then.'

Alix gasped. She crossed the room to them. 'Get out. Just get out. Get out of my house.'

The woman pulled at the man's arm, and said, '*Harold*,' but he stared at her, and drawled, 'We were just having fun. What's the harm in that?'

'I said, get out.'

'Don't be so stuffy—'

'Get out *now*—'

'My dear girl—'

A voice from the door said, 'Please. Do as the lady says. Out of the room and out of the house. Off you go, Harold.'

Harold went to the door. 'Derry Fox.' He had bunched his fists. 'What's it to do with you? I'm not going. Why the hell should I go? I paid for this.'

Rory moved in the bed, and moaned a little. Alix, her legs shaking, sat down beside him, stroking his head.

'Harold, if you don't leave *immediately*,' said Derry patiently, 'I shall ask my very large and very short-tempered friend to make you leave. Now, be a good chap, and be sensible, and make a quick exit.'

Alix, murmuring to Rory, bent and kissed the top of

his head, and he quietened. She was shaking. When she looked up, Harold and the woman had gone, and Derry was walking towards her.

He whispered, 'Is he all right?' and Alix nodded.

'There were gatecrashers, you see. Bill was dealing with the gatecrashers.'

She took a last look at Rory to check that he was asleep, and left the room. In the passageway, the remnants of her composure vanished, and she gasped, 'This is my house, Derry. Rory's *safe* here . . .' and he put his arms round her.

'They're all leaving now. Bill and Polly are seeing them out. I'd better help. You go and sit down in the library.'

Alix went downstairs. She sat in an old leather armchair, her feet tucked beneath her, her arms clasped tightly around herself, while the house emptied. Even the dim, mouldering peace of the library had been violated. There was broken glass in the fireplace, and a smear of champagne along the top of her desk. She sat perfectly still for a very long time, and then she rose and mopped up the champagne with her handkerchief. Stooping in front of the grate, she picked fragments of glass from the ash.

The door opened. Derry said, 'They've all gone.' He came into the room. 'I'm sorry. It was a bad idea. My fault.'

'You warned me. I wanted the money.' Alix felt drained and exhausted. 'Are they your friends, Derry? Are those people really your friends?'

Derry had collapsed on the sofa, his tie and collar undone. 'They are . . . useful.'

'Miranda.' She could not stop herself. 'Is she *useful*?'

'Very, actually.' He lowered his lids. 'I saw you leaving the terrace. I ran after you.'

There was a silence. Alix dropped the broken glass into the empty coal scuttle. One of the shards had scratched her thumb, she watched a drop of blood trail from the ball of her thumb to her palm.

Derry took her hand, and kissed the small, crimson droplet. 'I never seem to have a handkerchief, but this'll do, won't it?' When he put his arms round her, she pressed her forehead against his shoulder.

'Miranda just knows someone I'd like to know,' he said. 'That's all.'

'Another of your schemes, Derry?'

'Something like that.'

She pulled away from him. 'Jonathan was here a couple of weeks ago. I met the fabled Edith at last.'

'Really?' His voice was light.

'You were right. She is beautiful.'

'Isn't she?' He looked around. 'We should clear up . . .'

'Leave it till tomorrow. Polly will help.'

'A drink, then.'

Alix found a tumbler, and poured him a measure of whisky. 'Jonathan said he hadn't seen you for a while, Derry.'

'I've been busy. But I phoned him. Heard all the nuptial plans in immense detail.'

'The wedding isn't for ages, is it?'

'Next summer. But Jon seems to have organized everything, down to the last freesia in the last bridesmaid's posy.'

'Derry. What's wrong?'

'Nothing's wrong.'

'Nonsense. You haven't sat still for more than five minutes since you arrived here this afternoon.'

'Have I been annoying you?'

'Yes,' she said. 'Immensely.'

'Actually, I'm in a bit of a mess.'

'Money?'

He shook his head. 'There's someone . . . a woman.'

Her heart squeezed. 'And you're fond of her?'

'It's not that.'

'She's a friend?'

'I suppose. Only I think she wants to be more than a friend.'

She watched the movement of his features. 'And you don't?'

'No. *Can't.*' He held up his palms. 'Don't ask. I just can't.'

'Have you told her?'

'She knows it would be impossible. Disastrous.' He looked up at Alix. In the dim light, his eyes were two dark, empty pits. 'The thing is,' he said, 'that it's my fault.'

'You can't help what people feel about you, Derry. No-one can.'

'Oh, I can. That's what I'm good at. Didn't you know?' His voice was savage.

'Derry—'

'How do you make someone who is in love with you fall out of love with you? I've tried being obnoxious and I've tried being nice and I've tried being *dull*. And none of it makes any difference.'

'Then you must avoid her.'

'If you were in love with me – a real effort of imagination, Alix – then what would make you indifferent to me?'

She was glad of the darkness; that he could not clearly see her face. 'Oh – if you were your usual self . . .

234

difficult and conceited and opinionated. That would put me off.'

He did not smile. '*Coups de foudre* don't last, do they?'

'I wouldn't know. It's not something I've ever suffered from.'

'Of course. I forgot. You didn't marry for love, did you, Alix?'

She held his gaze. 'It was like that with Rory, though. I just looked at him and I loved him. I didn't expect it to happen. What I felt – it took me by surprise.'

He glanced at his watch. 'I'd better head off.' He rose from the seat. 'Are you angry with me about the party?'

Alix shook her head. He looked more cheerful. 'Thank God. I couldn't bear to lose all this.'

She smiled. 'You are just the same as me, Derry. You come here because Owlscote is your sanctuary.'

He turned to look at her. 'Not *Owlscote*,' he said. Then he left the room.

A few weeks later, Alix took the train to London. With Freddie Maycross's help, she had sold three articles about Owlscote to an historical journal. To celebrate, Freddie lunched her at the Savoy. Two hours later Alix emerged, blinking from the bright lights of the restaurant, into the street. The grey, ominous sky had begun to spit sleet. Glancing at her watch, she saw that she had just missed a train. She hailed a taxi to Derry's flat.

He opened the door to her. 'Alix, how lovely to see you. Have you changed your mind?'

'About what?' She stepped indoors.

'Maddy Ferraby's engagement party.'

Her hand flew to her mouth; she recalled the white paste card that had arrived at Owlscote weeks ago. 'I'd completely forgotten. And it was so kind of Maddy to ask me.'

'I have to go to it – there's someone I must see. I'm buying a tithe barn from a baronet. I'm planning to sell it to a Hollywood film mogul. They'll take it apart and number the bits and ship it to America in packing cases.' He looked at her. 'You're *blue*. And there are snowflakes on your eyelashes.'

There was a coal fire in the grate. Alix knelt in front of it, warming her hands.

'You'll come, then?'

'To the party? Derry, I can't.'

'Why not?'

She glanced over her shoulder at him. She thought how surprisingly tidy, how ordered his black and crimson room always was.

'I haven't a dress.'

'Buy one.'

'*Derry.*' Yet she remembered how he had stooped to kiss the drop of blood from her finger. And how he had turned to look at her, and had said, *Not Owlscote*. She said, 'There's Rory, you see . . .'

'Is Polly picking him up from school?' Alix nodded. 'Well, then.'

'I'd have to catch the last train.'

'Of course. Like Cinderella.' He raised her to her feet. 'Come on. Shops shut in an hour.'

They went to Oxford Street. Alix could not recall when she had last bought a dress – just walked into a shop and picked one off a rail and bought it. Beatrice made all her dresses. In Selfridges she tried on one after the other. She paraded them in front of Derry. Oyster-coloured satin ('Too bridal'); duck-egg-blue taffeta ('Like a lampshade'); black chiffon ('Terrifying. Just terrifying'). She finally settled on a russet silk with a handkerchief hemline – the colour, she thought, of autumn leaves.

In Derry's flat, doing her face, she paused, lipstick in hand. A sudden inexplicable moment of foreboding, and her hand shook, so that she had to erase the crimson scar of the lipstick with her handkerchief. She got hold of herself, and began to draw again. A dark, careful outline, her hand making a precise and perfect shape. When she looked in the mirror a different image stared back at her: red lips, pale face, eyes made more green by the contrasting russet of the silk dress. She gathered her comb, lipstick and powder in her bag. Armour, she thought. A sort of armour.

She left the bathroom. She saw the way he looked at her: the small, sudden widening of his eyes. The way his lips lingered, kissing her hand, as he complimented her on her appearance.

He helped her into her coat, and called a taxi. Maddy Ferraby's engagement party was held in a house in South Audley Street. Alix, stepping into the enormous and glittering reception room, whispered: 'I didn't think it would be like this. I didn't think it would be so . . . grand.'

'Maddy's very well connected. The niece of an earl.'

'But at Owlscote, she had darns in her jerseys!'

'It's the nouveau riche who don't have darns.' Derry looked round the vast, crowded room, and smiled. '*Everyone* is here. Come on, Alix.' Tucking her hand through his arm, he led her into the crowds.

Somehow he became separated from her. There was the baronet with the castle and the tithe barn. The baronet was mad, and desperate. Derry talked and coaxed and added numbers in his head. Then there was Andrée Garland, who hooked her hand round his arm, and drew him into the cool enclosure of a balcony and whispered, 'Three more issues, Derry. I only have cash enough for three more issues of *Chrome*. You must help me find a patron.'

He felt like a juggler, tossing coloured batons into the air. Catching them, sending them whirling into the sky, making the patterns he wanted to make. There was only one that threatened to slip from his hand. When he recalled the last time he had seen Jonathan and Edith, he felt nauseous. She had hardly spoken to him; he had made a fool of himself in his effort to distract Jon from her tense, coiled energy. He did not know which he feared most: that she would marry Jon, or that she would call the engagement off. He saw disaster in either. It had been desperation that had forced him to confide, as far as he dared, in Alix. Since that evening, he had avoided both Jonathan and Edith.

He found himself – he did not know how – trapped in a small side room, heavy with political discussion.

'All the great statesmen are gone.'

'The press lords and the bankers are running the country.'

'And the Bolsheviks. The events of the summer made that plain.'

'Parliament should pass a law—'

'Parliament should go. Parliament is an outdated institution.' The voice was clear and cold. 'The country needs one strong man to lead it. It does not need an assembly of flunkeys and liberals who know nothing of how to govern.'

The room was close and overheated. Derry pulled at

his collar. Feather boas, he thought, or quill pens or duck-down cushions . . . The cold voice went on: 'We must recreate the world we have lost, gentlemen, before it's too late. We must copy the example of other nations – Italy, for instance . . .'

Through the open doorway, Derry caught a glimpse of russet-coloured silk. Calling out Alix's name, he wove through the crowds. Hands reached out, slowing him, and voices said his name. By the time he had crossed the room he had lost her again.

Roma told Alix about the house she was decorating. 'Cream and lime-green and umber. No more black. Black is just too last year.' She looked at Alix. 'You should let me do Owlscote.'

Maddy Ferraby held out her left hand to show Alix her engagement ring. 'It was Henry's great-grandmother's. The sapphire once belonged to an Indian prince. Too romantic, don't you think?'

Alix drank champagne and ate tiny, delicious canapés. Someone asked her to dance, and she found herself foxtrotting with a stranger around the wide ballroom of the South Audley Street house. The music swept her up; dancing, she felt exhilarated and happy. She caught sight of Derry once, and saw his mouth form the syllables of her name, and then he was gone again, swallowed up by the crowd. With the rest of the guests, she listened to and applauded Maddy's fiancé's and uncle's speeches. The evening passed quickly, a flicker of bright colours and sparkling jewels.

She was searching for the powder room when a hand tapped her shoulder, so that she turned and looked up. Just a fleeting tap, as though he could not bear the touch of her. The sudden cold clutch to her heart, the dreadful dawning familiarity of his eyes. Her nightmares made real. Then he spoke to her.

Derry began to feel anxious, and then to feel angry with himself. He had taken it upon himself to coax Alix out of her shell, and yet, having persuaded her to come to the party with him, he had lost her. He began to search properly, methodically.

At the foot of the stairs, he encountered May Lanchbury. May said, 'You look *distrait*, Derry. Have you lost something?'

'Alix . . . I mean – my friend, Mrs North.' He blinked. 'Of course, you don't know her. A reddish-brown dress. Dark hair. Green eyes.'

May shook her head. He left her, elbowing his way through the reception hall. With sudden intuition, pausing only to grab his coat from the cloakroom, Derry went out into the street.

In the distance, he saw Alix hurrying along the pavement. She was not wearing her coat, and the pointed silk hem of her dress trailed in the dirty snow. Running to catch up with her, he called her name, and saw her pause for a moment, her high heels slipping on the flagstones.

'Alix! Where on earth are you going?'

'Home.' Beneath the gaslight, her face looked greenish-white.

'Your *coat*.'

She looked down at herself, as if surprised. 'I forgot.'

He glanced at his watch. 'You've hours till your last train. There's no need to hurry. Come back indoors – if you've had enough then that's fine, I'll get your coat and we can leave.'

'I'm going now.' She started to walk again.

Derry began to feel angry. 'I thought we were

enjoying ourselves – I thought we were having a good time . . .'

Alix said nothing, but continued to walk. Watching her, Derry saw that her hands were clenched, and that she had bitten her lip to stop herself shivering. He shouted, 'At least take my bloody coat!'

She stopped, her eyes closed. He shrugged off his coat, and draped it around her shoulders. When she opened her eyes they seemed like black smears against the white transparency of her skin.

He spoke more gently. 'Alix, what is it? What's happened? Has something upset you?'

The dead expression in her eyes altered to one of anger. She hissed, 'I don't like the company you keep, Derry! I don't like it at all! You *lower* yourself. You *sell* yourself!' Then she walked away. This time he did not follow her.

In the train, and throughout the taxi ride from Salisbury to Owlscote, and sleepless in her bedroom that night, the nightmare voice echoed.

I am surprised you show your face in society. I've been told you sell your services as a hostess. I'd recommend you to keep to that.

His voice. Charles Lanchbury's voice.

Alix had walked from the reception room to the powder room and Charles Lanchbury had touched her shoulder, and had spoken to her. She had known him instantly. She had not, as she had believed, forgotten. The dread that had forced her to run her finger down the guest list before each party, searching for the name of Lanchbury, had been justified.

Alix curled up on her bed, her knees against her chest, shuddering in the damp folds of Derry's coat. She remembered the intruders in Rory's bedroom. *I paid for this*. Charles Lanchbury had been right; she, like Derry, had sold herself. She had sold both herself and Owlscote.

She saw that she had been wrong to believe that she was closing a chapter, and wrong to believe that the loss of Charlie Lanchbury belonged to the past. Such a loss echoed through generations. Such a loss lived in the hatred she had tonight seen in Charles Lanchbury's eyes, in the silence that imprisoned Beatrice's tongue, and in the shame that lingered in her own heart. She had put her head over the parapet, and she had received a warning shot. Curled in her bed, her arms clasped around her head, Alix lay cold and empty and sleepless, remembering.

When, more than a year ago, Edith had agreed to marry him, Jonathan had believed that it was impossible to be happier. Only a few events had pierced the haze of delight – Derry's illness, his mother's reluctance to part with him (who would take her for her Sunday afternoon drives? Who would fetch her novels from Boots' library when she was not well enough to take the bus?). These difficulties had eventually been resolved; Derry had recovered, and Jonathan had reassured his mother that as he and Edith intended to buy a house not far from the Avenue, her routine need not be disrupted.

Then, in May, Edith had at last agreed to choose a wedding day. Because of Mina, and because of Eva Fox, they had set a date for the following summer. Jonathan should have been happier than ever. Yet over the ensuing weeks and months he began to detect a change in Edith. The brittleness he had once or twice previously noticed in her became more pronounced. When he attempted to soothe her she snapped at him. Then, seeing that he was hurt, she became apologetic and tearful. It's the summer heat, he thought. Yet with the coming of autumn, Edith's fractiousness persisted. Jonathan thought that her job was tiring her, but when he suggested that she give it up, she stared at him and said, 'And what do I live on, Jon? What do I eat?' About to offer to help her out, he had caught a glimpse of the pride in her eyes, and managed to stop himself in time.

In November, dining with the Winstanleys, talk turned, as it often did, to the wedding. Mrs Winstanley's niece, who would be a bridesmaid, was dining with them. They began to discuss the bridesmaids' dresses. Mrs Winstanley favoured lemon; the niece, who was rather sallow, preferred pink. Mrs Winstanley said, 'A nice *rose* pink, perhaps,' and Eva Fox said, 'Salmon, don't you think, Edith? So few girls have the complexion to wear rose—' and then Edith put down her knife and fork with a crash, and hissed, 'Salmon – rose – what on earth does it *matter*?' and ran out of the room.

Jonathan found her in the garden, sitting on the old swing on which they had played as children. Her face was patched red with tears. He took a deep breath and said, 'Edith, if you are having second thoughts you must tell me.' Though he did not see how, without her, he could go on living. When she did not immediately reply he seemed to feel the cold point of a knife touching his heart. He began, 'If you don't care for me—' and could not go on.

'Of course I care for you, Jon.'

'But perhaps not in that way. Perhaps not enough to marry me.'

The swing moved a little. Her face was turned away. She whispered, 'There is no-one I would rather marry.'

He closed his eyes for a moment, almost drowning in the intensity of his relief. He heard her say, 'It's just the wedding . . . so much fuss . . . I hate it!'

He managed to smile. 'I always thought,' he said, 'that women enjoyed that sort of thing.'

'Well, I don't.' Her blotched face and tangled hair reminded Jonathan suddenly of the Edith he had first loved: the Edith who had climbed trees with him, who had fished for tiddlers in the river with him.

'I wish we could just go away,' she said fiercely, 'go away and not bother with all this – go somewhere new, where no-one knows us, where we could start again.'

They had gone back into the house, and Edith had apologized, pleading a headache. But a seed of unease had been sown. *There is no-one I would rather marry.* Sometimes – often – that was enough. But at other times – during a bad night, for instance, when the sound of gunfire punctuated his dreams, waking him over and over again – there was an equivocation about Edith's reply that Jonathan could not bear to contemplate.

He needed to talk to someone, but there was no-one to talk to. His father worked long hours, and what little spare time he had was taken up by the golf club and the Conservative Association. His mother was not well enough to be burdened by other people's troubles. An evening that Jonathan had arranged in London with Edith and Derry had not been a success. Edith had hardly spoken a word; Derry had been exhaustingly talkative. Jonathan had sensed an antagonism between them. Since then, Derry had, once again, become elusive. He never came to Andover. He was rarely in his flat when Jonathan called. One evening, to his ringing of the doorbell there had been, at length, an answer. But

Derry had been bleary-eyed, and Jonathan had heard a woman's voice whisper something, and had seen a hand, all pale skin and scarlet talons, curl round his younger brother's neck. So he had apologized and left. Edith herself sometimes picked Derry's name from the gossip columns of the newspapers. 'Your little brother's moving in very high circles, Jon – I hope he doesn't run out of air!' There was a sour, vindictive tone to her voice that troubled Jonathan. He wanted Derry and Edith to get on: family squabbles upset him.

He thought of talking to Alix at Owlscote, but dismissed the idea. To his surprise, Edith had not taken to Alix. Jonathan had attempted to mollify Edith by pointing out that Alix had become more Derry's friend than his own, but that had not helped. Jonathan found himself unable to share his worries with anyone, so he did what he always did, and brushed his anxiety away, enclosing it within the area of darkness in his mind in which existed all unbearable, unfinished things: the war, and the dread of mutilation that had accompanied it, and the unnamable fear that one day all the ordinary routine he depended on might without warning change, and become unrecognizable.

There is no-one I would rather marry. The words lingered, exuding a slow poison. Sometimes Jonathan found himself looking at Edith's words and actions in a colder light. The long delay before she had agreed to name a wedding day. Her refusal to return to Andover during the General Strike. Her tense, nervous manner. That there was no-one Edith would rather marry did not necessarily mean that there was no-one she would rather love. The thought entered Jonathan's mind that she was in love with someone at the advertising agency. One of her married colleagues, perhaps. He tried to rub the suspicion away, seeing it as unworthy of both of them, but could not let it go.

In Town one afternoon, Jonathan's business was completed earlier than expected, so he went to wait for Edith in Golden Square. The roads were busy; he had to park some distance from the agency. At six o'clock, the doors opened, and typists and copywriters spilled into the street. Jonathan was about to press the horn and call out Edith's name when something stopped him. He would wait, he thought. Wait just a moment or two, and see whether she walked away with anyone else.

He almost lost sight of her as she left the square, but then he glimpsed her hailing a cab. He was surprised: he had expected her to head for the underground station. She was alone. He started up the car, and followed her, hating himself. The taxi drove along Piccadilly to Knightsbridge, and then turned down Sloane Street towards Chelsea. A few more streets and he knew where she was going. Edith was heading for Derry's flat.

Jonathan watched, bewildered, as she pressed the doorbell. There was no reply, and after a few minutes she walked away from the door, and went into the small café opposite. He saw that Edith had taken a seat by the window, and that her gaze moved continually back to the entrance of the block of flats. Through the condensation on the glass, her image seemed blurred and forlorn. He wanted to go to her, to take her in his arms, but he could think of no convincing explanation for his presence, so instead he started up the engine and drove away.

Driving out of London, the traffic was heavy, and Jonathan's head ached. The movement of his hands on the controls of the car seemed unfamiliar and clumsy. As he headed down the Goldhawk Road, he thought suddenly of Mina. He needed someone to talk to – what better person than Edith's sister? There was a screech of brakes as he swung the car off the road, towards the square in which Mina lived.

In her room, Mina made tea, and placed carefully on a plate a large and rather stale piece of fruit cake. Jonathan had not seen Mina's room since he had helped her move into it more than six months previously. Almost every inch of plaster was covered with posters. Many of the posters bore Cyrillic lettering.

Mina explained, 'A friend of mine went to Russia and brought them back for me.'

'They're splendid, Mina. Brighten the place up no end.' Jonathan stirred his tea. 'How's the novel?'

'My romance? I burnt it.' She smiled. 'Don't look so shocked, Jonathan. It was fit only for the fire. I'm writing something else now. Much more relevant. More intellectual.' She looked at him. 'But I'm sure you didn't come here to discuss literature.'

'I'm worried about Edith. She doesn't seem – happy.'

The brown eyes, behind their pebble lenses, surveyed him. 'Do you expect people to be *happy*?'

The question jolted him. He had always taken it for granted that one should pursue happiness. Yet when he considered his own family, *happy* was not the word that one would choose to describe either his father or his mother or Derry.

'Aren't you happy, Mina?'

Her mouth pursed. 'I decided a long time ago to think of my life as interesting or uninteresting. And yes, thank you, Jonathan, my life is rather interesting at present.'

He said desperately, 'But surely an engaged woman . . . an engaged woman should be happy?'

'It sounds to me, Jonathan, as though you're worried that Edith might be happier with someone else. Are you thinking of anyone in particular?'

His self-loathing returned. 'I wondered . . . one of her colleagues at work, perhaps . . .'

Mina shook her head. 'Gerald and Jimmy and Archie are just friends. Edith made that clear a long time ago.'

He felt both relief and shame. As he ran his fingers through his hair, Jonathan heard Mina say, 'Isn't the idea that marriage should automatically bestow everlasting bliss rather old-fashioned? Rather bourgeois, in fact.'

'Do you think so?'

'Middle-class marriage is as much to do with money as with love. It's an economic arrangement.'

He said hopelessly, 'Mina, I *love* Edith.'

She frowned. 'Edith isn't the sort of woman who feels particularly strongly about anything. Who particularly *wants* anything. Don't you know that, Jonathan? Whereas I – I have always wanted things. A pet rabbit – riding lessons . . . a lover . . . I wanted them until either I had them, or I managed to accept that I could never have them. But Edith isn't like that. She doesn't know what it is to long for something.' Mina glared severely at Jonathan. 'Men assume that the capacity for passion goes with golden hair and blue eyes. It doesn't, necessarily. If you are to marry Edith, then you must understand that.'

Jonathan rose to leave. As he reached the door, he said, 'Mina – does Edith ever mention Derry to you?'

Mina looked blank. He added, 'Because I thought she *disliked* him—' Seeing the incomprehension in her eyes, he broke off, and took his leave of her.

*   *   *

Jonathan drove to Richmond. Sitting in the car, waiting in the shadowy lane outside Edith's house, he began to feel calm again. It seemed to him that Mina was probably right. His anxiety and confusion faded away, and he knew that he would marry Edith even if her love did not match his. *There is no-one I would rather marry.* She had told him the simple truth, that she loved no-one more than she loved him. It was possible, he thought, that her capacity to love had been eroded by the long years nursing her mother. Horror brutalized, he had seen that for himself in France. In time, he would help her learn to love again.

After half an hour, looking up, he saw her walking down the lane towards him, a small, slender figure, her form intermittently picked out of the darkness by the street lamps. He climbed out of the car. He saw her eyes suddenly widen, and heard the words tumble out of her mouth.

'Jon! How lovely to see you! What a nice surprise . . . Have you been waiting long? I'm so sorry I'm late home . . . I was just . . . I was just . . .' and her gaze flicked from side to side, from the tall, heavily branched trees to the curtained houses on the far side of the street.

Then she said, 'I'm sorry I'm so late. Only, after work, I went to see Mina.'

Derry was invited to an End of the World party. Roma was there, and Miranda Hughes, and Ruth Duncan and her sister, Laura. Roma scolded him ('Never there when I want you, Derry. If you could just manage to occupy the same bed for a night or two . . .'), and Miranda pouted, and Ruth and Laura ignored him. Any moment, Derry thought, and Edith Carr would leap out from behind a curtain. The house, built on uncertain foundations too near the river, was to be demolished. Derry, making his way through gaudy, crowded rooms, saw the snaking cracks in the plaster, and the places where the floorboards had begun to twist and buckle. He would have liked the walls to twist and shake, and the dried mortar to begin to hiss in a stream from the cavities as the gilt façade crumbled to dust.

Someone said, 'Derry, you haven't dressed up,' and he said, 'I never dress up.' He looked down into kohl-circled eyes. 'Best to be dignified when you're facing damnation, don't you agree?' He saw the smile fade from her face, and he moved away.

In an upstairs room he watched Miranda Hughes lift the skirt of her long, red dress and put a needle to her thigh. The closing of her eyelids as she pushed in the syringe, the smile that stretched across her white, bony face. 'Too beautiful,' she whispered.

He did not speak to May Lanchbury until the early hours of the morning. He was caught up in the crowds, and then her hand curled round his arm, and she said: 'What crumbs are you scavenging tonight, my dear vulture?'

He held up a whisky bottle in one of his hands, a glass in the other. 'I'm having a night off.'

'I didn't think vultures took nights off.'

He smiled. He knew that he was very, very drunk.

'Are you enjoying your holiday, Derry?'

'Tremendously.'

'I don't believe you. Tears before bedtime, my old nanny would have said.'

'Have you been watching me, May?'

'It's my job.' She drew him away from the crowd. Then she muttered, almost to herself, 'And what on earth should I write about *this* . . . ?'

He said savagely, 'Write that it was a dignified and elegant occasion. A refined gathering of old friends.'

She frowned, looking at him. 'Your friend, Mrs North. Is she here tonight?'

Derry shook his head. 'Not tonight. Nor any other night.'

'You haven't seen her recently?'

He went to the window and looked out. A yellow fog clung to the river. 'I had a note from Roma Storm yesterday. Alix has cancelled the parties we arranged at Owlscote.'

'*Alix* . . .' she repeated.

He turned to face her. He could not read the expression in her eyes, and nor could he stop himself saying, 'She wrote to Roma and not to *me*, May. Rather pointed, don't you think?'

'Had you quarrelled?'

He shrugged. 'I suppose so. At Maddy Ferraby's engagement party. Not *quarrelled* exactly. She just – ran off.'

May Lanchbury's face had become very closed, very still. 'Did she say why?'

Derry shook his head again.

'Have you asked her why?'

He looked down. 'Alix disapproves of my way of life. She told me that she didn't like the company I keep.' He smiled unpleasantly.

May whispered, 'The company you keep . . .'

A voice called out to him, begging him for a dance; someone hailed him from across the room. He was about to turn aside when May said: 'Come home with me, Derry.'

'*May.* I hadn't realized . . .'

There was no answering humour. 'We need to talk.'

He followed her out of the house. He needed the cold night air on his skin, and an absence of chatter and music and people wanting things of him. And besides, he was curious. His besetting sin, curiosity.

May lived in a tiny terraced house in Kensington. The sitting-room was comfortable and elegant, as he would have expected. There were framed photographs of ballet dancers. She made him a cup of very strong black coffee, and sat down beside him.

'Mrs North . . . her name . . .'

'I told you – Alix.'

'I meant, her maiden name. Do you know her maiden name?'

'Gregory,' he said. 'When I first met her, she was Alix Gregory.'

May fell silent. Derry stared at her. 'May, I don't understand.' A sudden intuition. 'Do you know Alix?'

'A long time ago.' The words sounded like a sigh.

He wished he hadn't drunk so much. He battled against confusion and surprise. 'How? When?'

'There is . . . a family connection.'

'What sort of connection?'

She did not answer him. 'How well do you know Alix Gregory . . . I mean, Alix North, Derry?'

He ran his fingers through his hair. His head ached. 'Well enough.'

'How did you meet her?'

'Years ago, in a nursing home. My brother was wounded in the war. She was looking after him. I noticed her. There was so much that was *drab*, but not her. Alix isn't capable of being drab.'

She prompted him. 'And then?'

'Jon – my brother – recovered, and I went abroad, and I didn't meet Alix again until many years later. She'd been married and widowed, and she had a son.' He felt suddenly sober. 'Sometimes I think I know her well, and sometimes I think I don't know her at all. She's very *private*. But she's been a good friend. She sees me for what I am. She doesn't ask anything of me.'

'You love her.' It was a statement, not a question.

He looked at May, surprised. His heart was pounding: the whisky, the coffee.

'Oh yes,' he said simply. He remembered the first time he had seen Alix, at Fallowfield nursing home. She had been pale and snappish and tight-lipped. Eight years ago. It had been another six years before they had met again, at the party at the Rose Café.

'Have you told her?'

'Of course not.'

'Why not, Derry?'

'Because,' he explained, 'because Alix has Owlscote and all that goes with it. And I have nothing.'

'That may not matter to her.'

'But it matters', he said, 'to me.' He smiled. 'Give me credit for a little pride, May.'

She turned away. He heard her lighting herself a cigarette: the flick of the lighter, the indrawn breath. He added, 'And besides, there are – gaps.'

'Gaps?'

'I have this theory about Alix. That something bad happened to her. A long time ago – before the nursing home, certainly.' He was watching May carefully as he spoke. 'I have this theory, you see, that she is hiding from something. Or someone.'

May touched his hand. He saw, to his surprise, that there were tears in her eyes. She said, 'Go and see her, Derry. Go and see Alix, and tell her that May Lanchbury asked for her. Tell her that May Lanchbury sends her love and her best wishes.'

CHAPTER NINE

Alix had written to everyone who had booked parties, cancelling the arrangements and refunding money. She had written a letter to Roma, severing their business connection, but she had not written to Derry. She could not explain to Derry why she had left Maddy Ferraby's engagement party. She remembered the anger she had glimpsed in Derry's eyes when she had said, *You sell yourself.*

In the evenings, after she had put Rory to bed, she enclosed herself in the library and worked on her history of Owlscote. The excitement she had once felt in unpeeling the past had vanished utterly. Charles Lanchbury's voice echoed constantly in her ears. The blank page conjured up both his face and Charlie's. She would find that ten minutes had passed, and that the nib of her pen had made a blot on the paper as she had sat, her head in her hands, sick with remembering.

She dreamed the same dream each night. She was walking through the woods at Owlscote. A small boy was running ahead of her. He wore a blue velvet suit with a lace collar. He ran deeper and deeper into the wood, so that he became no more than a flicker of blue and white, a shadow child amid the darkness of the trees. Though she struggled to catch up with him, she hardly seemed to move forward at all, and her limbs battled against the resisting air. Every now and then she would lose sight of him, and then she would glimpse him again, in the shade of a beech's wide bough, or standing at the edge of a pool. When she called out his name he turned to look to her, and she saw his face clearly. It was then that she realized that she had been mistaken, and that the child lost in the forest was not Charlie Lanchbury, but her own small son.

Over the next few days, a frost settled upon Owlscote, stilling trees and grass, painting ice-flowers on the window panes. When one afternoon Alix walked across the grey lawn, the soles of her shoes crunched tiny fragments of ice. Frost edged the reeds that rimmed the lake, immobilizing their seed-heads in small, streaming banners. Testing the ice, Alix heard it creak, felt it bend.

Then she looked up, and saw Derry standing on the terrace. He walked across the lawn towards her.

'I know you didn't invite me, Alix.' Hunched in his jacket, he looked blue with cold. 'And perhaps you don't want to see me. But I have a message for you.'

She took him to the library. When the door was closed behind them, Alix repeated, 'A message?'

'From May Lanchbury.'

She sat down. In the fire, flames danced. She remembered the bonfire in the square of the village in France, the gypsy dancers, and May's rapt stare. She clenched her fists. 'How do you know May?'

'She's a friend of mine.'

'Her message?' Her voice shook.

'She asked me to give you her love and her best wishes.'

Alix closed her eyes, pressing her fingertips against the sockets.

'And she told me that there was a family connection.'

A silence. At last she said, 'May is my cousin.'

'*Oh*.' Another silence. 'You don't communicate—' Derry broke off. 'No. Stupid of me. It's obvious that you don't.' His eyes narrowed. 'You have three cousins.'

Ella, May and Daisy. Alix saw them again, with their white muslin dresses and their pink sashes.

She whispered, 'I've cancelled the parties, Derry.'

'I know. Roma told me.'

She was curled up against the end of the sofa, her arms folded around herself. 'After the last time – those awful people in Rory's bedroom – I saw that it wasn't suitable.'

He said nothing, but bowed his head in acceptance.

'My mother always disapproved. She was right. I won't change my mind, Derry.'

'I haven't asked you to.' A pause. 'Will you visit me in London again?'

Mutely, she shook her head.

'May I come here, then?'

She did not answer him. She saw him rub his eyes, and turn away.

'You look tired, Derry.'

He smiled. 'A long night. Selling myself.'

'I shouldn't have said that.'

He shrugged. 'You were justified. But then, it's all I've ever had to sell.'

'Still, I shouldn't have said it.'

'I don't mind.' He looked at her. 'You are my conscience, Alix. You always have been.'

Tears stung behind her eyes. She did not let them fall; she never let them fall. She patted her lap. 'Here.'

He lay on the sofa, his head in her lap. She stroked his black curls. She could then have told him. She began to say, *I had four cousins once, Derry, not three. Charlie died, and it was my fault.* But when she looked down at him, she knew from the fall of his eyelid and the regularity of his breathing that he was asleep, and she remained silent as the house enclosed them, quiet and safe.

Leaving Owlscote, he said, 'I won't say "Tell me" because you don't have to. I've never thought that loving someone meant being obliged to share all your secrets with them.'

He saw her become quite still. '*Loving . . . ?*' she repeated.

He flung out his hands. 'Well, what else is all this?'

Then he walked down the drive, and did not look back. On the train, he slept. When he arrived late that night in London, Edith Carr was waiting outside his house. The pallor of her face, and the way her hands, in their soft leather gloves, clasped and unclasped, told him that she had, perhaps, been waiting for hours.

'Rather late at night for a social call, isn't it, Edith?'

'This isn't a social call. Let me in, won't you, Derry?'

As he unlocked the door and she followed him into the flat, he heard the telephone ringing. He reached it just as the insistent chime died away; when he picked up the mouthpiece and said his name the line was dead. He looked around the flat. Uninhabited for more than twenty-four hours, it seemed cold, empty and unwelcoming. He realized that he never thought of it as home. If anywhere was home, Owlscote was.

Derry switched on the light, lit the fire, and offered Edith tea or coffee.

'I'd rather have a drink.'

He made her a gin and it, and poured a whisky for himself. His head still ached from the previous night's drinking.

Edith sat down beside the fire, her glass cradled in her hands. 'You needn't look so worried, Derry, I haven't come here to seduce you.' She laughed. 'I did consider it once. You weren't in, though. I'm not sure quite what I'd have done if you'd been at home – a difficult social situation, don't you agree? I'm not sure what one says on such occasions. I suppose I hoped that neither of us would have actually to *say* anything – that you'd just sweep me up in your arms – carry me into the bedroom and ravish me—'

'*Edith*,' he said.

'—but you'll be relieved to hear that I've changed my mind. We wouldn't do at all, would we, Derry? We'd hate each other within a week.'

Momentarily, he closed his eyes. Then, opening them again, he said, 'Why have you come here, Edith?'

'I remember that you once told me that you liked things to be like a cat's cradle. Complicated, and with you pulling the strings.'

He recalled the overheated room in his parents' house: Edith, and the fatal need to provoke a reaction. 'Not one of my better metaphors,' he muttered. 'I was always lousy at tying knots.'

'And untying them?' She laughed again. 'You are manipulative, Derry. You like to plot and plan. You like to persuade people to do what you want them to.'

He began wearily, 'I never intended, Edith—' but she interrupted him.

'Never?'

He remembered her blue, uninterested eyes.

'Momentarily,' he admitted, and looked away.

'It's all right. I'm not blaming you. After all, I manipulated Jonathan into offering to marry me. So we are alike, aren't we, Derry? You see, when Jon proposed to me I was afraid of being left on the shelf. There was a man – he's called Marcus Wenlock . . .'

Derry remembered Mina Carr, and a bouquet of lilies. *Marcus is madly in love with Edith.*

'I thought Marcus wanted to marry me, but then I realized that he was looking for something more. I wasn't good enough for him. I haven't the right background. Neither has Marcus, that's the trouble. His grandfather was a blacksmith. So he's looking for that little extra push up the ladder. A wife with a title, or at the least an old name.' Edith smiled, and then she said slowly, 'Yet I still see him sometimes. He waits for me.'

'Waits for you?'

'Outside my office. He just sits in his car and watches me walk out of the building. He doesn't speak, or wave. But there is such hunger in his eyes. A year ago' – she paused – 'a year ago, I wouldn't have understood. But I do now.'

There was a silence. Then she went on, 'Anyway, when I realized that Marcus was looking for a titled wife, I was afraid that I'd be left with nothing. And then Mina told me that she meant to leave home. And Mother was dead and I hated the house and my job bored me. I couldn't bear it, you see, Derry, to be left with nothing.'

There was a short silence. He heard the tick of the clock, the rumble of traffic. 'So I thought I'd settle for Jonathan,' she said. 'After all, we'd known each other for ages, and we'd always got on. It was easy. I seduced him.' Again, that short, humourless laugh. 'As far as one can seduce Jon.' When she looked at him again, he saw that there were tears in her eyes.

'There's never been anyone but me, Derry,' she whispered. 'Did you know that? Your brother has never loved any girl but me. I mean, literally, *no-one*.'

'You don't have to tell me this, Edith.'

'Oh, I do. You have to understand. Two passionless virgins. We seemed made for each other. Only I wasn't quite as passionless as I believed—' Breaking off, Edith took a large gulp of gin.

'When I visited you that day in Andover, Derry, you listened to me.' Her voice was calmer. 'You seemed to understand me. You seemed to understand about my mother. Jon never talks to me about my mother. I think he thinks it'll hurt me. He never talks about the war either. He never talks about anything bad. He just pretends it hasn't happened.'

'Perhaps,' said Derry, 'that's the only way he can bear it.'

'Perhaps. But it infuriates me, you see.' She looked away. 'But you listened. Most men don't. When they look at me, what do they see? Golden hair, blue eyes, and a doll's face.' Her voice was bitter. 'You seemed to see a little more.'

He felt, just then, utterly exhausted. He had, he calculated, endured two days with no sleep other than the catnap on the train. He wanted nothing more than peace and quiet, and to be able to lie still and alone long enough to unravel whatever chain it was that entangled Alix North and May Lanchbury.

He chose his words carefully. 'I never meant to spoil things between you and Jonathan. I didn't know, at that point, that you were engaged.'

Edith continued, as though he had not spoken,

'And then, when you made it clear that you weren't interested in me – that awful lunch – that horrid little restaurant . . .'

'I didn't mean to hurt you, Edith.'

'I know you didn't. But I saw the look in your eyes. So I let Jon set the date of the wedding. He'd been nagging me for ages, and I thought that by committing myself I'd get you out of my system. Only it didn't work out like that.'

He repeated, a weary and futile refrain, 'I didn't intend to cause harm.'

'You didn't cause harm. I'm grateful to you, Derry.'

He looked at her. 'For showing me', she said, 'that I mustn't marry Jonathan.' She knotted her hands together. 'I've talked to Mina as well. It's funny, we've never really been what sisters are supposed to be – too different, I suppose – but I found myself telling her the truth.'

Derry could not speak. His mouth was dry. He looked at Edith, his question written in his eyes.

'I can't go through with it. The wedding. That's the thing. I can't go through with it.' Edith put aside her glass, and said quietly, 'I shall write to Jonathan. I'll try to explain. And then – I don't know. I'm not clever, like Mina, or ambitious, like some of the girls at work. I just have this face, which doesn't really go with the rest of me. I'm not very good at understanding other people – what they want. I don't seem to be very good at finding a direction.'

'Not many of us are.'

She laughed shakily. 'There you go again.'

'What?'

'Understanding me. Even when I don't properly understand myself.'

262

He muttered, 'Sorry.'

'You shouldn't, you know. It's very . . . very *intoxicating*.' Her voice trembled. 'I came here to warn you, Derry. I told a stupid lie to Jonathan last week. I came here after work but you weren't in, as I explained, and when I went home, Jon was waiting for me. I was taken by surprise – I couldn't think what to say, and I panicked and told him I'd been with Mina. And then Mina told me that he'd visited her. So he knows that I lied, you see.'

'*Oh*.' Derry sat down, his head in his hands, trying to think clearly. 'Does he know you were here?'

'I'm not sure.' She looked up at him. 'I'm just not sure.'

The possibility had occurred to Jonathan that the two people he loved most in the world were betraying him. The idea, which had first come to him when Edith had looked up at him and said, *I went to see Mina*, grew and flowered over the ensuing days. He kept pushing the thought out of his head, knowing that he himself betrayed them both merely by considering such an outrage, but the image of Derry and Edith together would return to him as he lay awake in the early hours of the morning, or when, in his office, his hand suddenly froze on the page, halfway through the act of writing his signature.

Often he knew that he must be mistaken. His thoughts would twist themselves into their accustomed order, and he would know that Derry – charming, scapegrace Derry – would never betray him in that way. And that Edith's dislike of his younger brother was just that: dislike, and not a façade for something else. He pictured himself telephoning Derry and admitting his suspicions. He imagined Derry's hurt – no, far more probable, Derry's roar of laughter. He imagined confronting Edith. Her explanation, his relief. Yet, try as he might, he could not think of an explanation for the lie that she had told him. And sometimes, in his mind's eye, he saw Derry's dark eyes mask over, concealing the truth. And whenever he reached out his hand to the telephone, he withdrew it as soon as he touched the receiver, as though he had been stung.

The sleepless nights piled up. When he found himself nodding off in court, somewhere in the middle of the magistrate's summing-up, he knew he had to act. Arriving home that evening, he forced himself to choke down his fear and telephone Derry. There was no reply. At dinner, Jonathan ate little. For the first time he could recall, the familiar rituals and the repetitive nature of his parents' conversation seemed jarring rather than reassuring. The small pomposities: the silver napkin rings, each with its engraved initials; the complete place settings, even though his mother never ate dessert and he himself loathed cheese; and the parlour maid, disguising her yawns, condemned to remain on call until the last coffee cup had been drained. All these grated on his overstretched nerves.

After a while, he realized that he was seeing it all through Derry's eyes. He could almost see Derry's bored, amused stare, and hear his mocking voice. 'My *chaperon*, Jon . . .' And, 'I thought you'd be at home, Jon, fending off the forces of Bolshevism . . .' And from a long, long time ago, 'You have to make the most of opportunities, don't you?' He found himself wondering why, in 1919, Derry had taken up with a woman twice his age. Had it been out of love, or out of curiosity, or because there existed beneath that detached, attractive exterior a cold intelligence that liked to disrupt, to destroy?

Between dessert and cheese, Jonathan rose and made his excuses. His hands shook as he dialled the operator, and asked for the number. Again, no answer. Jonathan stood for a moment in the hall. The keys of the MG were on the silver salver by the telephone. He saw clearly just then that because he hated to confront, and because emotional scenes upset him, he had let events drift far too long.

He pocketed the keys, took his hat and coat from the peg and walked out of the house. Because of the cold weather, the car took a long time to start. As he left the town for the countryside he saw how brightly the stars glittered in the chill, black sky. He pressed his foot on the accelerator, and the London road unrolled before him. He drove fast and skilfully, enjoying the rush of cold air that seeped through the gaps between window and door. Driving, he felt confident and unafraid. The full moon lit the hedgerows and verges, and the beauty of the scene calmed him.

As the car approached a bend, Jonathan saw that the trees that lined the verge had fallen away, leaving the road unsheltered, with wide, flat fields to either side of it. He saw how the moonlight traced the long furrows in the soil, tinting them silver, and how a pale haze circled the flat bright disc of the moon. But because there was not the glitter of ice, he did not brake. And when the tyres of the MG lost their traction, and the rear wheels began to skid sideways, he felt, pulling futilely at the steering-wheel, nothing more than a mild, confused sort of surprise.

The cold weather persisted. Alix went through the routine of the day with mechanical expertise: helping Polly with the breakfasts, taking Rory to school, ironing sheets and making up beds. In the late morning, she tried to work in the library. But the words, tiny black birds' footprints on the white page, seemed meaningless. She put on her coat and hat and went outside.

The sky was a pale, crystalline blue. The familiar woods and gardens of Owlscote were reduced to shades of grey. When she walked to the edge of the lake, the fragile frozen leaves of the bulrushes snapped as she brushed past them. She stepped onto the ice. Now, after days when the temperature had remained below freezing point, the thick grey mass bore her weight easily. The soles of her boots left scars on the smooth white surface. The chill bit through to the soles of her feet. In the centre of the lake she paused, her hands tucked into the sleeves of her coat.

She thought, if I tell Derry about Charlie, will he think differently of me? And if I don't tell him, is whatever we have worth anything? She had thought to keep her secret for the rest of her life, but now she saw that she might not. The outside world pressed in on her. She imagined, one day, telling Rory. *I had four cousins, and one of them died.* Her eyes ached: if she let the tears fall, they would freeze and crack on her skin. She was not sure whether, after so long, she could unlock the words.

She heard a voice call out her name. Polly was running towards her across the frozen lawn. The still, cold air smothered her voice. Alix's heart began to beat faster. Something about a telegram, she thought.

The telegram was from Derry. It told her that Jonathan had been involved in a motor accident. Alix cycled to the post office in the village. There was no reply when she phoned Derry's London flat, so she telephoned the Fox household in Andover. The maid answered. Late on

Thursday night, Jonathan had left the house unexpectedly. His car had skidded on an icy patch on the London road, ending up in a ditch. The maid added, 'Mr Jonathan's very poorly, miss, very poorly.' There were tears in the distant voice.

Alix telephoned the hospital in Winchester. *We only give information about patients to relatives, Mrs North.* Taut with anxiety and frustration, she telephoned again, quarter of an hour later, pretending to be a cousin of Jonathan's. The sister listed Jonathan's injuries. Broken ribs, a broken wrist, a badly broken right leg, and concussion. The possibility of pneumonia because Jonathan had lain undiscovered at the side of the road for several hours. Alix made arrangements. Polly would take Rory to school, Martha would help with the housework and cooking. Beatrice, watching Alix button her coat as she made ready to leave Owlscote, said, 'That poor boy. And so handsome. How terrible if he should—' and then stopped, frozen into silence by her daughter's angry glare.

Mr Thompson gave her a lift in his motor-car to Salisbury railway station. Alix caught the train to Winchester. She watched the ploughed fields, with their edging of black hedgerow, speed by. She recalled Jonathan and Derry at that other hospital, so long ago. It worried her that Jonathan's most severe injury was to the leg that had been damaged during the war. In Winchester, Alix hired a taxi to take her from the station. Walking up the long drive to the hospital, she squared her shoulders, making herself ready to face the worst. She asked a nurse for directions to Jonathan's ward. She told herself that she was prepared for anything.

She was not prepared, though, for what Derry said to

her. He was alone in the waiting-room; she saw him first through the frosted glass of the door, a dark silhouette against the window. She pushed open the door; he spun round.

'Well, I've got what I want, haven't I?' he said. 'I'll be ahead for the rest of my life.' His voice was savage. 'And Jonathan, if he's lucky, will limp along behind me.' She made him sit down. He buried his face in his hands. He whispered, 'They say that he will live. They don't know if he'll walk again.'

She put her arm around his shoulders. After a long time, he added, 'Jon was coming to London to see me.'

She thought, so late at night . . . She knew that her question was in her eyes.

'He recovered consciousness yesterday evening.' Derry's voice had become low and expressionless. 'Dad spoke to him. I didn't know what was said until this morning – I'd fallen asleep, you see. But he was coming to London to see *me*.' His eyes were haunted.

'You can't blame yourself for that, Derry.'

'Oh, I *can*.'

'Derry—'

'Jon was worried about Edith. That's what he told Dad.'

Alix was bewildered. 'Derry, it's dreadful that this has happened, but you mustn't make things worse by imagining that it's your fault.'

'*Alix*.' He looked at her properly for the first time. 'What I meant was, Jon was afraid that Edith didn't care for him any more. He didn't say that to Dad, but I know that's what he meant.'

'How can you know that if you haven't spoken to him?'

'Edith told me.'

Her confusion deepened. 'Edith?'

'Edith was with *me*. If Jon had made it into London, he'd have found Edith with *me*.'

Through her bewilderment, voices echoed. Edith Carr's: *Derry's always busy. A busy little bee.* And Derry's: *There's someone . . . a woman.*

She whispered, 'It was Edith, wasn't it?'

The silence, which was both his understanding of her question and his assent, seemed to fill the room. She looked away, focusing first on the walls, with their brown wainscoting and bottle-green dado rail, and then on the linoleum, a swirl of muddy buff and grey.

'It was when I was ill, at home. I was in a foul mood one day, and Edith called, and I felt angry with her. Jonathan had asked her to call – that made it worse, you see, Alix, because I knew that meant that Jonathan pitied me. And I couldn't bear that. Edith didn't take the trouble to hide the fact that it was a duty call – in fact she made it plain that she couldn't care less about me. So I thought I'd *make* her care.'

She began to understand what he was telling her. 'You flirted with her.'

'Yes. Rather infantile, don't you think? I didn't even do it very subtly. Or very nicely.' Derry ran shaking fingers through his untidy hair. 'Then Jonathan told me about the engagement – so when I saw her again, with Jon, I thought I'd better be pleasant to her. Friendly and pleasant. Bad mistake. Made things worse. And then – since then – things have got out of hand.' He looked away. 'I keep telling myself that I didn't mean it to happen. That it was just unlucky – just an error of judgement, like Jon crashing his car into the ditch. But the truth is that, at the time, I did mean it.'

Alix remembered the girl in the garden: Miranda,

with her red dress and silvery hair. Derry's voice, coaxing and flirtatious. She rose and went to the window.

'I was angry,' he said, 'because everything seemed to have gone wrong for me, yet Jonathan had the job, the money, the girl. Jonathan had *done his bit*. So when Edith visited, I wanted to hurt – I wanted to prove that I was as good as Jon. Just that. For a minute – or for an hour, perhaps – that's all. Never again, I promise you. But it was enough, wasn't it?'

She had to look away, unable to bear the expression in his eyes. The chill weather had settled over the town, greying the naked branches of the trees, reducing the roofs of the houses to a silvery sheen.

'Either I provoked,' he said slowly, 'or I set out to destroy. Look at it any way you will, it's my fault.'

'Edith . . . ?'

'Came yesterday. Took one look at Jon, turned green, went home. She's in there with him now, though. Afternoon visiting hour.'

'And the wedding . . . ?'

'She'll call it off. Didn't want him in one piece, so why should she want him now?' His voice was bitter. 'She can't bear ill people. She told me that once.'

'If she doesn't love him—'

'If it wasn't for me, she wouldn't have known she didn't love him. Don't you see?' Derry held out his hands, palms up. 'If I hadn't been there, none of this would have happened. You forge links in chains, but you don't see it at the time. But without me, none of this would have happened.'

The door of the waiting-room opened. Edith Carr stood there, framed by the jamb. Her beautiful face was bone-white.

'Jon's asking for you, Derry,' said Edith. 'He wants to see you.'

Alix made herself useful. She did not see Derry again that afternoon. Mr and Mrs Fox arrived at the hospital in the late afternoon. She ran errands – smelling salts for Mrs Fox, a cup of tea for Derry's grey-faced, red-eyed father. She cornered the surgeon in a corridor and bullied the truth out of him. They had used fragments of bone from Jonathan's good leg to repair the injured leg. They thought the operation had been successful, but there was always the risk of infection. Alix felt as though the years had rolled back, and she had somehow found herself once more in 1918. When she pressed him, the surgeon said, 'The right leg will always be several inches shorter than the left, Mrs North. If he's lucky, he'll walk again.'

The surgeon continued up the corridor. Alix watched his retreating figure. She understood what he had meant. Jonathan will walk with the aid of a stick. He will never again run, or play tennis, or ride a bicycle. He will never again wade carelessly along a beach, Rory's hand in his.

She left the hospital, and wandered around the town. It was half past five. People were hurrying home from work, or rushing into the shops to buy a last pound of cheese or bag of apples before closing time. In a florist, she chose blooms from every bucket, a vast armful of them, and stood, knotting her hands together, as the girl wrapped up the stems in paper. Then she booked into an hotel. Back at the hospital, she gave the bouquet to the sister on Jonathan's ward, and caught Mr and Mrs Fox as they gathered up their belongings, making ready to leave the hospital. Quickly, before she could change her mind, she scribbled on a scrap of paper.

She spoke to Mr Fox. 'Would you give this to Derry? This is the address of the place where I'm staying tonight. Would you ask him to come and see me, please?' She took a deep breath and added, 'Say to him that it's important. Say to him that there's something I have to tell him.'

Alix was in her hotel room, writing a letter to her mother, when the maid knocked at the door.

'There's a gentleman to see you, madam. He's waiting in the lobby.'

She saw him from the top of the stairs. Derry was sitting in a chair, his head bowed, wearing the same crumpled jacket he had been wearing that morning. When she touched his arm, he looked up and smiled.

'Alix.' He was hollow-eyed. 'My father said you'd a message for me.'

She led him into the residents' lounge. Leather armchairs were grouped around small tables. Guests dozed over games of bridge or cups of coffee. A fire roared in the grate. Alix ordered brandy for both of them.

Derry curled his hand round the glass. 'I've been trying not to resort to this all day.'

'How's Jonathan?'

For a moment he closed his eyes. 'I don't know if he minds about the smashed leg more or less than he minds about Edith breaking off the engagement.' Again, he smiled. 'He apologized to me, Alix. Funny, isn't it? *He* apologized to *me*.'

'For what?'

'For thinking that Edith and I . . .' His voice trailed off. 'That's why he was driving to London – to find out whether Edith and I were having an affair. But Edith made it clear to him that there was never anything between us, and that her reasons for breaking off the engagement were nothing whatsoever to do with me. In fact, she told him that she disliked me. Which is probably true, and which I was immensely relieved about. Imagine, Alix – in all this mess, I can still find it in me to be self-centred enough to be relieved that I'm off the hook.' He gave a short laugh, and then he put down his glass. 'Jonathan told me that he wants to die, Alix. Because of Edith. How can I live with that?'

She said harshly, 'You'll live with it because you have to live with it.'

'I can't.' Again, that short, frightened smile. 'This afternoon – after I'd spoken to him – I had to get away. Out. Anywhere. I just walked and walked and walked – I can't remember where. And people were going on, doing all the things they usually do – fussing about how cold it was and what they were going to have for tea and whether they'd remembered to thank Auntie Madge for their Christmas present – you know, all that – and it just seemed . . . it just seemed *obscene*.' He looked at her. 'I'm sorry. What drivel. I'm not making sense.'

There was the click of cards from the bridge players on the adjacent table, a snore from the monocled man asleep in a chair. 'Actually,' said Alix, 'I know just what you mean. You wonder how the world can keep turning. And I meant what I said, Derry, you'll live with it because you have to live with it. I know, because I had to.'

She saw him rub at his forehead with his fingertips, as though the effort of thought was too great. She took a deep breath. 'The party we went to – Maddy Ferraby's party – I left because I met someone there. Someone I couldn't bear to see.'

'I assumed . . . May Lanchbury—'

'Not *May*. Her father. Charles Lanchbury. He was there too.'

She swallowed a mouthful of brandy. The liquid scorched her throat, but it enabled her to say, 'I told you that May is my cousin. Charles Lanchbury is my uncle – my mother's elder brother. I haven't spoken to any of the Lanchburys since I was fourteen, but Charles Lanchbury spoke to me at the party.'

Watching him, she was unsure whether he was listening to her. His features, usually so animated, seemed stilled and enclosed. But she persisted, remembering too clearly what it was to endure that press of despair and guilt and exhaustion, and understanding that she, and perhaps only she, could jolt him into life again.

'I had four cousins, you see, Derry, not three. There was a little boy, Charlie. When I was fourteen, and Charlie was two and a half, I went on holiday to France with my Lanchbury cousins. I was supposed to be looking after Charlie, but I lost him.'

She saw him blink. 'What do you mean, "lost him"?'

'Charlie disappeared.'

'But he was found again?'

Alix shook her head. Odd, how easy it had been, in the end. It had become, she realized, a part of her. Scarring her past, shaping her future, just as asthmatic lungs or a lame leg might help to dictate the course of someone's life.

And for a moment she forgot both Derry and Jonathan, and she was back in northern France, in the long hot summer of her childhood. The heat haze on the golden fields. The way the poppies on the verge had bent their heads as the motor-cars had sped past.

'It was May's ninth birthday. We were going on a picnic. All of us – Uncle Charles and Aunt Marie and Ella and May and Daisy. And Charlie, of course. But Charlie got lost. And we never saw him again. Never ever. And it was partly my fault, Derry. That's what I wanted to tell you. I drew pictures in my sketchbook and forgot to keep an eye on him. I misheard what Daisy said and thought that he was in the other car. I was tired and sleepy and didn't make sure he was safe. All little things, Derry. Such little things. And when the war broke out, and Uncle Charles came home from France without Charlie, I wanted to die. But I didn't. You don't. You go on living somehow. Because you have to.'

She did not realize that she was crying until he reached across, and with his fingertips wiped away the tears that trailed down her face. In the silence that followed, she thought that she could see Charlie's face, which had become blurred by the years, quite clearly. The copper curls, and his eyes, as blue as the summer sky.

She heard Derry mutter, 'Alix – dear God . . .'

'So much that I've done since has been shaped by that day. You were right, Derry – I have been hiding from something. I've spent the last twelve years of my life hiding from Charles Lanchbury. He hates me, you see. Because of me, his only son was lost.' She put her hand on Derry's knotted fists. 'Whatever you've done, Derry – whatever mistakes you've made – are nothing compared to mine. Jonathan is an adult, and will recover. Charlie was a child, and he died. But you can pick up the pieces. That's what I've learned. You're not quite the same person any more, but you can pick up the pieces, and start again, and make something good of your life. And you must do, because Jonathan needs you now.'

She saw him lean forward, and press his face against the palms of his hands. His hands were still wet with her tears. She sat quite still, watching the frost-flowers form on the window of the hotel.

PART FOUR

DISGUISES AND CONCEALMENTS

1932–1937

CHAPTER TEN

'. . . a little bird has mentioned to Oriana that wedding bells may be in store for Miss Marjorie Wood. At the Kelsey-Binghams' coming-out ball for their daughter, Lydia, Miss Wood was seen in animated conversation with Mr Alfred Withycombe, the only son of Colonel and Mrs George Withycombe. Miss Wood looked perfectly divine in powder-blue satin. Oriana predicts Miss Wood will be wearing a different shade of satin before the year is out . . .'

May Lanchbury thought, farmers' daughters and stuffed shirts! and helped herself to another chocolate. Her copy was late, and the office was emptying. She scratched her forehead with the end of her pen, and scribbled something about the Charmouths' at home, and the tedious party she had been forced to attend the previous evening. Parties, she thought, had grown duller these past few years. Or the people who attended them had become duller. In desperation, she wrote: 'Oriana will this Saturday attend the wedding of Miss Daisy Marie Lanchbury and Mr Philip Alfred Delavel at the Church of St Mary in the Fields. Miss Lanchbury, by common consent the loveliest debutante of her coming-out year, is the youngest daughter of Mr Charles

Lanchbury of Bell Wood, Cambridgeshire, and his late first wife, Mrs Marie Lanchbury née Boncourt. Miss Lanchbury will be attended by her elder sisters . . .'

. . . Miss Ella Lanchbury and Miss May Lanchbury, looking perfectly sick-making in pink chiffon, May thought gloomily, but did not write. If Ella, choosing her bridesmaids' dresses – an unlikely image – had selected such a colour, then May would have suspected her of spite. Daisy was incapable of spite; it was Daisy's fatal lack of judgement (evident in her choice of husband, May acknowledged grimly) that dictated that May herself would spend much of next Saturday looking like a blancmange.

May counted her words, yawned and stretched. One more paragraph. She thought of writing: *Oriana has just heard that Mr Nicholas Fox, father of Mr Jonathan and Mr Derry Fox, died suddenly last weekend.* But she did not, partly because one didn't, of course, waste column inches writing about the comings and goings of obscure country solicitors, and partly because she had an odd impulse to keep the possible return to England of her dear vulture, after so many years' absence, all to herself.

May bit the end of her pen. '*The* event of the coming week will be a charity ballet performance given at the Carlton Theatre in the presence of His Royal Highness the Prince of Wales . . .'

Derry's ship left Cartagena one Saturday morning in the April of 1932. He thought, watching the South American coast peel away behind him, that this journey fitted with the pattern of things. He had a distant memory of his housemaster at his prep school seeing him with trailing bootlaces and untucked shirt and unknotted tie, and yelling, 'Fox! You'll be late for your own father's funeral!' And he was. Several weeks late.

As the ship headed out to sea, the events of the last fortnight ran through his head. Jonathan's telegram: its arrival in La Paz had been delayed, of course, because telegrams to La Paz were always delayed. A hurried week of organization and leave-taking. The long journey to Cartagena, via Lima and Bogotá.

Adrift in the emptiness of the ocean, Derry forced himself to face memories he had evaded throughout his five years abroad. Jonathan, three months after the accident, smiling with exhausted pride because he had managed to walk from bed to chair. Jonathan, weeping over the announcement of Edith Carr's marriage in *The Times*. The daily scratch to his heart of the tap-tap of Jonathan's stick on the floorboards. He had gone away, Derry acknowledged, to escape that echo.

He had remained in England for six months following Jonathan's accident, six months in which he had cut himself off from his former life, staying in Andover throughout Jonathan's convalescence, putting all his energies into coaxing and bullying Jonathan into wanting to live again. He had not left home until he had seen that Jonathan would manage without him. He had been able to breathe again, Derry thought, when the boat had taken him from Southampton into open waters, and the distant grey coast of England had blurred into the equally grey Channel. He had made no farewells.

Jonathan's accident had made him see himself clearly. He had not liked what he had seen. South America had allowed him to begin again – yet another second chance, he had thought, with amused irony. In the aftermath of Jonathan's accident, all his old ambitions had fallen away. He had worked long hours, seven days a week, but not for his former goals. He had gone away to make something of himself, yes, but he had known by the time he left England that he no longer sought fame or recognition. His ambitions had become smaller, narrower, more focused. He worked so that he could send money home to help pay Jonathan's medical bills; he worked to help compensate for the shortfall in income to his father's practice that would be the inevitable consequence of Jonathan's slow recovery. He worked so that he might learn to live with himself again.

The shares that Mrs Kessel had left to him, in an emerald mine in Bolivia, had lain neglected in the bank too long. Travelling across South America, Derry had imagined perfect jewels of a fathomless, limpid green, torn from the earth. The reality had been different. After six months in Bolivia, he had known the emeralds to be substandard, and his shares overvalued. He had sold his stake in the mine and bought gold. Throughout the first nine months of 1929, he had watched, full of nervous doubt, as share prices soared. Then, at the end of October, the New York stock market had collapsed. The ripples of that falling-out continued to crash through Western economies like a tsunami. Banks had failed, and investors had hurled themselves from tall buildings, but Derry had sighed a huge sigh of relief, and had begun, in the early 1930s, to buy. He had bought carefully and cautiously, sound stock at rock-bottom prices.

He had, at first, intended never to return to England. He had seen clearly the harm he had done, and the chaos he had so carelessly made of both his and other people's lives. He saw himself as the vulture May Lanchbury had teasingly nicknamed him, pecking at other people's bones, making nothing new or good.

But against his expectations he had, after years of work and travel, found himself thinking of England. What he had once despised – England's smallness, its dullness – he now longed for. What had once seemed to him only complacency now seemed comforting and reassuring. What he had labelled mediocrity had become in retrospect a necessary and desirable lack of extremism. Derry had begun to feel restless; at night, he dreamed of chalk hills and green meadows.

And then the telegram arrived. He had slit it open and read it, and had then sat down at his desk and wept. Tears running down his face, trickles of sweat (it had been unbearably hot) down the back of his neck. He thought that this was his greatest punishment, never to be able to put things right. And he had known then that he must go home.

On board ship, he slept on deck, fighting seasickness, watching the first chill glimmer of sun on the distant horizon. Solitary at the gunwale before the daily social interactions of the ship began to stir, he thought about his father. He felt anger as well as grief. His anger was at the snuffing out of future possibility. A death was a line drawn under a relationship, a summing-up, a cessation of opportunity. In that series of grey dawns Derry acknowledged his own multitude of regrets and failures, but recognized also the mismatches contained within families. He and his father had been one such mismatch: a square peg and a round hole, a sore thumb and a . . . what? One of the many things he had failed to inherit from his father was, he thought wryly, an affinity with cliché.

In the spring of 1932, Alix had all Owlscote's windows and chimneys repointed, its doors painted, and guttering mended. When, bringing in the washing one Friday afternoon, she looked back at the house, it seemed to smile at her, clean and neat and in good repair. She would have liked to have fetched her sketchbook and drawn it, but there were sheets to iron and tables to lay, and three little girls would shortly be arriving for their drawing lessons. So she picked up the laundry basket and walked back indoors, a spring in her step.

She had started up the drawing lessons in the months following Jonathan Fox's accident. They had helped make up for the income that she had lost through cancelling the parties. Their success had taken her by surprise, and Alix had quickly gathered half a dozen pupils. She enjoyed the lessons immensely; even the most ham-fisted child would, with encouragement and perseverance, eventually produce something to be proud of. The income from the drawing lessons, and the continuing success of the guest house, had allowed her to make more improvements to Owlscote.

The drawing lessons had had another, less expected benefit. Alix had become acquainted with her pupils' friends and relations. She was invited to afternoon tea here, to a dinner party there. She had made friends; she had even found herself with a rather flattering succession of admirers. Though all of her companions had, in their various ways, eventually proved hopelessly unsuitable – one pined for a long-lost love, another shared a bed with his three Labradors and shed dog hairs to prove it, another had an unsettling penchant for women in uniform – the evenings at the theatre and cinema, the jaunts in motor-cars and picnics by the river, had been a welcome distraction from the routine domestic work of running the guest house.

That evening Alix had been invited to a cocktail party.

Seeing her pupils out of the front door, ironing the last of the sheets and hastily making up beds, she glanced frequently at her watch. The paying guests seemed to eat their dinner with infuriating slowness; Alix cleared away the last of the pudding bowls, and put them in the sink.

'I'll finish off.' Polly shook out a tea towel. 'You go and get ready.'

Alix looked up at the kitchen clock. 'I'll have to cycle.'

'In your cocktail dress?'

'Cycle clips,' said Alix firmly.

Polly snorted. 'Where are you going?'

'Only to the village. The Ritsons. It's not far.'

Alix went upstairs. From the wardrobe, she chose a dark green silk dress. She put her evening shoes in a bag, and wore brogues. When she had dressed and combed her hair, she went to Rory's room.

He was making something vast and complicated out of Meccano. His silky brown fringe flopped over his face as he fixed a bolt to a miniature strut, and Alix made a mental note to take him to Salisbury and get his hair cut. She sat on the floor beside him.

'That's terribly impressive, darling. What is it?'

'It's a bridge. I'm going to use it on my model railway. The engines'll go under here and along there.' He glanced at her. 'Are you going out, Mum?'

'Just to the village. And Polly and Grandma are here, of course.'

His hug squeezed the breath out of her lungs. At ten years old, the top of his head came almost to her shoulder. 'Teeth and face, remember, Rory,' she reminded him. 'And don't forget to say good night to Grandma.'

Alix called a hasty farewell to Polly, and dashed outside, grabbing her bicycle from out of the shed, pedalling fast beneath trees still dripping from the morning's rainstorm.

The Ritsons lived in a large, modern house on the edge of the village. They had one much-loved daughter, Veronica, whom Alix was attempting to teach to draw. Martha Ritson, who was vague and short-sighted and kind, introduced Alix to the other guests.

'This is Mrs Taylor – Mr Taylor works with Ronald, you see, Alix – and you know Lavinia Potter, don't you – and, oh yes' – Mrs Ritson squinted and waved – 'Celia, you must meet Mrs North! Mrs North teaches Veronica to draw! She is so talented. Veronica paints such beautiful pictures. She wants to go to art college. And this is' – Martha Ritson blinked, struggling to focus on the tall, fair man who had come to stand beside them – 'I'm afraid I can't remember your name, dear. How dreadful of me.' Martha Ritson blinked again. 'Did you come with Leonard? Or the Murchisons? I must apologize . . .'

'No apologies necessary,' he said, and smiled.

Mrs Ritson beamed. 'Well, I must dash – people still arriving – and the maid has forgotten the canapés . . .' She disappeared into the crowd.

He held out his hand to Alix. 'Allow me to introduce myself. My name's Kit Crawford.'

'Alix North.' They shook hands. He was well-dressed and well-spoken and, Alix guessed, much the same age as herself.

'Can I get you another drink?'

'Please.'

He plucked two cocktails from a passing tray, and handed one to Alix. 'So you teach drawing?'

'And I run a guest house.'

'Rather an eclectic mixture.'

'I'm very versatile. And you, Mr Crawford?'

'Kit, please. Oh, I'm in fine arts. That sort of thing.'

'Do you live nearby?'

'I move around a fair bit,' he said vaguely. 'Though' – his gaze caught hers – 'I've a feeling I might be happy to stay in the area for a while.'

'Do you like this part of the country?'

'I didn't think much of it at first,' he said, 'but I'm learning to appreciate it.'

They were flirting, Alix thought, and she was enjoying every minute of it. Kit looked around the room. 'It's a bit of a crush, isn't it? Shall we try and find somewhere quieter? One can hardly hear oneself think.'

In the large sun-room at the back of the house, Alix collapsed thankfully into a comfortable chair. She heard Kit say: 'Actually, this is my first visit to Wiltshire.'

'You haven't relations here?'

'I haven't any family at all.' His light grey eyes narrowed.

'I'm sorry.'

He shrugged, and ran a hand through his cropped fair hair. 'Oh, I've had plenty of time to get used to it. I was born in India, you see. Sent off to boarding school in England when I was six. My parents died of cholera when I was eleven. But by that time, I'd almost forgotten what they looked like.'

'How awful for you. *Eleven*.' Alix thought of Rory. 'I've a ten-year-old son,' she said. 'Too dreadful to imagine, sending him thousands of miles away.'

'It's what one did.' He looked at her glass. 'I say – drink up. I'll get you another one.'

She thought, as he left the room, Kit Crawford, you have passed the first test. The first test was telling them about Rory. Some men immediately found an excuse to leave, nervous that any widowed mother must be desperate for the security and protection of a man. And those who passed the first test and lasted a little longer often grew to resent the time she spent with her son, so that Alix herself, becoming tired of sulks and complaints, ended the relationship.

Kit came back into the room. 'Martha – Mrs Ritson – has just been telling me how talented her daughter is.' When he smiled, the corners of his eyes turned up, and his lips parted, revealing small, pointed white teeth. 'Another Leonardo, apparently.'

Alix, thinking of Veronica Ritson's square-jawed portraits and rubbery-legged ponies, also smiled.

He sat down beside her. He was looking at her closely. She was glad of the room's poor light; under his gaze, she felt herself redden.

Then he said, 'There's something about you that puzzles me.'

'What, Kit?'

'Why you choose to wear brogues with a cocktail dress.'

Looking down at her feet, she shrieked.

He insisted on driving her home that night. 'Bung the bike in the back of the motor,' he said. 'You shouldn't be wandering round by yourself at this time of night.'

When they drew into the courtyard and he looked up at the house, she heard his indrawn breath.

'Good lord.' He turned to look at her. His eyes shone, pale jewels in the moonlight. 'Yours?'

'My husband left it to me.' As always, looking up at Owlscote, Alix felt an immense pride. Now, the full moon gilded the roof and gable, and made a silvery patina of the weathered flint and brick.

He was silent for a moment, and then he climbed out

of the car, and opened the door for her. When he caught her hand and pressed his lips against her palm, a shiver ran down her spine.

'I'd love to see you again. May I, Alix?' His voice was soft and coaxing.

His fingers lingered on hers. 'Yes,' she whispered, and walked into the house.

They had lunch one day in a restaurant in Salisbury, and the following weekend they went to the theatre. After he had driven her home, Alix asked Kit indoors.

Owlscote was quiet and dark. In the library she poured out two brandies, and handed one to Kit. He circled the perimeter of the room, the tips of his fingers drifting against the leather-bound books, and the old, polished furniture. She enjoyed watching him: he was possessed of a seductively feline looseness of limb.

He smiled at her. 'I should love to see the rest of the place.'

'Come to tea on Sunday, then. You can meet Mother and Rory.'

'I'll show him the car. Small boys always like cars.'

'Three o'clock, then.'

He put down his glass, and crossed the room to her. He said softly, 'I shall look forward to it.' Taking her hands in his, he kissed them one after the other. His lips, soft and cool, sought her mouth, gently, almost cautiously at first. She felt his tongue flicker, touching first her lips, and then her teeth, searching, probing. His body, pressing against hers, was hard and firm. The top of the desk dug into the backs of her thighs. When his hand reached beneath her blouse – the glorious thrill of his fingertips on her bare skin – she gave a small gasp, and pulled away.

'Alix – I'm sorry . . .' He stepped back. 'I didn't mean to upset you.'

'You haven't, Kit.' Her voice shook slightly as she tucked in her blouse.

'Really?' He sounded anxious.

'Really. It's just that . . . you mustn't rush me.'

He tilted her chin so that she looked up at him. 'You're not cross with me, then?'

'Not at all.'

'And I can still come to tea?'

'Of course you can.' She kissed his cheek.

Derry's ship docked at Southampton in the early hours of the morning. Walking down the gangway, feeling the ground lurch wave-like beneath his feet, he realized that he had forgotten how bright and cold an English spring could be. The sky was a pure pale blue, and the clouds were tiny drifts of cotton wool. Strolling from the docks into the town, his rucksack slung over one shoulder, he could smell, above the traffic fumes, the sharp scent of early blossom and new leaves.

He exchanged money in a bank, and in a restaurant in the centre of the town ate his first decent meal in weeks. Then he headed for the railway station. Though his intention had been to travel immediately to Andover, the guard's announcement – *Eastleigh, Romsey, and all stations to Salisbury* – over the hiss of steam and clatter of pistons, gave a curious twist to his heart.

No time to think. Derry bought his ticket, and jumped on the train just as it was pulling out of the station.

On the train, he thought about her. Alix. In the murky reflection of the carriage window, he pictured her thick dark hair and her long green eyes. He remembered dancing with Alix at Owlscote, the two of them whirling round the perimeter of the Great Hall. He remembered her laughing with him, angry with him, cold with him. He remembered lying on the sofa in Owlscote's library, his head in her lap, and Alix stroking his hair as he drifted off to sleep. He remembered her forcing him to pick up the pieces after Jonathan's accident, to put aside his own shock and guilt so that he might care for Jonathan. He remembered all these things, but he did not remember when he had begun to love her. There had been no sharp, defining moment, no sudden, blinding revelation. There had just been an absence in his life, which Alix, without his at first realizing it, had filled.

He wondered whether love lasted, and whether she or he would have changed. He wondered whether, looking at her, there would still be that familiar twist to the heart, that familiar pang that had always accompanied his first sight of her.

Five years ago, docking in Cartagena, he had written to her, trying to explain his decision to leave England. He had known, though, that his letter had been thin, inadequate. He, who had always been good with words, had been unable to find those that could explain to her his sudden departure. Haunted by the remembered echo of Jon's slow, uneven footsteps, he had known himself to be unworthy of her. His pen had faltered on the paper, and he had found himself listing dry facts, excuses that had seemed unconvincing even to him. She had not replied.

Alighting at Salisbury station, Derry took a taxi to Owlscote. The brown-green tunnel of valley and trees enclosed them, and sunlight pierced the gaps between the branches, dappling the road. His heart lifted: it would be different, Derry told himself, when they saw each other face to face. He would find the words.

The taxi-driver dropped him at the entrance to Owlscote's drive. Derry walked down the narrow gravel path between the trees. Bulbs pushed their way through the dark earth, and the new leaves of the beeches were remnants of pleated bright green velvet. He saw the house first, just the same as he remembered it, sheltered, as it had been for centuries, by the hollow of the valley. Then he heard her voice, and his breath caught in his throat. 'Over here!' she called out, and for one foolish, heart-stopping moment, he thought she was speaking to him.

He saw Alix walk out of the woodland on the far side of the courtyard, a swirl of pleated skirt and blackberry-coloured jersey. He knew then that, for him, nothing had changed, that the compass of his heart was unaltered. He almost put down his rucksack, almost raised his arm and waved to her.

But then he saw the man, stepping out of the shadows. Tall, young, fair-haired. The smile on his face, the soul-destroying familiarity of the way in which he crossed the courtyard to her, putting his arms round her, lifting her up, embracing her.

Derry turned on his heel and, before either of them could see him, headed quickly back down the drive.

He spent a week with Jonathan and his mother in Andover, and then travelled on to London. His first evening in London, he called on Roma. She welcomed him with expressions of surprise and delight, and asked him in, and made him thick dark coffee, the sort that made his heart beat at twice its usual rate.

She told him all the news. 'Sophie's very well. She's still living in that awful little place, though Bernard's forever trying to persuade her to let him buy her somewhere nice. And Ruth Duncan's married and living in America. Her sister's divorce is through. Lawrence is just the same as he always was, though I'm afraid he's taken to wearing striped matelot tops and black berets. The café's closed – Eric's sister came back from Spain, and they bought a pub in the Lake District. Hard to imagine, isn't it, Eric among the daffodils.' She looked at Derry. 'How's your brother, my dear?'

He made himself smile. 'Jon's very well. Better than I expected.'

'And Alix? Have you spoken to Alix?'

He shook his head. In his mind's eye he saw a swirl of dark hair and pleated skirt and the bright spring day suddenly dimming.

'Alix and I had lunch together last month,' said Roma. 'I must say, I thought she looked blooming. Absolutely blooming.'

He said, 'And you, Roma? How are you? You look stunningly beautiful, as always.'

Roma wore a close-fitting purple sheath and a matching toque, pinned with an ebony brooch. She sat down beside Derry.

'I'm very well. I have a new friend called Caroline. She comes from Surrey and she adores horses and dreadful country pursuits, but she's the sweetest girl.'

'I'm glad. How's business?'

'It has been difficult, but things are beginning to look up. Last year was dreadful, Derry – I was desperately short of commissions. I was afraid I'd have to mortgage the flat. But I found some new clients – I sold my soul, I'm afraid, and went along with the sorts of frightful-nesses I'd normally have refused point-blank. So I've just about survived.' She looked at him. 'And you? You look thriving, my darling. Terribly *brown*. How was the jungle?'

'It wasn't *jungle*, Roma. The mines are in the mountains. Bandit country. One feels one should be riding a horse and lassoing things. But Bolivia was . . . profitable.'

'And now? What will you do now?'

He put aside his cup. 'That's what I wanted to talk to you about. Are you still planning to open a shop?'

Roma made a face. 'I don't think that's ever going to happen, Derry. I've almost stopped thinking about it, to tell the truth.'

'You haven't the capital?'

She shook her head. 'I had to eat into my savings just to keep going.'

'If you had the cash, would you still be interested in the idea?'

'Of course.' Roma looked sad. 'But I think it's going to stay a dream, Derry.'

He said, 'I have money, you see,' and she turned slowly, looking at him. Her grey eyes widened.

'Derry . . . ?'

'I have money,' he repeated simply. 'And I'm looking for something to invest it in.'

There was a silence. Then she whispered, 'Me . . . ?'

'Why not? We've worked together before.'

'Yes, but . . .' She was staring at him. 'Are you serious, Derry?'

'Never more so.'

She said faintly, 'Goodness,' and sat back on the sofa. 'A shop . . . ?'

'Yes. You'll need a good address – it gives the right impression.'

Roma's normally pale skin had gone even paler. 'Pour

me a drink, would you?' she said eventually. Her voice shook slightly. 'You've rather taken me by surprise.'

He poured two Scotches, and handed one to Roma. She took a cigarette from the case on the side table. After a while she said, 'What would be your role, Derry? I assume you'd want a little more this time than heaving furniture around and putting up decorations.'

He smiled. 'I'd want to keep an eye on the business side – that would free you up, Roma, and allow you to concentrate on the creative part. And I could source material for you – I did that for a couple of years in South America, importing rugs, exporting artefacts, that sort of thing. It would allow me to travel, which I'd enjoy. You have the contacts of course, and the reputation.' He looked at her. 'What do you think?'

Sitting back on the cushions, watching him, her eyes narrowed into thin grey slits. 'I think it's a simply marvellous idea.'

'I'll start looking for suitable premises then.'

She raised her glass. 'To us, Derry. And to success.' Their glasses clinked.

Polly Daniels said, 'Alix isn't at home, I'm afraid, Jonathan. She's gone out with Kit and Rory.' She added firmly, 'You'll come in, of course.'

'I bought cream cakes.' He held up a box, tied with string.

'I adore cream cakes. And you can help me collect the eggs.'

It was a command, not a request, so Jonathan didn't argue. He followed Polly into Owlscote.

'Eggs first, cakes as a reward after,' said Polly. She took a basket from the scullery and looped it over her arm.

The hens had escaped from their coop, Polly explained, and were laying eggs in all the most inconvenient places. Jonathan limped around Owlscote's vast garden, his walking-stick sinking into the soft, damp earth, holding the basket while Polly rescued eggs hidden beneath brambles and inside nettle beds.

After a while, Jonathan said, 'Who's Kit?'

'Alix met him at the Ritsons'. He came to tea last Sunday.'

'What's he like?'

Polly, straightening, placed another egg in the basket. 'Terribly handsome. Well-spoken. Generous. Charming.'

Jonathan, looking at her, said, 'Damned with excessive praise.'

She made a face. 'There's something not quite *transparent* about him. He reminds me of a friend that Stephen – my youngest brother – once had. It was when Stephen was about seven, and this little friend would come to tea and be terribly sweet and perfectly polite and pleasant, and then, when he thought I wasn't looking, I'd see him doing something dreadful – pulling the cat's tail, or stealing biscuits.' She caught sight of Jonathan's expression. 'Silly of me, Jon. I'm sure I'm just imagining it. And Mrs Gregory adores Kit.'

Jonathan changed the subject as they walked deeper into the copse.

'How are your brothers, Polly?'

Polly's mother had died in childbirth when Polly was twelve. Polly had spent her teenage years living in a rambling Hampshire vicarage, looking after her father and her five younger brothers. The kitchen at Owlscote was decorated with photographs of them and postcards from them.

'They're very well.' Polly told Jonathan about Leonard, who was twenty-six and had begun to work as a GP in Glasgow, and John, who had entered the Church, like his father. William and Patrick were both at Oxford, and the baby, Stephen, who was seventeen now, was still at boarding school.

'You must miss them all,' said Jonathan.

'Immensely. But we see each other as often as we can.'

'I envy you. I've always thought big families must have a lot of fun.'

Polly smiled. 'We do. Though it can be a bit of a bear-garden sometimes.' She looked at Jonathan. 'Does it hurt?'

'My leg? A bit. If I have to stand up a lot.'

Polly didn't fuss; Jonathan was glad that she didn't fuss. She just said, 'We've enough eggs,' and walked back to the house, slowing her pace a little.

In the kitchen, she arranged the cakes on a plate. 'Cream horns,' she said. 'Mmm. My favourite. And *two each*.' She offered him the plate. 'I'd love you to meet my family, Jon. All my brothers are home this weekend. You must come to tea. Are you free on Saturday afternoon?'

Derry had left his card at May Lanchbury's house. It was a fortnight before she returned his call. After they had embraced (May, always a plump armful, had, he noticed, become somewhat plumper), she said, 'So lovely that you're back. You look well, my dear vulture. Feathers sleek and black and glossy.'

'And you're as beautiful as ever, darling May.'

'I'm hideously fat. I've been in Le Touquet for a couple of weeks, and the food was divine and I ate *everything*.' Gloomily, she looked down at herself. 'I'm going on a diet. For the next three weeks I'm only going to eat pineapples.'

'A pity. I was going to offer to take you out to dinner.'

She smiled. 'The pineapples could wait till tomorrow, don't you think?'

Over dinner, he told her about South America, and she told him who had married whom, and who had divorced whom, and who was having an affair with whom. And who was rumoured to have lost everything in the Crash, but he had discovered that already, because it was his business to know that. Then, studying the pudding trolley, she said: 'And Mrs Wenlock has just given birth to her second child, I hear.'

He was taken off guard. 'Who?'

'Edith Wenlock. Née Carr. You know her, don't you, Derry?'

'She was engaged to my brother.' He shook his head to the puddings. 'Is the marriage happy?'

'I'm afraid I don't know.' May chose the trifle. 'He's a boor – new money, of course. Heavens – I sound like my father.'

Derry ordered a brandy. He heard her begin, 'Years ago—' and then she stopped.

'Years ago – what?'

'Before you left England . . . months before . . . that frightful party . . .' She touched his hand. 'Do you remember that I asked you to take a message? To Alix Gregory?'

'Of course.'

Her spoon had paused, halfway to her mouth. 'Did you take it to her?'

'Yes.' *I have a message from May Lanchbury*, he had said. And Alix had replied, *May is my cousin*.

'Alix explained the relationship,' he said. 'And then – and then, other things intervened.'

'Your brother's accident.' May squeezed his hand. 'So dreadful. How is he?'

'Fine. Fine.' Jon's walking-stick, tap-tapping along the shadowy corridors of his mind. Yet May's words had brought back to him stories unfinished, echoes unanswered. That suffocating hotel room – leather tabletops and old men snoring in armchairs – and Alix telling him about a lost child. And saying, *We never saw him again. It was my fault, Derry. Whatever mistakes you've made are nothing compared to mine.*

'Alix told me about your brother. About Charlie.'

He saw May put down her spoon, her trifle untouched. He remembered, too, saying, *I've never thought that loving someone meant being obliged to share all your secrets with them.* And he remembered the expression on Alix's face as she had told him about Charlie Lanchbury. She, Alix, had shared her darkest, most terrible secret with him. To comfort him.

He swirled brandy around his glass. 'Alix told me that it was her fault that your brother was lost.'

'No.' May shook her head.

Derry looked up. '*No . . . ?*'

'Of course not.'

Two such different versions of the same tale. He heard her mutter, 'I was afraid of that . . .'

Curiosity coiled and leapt. Derry saw May grope in her bag and take out her cigarette case. Her fingers fumbled with the clasp. He lit the cigarette for her.

'It was my birthday, you see.'

'Your ninth birthday.'

'Alix told you that? Yes.' She inhaled her cigarette.

'We always went to my grandparents' house in the summer. My French grandparents – they lived not far from Amiens, near a little town called Bapaume. My mama was half French. Each summer we'd go to Le Touquet, and stay there for a few weeks, and play with our buckets and spades. Nanny and the maid would look after us. Then we'd travel by train to the chateau, and meet Mama and Papa. They always motored – my father adores motor-cars. Anyway, that year, Nanny was ill, so Alix came instead. She was our cousin, but it was the first time she'd been on holiday with us.' May frowned. 'We saw Alix and Uncle Aylwyn and Aunt Beatrice once or twice a year, I suppose.'

'The two families lived far apart?'

May shook her head. 'Oh no. Bell Wood, our home, is in Cambridgeshire. And the Gregorys lived in Suffolk. Not far at all.' May raised her plump white shoulders. 'Some things you don't necessarily notice when you are a child, but since then I've understood how things were. Aunt Beatrice married beneath her. Aylwyn Gregory was a penniless drawing master. To my father, to marry out of one's class is an unforgivable sin.'

'So Alix came on holiday with you . . . ?'

'Because Nanny couldn't come. Alix came to help with the little ones – Daisy was five, and Charlie only two. I remember that I felt sorry for Alix. She didn't have the right clothes, and her hairbrush was bone, not tortoiseshell. Papa treated her like a servant. And so did Ella, of course, because Ella always copied Papa.'

'Was Alix unhappy?'

'I don't think so. She always seemed to me a very happy person. Very lively and funny and laughing a lot. She used to say such things . . . She wasn't like us at all. We were brought up not to speak until spoken to.' May smiled. 'Alix drew the most wonderful pictures. I remember that. Charlie took to her. And she adored him. She was always with Charlie. I remember that he sat on her lap all the way from Le Touquet to Amiens. I was jealous. I can remember wishing that I was small and sweet and cuddly like Charlie.'

Her voice trailed away. There was a long silence. Derry saw in his mind's eye a French railway carriage, and three little girls in old-fashioned dresses, and a much younger Alix, laughing and impetuous.

May stubbed out her cigarette. 'Anyway – my birthday. We went for a picnic. Every year, we went for a picnic on my birthday. We went' – she frowned – 'I can't remember where. There was a wood . . . a very dark, dense wood. I do remember that. Daisy was frightened. She thought there were wolves. I had a marvellous birthday cake. And Ella and I made a den. And . . . and we played cricket. And then we went to a fair. A wonderful fair, with dancing and music. When we arrived home it must have been very late, because I remember that it was dark and that I'd fallen asleep in the motor-car. Then . . . we were getting ready for bed, and Louise, the nursemaid, was cross with me because I'd lost my hair ribbon – and then we were told to go downstairs. I thought' – and Derry saw May take a deep breath – 'I thought that it was because of my birthday. A surprise present, perhaps. But it was because of Charlie. I didn't understand, at first. To tell the truth, I didn't understand for ages. No-one really ever explained it to us. People don't explain things to children, do they? I thought Charlie had gone away . . . or that he had fallen ill . . . I thought, for *years*, that he was going to come back.'

When she looked up at him, Derry glimpsed the

horror in her eyes. 'Poor Alix,' said May softly. 'Papa blamed her, you see.'

'Should he have?'

'Of course not. I told you. It was just one of those awful things. A terrible accident.'

'Why did your father blame her? Because she was supposed to be standing in for your nanny?'

'Yes.'

'But' – he frowned – 'the nursemaid . . . ?'

May took another cigarette from her case. 'You have to understand what losing his son meant to my father, Derry. You have to understand how important such things as name and land and bloodline are to a man like my father. Papa can trace back his ancestry to the Conquest. Bell Wood has been in the family since the seventeenth century. Charlie was his heir. Only Charlie could keep the family name, and only Charlie would have been able to pass that name on to his children in turn. The estate, of course, is entailed – neither Ella nor Daisy nor I can inherit Bell Wood. We three girls mean very little to my father, because we can't continue the family line. My father needed a son. How overjoyed he must have been at Charlie's birth – a son at last, after three daughters! And then – for Charlie just to *disappear* . . .' Her blue eyes, dark with old sorrows, focused on Derry. 'My father had to blame someone, you see. I think Alix was just unlucky. She was there and he didn't particularly like her, and he lost his temper.' May shook her head. 'Papa didn't treat Alix kindly or justly, Derry. But I can understand why he behaved as he did.'

'So Charlie died . . .'

'He must have.'

He glanced at her. '*Must* have . . . ?'

May had gone white, but she said clearly, 'They never found a body.'

'I assumed—'

'No body. No funeral. Nothing.'

There was a silence. Looking round, Derry saw that it was late, and that the restaurant was almost empty. He saw also that May's trifle remained in front of her, untouched. He said gently, 'I'm sorry. Asking questions . . . I didn't mean to put you off your pudding, May.'

'Grief, you see . . . better than pineapples.' She laughed. 'And I don't mind talking about it. I'm glad to, actually. No-one else mentions him. It's almost as though he never existed.' Her expression altered, and she said, 'For a long time, everywhere I went, any red-haired boy would always remind me of him. I could always picture what he'd look like, if he'd have lived. I could always work out how old he'd be. He'd have been twenty this April.' She smiled. 'And I used to find myself thinking . . .' She spread out her hands, a gesture of resignation. 'How it might have been. How it might have been all right. That the gypsies might have found Charlie and kept him safe . . . or some kind family might have taken him in – adopted him . . .' She looked up. 'Just fairy stories, Derry. Just wanting a happy ending.'

He squeezed her hand. She tried to smile.

'Have you ever been back?'

'To the chateau?' May shook her head. 'As far as I know, our two families – the Boncourts and the Lanchburys – haven't been in touch since 1914. There was the war, of course, and Mama died – of grief, I believe, Derry. Losing Charlie – it changed her. She was never the same after that. She hardly spoke – she shut herself away in her room. So I suppose that neither family wanted to open up old wounds. Though, some-times . . .' Her voice faded away.

'Sometimes . . . ?' he prompted.

'Recently, I've found myself feeling guilty about it. My French grandmother's still alive, you see. I should visit her – I write a letter at Christmas, but that's not enough, is it, Derry?' She paused. Then she said, 'And, though my father searched for Charlie – and though he told us that the police and the villagers searched too—' Again she broke off.

'What, May?'

She frowned. 'My father had to come home because of the war.'

'Your birthday . . . ?'

'Is at the end of July.'

'Just before Germany invaded Belgium.' Derry ran his hands through his hair. 'Damned difficult to search thoroughly when a war's breaking out around you.'

'Yes. I suppose it's the journalist in me . . . making up stories, looking at evidence . . . but sometimes I wonder whether my father simply didn't have long enough to search properly. Or whether he might, in the panic, have overlooked something. I imagine . . . I imagine that Charlie may have been alive, safe – taken into an orphanage. And perhaps displaced again because of the invasion. There could be records. Someone may remember something.' She looked across at Derry. 'You think that I'm deceiving myself, don't you? That I'm comforting myself with false hope.'

'I think,' he said gently, 'that if you want to go back to France, then that's what you should do, May.'

Derry ordered coffee. May spooned in sugar, and stirred it slowly. He heard her say, 'Have you seen Alix? How is she?'

'She's very well.' The sound of laughter. Strong arms enfolding Alix, whirling her into the air. 'Very happy.'

May just looked at him. 'I went back to Owlscote,' he said flatly. 'She was with someone.'

'Alix has married?'

'I don't know.'

May looked bewildered. Derry explained, 'I didn't wait for introductions.'

She put down her spoon. 'You didn't speak to her? You just upped and went? *Derry*.'

He grimaced. 'Ridiculous, wasn't it? But I felt such a fool. I shouldn't have turned up unannounced. I know that I've no right to expect that after five years' absence things would be unchanged.'

He saw the expression on her face, and explained, 'He had his arms round her, you see.'

May said crisply, 'My editor at the newspaper put his arms round me today. And he is sixty-five and has four children and ten grandchildren. And I assure you, Derry, that I'm not in love with him.' She reached across the table, and took his hand in hers. 'Write to her, Derry. Go and see her. Go and see Alix *properly*.'

Kit drove Alix north, along the valley of the Avon. It was early summer, her favourite time of year. Golden kingcups shimmered like jewelled carpets on the river, and in the shadowy woodland the forest floor was an azure mist of bluebells.

'Where are we going?'

Kit grinned. 'I told you. It's a surprise.'

The countryside swelled and rose, taking them higher, towards the ancient chalk hills of the Vale of Pewsey. Small, puffy clouds cast dark shadows on the grass. Alix could see, on almost every horizon, the smooth, egg-shaped tumuli that dotted the landscape.

'Avebury!' she exclaimed, delighted. 'My husband, Edward, spent most of his boyhood near Avebury, exploring the prehistoric sites. Our attics are full of clutter from the digs he worked on.'

'Attics?' he said. 'You didn't show me Owlscote's attics.'

She had given Kit a tour of Owlscote, enjoying his obvious fascination with the old house. She said, 'The attics are terribly gloomy, Kit, and full of the most awful old junk.'

He smiled. 'Archaeological finds . . . how marvellous. Did your husband only dig in Britain, or did he work abroad as well?'

'He was in Egypt for several seasons. And in Mesopotamia, of course. I was there with him.'

'You must promise me a tour of Owlscote's attics, Alix. I adore old junk.'

'And spiders?'

'Especially spiders. Now – look.'

She peered out through the windscreen of the car. Great grey stones, like a giant's teeth, rose from the grass. Small cottages, a church, and a herd of cows threaded through the stone circles.

Kit parked the car. 'My second surprise,' he said, and took a wicker hamper from the boot.

'A picnic! Kit – you should have let me—'

'It's your day off, remember, Alix.'

He took her hand, and they walked through the avenue of stones. In the shadow of one of the megaliths, he fed her fragments of smoked salmon and early strawberries, washed down with champagne.

He said, 'Your third surprise,' and handed her a small box. 'Go on. Open it.'

She lifted up the lid and saw a brooch, in the shape of an owl. Wide eyes glared at her. 'Kit, you shouldn't have—'

'Don't you like it?'

'I love it, but—'

'Put it on, then.' He pinned the brooch to her dress. 'They're only paste, I'm afraid. One day I'll buy you diamonds.'

She let her lips touch his. 'Kit, you are very sweet. And I don't want diamonds. This is perfect.'

'You deserve diamonds.'

She kissed him again. Threading her arms round his neck, the slight feeling of unease and unsettledness that had stayed with her throughout the day began to dissipate. His fingers ran the length of her spine, searching for the buttons at the back of her dress. Now, when his palm caressed her bare skin, she did not push him away, but heard herself moan as his fingertips brushed against her breast, her nipple.

Something warm and wet licked her foot. She shrieked, and sat up.

'Dear God.' Kit looked annoyed.

Seeing the cow chewing the grass by her ankle, Alix began to laugh.

They had afternoon tea in a small café, and walked around the stone circles. Kit told her a little about his childhood in India, his lonely years at boarding school, and the family in Scotland who had befriended him after his bereavement. When she asked him why he had never married, he smiled, and took her hand, and said, 'Never met the right girl, I suppose.' He questioned her about Edward, and Alix told him about the nursing home and the archaeological dig.

He frowned. 'With a young son . . . it can't have been easy. Didn't you ever think of marrying again?'

She shook her head, and said, 'Never,' and thought of the letter she had received that morning, and wondered whether she lied.

They drove to Silbury Hill. Almost without her noticing, the clouds had thickened throughout the afternoon, and as they climbed up the steep incline, a chill wind ruffled the tussocks of grass. Alix stood on top of the hill, her arms folded around herself, looking out at a sky that had blurred, a dark charcoal grey, into the horizon.

'Penny for 'em.' Kit had come to stand beside her.

'Oh . . .' She smiled up at him. 'Nothing important.'

'Really? You've seemed preoccupied all day, Alix. Is it me? Perhaps I'm taking up too much of your time – with your family . . . and the guest house . . .'

'It's not that.'

'If you're bored with me—'

'Not at all.' She linked her arm through his. 'Honestly, Kit.'

'Tell me, then.'

They began to walk back down the hill. She said, 'I had a letter from an old friend.'

He paused, putting his head to one side, looking at her. 'Nice things, letters, on the whole.'

'Yes. It was a perfectly nice letter.'

'And . . . ?'

'He wants to see me.'

'And you don't want to see him?'

'It's not that exactly.'

He looked at her more closely. 'An old friend . . . or a lover?'

She remembered the parties, the rows of coloured

lights glittering on Owlscote's terrace. 'Just a friend. He was a good friend, once.'

Kit was silent, waiting for her to go on. The wind buffeted her. She remembered, too, how she had felt five years ago, when she had received Derry's other letter, the letter that had told her that he had sailed to South America. Her utter disbelief and bewilderment. The realization that he had not loved her as she had loved him. And how, to begin with, she had expected Derry to return to England within six weeks, six months, a year . . . And how the years had since piled up, one upon the other.

She explained, 'He went away, you see, without telling me. Something awful happened, and he couldn't bear it, and he went away. And now he's written to me.'

'How long was he away for?'

'Five years.'

She heard Kit whistle. 'I see what you mean. Bit of a nerve, going off like that and then just turning up and expecting to pick up where you've left off.'

'It's just that I've got used to him not being there. I've put the past behind me.' She dug her hands into her pockets. 'That's always the best thing to do, isn't it, Kit? Move on. Start again.'

He had turned away, so that she could not see the expression on his face. 'You don't have to see this chap, Alix,' he said. 'If you don't want to see him, then you don't have to.'

She began to walk down the hill. 'I think I do though, Kit. I think I have to see him just once. For old times' sake, if nothing else.'

Alix wrote to Derry, suggesting they meet in London. He met her at Waterloo Station. Walking down the platform, hemmed in by the swarm of passengers alighting from the train, she saw him standing at the barrier. She was glad of those few moments of privacy as she walked up the platform: to observe him unobserved.

They kissed and exchanged pleasantries, their voices raised over the clattering footsteps and the scream of the engines. They agreed that each other was unchanged; she acknowledged, silently, that they deceived each other. He was stronger, older, and there was a leanness about his face and a weariness in his eyes that had not been there before.

They lunched in a quiet restaurant near the Embankment. Derry told Alix about South America, and then he asked after her family.

'Rory's weekly boarding now. He goes to school in Winchester.'

'How old is he now?'

'He's ten. Eleven in December. He's only a head shorter than me, and he looks more like Edward every day. He's terribly good at science – I can't think where he gets it from.'

'Not another archaeologist, then?'

'Rory thinks history is hopelessly boring,' Alix said ruefully. 'He adores cars and motor-cycles, things like that. I send him to this dreadfully expensive school, but I sometimes think he'll end up as a garage mechanic.'

Derry smiled. 'How's your mother?'

'Rather fragile, I'm afraid.' She said stiffly, 'I'm so sorry about your father, Derry. It must have been an awful shock.'

Derry frowned. 'The poor blighter worked himself to death, keeping the bloody business going. Even though I sent home enough—' He broke off. 'And poor Mother's just rather bewildered. After all, it was always Mother who was delicate, and yet Dad died first.' He had put down his knife and fork. 'Anyway, Mother's got poor old Jon running around after her. As far as Jon *can* run around.'

'Derry—'

'Oh, Jon's fine. Better than I thought he'd be. Planning to keep the firm going.' He muttered, 'It's just that I won't ever get used to it.'

'Jon's doing well, Derry.' Alix tried to reassure him. 'He came to Owlscote not long ago, and we walked for hours. He almost wore me out.' She saw him smile fleetingly. 'And when you remember how pessimistic the surgeons were at first . . . He's so much better than everyone feared he might be.'

And yet she knew that the other Jonathan, the golden Jonathan who had sprinted and swum and played tennis with skill and elegance, had gone for ever. The Jonathan who now visited Owlscote was slower, older, different.

Derry voiced her thoughts. 'He's changed, of course. He's become . . . darker. Or perhaps he was always like that underneath, and I just didn't see it.' There was a silence. Then he said, 'When I was away I missed you, Alix.'

'Did you?' Her tone was non-committal.

'I didn't come and see you before I left because—' He stopped, shaking his head. 'Unpardonable, I know.'

'I expect you were busy,' she said lightly. 'Packing. Buying sunhats and mosquito nets and quinine—'

'Alix—'

'—arranging shipping – hotels – that sort of thing.'

'To tell the truth, I didn't come and see you before I sailed, because I knew that if I did, you'd tell me that I was going away to escape from Jon.'

There was a small silence. 'And were you?'

'It was partly that. And – and I had to make something of myself.'

She looked at him properly for the first time, noting his well-cut suit and gold cufflinks. For one small, painful moment she remembered why she had, years ago, fallen in love with him. She thought, looking away, he stirs things up. That is his *métier*, to pick things apart and stir things up.

'And you, Alix?' he said. 'How are you? Are you still running the guest house?'

'We've a dozen rooms now. I opened up the two little box-rooms. And I teach drawing. To make up for not having the parties.'

'In South America, I used to think about the parties.' The corners of Derry's mouth curled in a smile. 'When it was unbearably hot and you could hardly breathe for the humidity, I'd imagine the terrace at Owlscote. In the early morning, at dawn. Guests wandering about on the frosty lawn. Do you remember?'

She could see it in her mind's eye, the weary couples leaning against each other, shadowed by the grey darkness of the box hedges. A sparkle of diamante headband and a swirl of brightly coloured feather boa among all the monochrome.

'The ghosts and ghouls party . . . heaving all those awful dusty skulls out of the attic—'

'The Chinese party,' he said. 'That wretched cardboard bridge . . . Some idiot insisted on standing on it, and fell in the lake.'

'And then everyone decided to go for a swim.'

'Kimonos all over the lawn . . .'

'My mother was so shocked . . .' Remembering the expression on Beatrice's face, Alix giggled.

'And Roma was furious about the bridge. She'd spent hours painting it, and wanted to hire it out to Lawrence's ballet company as a prop.'

'Cooking that awful haggis for the Scottish party . . . The beastly things burst.'

'It was fun, wasn't it?'

Looking at him, she caught the expression in his eyes, and no longer wanted to laugh. There was a silence, and then he said, 'I thought I might come back to find you married, Alix. A brood of children.'

She shook her head. She knew that their fleeting intimacy had been an illusion, nothing more than a shadow of their former friendship.

'There must have been suitors, though.'

'One or two.' She thought of Kit: pale, feline Kit.

'And now?'

She looked down at her plate. 'There is someone.'

'Ah.' Nothing more. Just *ah*, and a slight hardening about the eyes. And then he changed the subject.

'Has Roma told you that we're going into business together?'

Alix shook her head. Derry belonged to the past, she thought. After they parted that afternoon, their paths would rarely cross again. He had become a slight acquaintance, someone of little importance in her life.

She heard him say, 'I've been looking for premises. You wouldn't believe how difficult it is to find the right place . . .'

CHAPTER ELEVEN

May Lanchbury was making tea in the kitchen of her flat. Her sisters were sitting in the adjacent room. May found the sugar tongs and carried the tray into the drawing-room. Ella had telephoned the previous week to arrange to stay for a few days, and Daisy had turned up unexpectedly half an hour ago, puffy-eyed and wearing, May guessed as she looked critically at her younger sister, the frock in which she had gone out the previous evening.

'Sugar?' May offered the bowl.

Ella shook her head; Daisy scrabbled in the sugar basin and dropped four cubes from too great a height into the cup. Tea slopped onto the saucer.

'What a surprise to see you here, Ella,' said Daisy. 'You never come to London.'

'I had to buy dress material.' The bed in May's spare room bore lengths of tweed in the dark, murky colours that Ella favoured.

Daisy turned to look at Ella. Ella's grey flannel jarred beside Daisy's crumpled chartreuse silk. Daisy, chewing a lock of her untidy silver-fair hair, looked round anxiously.

'Papa isn't here, is he?'

'Papa's in Germany just now,' said May. 'That's why Ella took the opportunity to visit.'

'I'll have to go home tomorrow.' Ella was sitting bolt upright. In the sunlight that issued through the open window, her ash-blonde hair appeared faded and dull. Ella had almost turned thirty: the realization, and the resolute drabness of Ella's appearance, made May feel suddenly sad.

'I thought Papa was taking you to Germany, Ella,' said Daisy. 'I thought, at Christmas, you said you were going away with him.'

Ella's skin, always pale, lost its remaining colour. She said stiffly, 'Papa would have liked to take me to Germany, but there was too much for me to do at home. He says he will take me next year.' Since Charles Lanchbury's unsuccessful attempt to stand for Parliament in 1929, Ella had acted as her father's secretary, as well as his housekeeper.

'So awful for you. You should stay with Pip and me. Not now though, because we're having the drawing-room redecorated. Olive and cream and orange – so chic, don't you think? So beastly for you to be stuck in that horrid cold house, Ella, and—'

Daisy broke off. Ella had stood up, and was buttoning her jacket. 'I'm going out,' she said to May, 'to see a friend.' She did not look at Daisy. The front door slammed as she left the house.

Daisy looked bewildered. 'Did I annoy her? I was trying to be nice to her.'

'Ella is fearfully upset because Papa has gone to Germany without her. She was certain he'd take her.'

'*Oh*. I can't imagine anything worse than having to go on holiday with Papa, can you, May?' Daisy giggled. 'Anyway, good riddance to her. She makes me nervous, and then I say the wrong thing. So it's not my fault, is it?' She looked down at the tea tray, and added plaintively, 'Haven't you any cake, May? I'm absolutely starving.'

May shook her head. 'I'm dieting.' She glanced at Daisy. Slender, fragile limbs protruded from the creased silk of her dress. 'I could make you a jam sandwich, though, if you like.'

'*May*. You're a darling.'

May made the sandwich, and Daisy ate it quickly and messily, dripping jam over the front of her frock. May poured herself another cup of tea (no milk, just lemon, which would make up for the crusts she had nibbled in the kitchen), and said, 'You look as though you haven't eaten for days.'

'Not since' – Daisy scowled – 'not since last night. I didn't have a thing this morning.'

May glanced at Daisy's enviably flat stomach. 'Daisy, are you . . . ?'

'Preggers? Good lord, I hope not.' Daisy looked alarmed, and then she laughed. 'I'm sure I'm not. But I was out, you see, and busy, and we forgot breakfast.'

'You and Pip?' But May, looking at Daisy's dress (last night's *surely*) guessed her sister's reply before Daisy shook her head.

'Not *Pip*.'

'*Daisy*.'

'Don't look at me like that, May. Everyone does it. You know *that*. And Pip's being mean to me.'

'What do you expect?' May glanced at the clock. Almost four. She had work to do. She felt exasperated. 'You could at least be discreet.'

'He hit me, you see, May.'

May, who had begun mentally to compose her

description of the previous night's charity ball, was jolted back to the present. 'Hit you?'

'So I had to pay him back.' Daisy smiled. 'Blackie Barlow took me to see a wrestling match. It was the most marvellous fun.'

'Did he hurt you?' May pushed away her teacup; she felt sick.

Daisy began to undo the front buttons of her gown. She was, May saw, naked beneath the chartreuse silk. A bruise, which had begun to turn from pink to purple, flowered across her thin ribs.

'Does he hit you often?' May's voice shook.

'Oh no. Hardly at all.' Daisy looked at May. 'It doesn't *matter*, May. He just lost his temper. I expect it was my fault. He'll be sorry today.' She smiled. 'Pip'll be nice and buy me flowers and diamonds and all sorts of lovely things, and then we'll be friends again and everything will be all right.'

May wanted to explain to Daisy why it did matter, and why it couldn't possibly be her fault, and why all the flowers in the world wouldn't make it all right, but, looking at Daisy's sweet, uncomprehending face, she said instead: 'There's always a place for you here, Daisy. If Pip hurts you again, you must come and stay with me.' Though Daisy would, she knew, drive her to distraction within a week.

Daisy hugged her. 'Silly,' she said. 'There's no need for that. Pip and I love each other madly. And lots of married couples fight. Didn't you know that, May?' Her pretty face broke into a smile. 'Ella should marry, don't you think? Then she'd be less of a sourpuss. Only can you imagine what sort of man would want to marry Ella? Only the most awful old stick.' Daisy scooped up jam from the front of her dress, and licked her fingers. 'What about you, May? Any admirers?'

'There's someone at the paper,' May admitted. 'We go to the ballet together.'

'Is he terribly handsome and dashing?'

'He's called Cyril and he's a widower, and he has a daughter who's at boarding-school. And he's very kind and sweet.'

Daisy made a face. 'He sounds so *dull*, May. And . . . *Cyril*! Such a frightful name. Isn't there anyone else?'

May found herself thinking of Derry Fox. She and Derry had fallen into the habit of having a drink together once a fortnight or so. She knew that he was not in regular contact with her cousin, Alix North, whom he had once loved.

She said slowly, 'Perhaps . . . I'm not sure yet. I hope that there might be.'

It's our village fête. I've promised to help with the teas. Could you bear it, Jonathan? It's bit of an ordeal, I'm afraid. Tears over who wins the sack race.

Over the summer, Jonathan had visited Polly's family once a month or so. Polly had issued the invitation the previous weekend. She had added, 'I'm afraid we need help with the white elephant and the coconut stalls. You choose, Jonathan. I'd recommend the coconuts – the white elephants tend to be very musty.'

He chose the coconuts. Stephen, Polly's youngest brother, ran around collecting balls and balancing coconuts on stands, while Jonathan took the money and adjudicated. Stephen was brown-haired and blue-eyed, like Polly, like each of his four brothers. Each of the six Daniels siblings, Jonathan had decided when first he had met them, looked as though they had been shelled from the same pod.

At four o'clock Polly appeared with a cup of tea. 'How's it going?'

'Splendidly. A carter from Ragged Appleshaw appears every now and then and fells all five coconuts. I shan't have any left if he turns up again, and I'll be able to shut up shop.'

'Are you very bored, Jon?'

'Not at all. I can't think of a nicer way of spending an afternoon.' It was true: the vicarage garden, in which the fête was held, was charming, and there was something delightful and pleasant about the late summer sunshine, the murmur of conversation, and the click of wooden ball against coconut.

When the fête was over Jonathan helped clear away the debris, and then sat down to supper with the Daniels family. Henry Daniels, Polly's father, talked to Jonathan about fishing ('You must spend a morning with me, Jonathan. Next weekend, perhaps. I think of all my best sermons when I'm sitting on the bank of the Avon'). During pudding, a noisy argument developed about the National Government and the Means Test, with all Polly's brothers talking at once and gesturing wildly with pudding spoons. Then William and Patrick washed up, and Polly's father disappeared into his study, and Stephen and John went to look at Leonard's recently acquired motor-car. Jonathan gathered up his coat and hat.

'Won't you stay the night?' asked Polly. 'There's a spare room.'

'I can't, I'm afraid. I must go home, or Mother will worry.'

'I'm so glad you came. And I'm sorry about the noise at teatime.'

'That didn't matter at all. I enjoyed the company. I

don't go out much now,' he explained. 'Years ago, there was the tennis club, things like that – but since the accident—' He broke off, realizing that he was in danger of sounding self-pitying.

Polly was tidying the heap of coats and hats on the hall stand. 'I remember, when my mother died, thinking my life had been cut in two. That nothing that happened afterwards had much to do with anything that had gone before. Of course, I didn't think that way for long – there was Dad and the boys to look after, so there wasn't time to dwell on things – but I imagine your accident must have felt much the same.'

Jonathan shrugged on his coat. 'At first I thought I was going to die, and then when I realized I wasn't, I felt very angry, because I *wanted* to die.'

'And then . . . ?' she prompted gently.

A quick exhalation of breath. 'And then there were all the things I couldn't do – I couldn't even *walk* to begin with – which made me even angrier. I'd always been good at games, you see – cricket and tennis – anything – had all been so easy. I'd taken it for granted, I suppose – and to have that taken away from me . . . I'd have given up,' Jonathan said, 'if it hadn't been for Derry.' He smiled, remembering. 'He insisted I do things – get out of bed, dress myself, walk to the door, all that – when I didn't feel capable of anything. If I just sat there feeling sorry for myself he was hideously sarcastic. I remember wanting to hit him, but I couldn't move fast enough.'

'Do you still feel angry?'

'Sometimes,' he admitted. 'After such a narrow squeak in the war – I nearly lost my leg in a mortar attack – so to end up like this anyway . . . *and* it was my own bloody fault. Sorry, Polly. I suppose I should be thankful to be alive.'

She frowned severely. 'I've always especially loathed that school of thought. You know, the be-thankful-for-small-mercies and every-cloud-has-a-silver-lining one. As a vicar's daughter I've had a lot of that inflicted on me, so don't you start.' She patted his hand. 'You curse and swear as much as you like, Jonathan dear. I certainly did when my mother died. I remember that I didn't look at Stephen for a week – I blamed him, you see. Then my father left me alone in the house with him one afternoon, and he cried, so I had to go to him, and I fell in love with him, of course. Which was what Dad had intended all along. And now, if I've got a favourite, it's Stephen. But I still don't fall for that silver lining nonsense. It was a rotten thing to happen.' Polly looked at Jonathan. 'It must be very quiet at home with just your mother and you.'

'Sometimes,' he said savagely, 'I can hear the clock ticking.' He got hold of himself. 'But Derry visits, of course, and I go and see Alix whenever I can.' Suddenly, he smiled. 'Do you know, Polly, I used to wonder whether there was something between Alix and Derry. Of course, when he went away, I realized I'd got the wrong end of the stick. It's a pity, because I can't think of anyone I'd rather Derry married, but I suppose, with being widowed – and Rory – Alix thinks—' He broke off, seeing her face.

'What is it?'

Polly just said, '*Jonathan.*'

He felt bewildered. She placed her hand on his, and said gently, 'Jonathan, *of course* they were madly in love with each other.'

'*Oh.*' He struggled to arrange his thoughts. 'And now?'

'And now – I don't know.'

'This other chap . . . Kit . . . ?'

'She's still seeing him.' Polly looked at Jonathan. 'She seems keen on him, Jon.'

Jonathan frowned. 'Alix and Derry – how dense of me – I should speak to him, perhaps . . .' Jonathan felt exasperated with himself. 'Who should marry whom – I never seem to have a clue about that sort of thing.'

He saw her looking at him, and did not quite understand the expression on her face. Then he caught sight of the clock.

'Almost nine – I must go. Polly, *thank you* for a lovely day.' He held out his hand, and was both surprised and delighted when, ignoring it, she hugged him instead.

Alix found Rory in the shed, sawing a length of wood.

'Kit and I are driving to Salisbury. Would you like to come, Rory?'

'Where are you going? Not more boring shops?'

'I'm afraid so,' she admitted. 'It's the summer sales, and I have to get towels and things.'

'Yuk. I'd rather stay here, Mum. I'm making a mast for the boat. It'll be much better with sails.'

She watched him for a while, dragging the heavy saw through the narrow wooden pole, and then she said: 'You do like Kit, don't you, Rory?'

'He's all right.' Rory put aside the saw and began to rummage through a jar of nails. 'He's got a smashing car.'

He said nothing more, so Alix supposed she would have to be content with that. She kissed the top of his head. 'I'll be off then. And you'll be careful with the saw, won't you, Rory? And the hammer.'

'*Mum—*'

'And you won't take the boat onto the lake while I'm not here, will you?'

'Mum, don't *fuss* – I can swim—'

'Promise me, Rory.' Reluctantly, he promised.

Kit drove her to Salisbury. Emerging from the drapers', Alix thankfully unloaded an armload of table-cloths and bedlinen into the back of his car.

'You should have let me come in with you.'

'It was a battleground, Kit. You'd have been trampled to death. Fearsome ladies in tweed suits and forbidding hats hacking a path through the fray with their hand-bags.' She smiled at him. 'I'd love a cup of tea, though.'

They left the car in the Market Square, and walked to the Copper Kettle. It was market day, and Salisbury was crowded. Alix told Kit about the holiday she was planning to take.

'I've rented a cottage in Cornwall. Mother can sit in the garden, and Rory and I can visit Tintagel. He loves anything Arthurian – I gave him Edward's old *Morte d'Arthur*, and he read it in a couple of evenings.'

They were walking along Minster Street when there was a shout from the far side of the road. 'Christopher! Hey – Chris!'

Alix saw Kit glance across. Then he took her arm, and steered her away from the pavement, veering abruptly left along Butcher Row.

'I've just remembered that I had to wait hours to be served last time I had tea in the Copper Kettle. We'll go to Annie's instead.'

'That man . . .' She was slightly out of breath, hurrying to keep pace with him. 'Across the road – did you know him?'

He looked down at her, and his face broke into his now-familiar, charming wide-eyed smile. 'I'm afraid so. He's the most frightful bore. Do you mind that I dragged you away?' She saw him glance quickly over his shoulder.

'Not at all.' They had reached the teashop; Kit opened the door for her. '*Christopher*,' she said. 'I've never thought of you as a Christopher.'

They dawdled over tea and crumpets. Kit was, as ever, amusing and attentive, but Alix noticed that he seemed distracted, his smile a fraction slower than usual, his gaze darting every now and then to the window. She thought how little, after four months' acquaintance, she knew about him. That he had no family, that he had gone to public school and then to Oxford, that he owned a cottage in Scotland but lived there only infrequently, preferring to roam around the countryside. That he liked motor-cars, and old houses, and Impressionist paintings. That his parents' legacy allowed him to indulge his whims, and allowed him also, she guessed, to evade a settled sort of life. He had never introduced her to any of his friends; though he had mentioned colleagues in London, she had never met a single one.

She thought of him as a sort of gypsy. She did not question his desire for privacy; she, after all, had for a long time hidden even from those closest to her the events of the early part of her life. She thought that Kit's reticence was compounded of a mixture of courage and sorrow, the consequence of his early losses. Thinking of that small boy at boarding school, summoned to the headmaster's study to learn of the death of his parents, she reached across the table and squeezed his hand.

He said, 'Shall we go?'

They drove back towards Owlscote. There was a place where the tunnel of trees thickened, and a path spurred off into the woodland. Slowing the car, Kit swung up the path, parking in the shelter of the beech trees.

He climbed out of the car, and Alix followed him into the dark cavern of the wood. The forest floor, carpeted with beech mast and dog's mercury, curved upwards to form one side of the valley. The silvery trunks of the beeches soared above them, topped with a canopy of emerald leaves. He began to kiss her, his mouth exploring her face, her neck, and the hollow of her collar bones with an urgency she had not previously encountered. Her frock slipped to the ground, a fragile thing of white cotton and pink roses against the coppery leaves. He bent and kissed her breasts, and when he took her nipple into his mouth, she shut her eyes, almost faint with the ecstasy of it. So long, she thought, so long since I have known this pleasure. She remembered Edward, and the desert, and the stars, shining diamonds against the endless darkness. Then, as Kit drew her down to the forest floor, she was aware of nothing except his body against hers. Opening herself for him, welcoming him, the wave of pleasure overcame her, drawing him in, until he, too, shuddered, and then rolled away from her, his lips apart, one arm still around her, the other bent across his face as though he was sheltering his eyes from the shafts of sunlight that stabbed through the leaves.

She heard eventually, in the distance, the bark of a dog. She sat up, pulling her dress back on as a black and white spaniel broke through the undergrowth and scampered down the slope of the valley. Kit, too, rearranged his clothing. As the spaniel's owner came into sight, she thought that their intimacy, their complicity, must be plain to anyone who saw them. But the dog's owner just murmured a 'Good afternoon', and raised his stick, and walked on as Alix and Kit struggled to stifle their giggles.

Kit offered her a cigarette. Alix shook her head and combed the beech mast out of her hair with her fingers as he smoked.

'I'm never quite sure, Alix,' he said slowly, 'how you feel about me. This afternoon – this afternoon has been wonderful, of course. You've made me so happy. But – well, most of the time we're lucky if we see each other once a week.'

'There's the guest house,' she reminded him, 'and Rory.'

'I know. But we've known each other for almost six months. I've tried not to rush you, Alix, but . . .' His face had a slightly bruised, defenceless expression.

She began, 'You know that I'm fond of you, Kit—' but he interrupted her.

'*Fond* . . . Weasel words, Alix.'

There was a silence. He said, more gently, 'Is there someone else?'

'Of course not.'

'That chap . . . the one you met in London a couple of months ago. What about him?'

She had neither seen nor heard from Derry Fox since that afternoon. She thought of the various men she had dated during the last five years. She wondered whether she had deceived herself, and whether she had found fault with them because she had, unconsciously or otherwise, compared them to Derry and found them wanting.

If she had, she thought, then she had been a fool. She looked at Kit. 'Derry means nothing to me now, Kit,' she said. 'Nothing at all.'

His eyes lightened. He stubbed his cigarette out in the soil. 'I want to see more of you, Alix. I adore you. I want to be with you morning, afternoon and night – I'll do whatever it takes. Do you understand?' His eyes gleamed, vivid and intense, as he took her hands in his, and kissed her fingertips, one by one.

They celebrated the signing of the lease for the shop with a bottle of champagne in Roma's flat. Jonathan, who had carried out the legal work, joined in the celebrations.

Jonathan raised his glass. 'To . . .' He paused, frowning. 'What are you calling the place? *Roma's*, I suppose.'

'*Storm*,' said Roma. 'Much more stylish. Silver lettering on a black background.' She smiled.

'When do you hope to open?'

'Next month,' said Derry.

'Bit of a rush.'

'We're losing money all the time we're not open.'

In the hall, the telephone rang. 'That could be Caroline,' said Roma. 'Excuse me.'

She left the room. Jonathan, looking at Derry, said, 'Have you seen Alix?'

'Just the once. When she came to London.'

'You haven't been to Owlscote?'

A shake of the head. Everything about Derry's demeanour warned Jonathan not to continue. But, leaping in feet first, he said: 'I thought you were *fond* of her.'

Derry glanced up sharply. 'That was a long time ago.'

'You don't care for her any more?'

He saw Derry frown. 'It's not that. There's someone else, you see.'

'I know,' said Jonathan. 'Kit. Polly doesn't think much of him.'

He had Derry's attention now. 'Have you met him, Jon?'

'Just once. When I picked Polly up from Owlscote.'
Jonathan shrugged. 'He seemed a nice enough chap.'

'I'm glad,' said Derry. He turned aside, and lit a cigarette. Jonathan knew that every movement, every gesture, was intended to convey to him that the subject was closed.

From the hall, he could hear the rise and fall of Roma's voice. Jonathan felt a surge of impatience. 'Have you told Alix you still care for her?'

Derry had gone white about the mouth. 'That's none of your business, surely, Jon.'

He persevered. 'Only, if you haven't told her, then perhaps she doesn't know.'

'If she's seeing someone—'

'She was terribly low after you went away, Derry. Polly told me, and besides, I noticed it myself.'

Derry's entire body had become taut. Jonathan thought he might just walk out of the room. He could almost hear the door slam.

But instead Derry bent his head and groaned, and ran his hands through his hair, and after a while he looked up, and said, 'I've left it too late, haven't I?' His eyes were bleak.

Jonathan said gently, 'It's worth another shot, surely, Derry?'

A silence. Then, 'Perhaps.'

'Only' – and Jonathan remembered Polly saying, *She seems keen on him* – 'don't leave it too long, will you, old chap?'

Over the summer months, Derry had begun to despair of finding shop premises that were not either too small, too big, or far too expensive. Then a friend had mentioned the place for sale in a side street off Campden

Hill. Derry, visiting, had found the rooms to be small and narrow, but with plenty of natural light and scope for improvement. There was a shop and an office and space for storage. When he had taken Roma there, her eyes had lit up, and she had whispered, 'Perfect. It's perfect, Derry.'

The search for the shop, all the rest of the work involved in setting up a business, the purchase of a flat and a motor-car, had fully occupied the months since he had lunched with Alix. He had not brooded, he had not pined. He needed to make a success of *Storm*. Yet sometimes, alone in his flat in the evenings, or walking through London's dusty streets, he had thought of Alix, and there had been that small, painful twist to his heart, an acknowledgement of unsaid words, unfinished business.

Now, walking home from Roma's flat, Derry recalled Jonathan's clumsy, well-meaning attempt to intervene. His brother's words echoed in the darkness. *Polly doesn't think much of him.* And, *Don't leave it too long, will you, old chap?*

Derry found himself questioning his own motives in staying away from Alix. Was he merely trying to avoid further pain and humiliation? Had he, meeting Alix earlier in the year, explained things properly to her? Or had he, as Jonathan had suggested, allowed her simply to go on thinking that he did not love her, had never loved her?

He recalled the silences, the evasions of that conversation. He wondered whether Jonathan was right. One last shot. And besides, he thought, smiling to himself in the darkness, he had nothing much to lose.

Derry left London early the next morning. It rained until he crossed the Hampshire border. The first autumn leaves were tossed from the trees by the gusty wind, adhering like copper pennies to the windscreen of the car.

By the time Derry reached Owlscote the wind had got up, blowing the clouds away, and the sun had come out. The tyres of his car churned up puddles in the driveway. Parking in the courtyard, he sat for a moment, looking up at the house, and then he climbed out, slamming the door behind him.

Polly Daniels answered his knock, and directed him to the garden. At the back of the house, he stood still for a moment, watching Alix at the washing-line, wrestling with wet, flapping sheets and tablecloths. Then he crossed the lawn to her.

'Let me help,' he said. 'Or you'll sail off like a kite over Salisbury.'

Seeing him, she gasped. He pinned down the sheet with pegs. He heard her say, '*Derry*.'

'I'm sorry for turning up like this. I know you're busy, Alix. Can you spare a moment or two?'

She was silent, staring at him, and then she said, 'Of course.' Her long, dark hair was tangled by the wind, so she tucked it behind her ears.

'Shall we walk?'

They headed down to the lake. Alix was wearing a red skirt and navy-blue jacket. She dug her hands deep into the pockets of the jacket as they walked, and did not look at him.

He heard her say, 'Why have you come here, Derry?'

'Because there were things I should have said to you when we spoke before. And I wanted to say them now.'

They had reached the lake. The shaggy seed-heads of the reeds trembled in the breeze. She remained silent, so he took a deep breath.

'I realize what you must have thought when I went away. You were right to be angry with me. I can see how it must have looked.'

She whispered, 'So sudden, Derry . . .'

'You must have thought that I didn't care for you. That I'd never cared for you. Damn it' – he almost spat the words out – 'had never *loved* you.'

'You shouldn't say these things.' She had turned her face away, and she sounded cold, distant.

'Oh, I think that I should. I think that I should have said them a long time ago.'

There was a silence. He saw her snap one of the reed-heads, tearing the seeds off, crumbling them between her fingers.

'You see, I felt that I had nothing to give you.'

She turned to face him at last. 'I didn't want you to *give* me anything, Derry.'

'I meant . . .' He tried to explain. 'You have *this*.' His gesture encompassed the lake, the house, the grounds. 'And I had nothing.'

'That didn't matter to me.'

Another silence. The wind made ripples of the surface of the lake. Derry stared across the water. 'After what happened to Jon, I hated myself, Alix. I had to go away, start again. *You* may not have minded about the differences between us, but I did. I had to . . . even things up.'

'And did you?' Her voice, small and chill, echoed.

'I think so.'

She began to walk again, her shoes leaving small indentations in the muddy perimeter of the lake. He called after her, 'I know that you have every right to be angry with me . . .'

She stopped, turning and looking at him. 'I'm not angry with you, Derry.'

'Then—'

'But we can't just take up where we left off. It simply isn't possible.'

There were the beginnings of pain, raw and unwelcome, flowering in his heart. Mutely, he looked at her.

'I'm sorry, Derry, but we just can't.' The wind whipped her hair against her face. 'I am engaged to be married, you see. I'm engaged to be married to Kit Crawford.'

Derry went back to London. With Roma, he worked night and day to make ready the shop for opening. He had thought that work would take his mind off things, that it would erase the memory of Alix saying, *I am engaged to be married to Kit Crawford*, but it did not, and, helping to put up shelves, or poring over ledger books, he would find that the minutes had drifted by and he had not seen the numbers on the page, but had instead envisaged Alix's face: her green eyes sparking with anger, her hair blown about by the wind.

They gave a party to celebrate the opening of *Storm*. The shop, which was black and pale gold and ochre, was crowded. The *pop* of champagne bottles echoed against the high ceiling, and couples mingled, shoulder to shoulder, amid the rugs and lamps and vases. A hundred people crammed into the long, narrow room.

A hand touched Derry's elbow. Looking round, he saw May Lanchbury.

'You look tired, my dear vulture. And as though you're not really enjoying yourself.'

He bent to kiss her cheek. 'I'll enjoy it more now that you're here, May.'

'I can't stay long, actually. I came to tell you that I'm going away for a while.'

He led her away from the chatter and music, into the little back room that served as an office.

'A holiday?'

'In a way. I'm going to France, Derry.'

He looked at her. He remembered their conversation earlier in the year. 'Not Le Touquet, this time, May?'

'I'm travelling to Picardy.'

'You're going to visit your grandmother?'

'Yes.'

'And to look for Charlie?'

'I haven't told anyone else I'm going, Derry. We don't talk about Charlie, you see. Papa can't even bear to hear his name.' May looked up at him. 'Do you think I'm being foolish?'

'Not at all. One shouldn't put off following one's dreams.' He knew that he sounded bitter.

'Derry, what is it?'

'Nothing.' He tried to smile. 'It's been a long month. I need a break, I suppose.'

She peered back into the shop. 'I wondered . . . I wondered whether Cousin Alix would be here.'

He shook his head. Suddenly she touched his arm. 'Come with me, Derry. Come to France.'

'Can't, May. I'm sorry. The business . . .'

'Of course.' She smiled. 'Silly of me.'

She began to gather up her bag and gloves. Derry remembered the suppliers he should visit in Paris and Brussels. And he thought how much he needed to get away, if only for a little while.

'Northern France, you said?'

May was opening the door. She swung round. 'Derry . . . ?' Her pale eyes brightened.

'I wouldn't want to be in your way . . . Family reunions . . .'

'You speak French, don't you, Derry?'

'Of course.'

'My French is rather terrible,' she explained. 'Strictly from the schoolroom.'

'I imagined that your mother—'

'I don't think Mama ever spoke French to us. So, though I'm awfully good at the *plume de ma tante*, train timetables and hotel rooms can be a bit of a battle.' She touched his hand. 'Do you mean it, Derry? Would you come to France with me?'

He thought of crossing the Channel; the cold salt air, and the certain and unalterable excitement of another country.

'I'd love to,' he said.

Jonathan called at Owlscote one evening to thank Polly for the fête and the supper. He took her a huge bunch of snapdragons and asters gathered from his garden. She was making crab-apple jelly, and the kitchen was over-flowing with Kilner jars and muslin and vats of bubbling apple pulp. He helped her spoon the apple into the muslin bag, and label the jars when they were full of coral-coloured jelly. Afterwards, she made sweet omelettes, light and foamy and oozing with jam. It surprised Jonathan to look up at the clock, and see that it was almost midnight: odd, he thought, that the hours could pass so quickly.

The memory of that evening lingered through the remainder of the week, so that, enclosed with a client or listening to his mother's worries about her health, Jonathan found his mind drifting to a recollection of Polly, dripping apple juice onto a saucer to test its set, or frowning as she glued the labels to the jars. The sweet scent of the boiled apples seemed to linger on his clothes, his skin. At the end of one particularly distracted morning, he hastily scribbled a note suggesting Polly accompany him to a piano recital on Friday evening.

After the concert, she invited him to Sunday lunch at the vicarage. Jonathan made tortuous and deceitful plans, arranging for one of his mother's friends to issue an invitation for whist and afternoon tea. When at mid-morning he headed out of Andover, his mother's voice echoed in his ears. '*Jon*. Sunday *lunch*. Our special time . . .'

An enormous lunch, a walk by the river, and a game of French cricket with Stephen and Polly (you didn't have to run to play French cricket) drove most of the guilt out of his head. After tea, Polly and her father washed up, and Stephen asked Jonathan to help him mend his bicycle.

'The brakes don't work, and Poll's convinced I'm going to brain myself.'

'It helps', Jonathan said as he fiddled with blocks and cables, 'to have brakes.'

'Bicycles are so slow. I'd like to drive a motor car. I wish Leonard lived nearer so that I could drive his motor. Though,' Stephen scowled, 'he probably wouldn't let me.'

'Why not?' Jonathan peered at the bicycle. 'I think that this is the difficulty, Stephen old chap. The cable's loose.'

'They all think I'm an idiot. Just because I'm the youngest.' Stephen pushed back his floppy brown fringe with an oily hand. 'When you and Polly are married, Jonathan, will you teach me to drive?'

There was a silence, filled only by the distant sounds of a dog barking, and someone trying to tune in a wireless.

Stephen, suddenly realizing what he had said, went red. 'It's just that Leonard and William both think—' He broke off.

'Leonard and William . . . ?' repeated Jonathan, looking severely at Stephen. 'And John and Patrick, I suppose?'

'Not *John*. John doesn't notice things like that. Oh lord.' Stephen stared at Jonathan. 'You're not cross, are you? It's just that it's about time Poll got married – and some of the chaps she's dated in the past were the most frightful asses, and . . . you're not cross, are you, Jonathan?'

'Stephen,' said Jonathan gently. 'I'm not cross at all.' He rose from his seat, and looked down at Polly's youngest brother. 'All I'd suggest is that when you're considering your future career, whatever you do, you don't attempt the Diplomatic Corps.'

He walked across the lawn. It was evening; he knew that he must go home soon. There was an area of the Daniels' garden he particularly liked, where the cultivated part dissolved into wilderness and weeds. He stood among the ragwort and poppy-heads and long grass. His leg ached, but he did not notice it.

He looked back over the past six months, and saw that all the moments when he had been happiest – the moments that shone like diamonds – had been spent with Polly. Making crab-apple jelly, searching for eggs, or just sitting and talking in the kitchen at Owlscote. He tried, and failed, to remember the first time he had met Polly. At Owlscote, surely, when he had been engaged to Edith. He supposed that he had not noticed her then because his mind had been full of Edith Carr's smooth, perfect features and aquamarine eyes. He saw that his feelings for Polly were not the same as his feelings had once been for Edith. That he had somehow muddled up friendship and passion. He had believed Polly to be his friend, and Edith to be the object of his desire, whereas in fact it was the other way round. He had never particularly wanted to touch Edith. He had liked to watch her; he had, he had since realized, put her on a pedestal, and in doing so made her untouchable. Yet just the memory of Polly's warm hand in his made him shiver. He knew also that he would have loved her had she a spot on the end of her nose, had she taken to wearing pebble-lensed glasses. His need for perfection had gone, driven away by his enforced acceptance of his own vulnerability. He had learned to appreciate common sense, gentleness and compassion.

Jonathan glanced at his watch. Seven o'clock. Mother would be waiting for him. He walked back into the vicarage. Standing on the threshold of the kitchen, he saw that Polly was now alone, and that she was standing in front of the window, polishing glasses with a cloth. The light from the setting sun, through the window, turned her brown hair to gold. He crossed the room to her.

Throughout the year, Beatrice Gregory's health had been failing. Her bones ached and, climbing the stairs, she had to pause halfway and catch her breath. She could not attend church on Sunday unless Kit, or one of the parishioners, offered her a lift. Dr Arthur visited one afternoon and listened to Beatrice's chest, and muttered vaguely about rheumatism and the damp weather. Alix, looking at her mother's small, stooped frame, worried, and made sure there was always a fire lit in Beatrice's bedroom.

A succession of anxieties plagued her that autumn.

Rory broke his arm climbing a tree, and had to be taken to hospital to have it set in plaster. The paying guests seemed particularly querulous and demanding. They forgot to change their shoes when they came into the house, and left a trail of mud along the hall and stairs. They complained when their egg-yolks were the tiniest bit hard, or their toast a shade or two darker than it should have been.

These were minor niggles. Alix's growing certainty that one of the paying guests was a thief was a much greater worry. She noticed first that a Meissen shepherdess, one of a small collection that had once belonged to Edward's mother, was missing from the cabinet. Then, a few weeks later, dusting bookcases, she realized that a tiny Book of Hours, Owlscote's particular treasure, was no longer in the library. She had taken it out of the cupboard to show it to Kit a week or so earlier; she thought at first that she must have put it back in the wrong place, but, searching through every shelf, running her finger along the spine of each book, she was unable to find it.

Over the next few weeks, other small items disappeared. A Jacobean goblet, a Georgian candlestick. Alix wondered whether to telephone the police, but in the end decided not to. It would upset her mother, and would also be bad for the reputation of the guest house. Instead, she locked away everything that was small and valuable in a chest in her bedroom. And she watched the guests. She found herself becoming suspicious of them, seeing in their friendly smiles and casual conversation an ulterior motive. At night, she slept badly, part of her continually listening out for the creak of the stairs, or the sound of an invasive footstep along the passageway.

Her engagement to Kit remained a secret. 'Do you

mind, darling?' he had said. 'I'd love to tell the world, but I'm duty bound to break it gently to the people I know in Scotland. The old chap's set his heart on my marrying his youngest daughter, I'm afraid, and I don't want to hurt him. He's been like a father to me. You don't mind keeping things under wraps for a while, do you, darling?'

Alix had agreed, of course, and Kit had promised to travel to Scotland as soon as possible. Kit continued to visit frequently, and was attentive to her in every way. Yet over the ensuing weeks, Alix was aware of an increasing unease. One morning, Polly told her of her engagement to Jonathan. 'He's putting an announcement in the *Telegraph*. I think Jon would like to stand on the rooftops with a loudspeaker, and let the whole of Andover know we're engaged. Or broadcast it on the wireless.' Though she had hugged Polly, delighted and unsurprised that her two closest friends were to marry, Alix had been aware of a flicker of envy at Jon's obvious pride in Polly. That the nature of her own attachment to Kit remained undisclosed left her in a sort of limbo.

She had told only one person of her engagement: Derry Fox. She was reluctant to admit even to herself that Derry's visit to Owlscote had also unsettled her. After he had gone, she had found herself looking back, seeing clearly her own role in the failure of their relationship. In all the years they had known each other, she had never once told Derry that she loved him. The reticence that her early years had given her, and the habit she had acquired of holding a part of herself back, had lingered. When, five years earlier, Derry had written to her from South America, trying to explain his decision to go away, she, full of hurt and anger, had not even attempted to understand him.

Bruised by his absence, she had assumed a lack of love on his part.

And yet, and yet . . . Alix remembered travelling to Mesopotamia with Edward in 1919. The utter relief of putting Europe, with its burden of horrors – the war, and the loss of Charlie Lanchbury – behind her. She knew that Derry, five years ago, with the disaster of Jonathan and Edith close on his heels, had felt the same. And sometimes, waking in the night, she found herself comparing her love for Kit to the love she had once felt for first Edward and then for Derry, and finding it wanting.

It was better that way, she told herself firmly. Less frantic, less exhausting. She was thirty-two now, and she must put the seesawing passions of her youth behind her.

CHAPTER TWELVE

Derry and May took the steam ferry to Calais, and then a train to Amiens. Rising in the morning, Derry could see from the hotel window the lacework of canals and waterways that criss-crossed the town.

He hired a Citroën from a garage in the centre of Amiens, and drove north-west towards the Chateau Boncourt. May spoke little, but stared out of the window of the car. Monuments to the war dead littered the fields, and heaps of shrapnel were gathered in steel-grey pyramids at the sides of the road. Lines drawn on the earth showed where trenches had scarred the green meadowland. It had begun to drizzle and, gazing out through the windscreen, Derry could almost imagine that the blurred brownish-green trees on the skyline had become columns of men, marching across the horizon, and that the ploughs and carthorses that dotted the fields had fleetingly metamorphosed into field guns, mortars and a tangle of barbed wire. As they journeyed through the Picardy countryside, the succession of dreary hamlets began to depress him. The shabbiness of the buildings, and the cluttered ruins that indicated where homes, barns and farmhouses had once stood, weighed upon him. He found himself thinking of Jon, nineteen years old, enduring all this.

'Just here,' said May at last.

Derry pulled up at the side of the road. Dark hedgerows cut the house off from the surrounding fields. The roof of the chateau was patched with differently coloured tiles, and some of the chimney pots were broken.

May, looking out of the window, had become very still. She whispered, 'There were trees, tall trees. Poplars, I think. And the house was splendid . . .'

Broken walls marked the margins of the chateau's gardens, and clumps of ragwort and fireweed lined the courtyard. A shaft of autumnal sunshine glittered on puddles that mirrored a pewter sky.

Derry remained in the car as May walked into the courtyard and climbed the steps to the front door of the chateau. He found himself imagining Alix here – laughing, playing with the Lanchbury children – the scene soaked in sunshine, and the hedgerows thick with flowers and buzzing with insects. But he cut the thought off ruthlessly, and, climbing out of the Citroën, leant against its bonnet, waiting.

In less than half an hour, May emerged from the house. Her face was white, her lips tightly compressed.

'Isn't it odd, Derry,' she said, 'how in spite of all common sense one imagines that everything will be just the same? Almost twenty years have passed, and a war has been fought in these fields, and yet still I thought—' She broke off.

He said softly, 'May . . .'

'Apples growing in the orchard, and *Grand'mère* in her old chair by the fire.' Her eyes were bright with unshed tears. 'Only the orchard doesn't exist any more, and *Grand'mère* is quite, quite dotty.' She looked up at him. 'Because the roof leaks and none of the bedrooms are habitable, my grandmother lives in two rooms on the ground floor. She didn't know me, Derry. She thought I was the girl who came to do the mending. Or the girl who came thirty years ago to do the mending. She told me that Marie was a good girl but a bit of a one for the boys – my *mother*, Derry – and that I must take more care of my work because the lace is coming unstitched from her petticoat.'

He watched May walk away, and blow her nose. After a few moments she returned. 'So sorry. I didn't mean to blub. Anyway, the maid told me what happened. The chateau was used by German officers during the war. When they retreated at the beginning of 1917, they destroyed much of the area. They mined the farm and the orchard. There was nothing valuable left by then, of course, because the house had been looted in the 1914 invasion. And when *Grand'mère* came back from Paris in 1918 and saw what had happened to her home, it turned her wits.'

There was a silence. Then May said, 'The maid did say something that interested me, though. I asked after the people I remembered from my childhood. I asked after Robert, the Boncourts' stable-boy.'

'And . . . ?'

'Robert Desvignes died in the war, Derry. He was killed in 1915. But before he died, he married. His wife's still living in a village near Bapaume. Derry, Robert married Louise, our nursemaid.'

Derry had agreed to accompany May Lanchbury to France because he had needed to put Alix North, and the feelings he had once had for her, behind him. Yet, driving towards Bapaume, he found himself, against his expectations, caught up in May's quest. The long-ago disappearance of Charlie Lanchbury provided a puzzle, a welcome distraction from other, more painful thoughts. Both May and Alix had described to him the distant day on which Charlie Lanchbury had disappeared. The picnic, the game of cricket, the night at the fair. These events had not seemed real to him. They existed in his imagination as a shadowy narrative, fiction and fact blurring until they were indistinguishable and of almost mythic substance. To meet the Lanchburys' nursemaid would, Derry thought, be like knocking on the door of Bluebeard's castle, or coming face to face with Snow White's malevolent stepmother.

But the woman throwing corn from a bucket to the hens in the garden of the Desvignes' house was solid enough, and not, thought Derry, a creature from a fairy tale. She wore gumboots and a faded print dress, and her chestnut hair was bobbed. May called out, 'Madame Desvignes?'

The bucket was lowered, and the woman looked back. Incurious eyes surveyed May. 'Yes?' Louise Desvignes' gaze, moving slowly to Derry, became slightly less bored. She put up her hands to smooth back her hair, displaying to advantage her full breasts.

'We knew each other a long time ago, Madame Desvignes,' said May. 'You once worked for the Lanchburys.'

A curl of the lip. 'More fool me.'

'I'm May Lanchbury.'

A pause, then a flicker of recognition. '*Lord. May.* When the little boy was lost . . .' Louise Desvignes, staring at May, walked slowly towards them. 'Little May,' she said again. 'Well I never . . .'

'May we talk to you, Madame Desvignes?'

Derry thought for a moment that she would refuse. But then Louise Desvignes' lids lowered, and she shrugged and said, 'I'd ask you into the parlour, but the old dragon's always there in the afternoon. Mother-in-law. But there's the kitchen, if you're not fussy.'

Her hips swayed, leading them across the grass, back to the house. The kitchen was warm, scented with the basket of apples that stood on the window sill, and the coffee brewing in the pot.

'Lost my place because of that wretched kid,' muttered Louise Desvignes, as she poured coffee into tiny china cups. 'Mr Charles bloody Lanchbury said I hadn't been doing my job properly. Gave me the push as soon as he got back from France. The chauffeur, too – poor old Ginger.' Louise accepted the cigarette that Derry offered her. 'He was a card – Ginger, I mean. Don't know what he'd done to get on the wrong side of the old devil.' She looked at May. 'Why have you come here, Miss Lanchbury?'

'I'd like to talk to you about the day of the picnic. The day that Charlie was lost.'

There was a silence. Then Louise Desvignes said, 'What do you want to know?'

'Anything. Whatever you can remember.'

'I wasn't there when it happened. He – Mr Lanchbury, your father – sent me back early to the house. He said that Robert and I were – you know. He said he'd seen us together. He must have been spying on us, the horrid old man. I beg pardon, Miss Lanchbury, if I'm causing you offence, but I speak as I find. Next thing I know, everyone's saying the kid's gone missing. Then the following day we're all packed off back to England, and a few weeks later, I'm given the sack.

Mind you' – Louise smiled – 'by then I knew I'd made a little miscalculation.' Looking at May, she added insolently, 'A bun in the oven, you might say.'

'Robert's?'

'Course. So I legged it back to France. Needed a ring on my finger, didn't I?'

'And you and Robert married?'

'He'd joined up, so I had to wait until he had leave. I'd realized what I'd let myself in for by then – had *her* breathing down my neck.' Louise nodded at the door. 'We weren't living here, of course – we'd had to up sticks and stay with her cousins further south, because of the war. I made sure I was married in white, though. I wasn't going to be cheated out of that.'

May stirred cream into her coffee. 'And your baby . . . ?'

'A boy. I'd just had the telegram telling me his father had been killed when he was born.'

'I'm sorry.'

'It hasn't been so bad.' Louise shrugged. 'The Boche tried to burn this place down, but it didn't catch. We were luckier than most. And the boy hasn't been much trouble, and the old lady's no-one else to leave the farm to when she goes.'

'How old is your son?'

'Seventeen. Robert and I were both seventeen when we met. Robert was eighteen when he died.' There was a silence, then Louise said suddenly, 'Charlie was a nice little kid. Shame it happened to him . . .' Then she tossed back her hair. 'Though I was glad to be shot of all that. I'd wanted to be a ladies' maid, not a nursery-maid – can't stand kids, to tell the truth. The day of the picnic . . .' She narrowed her eyes. 'That morning . . . there was some sort of fuss, wasn't there?'

Derry noticed that May had gone pale. She shook her head. 'I can't remember.'

'Yes. We almost didn't go.'

'Because of the war, perhaps,' suggested Derry. 'Events must have begun to look pretty ominous by then. But you went on the picnic in the end?'

Louise nodded. 'I was glad we were going out – better than being stuck in the nursery, and I thought I might see Robert.' Just for a moment, Louise's features softened, and Derry was able to glimpse the sweet, pretty girl that the Boncourts' stable-boy had long ago fallen in love with.

Then Louise Desvignes pursed her lips. 'We went to the woods near Albert. Nasty, dark place.'

'I've a map,' said May. She unfolded it on the table. 'Would you show me, Madame Desvignes?'

Ten minutes later, they took their leave. At the door, Louise looked at May, and said, 'Why are you doing this, Miss Lanchbury? You'll only make yourself miserable, digging up all those memories. It's better to leave the past alone, you know. So many children suffered because of the war. The woman up the road – Madame Dufèvre – lost her three when a mortar landed on them. A couple of boys were killed only last week, playing with an unexploded shell they found in a field. That sort of thing happens all the time. At least poor Charlie had a good couple of years. At least he had food and warm clothes and a family to care for him.'

In the place that she had begun to think of as their wood, Kit and Alix made love once more. As always, she lost herself in the nearness of him, the touch of his skin on hers. As his fingertips stroked the secret place between her thighs, and his body became a part of hers,

347

all the other taunting, nagging thoughts were erased from her mind. But afterwards, cradled in his arms in the back of the car, she was aware of a feeling of unease, almost of melancholy. Something had altered, and she could not quite pinpoint what it was. The change of season, she thought. The cramped back seat instead of the forest floor; the steely sky glimpsed between bare black branches, instead of the canopy of green.

Alix invited Kit to Sunday lunch, and he arrived bearing a huge bunch of chrysanthemums for her and a box of chocolates for Beatrice. Rory had stayed at school that weekend for a rugby match, Polly was spending the day with Jonathan, and the house was empty of paying guests. After lunch, they sat in the drawing-room. Kit offered to make coffee, and Alix kicked off her shoes and held out her stockinged feet to the fire. She noticed that Beatrice, in spite of the flames roaring in the hearth, shivered.

'Shall I fetch your shawl, Mother?'

'If you wouldn't mind, dear. Such a damp day. I think I've left it in my bedroom.'

Alix was halfway up the stairs when she heard the sound. A pitter-patter on the ceiling overhead. She thought, with a shiver, *mice*. But then the sound changed in timbre. Not mice, she thought. A door opening.

Her mouth was dry as she walked along the passageway. Climbing the small run of stairs at the end of the corridor, her stockinged feet made no sound. The noise of her heartbeats pounded in her ears as she peered through the open door leading into the first of the attic rooms.

When she saw Kit, she almost called out to him. But something stopped her, and instead, clamping her knuckles over her mouth, she stood still, silent, watching. He was searching through the cupboard in which Edward's Egyptian artefacts were kept: the scarabs, the canopic jars, and the rather horrid mummified cat that Rory had had nightmares about when he was younger. She watched as Kit picked up a gold amulet and looked closely at it. Then he slid it into his pocket.

She must have made some sort of sound, because he turned and saw her, standing in the doorway. He blinked, and then his gaze darted from one side of the room to the other.

'Good lord, how silly of me. Just absentmindedness, Alix. So sorry.' He took the amulet out of his pocket.

She longed to believe him. Yet she still saw in her mind's eye his long, tapering fingers searching methodically through the cupboard.

'So sorry,' he repeated. 'Just a mistake.'

A thought occurred to her, chilling her heart. 'The other things' – her voice trembled with shock – 'the shepherdess . . . the goblet . . . did you take them, Kit?'

'*Alix.*' His voice was coaxing, his smile charming. 'You mustn't jump to conclusions. I told you that it was a mistake.' The amulet was still nestled in his palm.

She remembered showing Kit the Book of Hours in Owlscote's library. A few days later she had discovered it missing. 'No. No, I don't believe you, Kit.'

He reached out a hand to her, but she took a step backwards, shaking her head. 'Don't make it worse, Kit, please. You took them. I know that you did.'

She heard his slow exhalation of breath, and saw once more his familiar, lazy smile. Then he glanced down at the amulet, and said, 'You can get a fortune for these things in London, you know.'

'Put it back in the cupboard.'

He did so. She whispered, 'Why, Kit?'

'Does it matter now?'

'Tell me. I want to know. Or I shall call the police.'

He looked at her, eyes wide. 'Well then. Because I needed the money, of course.'

'But your legacy – and your old friend in Scotland . . .'

'It's not quite like that, actually.'

Alix's legs felt weak. She sat down on an old, three-legged chair. She was aware of the beginnings of a terrible humiliation. She saw Kit look back regretfully at the chest of drawers.

'You've a lot of valuable things in this house, Alix,' he said. 'You should take more care of them.'

'Everything . . .' Her gesture took in the cluttered attic, and the fabric of the ancient house. 'Our engagement. It was just for *this*?'

He looked away. 'Not', he said, 'at first.'

'Don't lie to me, Kit.'

'It's the truth. When I saw you at the party, I noticed you because you were beautiful. That was why I spoke to you, Alix. I've always liked beautiful things.'

'The Ritsons—'

'Don't know them from Adam. I saw the cars parked outside, and I just walked in. Gatecrashed. I've done it before.' Again, that quick, fleeting smile. 'It works, Alix.'

She could not bear even to look at him. She rose and went to the window. Through the covering of cobweb and dust, Owlscote's lawns and gardens were reduced to a greying mist.

She heard him add, 'But when I saw this house, I told myself that I'd have to be a little more practical. It's how I make my living, you see.'

She swung round. 'Stealing?'

'Sometimes. And sometimes people give me things.'

'*Women* give you things?'

He inclined his head. She hissed, 'Only I wasn't so generous, was I, Kit? Do you know why? Because these are not *my* things. Everything belongs to *Rory*. This house was left me by Rory's father. I keep it for Rory. For Edward's *son*!'

She wanted, just then, to strike his smiling, handsome face. But instead she clenched her fists and, turning back to the window, said: 'That man in Salisbury – the one who called out to you . . .'

'An old friend. Who knows me rather too well, I'm afraid. That's when I realized things were going to get difficult. That I was running out of time.'

Tall trees above her, and their bodies naked on a bed of beech mast and dog's mercury. She closed her eyes and put up her hand to the pane, feeling the icy glass beneath her palm.

'I'd like you to go, Kit.'

'You're not calling the police?'

'I think,' and she struggled to keep her voice level, 'I think that that would only add to my humiliations, wouldn't it?'

He did not reply. She remained quite still, looking out at the sombre sky through a tangle of spiders' webs. After a while she heard him turn on his heel and walk out of the attic.

May Lanchbury could remember quite clearly the first time she had seen Derry Fox. She had been at a party in Grosvenor Square, and Andrée Garland had pointed him out to her. *He writes me a piece each week for the magazine. Terribly amusing. And rather beautiful, don't you think?* And May had looked and had mentally filed

Derry Fox into the category of possible friend, never lover. May knew her level.

And they had become friends. And if she had, against her better judgement, allowed herself to begin to love him, then she had kept that small, private yielding to herself. Friendship, May had told herself, was enough.

And then Derry had gone away to South America and, returning, it had seemed to May that his long acquaintance with her cousin, Alix North, was over. When he had offered to travel to France with her, she had found herself, despite her resolve, hoping. Derry's company had compensated for the bleakness of this journey. Looking for connections to the past, she had discovered only absence and loss. She retraced the route they had taken on the day of Charlie's disappearance, not because she hoped or expected to find out what had happened to her little brother, but to lay a ghost.

They drove to the woods near Albert, where the Lanchbury family had picnicked in the July of 1914, and where tall trees rose overhead, their black branches meshing, shutting out the sky. The dying leaves were edged in grey frost. Cold even in her sealskin coat, May walked into the shadows. Later that day, in churches that had survived the holocaust of the years of war, she turned the pages of huge, leather-bound record books. And in graveyards where headstones were still pocked by shrapnel she studied pathetic monuments to unnamed children.

There remained in May's memory a clear impression of the village with the fair, the village in which Charlie had been lost. She remembered the square in which the gypsies had danced, the *mairie*, the narrow, winding streets, and the forest that had surrounded them. May and Derry drove for an entire day, searching for the village, criss-crossing the small triangle of northern France that lay between Bapaume, Albert and Boncourt. It wasn't until mid-afternoon, when the sky had already begun to darken, that May started to realize what had happened. Talking to an aged curé in a churchyard, describing the village to him, May saw recognition, and understood then that no matter how diligently she searched, she would never, ever, find the place where her brother had been lost.

The village of Herleville-aux-Bois had been occupied by the Kaiser's troops during the last week of August 1914. The battles that had been fought in the streets of Bapaume and Cambrai had taken place at much the same time in the small, wooded hamlet of Herleville. The spire of the church had been felled by a mortar, and the houses and shops first ransacked, and then set alight. When battle lines had been drawn up in the autumn of 1914, Herleville-aux-Bois had remained occupied, close to the front line. When the German army had been forced to retreat in 1917, there hadn't been much of Herleville left to lay waste. The men who had taken part in that last, desperate advance south in the summer of 1918 would not have known that the village had ever existed. Only the ragged remains of the wood that had once surrounded the houses and market place lingered.

Where Herleville-aux-Bois had once stood, the lines of trenches were visible beneath the green blanket of grass. Broken stumps of trees were dwarfed by the new saplings that had grown between them. Dark water, gathering in ruts, swilled around May's shoes. 'It was so magical, Derry,' she whispered, her gaze flicking to the desolation that surrounded them. 'The village . . . and the fair. The gypsies dancing around the bonfire – I thought I'd never seen anything more beautiful.' She looked up at him. 'It's like a fairy story, isn't it? The child is stolen, and the village is cursed and turned to dust.' There were tears in her eyes, and when he put his arms round her, she pressed her face against his coat.

Throughout the days, Derry was beside her. Against her better judgement, May found herself becoming accustomed to his presence. When, asking questions of the proprietors of small, smoky cafés ('A small boy . . . just before the invasion . . . the child was lost in Herleville-aux-Bois . . .'), he was there beside her, translating when her own French stumbled, comforting her when, yet again, her question received the answer of a shake of the head or an uninterested shrug.

And when the woman in the *pâtisserie*, listening to May's description, nodded, and said, '*Ah oui. Il y a longtemps de cela . . .*' and May's heart began to beat with unaccustomed rapidity, and she forgot every word of French she had ever known, it was Derry who continued to ask the questions, Derry who let her hand curl round his own, squeezing his fingers until her own knuckles ached.

She heard him say to her, 'May, this lady – her name's Mme Bonneville – remembers seeing a neighbour with a little boy. She was curious because she knew that her neighbour had no children of his own, and because she noticed the child's clothes – expensive clothes, of velvet and lace.'

Another long flurry of French. The blood pounded in May's ears. She pulled at his sleeve. '*Derry.*'

He licked his lips. 'Mme Bonneville says that although the child's clothes had been good, they had become ragged and dirty. When she tried to speak to the little boy, he wouldn't reply, so she thought he was mute, or simple.' When he turned to look at her, she saw the pity in his eyes.

Derry said softly, 'The little boy was red-haired, May.'

She could not at first speak. Then she whispered, 'When? When was this?'

More questions. At last May's mind seemed to click into gear, so that she was able to understand the heavily accented French. Mme Bonneville remembered seeing the child just before Bapaume fell. That had been in the last week of August 1914. Mme Bonneville remembered every detail of that terrible day. The townspeople had known that the Kaiser's troops would take the village in a matter of hours. Which was why, Mme Bonneville explained, she hadn't looked more closely into the business of the child. Everything had been topsy-turvy.

Mme Bonneville fixed May with sombre eyes. 'Hell is not pitchforks and flames, madame. Hell is when everything you know, everything that is familiar and beloved, is taken away from you. I remember those days clearly. All the shops had been shut up, and no trains were running. The noise of the trains was like the heartbeat of the town – you didn't notice it until it had stopped. The last hours before the Germans came were terrible. We were all so frightened. We tried to hide. One old man hid himself inside a grandfather clock. The mothers of sons were terrified, because they'd heard that German soldiers cut off the hands of little boys. So they hid their sons in trees, in hayricks, in cupboards. When I saw my neighbour, I was worried for the child. I asked him why he hadn't hidden the boy.'

A silence. May whispered, 'What did he say, madame?' and, listening to Mme Bonneville's reply, a shiver ran the length of her spine.

*   *   *

'If it *was* Charlie . . .'

They had returned to their hotel in Amiens. It was late evening, and they had dined. The maid had poured out the coffee; absently, May spooned sugar into her cup.

'I won't ever know for certain, will I, Derry?' Mme Bonneville had told them that she had not seen her neighbour, the neighbour with the little boy, since that fateful day in August 1914.

'If it was Charlie,' Derry repeated, 'then it's possible that he survived the war.'

'Do you think so?' May frowned, looking down at the table. 'I always assumed he'd died, you see, Derry. Of starvation, perhaps – or he'd drowned . . . or someone – some madman – had just taken him away . . .' Her voice faded. Then she smiled at him. 'So kind of you to come to France with me, Derry.'

'It's funny, isn't it,' he said thoughtfully, 'how the space of a few days can make you think quite differently about something. How the way you *feel* can change.'

She did not, suddenly, want to drink her coffee. Rising, she went to the window and, drawing aside the heavy velvet curtain, looked out to the canal beyond.

'When I left England – well, to tell the truth, May, I felt bloody awful. Tired. Bitter. Hopeless.'

'Alix?' she whispered.

A fleeting smile. 'Of course.' He blinked. 'I went to see her a few weeks ago, you see. And she told me that she was involved with someone.'

'Oh.' Just a small sound, but there was within her the seeds of a great happiness.

'And I thought, well, that's it, you had your chance, Derry Fox, and you made a mess of it, and the best thing you can do is to leave her alone, forget about her.'

May could not speak. Twisting her hands together, she stared out of the window and saw the small ripple of the canal, and the moon's reflection, a shimmering silver sphere.

'And then, these days that we've spent together . . .'

She whispered, 'Yes . . . ?' and the moment seemed to pause, suspended in silver, like the moon on the water.

'It made me see things differently. You lost your brother almost twenty years ago, May. Yet you're still looking for him. You still *believe* in him. You haven't given up on him. And I found myself thinking, how can I give up on Alix?'

She remained motionless, steeling herself against the pain she must soon begin to feel, thankful that her back was to him so that he would not be able to read the expression in her eyes. Thankful also that she had not spoken, had not betrayed herself to him.

She said softly, 'You still love her?'

'Oh yes. I think I always will.'

There was a silence. Then she heard him say, 'I'll have to head on to Brussels tomorrow, I'm afraid. What are your plans, May?'

She made herself turn round, face him, smile. 'I'll go to Paris. I promised to stay with friends for a day or two. And then I'll go home. Work to do . . .' The words trailed away.

'And Charlie?'

May could see, in her mind's eye, a small boy clad in ragged lace and velvet. She said, 'One day, I'll come back. When I can, I'll come back here.'

Shortly afterwards, she excused herself and went to her room. In the looking-glass, she caught sight of her reflection. Her pale blue dress, which she had thought echoed the shade of her eyes, merely robbed them of what little colour they had, so that they seemed translucent, glassy, and devoid of expression. The satin bodice of her dress pulled across her bust. She had put on weight, she thought. The finger-waves that she had carefully set that morning had fallen out, so that her fine, fair hair clumped in pale strings.

She remembered Alix Gregory. Her quick movements and equally quick laughter, her impetuosity. Her thick, curling dark hair, and green eyes like emeralds. Fleetingly, May was aware of a stab of envy.

But the moment passed, leaving her exhausted and numb, and, taking down her suitcase, she began to pack.

Alix took Beatrice to see a doctor in London. After he had examined Mrs Gregory, he suggested she remain in the clinic overnight for tests. Alix settled her mother at the clinic, and booked herself into an hotel. The long evening stretched before her. Putting her coat back on, she went outside.

Gaslights shimmered in the thin drizzle. She walked aimlessly at first. Thoughts she did not wish to contemplate returned continually to the forefront of her mind, taunting her until she pushed them away. Finding herself outside the gaping dark maw of an underground station, she went inside and bought, before she could change her mind, a ticket to Kensington High Street.

The lettering on the shop front, *Storm*, a dark, metallic swirl, gleamed in the charcoal light. Alix saw the 'Closed' sign on the door. She glanced at her watch. It was two minutes past six. Glimpsing movement in the interior, she rapped on the window. There was a clink of chain as Roma unlocked the door.

'*Alix!* What a wonderful surprise!' Roma embraced her. 'I've company,' she explained. 'Sophie's here. We're having a drink. You'll join us, won't you, Alix? Derry's away, I'm afraid. He's gone to France.'

Alix was aware of a pang of disappointment. Roma added, 'He travelled with that fair-haired girl. Fish-eyed, and rather plump . . . the gossip columnist . . .'

'May Lanchbury?'

'Yes.' Alix followed Roma through the shop. 'I have to say,' added Roma, 'I hadn't realized they were that close. Not Derry's *type*.' She opened the door to the office.

Sophie Berkoff greeted Alix with a hug. 'Have a drink, dear Alix.' She was handed a glass.

'Are we celebrating?'

'Commiserating. Vodka is good for broken hearts, don't you think?'

Alix looked at Sophie. Roma said, 'Not *Sophie*'s heart. Sophie's heart is unbreakable.'

'Yours, Roma?' In the brighter light of the office Alix noticed that Roma's eyes were red-rimmed.

Roma made a face. 'Caroline has left me. Sent me a note, the wretch. Didn't even have the guts to tell me face to face.'

'So we are drowning our sorrows . . .'

'I'm through with love. Never again.'

'You say that every time, Roma dear.'

'This time I mean it. I shall become like you, Sophie. Cold-hearted.'

Sophie snorted and refilled Roma's glass. 'It's so lovely to see you, Alix. It seems an age. Are you well?'

'Perfectly well.'

'Derry's handsome brother mentioned that you had a new friend.'

Alix mentally cursed Jonathan. 'I did for a while, but I don't now.'

Two pair of eyes gleamed, looking at her expectantly. 'Now, you can't possibly believe, my dear,' said Sophie, 'that we won't worm the truth out of you.'

'You must', said Roma, 'tell us. All the gory details.'

The vodka, ice-cold and flavourless, had made Alix feel pleasantly muzzy, blurring the humiliation that still stung after the end of her affair with Kit.

Sophie asked, 'Was he handsome?'

'Terribly.' She thought of Kit's pale hair and cobweb-grey eyes.

'Then . . . ?'

Alix shrugged. 'He wanted the house. Owlscote.'

Sophie's dark eyes widened. 'A fortune-hunter?'

Alix sat down. 'I made enquiries.' A slow exhalation of breath. There was a sense of relief in being at last able to share her misery. 'I spoke to a few people. Discreetly, of course. I didn't want anyone to know.' She grimaced. 'But Freddie Maycross had heard of him, and so had Maddy. His real name's Christopher Crawford-Hardy. He told me that he was an orphan, but that wasn't true at all. His mother's still alive, and he has several brothers and sisters. His family were once well off and respectable, but they lost most of their money in the war. He makes his living, if one can call it that, by preying off women. Stupid women, like me.' She bit her lip. 'He *stole* things, Roma. A china statuette . . . a book . . .' Alix put her head in her hands and groaned. 'I feel such a *fool*.'

'We all make mistakes, Alix darling.' Sophie patted her shoulder.

'My marriage', said Roma, 'was the most terrible mistake.' She shuddered.

Sophie topped up Alix's glass. 'Were you lovers?'

She nodded mutely, and thought of the high trees overhead, and Kit's body against hers.

'Was it fun?'

'*Sophie*—'

'No, you must tell me – was it fun?'

She said honestly, 'Yes. Yes it was, actually.'

'Well, then.'

Alix stared at her. 'What do you mean, *well then*?'

Sophie raised her shoulders. 'You enjoyed it. This person—'

'Kit—'

'—he gave you pleasure.' Another shrug. 'He helped himself to a few trinkets, and you enjoyed yourself. It seems not such a bad exchange.'

Alix gave a watery smile. 'I suppose that's one way of looking at it.'

'A perfectly reasonable way, I should say. And you, Roma' – Sophie glared fiercely across the table – 'why do you mourn your lost Caroline? You adored her, and she adored you for a while, and now you have parted. Nothing lasts. That is the way of things. You must enjoy what you have while you can.'

Alix said, remembering, 'Kit moved like a cat. He *loped*—'

'A cat-burglar.'

Alix giggled.

'Terribly exciting, consorting with the criminal classes. I rather envy you.'

'I once knew a man who was part of a revolutionary cell. He was on the run from the police. Whenever I kissed him, I'd be listening for the footstep on the stairs, or for a hand to tap my shoulder.' Sophie looked dreamy. 'He was rather ugly, but I went to bed with him all the same. Danger is such an aphrodisiac, don't you think?'

Derry remained another fortnight on the Continent, visiting suppliers, searching junk shops and street markets to find treasures to bring back to Roma. Returning to London, emerging from Victoria Station, he discovered that it had begun to snow, soft white specks floating from a leaden sky.

He went straight to the shop. It was midday, and Roma was nibbling sandwiches in the office. She kissed his cheek. 'You look green, Derry. A bad crossing?'

'Pretty grim.' He had travelled for a day and a night without stopping. He had not slept on the ferry; he never slept on ferries.

Roma made tea. 'The order book's full till the end of January,' she told him. 'Annabel Fielding has commissioned me to redecorate her entire house.' She offered Derry a sandwich. 'How is Miss Lanchbury?'

'Fine, I dare say.' He flung off his coat; crystals of snow still adhered to the shoulders. He saw that Roma was looking at him, so he explained, 'As far as I know, May came back to England a couple of weeks ago.'

'*Oh*,' said Roma meaningfully. 'I thought—'

'May and I are friends, Roma. Good friends. That's all.'

He stirred sugar into his tea. He heard Roma say, 'Alix was here. She asked for you.'

He was suddenly alert. 'Alix? In London?'

'Her mother's ill, apparently. Cancer, I'm afraid. Terribly grim. Not much hope, as far as I can gather. I didn't ask for details because she didn't seem to want to talk about it. I told her that you'd gone away with Miss Lanchbury. She seemed disappointed.'

'Was she on her own? Was she—'

Roma had come to sit beside him. 'Alix told me that she has broken off her engagement.'

Derry stared at Roma blankly. His mind, exhausted from lack of sleep, struggled to take in such a turn of events.

'Did she say why?'

'The man was a complete cad, apparently. After her money.'

He was aware of an almost overwhelming mixture of anger (directed at the wretched Kit Crawford) as well as confusion and relief. He sat for a while in silence, and then he muttered, 'I should go to her.'

'Take my advice, Derry, and wait a while. Something like that – it humiliates, you see. Give Alix time.' Roma squeezed his hand. 'Be a *friend*, Derry. That's what she needs just now. A friend.'

Polly and Jonathan were married in December, a week before Christmas. Though it rained at dawn, by mid-morning, when the bride and groom came out of the church, the sky had almost cleared, and only a few ragged clouds flitted across the face of a pinkish-gold sun. Confetti mingled with the last yellowed leaves blown from the silver birches, so that petals and leaves glued themselves both to the bride's fur-trimmed gown and to the shoulders of the groom's morning suit. The breeze tugged at wedding hats and lace veils.

The guests cheered as Polly threw her bouquet into the crowd, and clapped as it was caught. Cameras flashed, competing with the watery light of the sun. After a while, the wedding party began to drift out of the churchyard, carefully avoiding the puddles, and the rain started up again, as though it had left off for the duration of the ceremony only as a special concession, gently at first, and then darkening the lichened stones in the graveyard.

Derry caught up with Alix and Rory as they walked from the church to the vicarage. During the ceremony, Alix's gaze had drifted to Derry as he had stood at Jonathan's side, as he had handed his brother the ring. Alix had thought of May Lanchbury, her cousin, who had accompanied Derry to France, and she had looked away, focusing instead on the wooden angels that adorned the roof of the church.

He said, 'Thank God that's over. I was convinced that I'd lose the ring or forget my lines.' Derry put up his umbrella, sheltering them from the rain.

She thought that he looked well and happy. Love suited him, perhaps. 'It went splendidly, didn't it, Derry?'

'Though even poor Jon, who has faced enemy fire, was quaking in his boots.'

They had almost reached the vicarage. Alix began to talk again – something banal about Polly's dress, and the bridesmaids – but Derry interrupted her.

'I need to speak to you, Alix. In private – not surrounded by the hordes. When the worst of this is over, if you have time.'

She nodded, and then was divided from him by the swarm of guests who milled around the entrance to the vicarage. Cold rain stung her face, and, smiling at friends, talking to acquaintances, she was aware of an emptiness in her heart.

Later, after the wedding breakfast, Alix went up to Polly's bedroom. She handed her a package. 'Here's a little extra present, Poll.'

Polly was changing into her going-away outfit. She

glanced inside the paper bag. 'Silk stockings! *Alix*. And . . .' she counted them. 'A dozen pairs! Alix, you *shouldn't*.'

'I couldn't have you honeymooning in a smart hotel in lisle.'

'And from *Harrods* . . .'

'Don't you dare cry, Poll.'

Polly wrapped her white satin shoes in tissue paper. 'To tell the truth, Alix, I'm so glad it's over. I do hate *fuss*.' She placed the shoes in the wardrobe.

'You could hardly slip away to a register office.'

Polly smiled. 'No. And Dad read the service beautifully, didn't he?' She turned to the window. 'Oh, Alix, *look*. They are so dreadful. They're tying things to poor Jonathan's motor-car.'

Alix glanced down at the drive. Stephen and Patrick crouched on the gravel. Tin cans and boots trailed from the back bumper of Jonathan's car.

'Mrs Gregory' – Polly was hesitant – 'how is she?'

'Not so good, Poll.' The London doctor had been able to do little for Beatrice. Her health had deteriorated with alarming speed over the last few weeks, and now she divided her time between her bed and the drawing-room sofa. It hurt Alix to watch her mother slowly hobbling around the house, her pain written on her face.

'I feel as though I'm leaving you in the lurch, Alix.'

'Nonsense. I'll take Mother a slice of cake and put your lovely bouquet in a vase in her room, and I'll describe in great detail every stitch you wore, Polly.' Alix smiled. 'And you've left the place so organized.' Yet now that the prospect of Polly's leaving had become reality, she had to damp down a sharp tug of misery.

But she said lightly, 'And you, Polly? Will you manage? I mean . . . Mrs Fox . . . ?'

After the honeymoon, Polly would move into Jonathan's Andover home. It had, in the end, been the easiest solution.

Polly smiled. 'I have plans,' she said mysteriously. 'You'll see, Alix – everything will work out.'

Leaving Polly's room, Alix saw that Derry was waiting for her at the bottom of the stairs.

'Jon told me you were with Polly,' he said. 'The house is such a crush – I know it's damnably cold, but shall we walk in the garden?'

He fetched her coat and they wandered through winding paths edged with faded asters and arched by dripping rambler roses. Alix waited for Derry to tell her about May. *I wanted you to know first because she's your cousin . . .*

But he said only, 'Roma told me that she'd mentioned to you that I went to France with May Lanchbury.'

Alix hugged her arms tightly around herself. 'Did you enjoy your holiday, Derry?'

'It wasn't a holiday. We went to Picardy. To Boncourt.'

She paused, confused. '*Boncourt . . .*'

'To visit May's grandmother.'

She had a sudden clear recollection of the Boncourts' chateau, set in an orchard, hedged by poplars, backed by endless golden fields.

'M. Boncourt is dead, and Mme Boncourt – well, May spoke to her, but she's not too good.'

'She's ill?'

'Lost her wits, I'm afraid.'

Alix remembered Mme Boncourt's sweetness, her gentleness. 'How dreadful,' she whispered. 'She was kind to me. Even when Charlie was lost.'

Derry ducked beneath a trailing frond of clematis. 'It was Charlie I wanted to speak to you about, Alix.'

They had reached a bench, sheltered from the rain by a tangle of honeysuckle. He said, 'Perhaps you should sit down,' and threw his coat across the cold, damp slats. He stood at the margins of the small, circular terrace. He told her about Robert Desvignes, the Boncourts' stable-boy, who had married Louise, the Lanchburys' nursery-maid. And about a journey through the French countryside. And about a woman who remembered seeing a red-haired child, dressed in ragged velvet and lace.

When he had finished, he sat down beside her. 'There's something more. Mme Bonneville told us what her neighbour had said to her when she asked about the little boy. She asked him why he hadn't hidden the child from the Germans. Her neighbour told her that he was leaving town. And then he said to her – and Mme Bonneville told us his exact words – *that he wasn't going to give his prize to the Boche.*'

Alix stared at Derry. 'I don't understand. What did he mean?'

'That's it. I'm not sure. That the child wasn't his – I think we can be sure of that. And that the child represented something of value to him. But more than that, I just don't know.' He was silent for a moment, and then he added: 'It shocked me, Alix. I'd gone to France with May because I needed to get away from England for a while. I was happy enough to spend a couple of days wandering round the French countryside – May's good company, and it took my mind off things. But I expected to find – nothing. And I think that even to May it was always more about laying a ghost than about finding out what had happened to her brother.'

She had discovered, Alix thought, that a story, begun long ago, had not yet quite ended. 'So Charlie may have survived . . . ?'

'The first month at least. Yes.'

She touched his hand. 'Thank you for telling me this. Thank you, Derry.'

She sat for a long time on the bench, looking out at the rainswept garden. The shadow child had altered, she thought, the tentative pencil strokes becoming firmer. He had survived the first month, and having endured that terrible solitariness his luck had held, perhaps. She saw him more clearly now: he had left the forest behind, and the late summer sunshine glinted on his auburn curls.

CHAPTER THIRTEEN

Polly's replacement at Owlscote, whom Polly herself had interviewed, vetted and chosen, left unexpectedly in the spring when her father fell ill, amid a flurry of apologies and explanations. Alix advertised for a cook. A succession of women, all in their ways utterly unsuitable, shuffled down the drive to the house. Alix chose the least worst, and was unsurprised when the girl failed to appear one morning, having crept out of the house in the middle of the night and run home. The homesick cook's successor lasted six weeks, and then dropped a cast iron frying pan on her foot and had to be taken to hospital. The next one was, simply, mad, and saw things that weren't there. Ladies in white walking across the terrace, nuns walled up behind the plaster. That would have been bearable, Alix thought, had the wretched creature been able to cook. But after a week of complaints from the paying guests, Alix cut her losses, offered a week's wages in lieu of notice, and sent the girl packing.

The trouble was, she reflected, that no girl with an ounce of common sense would choose nowadays to go into service. Anyone with ambition would work instead in an office or shop, where she would have company and could earn good wages. Owlscote's isolation was an added disadvantage. Most girls wanted dance halls, cinemas and shops. Polly had, of course, been a shining exception, but Polly was now blissfully happy in Andover with Jonathan. Without any great optimism, Alix put another advertisement in the newspaper.

The increasingly dispiriting succession of cooks at least managed to distract Alix temporarily from her worries about Beatrice. Part of her knew that Beatrice was dying, yet part of her refused to accept it. The flesh continued to fall from Beatrice's bones, and her skin had acquired an oddly golden hue. In the evenings, Alix sat beside Beatrice's bed. You can't die, Mother, because there's so much we haven't said. You can't die, Mother, without filling in the gaps.

Without Derry, she often thought, the first six months of 1933 would have been almost unendurable. The guest house business and Beatrice's illness kept Alix tied to the house. Derry visited once a month or so, his arms laden with presents – not dull things like chrysanthemums and chocolates, but the latest racy novel, or a board game which kept them up to past midnight, or a box of sugared plums, round and sweet, and tasting, Alix thought, of summer. He would sweep her up and take her out for drives in the countryside, or they would walk along the river, their gumboots squelching the mud between the clumps of marsh marigold and lady's smock. Sometimes, when she could not leave her mother, Derry took Rory out, expeditions from which Rory returned more cheerful and talkative. It saddened her that Rory, too, had to endure at weekends the atmosphere of quiet melancholy that seemed to have settled on Owlscote.

When she wanted to talk about Beatrice, Derry

listened. He never tried to cheer her up with false optimism, and he didn't flinch when she found herself describing to him the most distressing symptoms of her mother's illness. He just listened, and when she wept, he held her. When she wanted distraction, he talked to her. He told her about their friends in London. He told her the gossip: the engagements, the love affairs, the betrayals. He told her about Roma's plans for the shop, and his own travels to the Continent.

She accepted, as the months passed, that she had been mistaken in thinking that Derry was in love with May Lanchbury. She knew also that she had been wrong to believe herself in love with Kit Crawford. She had had a lucky escape, she told herself. Slowly, as some of the humiliation of that encounter faded, she acknowledged that she had mistaken desire for love. Kit Crawford had taught her, she thought, that desire was only a part of love.

Derry, taking Rory out one Saturday afternoon, let him choose their destination.

'The railway station,' said Rory.

Derry found himself on a chilly platform at Salisbury station, being instructed by Rory in the art of train-spotting. 'You have to write down the numbers in this book.' Rory drew from his pocket a tattered notebook and a stub of pencil. 'A fortnight ago, Hollingsworth and I got three new ones. It was really ace. Oh blast, the point's broken and I haven't a sharpener.'

Derry offered Rory his fountain pen. Engines shunted in and out of the platforms, enveloped in clouds of steam and noise. Derry watched Rory dart among the crowds, and later bought him lemonade and Cadbury's Dairy Milk in the station buffet.

Rory, peeling the silver paper from his chocolate, said seriously, 'Trains are better than motor-cars, don't you think, Derry?'

Derry considered. 'Definitely.'

'And aeroplanes are better than both.' Rory wiped chocolate from his inky fingers onto his blazer. 'Have you ever been in an aeroplane, Derry?'

'Once or twice.'

'I'd love to fly. Would you take me?'

He said carefully, 'One day, perhaps. In a while. When you're older.'

'That's what Mum always says. She's afraid the aeroplane might crash. But I'd far rather die in a plane crash than be ill for ages like Grandma, wouldn't you, Derry?'

He felt a pang of sympathy for Rory, and thought that he wasn't doing too good a job in taking the poor kid's mind off things. But he said honestly, 'Yes. But I'd rather not die at all yet. And I promise that I'll arrange a plane trip for you as soon as possible.'

He went back to London that evening, and bought May Lanchbury pink gins in a club in Jermyn Street.

'Will you go away for the summer, May? Stay with your family, perhaps?'

'Family holidays,' said May, making a face. 'Too frightful.'

'Quite. But Bell Wood sounds rather splendid. I imagine you serving tea on the lawn, May – wearing a white dress and a wonderful hat – or punting on the ancestral lake.'

She smiled. 'I don't think we've had tea on the lawn since Mama was alive. And Papa is trying to sell the ancestral lake. *And* our lovely summer house.' May ate the cherry from her cocktail stick. 'My father's in London just now, actually. He'll go back to Bell Wood in time for the Twelfth, of course. Keeping up appearances, you see, Derry. Poor Ella will do her duty as the lady of the manor – though as she's lacking in any sort of charm she never makes too good a fist of it. And all Papa's friends and neighbours will enjoy themselves complaining about how the country's gone to the dogs, and how Something Really Ought To Be Done About It.' May scowled, looking down at her glass. 'I should call at Papa's club, shouldn't I, Derry?'

'I don't know,' he said. 'I never really got the hang of filial duties.' But he found himself thinking of the windy station platform, and Rory, frowning, bent over his notebook, scrawling blotted, illegible numbers.

'Not tonight, though,' said May. 'I have to go to an at home. Frightful Bloomsbury thing. Mina Carr is invited – you know her, don't you? Her latest novel . . . so extraordinary . . . They'll all be wearing homespun and talking about their complexes. I wouldn't go, but Beryl Kirkpatrick will be there, and I need to ask her a favour.' She looked up suddenly, and touched Derry's hand. 'Come with me, won't you, Derry? You'd adore it.'

'It sounds simply marvellous,' he said regretfully, 'but I'm afraid, darling May, that I shall have to decline. A prior engagement.'

'Oh, well.'

'You look glum, May. Is there anything I can do?'

She shook her head. 'My sister is staying with me,' she explained.

'Daisy or Ella?'

'Daisy. She's quarrelled with her husband.'

'Don't you get on?'

May sighed. 'I'm very fond of Daisy, but she is rather maddening. She can't bear to be by herself, so she fills the house with her friends. And they're the sort of people who think that it's too, too amusing to stay up dancing until dawn, or to pick up the most awful people – wrestlers or stevedores or cheap little girls they find in nightclubs – and bring them home. They still think it's the Roaring Twenties, Derry. They still wear feather boas and headbands, for heaven's sake. They don't have to work, and I find myself fleeing to the office each morning with a splitting headache and in a foul temper.' She grimaced. 'I fell asleep over my typewriter this morning.'

'Poor May.' Derry signalled to the waiter, and ordered her another drink. 'Will your sister go back to her husband?'

She sighed again. 'Oh yes. She always does, you see.'

Alix had engaged a nurse to look after Beatrice at night. The nurse sniffed about the cobwebs in the corridor, and the distance from bedroom to bathroom. Some days Beatrice talked for hours, during others she hardly spoke at all, but flickered fitfully between sleeping and waking. When she spoke, it was of her childhood, and the distant past. The organza party dresses, the pony rides. The mornings in the nursery, the afternoon walks around Bell Wood's grounds, and the visits to the drawing-room in the evening, to see her parents. The games that she and Charles had played. Beatrice's admiration and affection for her stronger, handsomer, cleverer elder brother.

Alix thought that if she looked hard enough, she would see the bones through her mother's translucent skin. When the nurse turned her, Beatrice whimpered like an animal. One night, she gripped Alix's hand, and whispered, *Charles*. Alix wrote a letter to Bell Wood.

374

There was no reply. Uncle Charles has gone away, she thought. He cannot know that his only sister is dying.

Curled up in her bed, she sought solutions, resolution, a means of conciliation. Sleepless, she wrapped her coat around herself one night, and tiptoed downstairs to the library. Her pen scratched the paper. Just a few lines; she blotted it carefully. She walked to the post box. The night was as dark as ink. The hem of her night-dress trailed on the gravel. She had an odd premonition that she was starting a fire: something that could not be put out.

Derry had spent the day at a house sale in Ascot. Returning to his flat in the early evening, he picked up the letters from the mat, and glanced through them. Recognizing Alix's handwriting, he slit open the envelope.

Alix's letter explained that Beatrice Gregory had asked to see her brother. She herself could not leave Owlscote, Alix explained, so she begged Derry to speak on her behalf to her cousin, May Lanchbury. She enclosed a note to May. A footnote at the end of Derry's letter said bleakly, 'I must ask you to broach this matter with May soon, Derry. The doctor believes that my mother has only a few days – weeks, at the most – to live.'

Derry stuffed the letter into his jacket pocket, and left the flat. May's house was within walking distance. He heard the noise of the party as he turned the corner of the street. The front door of the house was slightly ajar, so when his knock remained unanswered he walked inside.

May's house was unrecognizable. It would have been impossible, Derry thought, to have squeezed more people into such a few rooms. One would have had to use a shoehorn. He wormed his way through the hallway, searching among the crowds for May's familiar face. Someone thrust a drink into his hand, but he abandoned it on a mantelpiece. He searched methodically: drawing-room, dining-room, kitchen. Then he went upstairs. There were guests drooped over the banisters, and guests sitting, arms round each other's shoulders, on the treads.

The bedroom door was open. He heard a woman's voice.

'Is it because you're *married*, Ronnie? So *old-fashioned*. *That* doesn't matter. Everyone has affairs. I've had *loads* of affairs. My husband has affairs. Even' – a peal of laughter – 'even my *mother* had affairs. So it must be all right, mustn't it, darling?'

Derry peered round the jamb, and saw a man and a woman. The woman's short, fluffy hair was platinum blonde, and she wore a dress of silvery fabric that clung to her, shimmering like a mermaid's tail. When she turned to look at him he saw the violet bruise that ringed one of her large grey eyes.

'I'm sorry,' he said. 'I was looking for May.'

'May's not here, darling.' She crossed the room to him. 'Won't I do?'

The man – Ronnie, Derry assumed – hissed, '*Daisy* . . .'

May's sister was called Daisy. *My sister is staying with me. She fills the house with her friends.*

'I need to find May urgently, Mrs—' he explained, and then stopped, unable to recall Daisy's married name.

'Delavel,' she said. 'Daisy Delavel.' She held out her hand.

Derry introduced himself. He thought how unalike

the sisters were. Daisy Delavel glittered, small and pale and fragile. Her great, damaged eyes – a narrow ring of grey round distended pupils – were set in a white, bony face. Only the shape of her eyes – the fringe of black lashes, and the smooth downward sweep of the inner lid – reminded him of both May and Alix.

'Do you know where I can find May?'

Daisy looked blank. 'I've no idea, I'm afraid, dearest. She did say something, but I'm afraid I can't remember. She's gone to the country, perhaps.' She smiled apologetically, showing tiny, wide-spaced, perfect teeth. 'Are you sure I can't help you, Mr Fox?'

Her small fingers stroked his lapel. Ronnie, behind her, coughed. Derry, muttering excuses, escaped from the room.

Outside he stood, momentarily irresolute, on the pavement. As the warm summer air cleared his head, he took Alix's letter from his pocket, and slit open the note to May. Reading it, he recalled their conversation of the previous evening. *My father's in London just now. I should call at his club, shouldn't I, Derry?* He headed for the nearest telephone box.

Derry discovered that Charles Lanchbury's club was in New Cavendish Street. Inside, he followed a man-servant up narrow, wainscoted stairs. There were prints of cricket matches on the walls, and the rooms smelt of beeswax and pipe tobacco and school dinners.

As the manservant showed Derry into a room, he was aware of feeling unexpectedly nervous and utterly out of place. He looked around. Though it was July, a fire burned in the grate. There were leather wing-chairs and newspapers in wooden racks and he could hear the clink of cut glass. The servant bent over the wing of a chair. There was a low murmur of conversation.

'Fox?' He heard the voice first, dry and cold and clear. Then he glimpsed the white flicker of his own card, gripped between long, pale fingers.

'Derry Fox,' he said. The manservant moved aside, and Derry stepped forward. 'Mr Lanchbury?' When he offered his hand, the older man's grasp was dry and fleeting.

'I apologize for barging in like this. I don't intend to take up too much of your time.'

He saw Charles Lanchbury clearly at last. The long narrow face, the droop to the corners of eyes and mouth. Only in the colour of his eyes – a pure, pale blue – was there any obvious similarity between father and daughter.

'Perhaps you could explain, Mr' – another glance at the card – 'Mr Fox, why I should be inclined to allow you to take up *any* of my time?'

Derry took a deep breath. 'I've a message to you from your niece. It's about your sister, Beatrice Gregory. I'm sorry to have to tell you that she's very ill.'

'*Sorry?*' For the first time, the pale irises focused on Derry. 'Why are you *sorry*, Mr Fox?'

'Because one doesn't care to be the bringer of bad news.'

A small shrug. 'The news you bring is of no consequence to me.'

Derry found himself beginning to resent being left standing like a guilty schoolboy brought before his headmaster. But, realizing that he had not explained matters properly, he swallowed down his anger and tried again.

'Your sister has very little time left, Mr Lanchbury. Alix thought you would like to see her before she dies.'

'She was mistaken.'

Three small, cold words. Then Charles Lanchbury picked up the newspaper. Afterwards Derry thought it was that gesture that chilled his own heart: the flick of the page, pale blue eyes scanning the lines.

But for Alix's sake, he persevered. 'A letter, then,' Derry's mouth was dry. 'A note – affection and forgiveness – something like that. A few lines, that's all. To Beatrice, if not to Alix.'

The newspaper lowered. 'I have no sister. I have no niece.'

'The woman's dying, for God's sake!' Derry, who never lost his temper, did so now. Heads peered round the wings of chairs, and monocles focused on him.

'You seem upset, Mr Fox,' said Charles Lanchbury. 'Of what concern are these people to you?'

Derry made himself speak calmly. 'They are my friends.'

'*Friends*. Such a multitude of sins that word covers these days.' Charles Lanchbury smiled. 'I dare say Mrs North has a great many *friends*. That sort of woman always does.' The smile faded as Lanchbury leaned forward in the chair. 'I think you should go, Mr Fox. You have no business here. Shall you find your own way out, or shall I ring for the manservant?'

'I'll find my own way.' Derry's voice was hoarse.

He headed back to his flat. Walking, he tried to think of the kindest phrases to write to Alix.

Yet the intensity of his loathing shocked him, forcing the oxygen from his lungs. It was hard to breathe, he thought. Not, this time, feathers, but the dry, choking air of unforgiveness, and old hatreds.

Beatrice died at the beginning of August. She had had a bad night; Alix and the nurse had sat with her since the early hours of the morning. She died just before dawn. How unbearable, Alix thought, not to see the sun again, and then she closed her eyes very tightly and sat motionless, her fingers still gripped round Beatrice's.

The funeral was three days later. Rory stood beside Alix in the church, and Polly and Jonathan came, and Derry, and Maddy and her husband, and a great many people from the village. But not Charles Lanchbury. Alix had put a notice in *The Times*. Charles Lanchbury must know that his only sister was dead. Sitting in the front pew, Rory at her side, Alix looked round the church once, and felt a mixture of anger and relief at his absence.

She turned down Derry's invitation to go back to London with him, and Polly's to stay in Andover. She could not, she thought privately, have just then borne the proximity of Jonathan and Polly's almost tangible happiness, and besides, there were things she had to do. She told herself that she preferred to be alone, and yet the house seemed echoing and empty. A door, slamming in the wind, made her start. She found herself listening for her mother's slow steps along the corridor.

She sorted through Beatrice's belongings. Three heaps: things to keep, second-hand shop, jumble sale. She knew that she had half hoped to find letters, diaries, something to help her understand the enigma that her mother had always been to her. But there was nothing. She kept a pair of gloves, a silk scarf, a fur muff. Jewellery and photographs, and for Rory a watch that had once belonged to her father.

When the room was cleared, she drifted around the house, beginning tasks she was too tired to complete, unsure what direction to take. Because it was August, Owlscote was empty of paying guests. At the end of the week, she heard a motor-car drawing up in the drive. Looking down, she saw Derry climbing out of his car.

He had booked, he told her, a week in a hotel in Bournemouth. She threw a few clothes into a bag, and told Rory to pack his shrimping net, and they headed for the seaside. Sitting on the beach, Alix watched Rory swim through the sparkling waves. As the tide ebbed and flowed, all the cluttered, disparate thoughts in her head began to fall into place again. One afternoon, a butterfly perched on the arm of her deckchair. Every now and then the breeze would catch it, so that it fluttered away for a few moments, but then it would return to the deckchair, spreading out its great wings with their dark, velvety peacock's eyes, and sunning itself. She thought of Beatrice, poor, fragile Beatrice, and how life had buffeted her this way and that and, amid the crowds and glitter of the beach, Alix wept for her mother.

Derry, returning to London, went to meet Roma in the bar of the Ritz. She had chosen the Ritz as her fiftieth birthday treat. He caught the words as he wove through the crush.

'. . . my own cinema screen. At Marblehurst. Should be finished much the same time as the swimming pool.'

'Darling Roma.' She was sitting in a corner, smoking a cigarette. He kissed her. 'Many happy returns,' he said, and placed a small box, wrapped in gold tissue paper, in front of her.

He watched her open it, and take out the jewelled scarab and smile. 'It is delightfully malevolent,' she said. 'I shall have it made into a brooch. Dear Derry. So clever.' As she spoke, Derry thought, *My own cinema screen. At Marblehurst*, and the nagging memory fell into place. He recalled Mina Carr, her fingertips powdered with ochre pollen from a bouquet of white lilies, saying, *Edith's friend sent them. Marcus Wenlock. He has a country house called Marblehurst.*

'You could *pretend* to be listening to me, Derry.' Roma's long, lacquered fingernails dug into the back of his hand.

He blinked. 'Sorry. Miles away.' He glanced over his shoulder into the crowds. 'Marcus Wenlock . . .'

'Dreary little ginger-haired man?'

'Not *ginger*.' Derry found him again. His guest had just risen from the table, leaving Marcus Wenlock sitting alone, a glass of whisky in front of him. Derry saw a pink, fleshy face, tow-coloured curls, and a short, thick neck rising from massive shoulders. Derry tried, and failed, to imagine Edith Carr married to such a man.

'Sandy, then.' Roma smiled. 'I did a room for him not long ago. Simply frightful. Faux Regency – stripes and gilt and spindly little chairs. He insisted. I was short of clients at the time, so I couldn't refuse. But I was so ashamed of myself I had to go to confession afterwards. Oh *heavens*' – she glanced across the room – 'he's seen us, Derry. He's coming over.'

'Could be good for business . . .'

She made a face. 'He'll talk about hunting,' she hissed, 'or something dull and financial . . .'

Roma subsided as Marcus Wenlock approached their table. Derry introduced himself, and they shook hands.

'It's Mrs Storm's birthday,' he explained.

'Then I shall buy champagne.' Marcus Wenlock signalled to the waiter. 'Are you still in business, Mrs Storm? Yes? Because I've made a few improvements to Marblehurst . . .'

The conversation proceeded, oiled by champagne. Marcus Wenlock described at length Marblehurst's tennis court and ornamental maze. The Chinese room, for his collection of jades. The Belgian tapestries, housed in an Elizabethan gallery that ran the length of the house. His sons' nursery, with its own bathroom, kitchen and sitting-room. The master bedroom had two bathrooms, Marcus Wenlock explained, one for himself and one for his wife. Edith's bath was in the shape of a shell. Inspired by Botticelli. Venus rising from the waves.

'And the swimming pool's well under way. That's what I wanted to speak to you about. I wondered whether you'd have a look at it for me. I had a thought. Perhaps we could do it up to look like the Alhambra. Have you been there? Those little tiles and mirrors. I thought that would be nice. And fountains. And a statue or two.'

Derry frowned. He knew that Charles Lanchbury had recently put up for a sale both a statue and a summer house. Derry imagined Marcus Wenlock's swimming pool, a riotous collision of garish colours and unsuitable borrowings from inappropriate sources. How proud, artistocratic Charles Lanchbury would *hate* his treasures to be displayed in such a setting.

He saw then a way of repaying a debt. Of making Charles Lanchbury endure just a fraction of the suffering he had inflicted on Alix. He thought, with a fleeting pang of regret, of May. But Charles Lanchbury's cold voice echoed too loudly. *I have no sister. I have no niece.*

'A statue,' said Derry, 'might just set it off.' Roma glanced at him.

Marcus Wenlock tapped the ash from his cigar. 'Know of something, do you, Fox?'

Thick blue smoke clouded the air. Derry tried not to cough. 'As a matter of fact, I do . . .'

*　　*　　*

At the beginning of September, Alix caught the train to Andover, to stay the weekend with Jonathan and Polly. After they had eaten, Polly began to clear up. Jonathan said, 'Let me—' but Polly interrupted him.

'Alix will help me, won't you, Alix? You go and show Rory your new fishing rod, Jon. You'd like to see it, wouldn't you, Rory?' The men disappeared. Polly and Alix took the plates into the kitchen.

'Mrs Fox . . . ?'

'Is in London, seeing her analyst.'

Alix's eyes widened. '*Analyst*—'

'A marvellous man. I've known him for ages. Max was at university with my father.' Polly ran water into the sink. 'Max is very sympathetic, particularly with anxious patients. He'll listen for *hours*. Eva goes to see him three times a week.'

'*Polly.*'

'And then there's the chiropodist and the oculist and the masseuse . . . They all take up so much of Eva's time, you see.'

Alix wanted to laugh. 'Polly, you are *wicked*.'

'I did think of a faith healer, but my father disapproves terribly of that sort of thing. But I shall keep her up my sleeve, just in case.' Polly turned to face Alix. 'And now, I have something to tell you. The most marvellous thing. I wanted to tell you before, but with your poor mother . . . and I wasn't certain. But now I am absolutely sure.' Polly's eyes were shining. 'I'm going to have a baby, Alix. In the spring. Isn't it wonderful?'

Alix went back to Owlscote, and everything seemed to go wrong at once. The geyser exploded, drenching the scullery, and the library ceiling, which she had for years intended to replace, collapsed one night. Every book in the library, and all the papers that comprised her history of Owlscote, were powdered with plaster and horsehair. She spent an entire weekend dusting furniture and books. When the workmen came to repair the ceiling, their boots left white footprints on floors and corridors. A thin film of white covered every surface, like a layer of snow.

She remained unable to find a replacement for Polly. A woman from the village came to the house in the afternoon for a couple of hours to help peel potatoes and clean the grates, but that was not enough. Alix found herself beginning to loathe the paying guests. Wanting to slam down their plates in front of them, and tell them to hurry up and finish their supper. Increasingly she found herself growing impatient with them when they told her their troubles, or worse, attempted to flirt with her.

And she began to realize that she had become vulnerable. The presence of Beatrice and Polly had shored up her position at Owlscote, and had guarded her from the advances of all but the most unsubtle. Losing their company, she was in danger of also losing her reputation. A single woman living with a dozen men – in the village, some of the more respectable families began to cut her in the street. She did not care about that, but she found herself locking her bedroom door at night, something she had never done before.

Before term had begun in mid-September she and Rory had spent an enjoyable day in London, visiting the Natural History Museum and seeing a play. Then Rory returned to school, and the house had echoed once more, all those rooms, with the memories contained in them pressing down on her. She often woke early in the morning, before the first coppery fingers of dawn crept around the gaps between the curtains, watching the hands of the clock move slowly from four, to five, to six. She was, she acknowledged, lonely. The house, without Polly and her mother, was vast and silent.

After breakfast, one of the guests, Mr Charnley, spoke to her.

'A moment of your time, if you please, Mrs North?'

Alix had taken a dislike to Mr Charnley: his shiny black hair, his toothbrush moustache. The way he touched her at the slightest opportunity, a tap on the shoulder to gain her attention, a pat on her hand to accompany a request for extra custard. The small, disbelieving emphasis on the *Mrs* of Mrs North.

'A slight' – a small cough – 'problem.'

'Yes, Mr Charnley?'

'Not here.' They were standing in the hall. 'I think you'd prefer this to remain private. And besides, there is the *evidence*.'

Ridiculous man, she thought. Mr Charnley sold face powder and vanishing cream to chemist's shops. He had several times offered her gifts of face powder. She always refused.

Yet she followed him upstairs. Standing in the doorway of his room, Alix watched him crouch by the wardrobe, and take something from the bottom shelf.

'This', he said portentously, 'is the problem, Mrs North.'

'This' was a large brown rat. Alix's stomach churned at the sight of the whiskery snout, the naked pink tail. She struggled to speak calmly.

'Where did you find it?'

'In' – he paused impressively – 'this very room.'

In the eleven years Alix had lived at Owlscote, the house had been plagued by wasps, ants, silverfish and mice. But never rats. Never in the house.

'I'm sure you're grateful,' Mr Charnley said, 'that I kept this little – *incident* – quiet.'

'What do you mean?'

'Oh, come, come, Mrs North. I'm sure you know exactly what I mean.' He smiled. 'Not exactly good for business, eh? Vermin in a guest house.'

She said coldly, 'I apologize for any inconvenience or distress, Mr Charnley, but I'm certain this is an isolated incident. There have never been rats in Owlscote. I'll ask Jacob to dispose of it.'

She turned to go. He said, 'What about my reward?'

'Reward?'

'For keeping mum.' His hand rested on her arm, staying her. 'You'd like me to keep mum, wouldn't you? You scratch my back, and I'll scratch yours. Tit for tat, that's what I always say.'

'Mr Charnley—'

'You oblige me, and I'll oblige you. Because you can be obliging, can't you?' His hand moved; he squeezed her breast. 'I know that you can, Mrs North.'

She jabbed him so sharply with her knee that he yelped and went white. She snapped, 'Have your bags packed and be out of here by ten o'clock, Mr Charnley. And don't come back.' Then she walked quickly down the corridor.

His voice followed her. 'Don't come the ice-maiden with me! I've seen you with your fancy men! Your followers! I know your sort! You shouldn't be so fussy!'

Alix took a torch and a broom, and searched the house from top to bottom. Attics, bedrooms, living-rooms, outhouses. She wore gumboots and gloves, afraid of what she might disturb behind stacks of trunks and suitcases that had not been moved for decades, afraid of the teethmarks she might find in the packets of dry goods in the back of the larder. When she had finished, and had found no trace of a rat, she collapsed on the kitchen sofa. It was three o'clock. I'll sleep for ten minutes, she thought, and then she closed her eyes. When she woke up, the hands of the clock had moved with extraordinary speed, and were now pointing to half past four. It was the daily help's afternoon off, and the vegetables were not peeled, and the shopping not done. The dishes from breakfast were still stacked in the sink, bacon fat congealing on the plates. In less than two hours the men would be sitting at their tables in the dining-room, waiting for their supper.

She stood up. Her legs felt wobbly, and she realized that she had eaten nothing all day. Her skirt and sweater were grey with cobwebs and dust from crawling through the attics. There was a hole in her stocking. She went to the sink and turned on the tap. When she picked up the household soap, it slipped out of her nerveless hands, and leapt bloody-mindedly beneath the sofa. The sofa was too heavy to move, and there was no more soap in the cupboard. She threw on her coat and left the house, taking her bicycle out of the shed. In the shop, she bought soap and potatoes, and dumped them in her bicycle basket. The telephone box was outside the shop. On impulse, she opened the door and went inside. Enclosed in the dusty, fuggy interior, she asked the operator for the number of Derry's flat and, when she heard his voice, pushed pennies into the slot.

'Derry?'

'Alix? Are you all right, Alix?'

'Fine,' she said, but her voice wobbled a little. 'I just needed to talk to someone.'

'Fire away.'

She thought how nice it was to hear his voice. She told him about the rat, and Mr Charnley. 'He wanted me to go to bed with him, Derry. He looked like a rat himself – horrid brown whiskers and little pink eyes.'

'Squeaked like a rat, I should imagine, by the time you'd finished with him.'

She giggled, and realized that was the first time she'd laughed in weeks. Then she sighed. 'Oh well, I'd better go home, I suppose. I'm running out of pennies. And the washing up isn't done, and there's nothing for supper.'

He said, 'Marry me, Alix.'

She thought she had misheard him. The scratchings and whistlings of the telephone line. She whispered, 'Pardon?'

'I said, marry me, Alix.'

The operator interrupted, asking for more money. Alix fumbled, trying to fit her pennies into the slot, her fingers cold and clumsy.

Derry said, 'I've been meaning to ask you for ages, but it's never seemed to be the right time. But perhaps there isn't a right time. And it's not such a bad idea, is it? You and I. Better than struggling on with the guest house, don't you think?'

She forced her last penny into the slot. 'I like the guest house.' Yet that was no longer true, she thought. She was thoroughly fed up with the guest house, and had been for months, but had been reluctant to acknowledge it.

'You've done a good job,' he said gently, 'but you've done it long enough. Perhaps it's time to try something new. Marry me, Alix,' he said again, 'and if it doesn't work out, I'll go, I promise. No fuss.'

At last, she heard herself speak. 'Yes,' she said. 'Yes, please, Derry.' Then the phone went dead.

Jewels gleamed, satin shimmered, and cut-glass chandeliers swayed in the vast ballroom. Heads – fair and dark and red, ornamented with pearls and diamonds and tortoiseshell clips – bowed and swayed and huddled, almost touching. May Lanchbury thought of waves crashing on a beach, casting pebbles one against the other, white against grey, pink against tan-coloured. The seawater rearing back, falling once more, jostling the stones into different places.

May saw Derry Fox talking to her sister, Daisy. The dark curls almost touching the smooth platinum chignon. Then Daisy moved away, and was caught up in a different circle of people.

May walked from the ballroom to the dark, cool shelter of a balcony. She did not wish to speak to him tonight; she did not want him to see her. Not yet. She knew that if he spoke to her he would see the hurt in her eyes, and if he spoke to her she would forgive him. And she was not yet ready to do that.

From the balcony, May looked down to the garden of the house. Moonlight feathered the leaves of the evergreens, and snaked along the bare branches of birch and willow. A few dead leaves, curled and transparent like chrysalids, lay scattered on the lawn. Above, the sky was clear. There would be a frost tonight. The first frost of winter.

Taking a deep breath of cold, still air, May closed her eyes. She found herself longing, for the first time in years, for Bell Wood. In her mind's eye, May walked from the house up the wide avenue of limes that her great-grandfather had planted almost a hundred years before. Frost crisped the grass, and the branches of the trees twisted like wrought iron against a sapphire blue sky. The avenue debouched into a circular lawn, walled with high hedges of hornbeam and box. A small girl, she had liked to walk the circle with her eyes closed, her palm flat against the hedge, her route guided by the smooth sweep of the greenery. She had never opened her eyes before she reached the narrow gap in the hedge. She had always been seized by a sense of wonder as she looked out at the broad sweep of the meadow, and saw, in the distance, Bell Wood's lake, and its white marble summer house.

And in the summer house, protected from wind and rain, was the statue of the sea nymph Thetis, the mother of Achilles. May recalled the graceful droop of her body as she bent towards the water, seemingly about to plunge into the lake. And the shells, starfish and seaweed that had littered the plinth on which she stood. And the nymph's robes, a gauzy swirl, and the single curl that had strayed across her forehead.

The Italian sculptor Antonio Canova had made the statue at the beginning of the previous century. May's great-grandfather had bought it a few decades later from an impoverished Frenchman. It had remained in the summer house by the lake at Bell Wood ever since.

But now the lake was sold to a farmer who would rent it out for coarse fishing, and the statue of Thetis had been removed to the grounds of a banker's mock-Tudor house in Surrey. May's father had sold both lake and statue, because he had seen no other way of keeping the house that had been his family's inheritance for centuries. And Derry Fox had bought the statue of Thetis, and had sold it to Marcus Wenlock.

Ella had written to May. *Papa is very angry because some frightful no-person has bought our Canova statue.* *No-person* was private Lanchbury family slang for an arriviste. The sort of person for whom her father always reserved his most bitter contempt. May herself, visiting Bell Wood, and keeping her ear to the ground, as she always did, had worked out what had happened. Derry Fox had asked Papa, on Cousin Alix's behalf, to visit Aunt Beatrice, who was dying. Papa had refused. Papa, May supposed, had been insulting. So Derry had bought the statue anonymously, through a third party, and had since sold it to Marcus Wenlock, whose wife had once been engaged to Derry Fox's elder brother. May did not doubt for a moment that Derry had both bought and sold the statue with the particular intention of enraging her father. There was a special sort of mockery in it: the purity of the Canova nymph now diminished by the opulent vulgarity of a faux-Moorish swimming pool. It was, May thought, a sort of violation.

What Derry had done was understandable, forgivable even, if one thought of Cousin Alix and Aunt Beatrice. Hatreds should not linger so long. But May's hurt remained. She remembered saying to Derry, *Papa is trying to sell the ancestral lake.* Her own chance comment had aided Derry in her father's humiliation. Unwittingly, she had helped Derry Fox destroy the magical vista of her childhood. He had used her, and it was that betrayal which stung.

Yet, looking down at the moonlit garden, May found herself questioning whether her father's humiliation was the true cause of her hurt. A second piece of news about Derry Fox had hurried hard upon the first one. The news of his marriage.

Derry Fox had married Alix North a week ago. A small, quiet wedding, by special licence. The news had reached May as news does, by word of mouth, rumours handed from one person to another. She had wondered at first whether the rumour-mongers had been mistaken, as they so often were, but she had quickly discarded the notion. She had, after all, known for a long time that Derry loved Alix.

Yet the pain remained, quiet and secret, hidden at the core of her heart. She knew that she would learn to live with it. Just as she would eventually pick up the pieces of her friendship with Derry, partly because he would charm her into doing so, and partly because her pride would not permit her to do otherwise. Plump, plain May Lanchbury, a spinster in her late twenties, could not be seen to have been wounded.

She heard a footstep, and the rustle of a curtain, and turned round. Daisy stepped onto the balcony.

'Such a glorious party, May! Why on earth are you hiding out here? I've brought you champagne.' A glass was pressed into May's hand. 'Pip is being terribly dull and insists on playing cards, but simply everyone is here. And, the most extraordinary thing! The most beautiful man – I'm sure I've seen him before, but I simply can't remember where – and he is married to – you'll never guess—'

'Cousin Alix,' said May. 'Yes.'

Daisy looked slightly deflated. 'I'm going to make sure he dances with me. After all, we're almost related, aren't we?'

'You shouldn't dance with Derry Fox.' The words were out before May could stop them. 'You should keep away from him, Daisy.'

'Why?' Daisy's dark grey eyes were blank.

Because he's much, much cleverer than you. And because he's looking for carrion.

'Because he's not our sort,' said May crisply, and put aside her glass of champagne, realizing that she did not want to drink it at all.

CHAPTER FOURTEEN

Daisy said, 'I am in the most frightful pickle. You will help me, won't you, May?'

The sisters were shopping in Selfridges; Daisy's fingers dabbed nervously at the silk camisoles spread out on the counter for her inspection.

May glanced quickly at Daisy. 'Is it Pip? Has he—'

'He wants a divorce.'

Only in a slight widening of her eyes did the salesgirl show that she had heard, but May said clearly: 'Half a dozen of those, please.' She indicated, at random, an apricot silk. 'Have them parcelled up and sent to Mrs Delavel's address.' Then she seized Daisy's elbow, steering her away from the counter.

'*Divorce . . . ?*'

Daisy nodded. 'Some frightful sneak told him about Blackie.'

Daisy, huddled in white fox fur, looked utterly miserable. Studying her sister, May felt the usual mixture of pity and exasperation.

'If you talked to Pip . . .' May's voice was low. 'If you talked to him . . . He's had affairs, after all. I'm sure he'd forgive you.'

Daisy came to a halt. They were in the haberdashery

department. She looked at May. 'Don't be silly, May, of course he wouldn't. It's different for girls, you know that. And anyway' – and her hands fluttered like white moths against the trays of brightly coloured buttons – 'I don't mind about the divorce. Pip has promised to be a gentleman. It's just the other thing.'

'What other thing?'

'I'm expecting a sprog, you see.'

May felt a rush of relief. 'If Pip knew that – I'm sure he'll change his mind about divorce – I'm sure he'd—'

'It isn't his.' Daisy's tone was expressionless. There was a silence. 'Pip and I haven't done *that* for months.'

May found herself thinking, I don't want to know, I just don't want to know. But she forced herself to ask, 'Is it Blackie's?'

A small shrug. 'Perhaps.'

May had to look away from Daisy, focusing instead on the rush of people, hurrying through the shop.

'So you see,' Daisy went on, 'if Pip knew, there'd be a frightful scandal. He'd say that it was *my* fault. In court, I mean. It would be in the newspaper – that I was an adulteress . . .'

You should have thought of that before. But May managed to remain silent.

'Papa would be *furious*.'

May looked back at her sister. Daisy's dark grey eyes were round and frightened. She said gently, 'Daisy, does it matter what Papa thinks? It's not as though you *love* him.'

'Love him?' Daisy giggled. 'How ridiculous.' Then she became anxious again. 'He'd say that I'd dragged the Lanchbury name into the mud. He would be angry with me. I hate it when he's angry with me. He frightens me.' She was winding a length of pale pink ribbon around her fingers. 'So you have to help me, May. You know simply everyone, don't you? You have to help me find someone.'

May didn't understand at first, and then she did, and was aware of a mixture of resentment and shock and rage. But she repeated evenly, 'Find someone?'

'To get rid of it.'

She thought, such a *barren* family. Ella, with her stale allegiances; Daisy, with her wantonness and promiscuity; and me, loving only the wrong men, and protected by the acres of flesh that guard my virginity.

'Daisy, I can't.'

The pink ribbon had become twisted and grey. '*May*—'

'I can't, Daisy. I just can't.'

Tears trembled on Daisy's lids. 'But you've always helped me, May.'

'I can't this time.' She was unable to keep the revulsion out of her voice.

Daisy shifted her weight from one foot to the other. She looked agonized. The bright warmth of the department store had begun to seem oppressive and airless. Daisy muttered, 'Then I'll have to sort it out *myself*,' and walked away, leaving May standing among the buttons and the sequins.

She should have felt, May thought, some sense of pride in having done the right thing. She did not, though: she was aware only of an uncomfortable self-righteousness, and a suspicion that her refusal to help Daisy was founded more on envy than on principle. Daisy, however indiscriminately, loved. Daisy knew ecstasy, the ecstasy that had sparked the life in her womb. An ecstasy denied her elder sister. In the middle of Selfridges, May stood, her eyes closed and her arms folded around her, trying to remember when she herself had last experienced joy. She found herself recalling the gypsy dancers that she had seen so long ago in the square in the village in France. The sparks from the bonfire leaping into the sky, the dark faces full of rapture, and the whirling limbs golden in the firelight.

Polly, visiting Owlscote, wore capacious smocks and talked about her backache, and the tiny clothes she was crocheting. Jonathan had bitten fingernails and a haggard appearance: beside him, Polly bloomed, large and plump-faced and pink-cheeked.

In March, Jonathan telephoned to announce that Polly was safe and well, and that he himself was now the father of twin boys. Visiting the Andover nursing home a few days later, Alix hugged both Jonathan and Polly.

'I didn't know,' said Polly, still dazed. 'I mean – there was Nicky, and I was delighted with him, and so relieved it was all over, and then the nurse said, "What's that funny lump?" and the funny lump was Harry.'

Polly's boys were tucked into one cradle, face to face, a mirror image, red wrinkled hands drifting across each other's crumpled features. Alix stroked a tiny, fragile head, velvety with golden down, saw the violet skin about the eyes and nose, and breathed in the beautiful, unique scent of a newborn baby. Driving back from the nursing home, she thought of Rory, and how he had howled from Naples to Salisbury, and had not quietened until they had reached the safety of Owlscote.

That had been more than twelve years ago. Now Rory was almost the same height as herself, and would next year leave his prep school for a public school in the neighbouring county of Hampshire. It was a source of great pleasure to Alix that Rory and Derry got on so well. Shortly after she had accepted Derry's proposal she had travelled to Rory's school and told him about her forthcoming marriage. 'Do you mind?' she had said, filled with sudden anxiety. He had not spoken, he had just hugged her, checking first, of course, that none of his schoolfriends would see.

Maddy came to stay at Owlscote, and so did Sophie Berkoff and Freddie Maycross. Freddie, frail now, and leaning heavily on his walking-stick, shook Derry's hand. 'Pipped me at the post, dear boy, pipped me at the post.' Derry coaxed Roma to Owlscote. Roma's high heels sank in the muddy drive, and she did not venture beyond the terrace to the garden. But she and Alix painted a vast, colourful mural on the dining-room wall.

'Such *scope*!' muttered Roma, a paintbrush in the mouth. 'You are so lucky!' Then she looked narrowly at Alix.

'You must work for *Storm*.'

'Painting?'

'Of course. Masses to do, and you must have time on your hands now, without the guest house. What do you think?'

She accepted, of course. Roma taught her the tricks of her trade. Alix learned how to make brand-new factory-made cupboards look battered and old, by applying two layers of paint and rubbing off the top one. She learned to gild mirrors, and how to make an undistinguished desktop appear to be made of marble or malachite or tortoiseshell. She painted raw wooden tables with an antique craquelure, so that they looked centuries old. She decorated cabinets and fireplaces, writing-desks and blanket boxes. On the old crockery and trays and pieces of furniture that Derry bought through house auctions, she painted colourful wreaths of flowers, plump fruit and butterflies. They sold them through the shop for ten times their original price. She practised the art of concealment, she thought, making the new old, and the plain fanciful.

Her first commission was a mural for a dining-room in a house in West London. Roma said, 'Oh, *just* the job for you, Alix,' and accompanied her there. The house faced onto the river, so that a reflected watery light flickered on the pale plaster. Roma introduced Alix to the owner of the house, an actor, and Alix stared at the vast expanse of wall. Just for a moment, her heart faltered, and she whispered, 'Roma – I'm not sure—'

But Roma said sternly, 'Nonsense. You'll do a wonderful job. Just nothing *affected*. No mermaids. Definitely no mermaids.'

So Alix picked up her paintbrush and set to work. She painted a river scene, the painted water on the wall reflecting the mutable grey of the Thames. Barges and tugboats plied the real river, tea-clippers and barquentines the painted one. The actor was delighted, and gave a huge dinner party, and invited all his friends. Further commissions followed.

Alix worked steadily throughout June and July. She and Derry lived in London during the week, and at Owlscote at weekends. Throughout his long summer holidays, Alix remained at Owlscote with Rory.

Clients began to ask for her by name. In the autumn, Alix was commissioned to decorate a room in a cottage in Sussex. She sketched out on the wall *trompe l'oeil* niches, and inside each niche she painted a small, precious object. She copied the treasures from the clutter in Owlscote's attics, and from her own sketchbooks. An Egyptian amulet, a Mesopotamian statuette.

A Greek vase, and a blue bead from the Eagle's Nest.

Working at the cottage, she slept each night in a small inn in the village. She realized after a while that she was not far from the nursing home in which she had worked during the war. She borrowed a bicycle from the innkeeper's wife, and cycled over to Fallowfield one afternoon. It was boarded up, used only for furniture storage, so Alix clambered over a locked gate, and wandered around the garden. The summer house in which Edward had first shown her his sketch of Owlscote was gone, and the tangle of trees and rhododendrons had thickened, so that one could no longer walk through the copse to the Downs. Dead leaves smudged the grass, and the bare, black branches of the trees were silhouetted against a pale sky. There was a muted melancholy about the place, as though the house itself remembered all the maimed and brutalized young men who had passed through its doors. She did not remain there long: the house, with its memories of youth and war, saddened her.

Yet she had never, she thought, spent a happier year. Sometimes, at the end of the day, she would let herself into the London flat and wait for Derry. She would draw the curtains, and pour herself a drink, and wander around the familiar rooms, letting her fingertips trail across a stack of old books, a musty, folded tapestry, an orange box full of china. And then she would undress, and slip between the silk sheets, and wait for him. And he, coming home, would not speak, but would draw back the coverlet and make love to her as she lay in the darkness. Neither sight nor sound distracted them: there was only his lips, tracing the contours and hollows of her body, and the pleasure coiling and leaping inside her.

*   *   *

In the autumn of 1934, May travelled to Bell Wood for Ella's birthday. It was years – *decades*, May thought – since she had done any more than send a present and a note, but this year, as she searched for brown paper to wrap the parcel, she had felt a flicker of guilt, a flicker which sparked and glowed and could not be put out.

Sitting in a railway carriage, May watched the rolling Essex countryside flatten and extend into the fields and hedgerows of south Cambridgeshire. She felt guilty, she acknowledged, because of Daisy. It was not that she regretted refusing to help Daisy, but she saw, looking back, that during the months that had followed their conversation in Selfridges she had evaded her younger sister. There was a sticky messiness that clung to Daisy, that May had always tried to avoid, afraid that it might drag her too down into chaos. Left to her own devices, Daisy had resolved the problem of her unwanted pregnancy in her own way, with a butcher in a clinic with smart lettering on the door and poorly sterilized equipment in the operating theatre. Daisy had nearly died; Daisy would have no more children. The episode had been hushed up: a late miscarriage, poor creature. Yet there were whispers, of course.

There was no need to whisper about Daisy's divorce: banner headlines in the more lurid newspapers proclaimed the history of Daisy and Pip's marriage to the world. Though Pip had, rather to May's surprise, honoured his promise to do the decent thing and take the blame, gossip, and Daisy's fatal carelessness, had ensured that plenty of juicy details had been made public. So Papa had, as Daisy had predicted, been furious, and had, as May had dreaded, cut off all contact with his youngest daughter. Thus the journey to Bell

Wood, a belated attempt to piece together what remained of the Lanchbury family.

At Cambridge station, May hailed a cab. There was a time, she recalled, when a uniformed chauffeur would have met her at the station. There would have been travelling rugs and a flask of cocoa in the back of the car. It was not that she missed *that*, it was just that she had begun to mind the breaking up of her family. May recalled her childhood at Bell Wood. It had been divided in two, of course: before and after 1914. She saw that though the seeds of their falling-apart had been sown in 1914, there had been happy times both before and after that fateful year. Indeed, the loss in close succession of first Charlie and then their mother had, if anything, made the three sisters closer.

They had never talked much about Charlie. That had been, May thought, a silent, mutual agreement, born of bewilderment and a reluctance to voice their worst fear – that one could just cease to exist, there one moment and gone the next. Later, they had laughed together about their stepmother, whom Papa had married six months after Mama had died; and they had huddled together under the blankets, their fingers in their ears, when their stepmother had left one night, and Papa's sharp tongue and pacing footsteps had echoed around Bell Wood.

Together the three sisters had endured incompetent governesses, poorly cooked food, and Bell Wood's icy corridors. Together they had played hide-and-seek in the house's vast, cold attics, and had performed the plays that May had written to an audience of cook, housemaid and gardener. Together they had fallen off horses while learning to ride, and trodden on each other's toes learning to dance. Together they had witnessed the relentless stripping-away of the Lanchbury fortunes. They had shared words, phrases and gestures that (only to the Lanchbury sisters) had special meanings. They had loved each other, May thought, because there had been no-one else to love them.

Yet she had longed to escape, seeing how narrow her life must remain at Bell Wood, and at the first opportunity she had fled to London. Papa had disapproved, of course; daughters should remain at home until they married. Papa had disapproved even more when May had begun to earn her living through journalism. Settling in London, she had become caught up in a different world. She had deliberately distanced herself from her sisters. Neither Ella nor Daisy possessed either insight or intellect. Those were qualities May prized, and had discovered in abundance among her many friends.

Yet lately, unexpectedly, she had begun to see that however many friends you had, they did not quite fill the gap left by family. I am becoming like Papa, she thought wryly, as the cab approached Bell Wood's gates. Soon I shall be singing the praises of name and breeding and blood.

May paid the driver at the gates, and walked up the long gravel drive. Ragged clouds skittered across a blue-grey sky, and every now and then a little rain spat, breaking the surface of the puddles. A maid explained that Miss Lanchbury was out, but would be home presently. The house, which was dignified rather than beautiful, was unexpectedly soothing after May's last few hectic weeks in London. Yet she found herself noticing the squares on the silk wallcovering that were lighter in colour, showing where a picture or a print had been sold, and the marks on the parquet where pieces of furniture had once stood.

May walked from the library onto the terrace. From the terrace she could see the avenue of limes, and the circle of box and hornbeam. Bell Wood's garden was its chief joy, its inalienable beauty. No-one, she thought, could take its serenity from them. A young girl, she had liked to curl up on a corner of the terrace with a book, sheltered by jasmine and wisteria, the long, sweeping line of the avenue before her.

She did not walk down the avenue because she knew what she would find – the barbed wire that separated the lake from Lanchbury land, and the signs that now declared it to be private fishing. The absence, of course, of summer house and statue. She had months ago forgiven Derry Fox for that small betrayal, just as she had months ago offered him congratulations on his marriage, partly because she was fond of him, and partly because her pride would not let her do otherwise. Yet, since then, a part of her had remained wary of him. They had never quite regained their earlier closeness, and she had never renewed her acquaintance with Alix, Derry's wife, her cousin. Throughout her teenage years, May's family history had kept her distant from Alix, a distance that would now be hard to make up. And besides, May thought, there was a peculiar irritation about witnessing happy marriages – the pet names, the casual, incessant touching – that she found hard to endure. *That* happy marriage in particular.

'May?'

May turned and saw Ella, standing on the terrace. The two sisters kissed awkwardly. May fished a small parcel out of her coat pocket.

'Happy birthday.' She watched Ella peel back the

paper. Ella looked well. Her fair hair shone, and her complexion, though innocent of powder and lipstick, was slightly pink. If only, May thought, she had not chosen such dreary colours. Ella's straight skirt and mannishly tailored blouse were a dark olive-brown.

'Thank you, May.' Ella pinned the brooch, a tiger's eye set in silver, to the placket of her blouse.

They went back into the house. May asked, 'How's Papa?'

'He's very well. He's in London just now. I've been typing an article for him. It's for a magazine. I've just been to post it. He dictates and I write it down, and then I type it up later, and then he reads it through to see whether everything's right.'

Reams of foolscap, covered in Ella's childish handwriting, were piled on a desk in a corner of the library. May caught glimpses of odd words – 'threat' and 'degenerate' (misspelt) and something long and multi-syllabic in German. She said absently, 'You should learn shorthand, Ella. It would make it so much easier.'

'Do you think so?' Ella bit her lower lip. 'I'm learning German. Herr Schwartz is teaching me.'

They lunched alone, perched on a corner of the huge kitchen table. The room was cold, as all Bell Wood's rooms were, and May wished she had kept on her coat. Ella talked continuously.

'We had so many visitors last weekend. I had to take the dustcovers off Daisy's old room. We had six courses. Just like when Mama was alive.'

'How do you manage, Ella? With so few servants.'

'There's Lily. And Mrs Pagett.'

'But—'

'I *can do it*, May.' Ella's bright smile became a fierce glare. 'I know you don't think I can – I know you're cleverer than me – and that you think I'm a dunce . . .'

May touched Ella's hand. 'I didn't mean to imply that, Ella,' she said gently. 'I'm sure everything went splendidly.'

Ella was slightly mollified. 'Some girls from the village come up to help. And I make lists. I have a list for the laundry, and a list for the meals. I check every room myself. Papa said' – Ella's eyes shone with pride – 'Papa said that Lady Compton told him that her room was quite comfortable.'

May felt a mixture of anger with her father and pity for Ella. Such *crumbs*, she thought. Ella's contentment depended on such meanly rationed approval.

Ella dabbed her mouth with her napkin. 'Papa's always trusted me, May. Even when we were children. He tells me things, you see. All sorts of things.'

There was, in Ella's eyes, a fanatical gleam. May was aware of a sudden frisson of concern for her elder sister. She pretended to be interested. 'What sort of things, Ella?' Dreary little secrets, she assumed. Snatches of gossip about Papa's tedious *ancien régime* cronies.

But Ella only scowled. 'Nothing. Nothing at all.'

May looked closely at Ella. Yes, it seemed to her that Ella looked happier and healthier than she had for years. May doubted whether their father was responsible for that. Ella glowed, thought May, as though she was in love. Perhaps one of Papa's dreadful old friends had a son, or a cousin . . .

They had finished eating. Ella said, 'Would you like to see my room, May?'

'I'll have to leave soon.' Or my feet, she thought, will have turned to ice.

'I've decorated it specially.'

May made herself smile. 'I'd love to see it, Ella.'

She followed her sister upstairs. Here, the Lanchburys' losses were more evident. The corridors, empty of rugs and ornament, echoed.

'Look,' said Ella. She opened her bedroom door. The curtains were half drawn, and May had to blink several times before she was able to focus in the darkness. Then, the chill that had already touched her fingers and toes began to spread, reaching for the core of her body.

The room was a shrine. There were photographs on the mantelpiece and dressing-table, and banners crossed over the fireplace. Each of the banners bore a swastika, carefully stitched in black felt. The framed photographs were of faces that were already familiar to May from the pages of the newspaper she worked for: the German Chancellor, Herr Hitler, and his henchmen, Goering and Goebbels.

Ella said softly, 'We stayed at Herr Goering's house when we went to Germany. It was *wonderful*.' Her eyes were shining.

'*Wretched* woman,' said Roma. 'So *unreliable*.' She put down the telephone receiver.

Roma and Derry were in the office behind the Kensington shop. Derry looked up at Roma. 'Who?'

'Mabel Barker. Light me a cigarette, won't you, Derry?'

He lit a cigarette, and passed it to her. 'Mrs Barker doesn't like the curtains . . . ?' he hazarded. 'She insists on cerise walls and puce rugs . . . ?'

Roma exhaled a cloud of smoke. 'She has just cancelled. And I've spent *weeks* – simply *weeks* – planning for her – the most wonderful colours, Derry – and the *fabrics*! From *Paris*! – and now the wretched creature has cancelled!' Roma glared at him. 'She's the fourth this month.'

'Surely not.'

'Oh yes. And three of my best clients let me down last year. I simply can't understand it. I've been designing for Violet Parminter for *ages*. I saw her in Harrods a fortnight ago, and she avoided me, the ridiculous woman. I did wonder,' said Roma thoughtfully, 'whether there had been *gossip*—'

'Gossip?' Derry looked up.

'—but there hasn't been anyone since Caroline, and besides, I've always been discreet, you know that, Derry.'

He said mildly, 'I'm sure it's just coincidence. Someone's lost money on the stock market – or a legacy they've been expecting hasn't come up to scratch – and they realize they simply haven't the cash to redecorate their house.'

Roma took a ledger book from a shelf and opened it. 'There were half a dozen late cancellations last year, and the same number already this year. I'd meant to mention it before, Derry, but you've been so busy. But it's beginning to worry me. Look at the figures. If things don't improve, we shall have to retrench. Move to a less expensive part of London, perhaps.'

She went back into the shop, leaving Derry alone in the office. Opening the ledger book, he turned pages, checked figures. What he discovered disturbed him. A tailing-off of orders, a series of ill-timed cancellations and rejections. There was a pattern to it. Roma would be invited to tender for the redecoration of someone's Knightsbridge town house or country mansion. She would put in hours of work, planning and sourcing samples. Then, at the last moment, the client would change their mind, cancel the commission, and weeks of effort would be wasted. Roma would meanwhile have refused several smaller commissions in favour of the larger one. The order book resembled, Derry thought, a rusty can, full of increasingly leaky holes.

Roma had closed up the shop. She came into the office, buttoning her coat. 'I am becoming unfashionable, I suppose.'

'No. Never that, Roma. But I think we need to be careful for a while.'

'Are you coming? We could drown our sorrows.'

'I'll stay a while, I think,' he said absently. 'Things to do.'

He left the shop only briefly to buy whisky and cigarettes. Back in the office, he took all the ledger books down from the shelf, poured himself a glass of Scotch, and settled down for the evening.

He studied the pattern of late cancellations. One or two in the earlier part of 1934, and then several more as the year had gone on. Half a dozen, as Roma had mentioned, this year. And April was only halfway through. Derry studied the names of the clients who had cancelled or withdrawn. All were well-off and well-connected, as most of the people who commissioned Roma's services were. Yet these people, he thought, looking at the list, were old money. Landed gentry, patricians. Not merchant bankers, or newspaper moguls, or film actresses. As he folded up the list and put it in his pocket, Charles Lanchbury's cold voice whispered in his ear. *I have no sister. I have no niece.*

At ten o'clock, Derry left the office. He walked out into the chill spring night. London, a spider's web of connections, spread out before him.

*   *   *

It took him a week to be sure, and then, late one evening, he went to Roma's house. Climbing the steps, pressing the doorbell, Derry found himself remembering his first visit to this house, more than ten years ago. He had been struggling to survive by taxi-driving and by clerking for Jack Swinton. Roma had introduced him to her friends, to her world. He knew that he owed Roma a great deal.

She made him a drink, offered cigarettes. He said, 'The cancellations – I think I've found out what's behind them.'

She looked at him sharply. '*Behind* them?'

'Yes.' He grimaced. 'They're not random, Roma. I made a few enquiries. All the people who've cancelled have one acquaintance in common.'

Roma put down her glass. 'Derry. What on earth are you talking about? So *melodramatic*.'

He was standing at the fireplace. There was an Art Deco mirror on the chimney breast, and two stylized china cats, arching and spitting, on either end of the mantelpiece.

'I – um – fell out with someone. And I think he has spoken to his friends.'

There was a silence. 'If what you are implying is true,' said Roma slowly, 'then *fell out* is hardly the appropriate term.'

'No.' With the tip of his toe, Derry nudged the burning logs in the grate. 'It goes a bit deeper than that.' He thought of the statue of Thetis, all exquisite white limbs and shy, darting glances, set against the riotous vulgarity of Marcus Wenlock's swimming pool.

'A quarrel?'

'I suppose so.'

'Then resolve it, Derry, for heaven's sake.'

'I can't, Roma.'

'But the *business*—'

'Sorry. No.'

Another silence. Then Roma said, 'Who is he? What's his name?'

Derry shook his head. 'I can't say.'

'*Derry*.' Roma's face was white with anger.

'It concerns someone else, you see.'

Roma opened her mouth to speak, and then shut it again. 'Very well. You are involved in some ridiculous feud with a man whose name I am not permitted to know, but who has persuaded his friends to take their business elsewhere. You must see, Derry, that it affects me as much as it affects you. More, perhaps. The shop is my livelihood. I do not, like you, have other interests.'

'I don't think that my grovelling on bended knee would make any difference, you see. He's not that sort of man. Not a *forgiving* sort of man.' Derry looked at Roma. 'If you want to bale out – if you'd prefer that we go our separate ways – then I understand perfectly.'

This time, the silence seemed to last for ever. At last Roma said softly, 'No.'

'Good. Then there are things we can do. Precautions we can take. I thought we should discuss them.'

A few weeks later, Derry travelled to the continent, running errands for *Storm*. After visiting suppliers in Rouen and Paris, he continued north to Brussels. As the train sped across the plains of northern France, Derry found himself recalling the weeks that he and May Lanchbury had spent there more than two years ago. The extent of the destruction he had discovered had shocked him. He had been reminded, witnessing those ruined villages and vast memorials to the dead, of what war could do. Although he suspected that the child that Mme Bonneville had seen had indeed been Charlie Lanchbury, he doubted that such a young infant could have survived the war. He thought of Jon's tiny sons, so fragile, so defenceless. Charlie Lanchbury had been only two years older than Nicky and Harry. War, a grim Leviathan marching across the French countryside, must have crushed him.

Since his marriage, Derry had seen May less frequently, and always in company. He knew that May had gone back to France once more, and that she had found no further trace of her brother. He knew also that she had spoken to her sisters, Ella and Daisy, and that neither remembered anything at all of the day that Charlie Lanchbury had been lost. There remained a niggling doubt at the back of Derry's mind. Now, sitting in the railway carriage, he found his thoughts drifting once again through the ragbag of fact, opinion and recollection that made up both Alix's story and May's. It seemed to him that in both versions there were omissions and misconceptions. He thought of Charles Lanchbury's failure to trace his only son, and the child's reappearance, less than a month after May's birthday, only a few miles from where he had been lost. *He told me that he wasn't going to give his prize to the Boche.* And he remembered the malice in Charles Lanchbury's pale blue eyes. *I have no sister. I have no niece.*

Derry visited furnishing suppliers on the outskirts of Brussels, and then, on an impulse, travelled on to Berlin. He had visited Berlin for the first time many years ago, with Mrs Kessel. The city's mixture of decadence, tolerance and grandeur had always fascinated him. He remembered walking down Unter den Linden, and drinking coffee in the Hotel Adlon. Years later, after he had parted from Sara Kessel, he had visited the Resi café-bar, and the Lunapark, a vast fairground. A decade ago he had been fond of Berlin.

He called on old friends, and explored antique shops and secondhand bookshops. He saw that the city had changed, but he did not fully appreciate the extent of its alteration until he visited Steffie Wolff in her apartment in Wilmersdorf. Frau Wolff had been a close friend of Sara Kessel; her family were bankers and businessmen. Now in her sixties, Frau Wolff's apartment was a treasure-cave of rare prints, medieval books and paintings, antique furniture and ceramics.

Steffie made Derry coffee and Schnapps. 'Such a great pleasure to see you, Derry. So long since you have visited.' She peered at him. Steffie had a face, he thought, like some ancient, brooding bird, all hawk's nose and black, shining eyes and thin, feathery hair.

'You look well,' she said. 'So handsome. Have you married, darlink?'

'Yes. She's called Alix, and she's very beautiful.'

'That's good.' Frau Wolff nodded approvingly. 'Young men should marry. Have you children?'

'Alix has a son, Rory. We have no children of our own yet.'

'You must have children, Derry. Lots and lots of children. I have four children and twelve grandchildren, and they have, till now, brought me only pleasure.'

He looked up at her. She shrugged. 'Berlin has changed. You have seen that, surely, darlink.'

'The trees – in Unter den Linden . . .' He had noticed that the great lime trees that had once lined the broad avenue had been felled, replaced by small saplings.

'Herr Hitler cut the lime trees down to make room for his processions.' Frau Wolff's tongue curled in distaste around the word *processions*. 'There is a song, Derry, which says that as long as the old trees bloom on Unter den Linden, nothing can defeat Berlin.'

There was a silence. 'How are the others?' he asked. 'Rosa and Tilly and Pieter . . .'

'Rosa married Hans Fischer – the draughtsman – you remember him, don't you, Derry? They have two children, a girl and a boy. Tilly lives in Paris now. She realized that it would be impossible for her here.'

He said slowly, 'Because she's Jewish?'

'Of course. As I am. You saw Tilly in *Faust*, didn't you, Derry? Such a marvellous Gretchen. Tilly tried to stay – she wanted to stay – but they wouldn't give her any work. Imagine – an artist of Tilly Dorfeld's greatness, being reduced to walk-ons and single lines.' Frau Wolff's old, sad eyes fixed on Derry. 'Pieter, too, must leave. The Nazis do not like homosexuals. They do not like anyone who is different. Anyone who *thinks*.'

She refilled his glass of Schnapps. 'That is why I said to you, Derry, that until now my children have brought me only pleasure. I tell them they must leave Berlin, you see. They must leave Germany. That there is nothing here for them now. Yet they insist on staying.'

Derry thought of all the people he knew who were *different*. He preferred people who were different.

'And you, Steffie?' he said. 'Will you go?'

Steffie shook her head. 'No, darlink, I won't. I am too old. Too *creaky* for such a journey. And besides, Berlin is my home. I love Berlin. And I love my country.' She looked around the room. 'I help my friends to leave, though. I buy their trinkets – their ornaments, their jewellery. Their treasures. It costs money for a Jew to leave Berlin, Derry. A lot of money.'

* * *

Alix was asleep in the London flat when Derry arrived home in the early hours of the morning. Hearing the scratch of his key in the lock, and his quiet footsteps in the adjacent room, she called out his name.

He opened the bedroom door. 'I was trying not to wake you, darling.' He kissed her.

'I was only dozing.' He sat down on the edge of the bed. She looked closely at him. 'You look exhausted.'

'Sea crossings,' he said, with a wry grin. 'You know how hopeless I am.'

Sitting up behind him, she put her arms around his neck, and kissed the back of his head. 'So well travelled, Derry,' she said mockingly, 'and still suffering from *mal de mer.*'

He made a face. She said, 'Was it a good trip?'

'Useful. The place in Brussels agreed to give me a ten per cent reduction if I put in a larger order. That'll please Roma.'

She saw him pass the back of his hand across his eyes. 'Derry?' she said. 'What is it? Tell me.'

He was silent for a moment. 'There have been – problems.'

'What sort of problems?'

'Late cancellations of big orders. So Roma's had to play safe and take on a lot of small commissions instead. And . . .' He paused. 'Charles Lanchbury's behind the cancellations, Alix, I'm sure of it.'

She did not speak, but sat back on the bed, listening to him as he described the pattern of the late cancellations, suddenly cold, wrapping the coverlet around her. The dim light in the room shadowed his face, marking runnels of black below his eyes, around his nose. As Derry spoke, Alix thought of Charles

Lanchbury. She recalled herself, fourteen years old, not much more than a child, the target of her uncle's cold, terrifying anger. No, not anger, she thought, suddenly, looking back, remembering. *Venom* – that was the word. As though the discarded snakeskin that Charlie had found in the wood had somehow come to life again and taken on form and substance, and had fixed its frozen gaze on her, eyes gleaming, forked tongue spitting.

She shuddered. Derry had fallen silent. Then she heard him say: 'And . . . I went to Berlin. I've always loved Berlin.'

She saw that his eyes were sad. 'And now . . . ?'

He ran his hands through his hair, so that his short black curls stuck out in a spiky aureole. 'I visited an old friend. Steffie Wolff. She knew Sara well. Steffie and I discussed mutual acquaintances. So-and-so has been imprisoned by the Nazis, and so-and-so has been beaten to a pulp by the SA. And some of her Jewish friends have emigrated, and others are waiting, knowing they should go, but praying that things will change, or struggling to find the cash. And I couldn't help thinking – what if something like that should happen here? What would happen to *my* friends? Sophie is Jewish, of course, Alix. She's a Communist, too. There are plenty of Communists in Dachau. And then there's Roma, who prefers girls, and Lawrence, who prefers boys, and—'

Alix said softly, 'It won't happen here, Derry. It just won't.'

'You can't be sure.' She hardly caught the whispered words. Turning, he held her tightly, as though her presence, her solidity, gave him reassurance.

Then he sighed. 'And I felt – useless. Caught up in all

417

this trivia.' The wave of his hand indicated the clutter of books, furniture and ornaments which Derry bought at house auctions and sold on, which so often crowded the flat.

He rose from the bed. 'So I bought some things from Steffie.' He stooped to unbuckle his rucksack. Alix saw him draw out an ivory plaque, a necklace, a book. 'Just little things,' he said, looking down at them, 'but I mean to buy more next time. Steffie bought them from friends of hers. Jewish friends who need hard cash to get out of the country. Only Steffie hasn't much money herself now. The Nazis intend to bleed the Jews dry, you see, Alix. So I bought these things from Steffie, and gave her what currency I had with me.' He looked at Alix. 'They're not worth much – just trinkets.' He let the necklace trail through his fingers. Blue stones gleamed as they caught the light. 'The chap who sold Steffie this necklace thought they were sapphires. But they're not, of course. Just glass. But Steffie didn't tell him that.'

He sat back on the chair, silent, staring into the darkness. After a while, he said, 'I used my own money, Alix. This is nothing to do with *Storm*. And I told Steffie I'd come back to Berlin as soon as I could.' He looked at Alix. 'Do you mind?'

'Mind?' She stared at him. 'Why should I mind?'

'Because, with the problems with the shop, we may run short of cash. We may have to be careful.'

She smiled. 'Six months after I first went to live at Owlscote, Derry, I had thirty pounds in the bank. Thirty pounds in the whole world. And the ceilings were falling down, and we were running out of coal, and Rory was growing out of his boots. I'm used to being careful. I don't mind being careful.'

She rose from the bed and went to him. She put her arms round him, resting the side of her face against his shoulder, closing her eyes. 'And of course you must go back to Berlin, Derry. And of course you must do whatever you can to help.'

He reached up his hand, and threaded his fingers through hers. After a long time, he said softly, 'Before I went away, Alix, you thought you might be—'

She felt a pang of sadness. She whispered, 'No, Derry – I'm not pregnant.'

She had been a week late. She had begun to hope, she had begun, almost, to be sure. And then, early that morning, she had felt the familiar ache in her belly. Each month, the disappointment seemed more crushing.

But she said lightly, 'We'll just have to try harder, won't we?' and he drew her to him, lifting her onto his lap, and began to kiss her.

In mid-September they drove Rory to his new school. Leaving him in the care of his housemaster, driving away through crowds of bewildered parents and nervous new boys, Alix wept. The following day Derry went back to Berlin. He had cashed in some shares. From Steffie, he bought a tortoiseshell mantel clock, a Delft plate, and an enamel goblet.

He took two more journeys in the autumn of the year, tagging them onto necessary business trips for *Storm*. In an icy December, a fortnight before Christmas, he met by arrangement the owner of a small collection of jades in a quiet corner of a park in Berlin. There was snow on the ground, and desperation in the man's dark eyes as he handed Derry the package. Unfolding the wrapping, Derry saw the figures – bat, dragon and fish – carved from opaque green stone.

The park bench by which he and the jades' owner had met was painted yellow. Yellow park benches were for the use of Jews. That same year, laws had been passed in Germany forbidding marriage between Jew and non-Jew, and forbidding Jews to work in non-Jewish households. The owner of the jades had asked of Derry two thousand pounds in cash, so that he and his wife could emigrate to Palestine. Derry hid the jades in the lining of his suitcase.

Crossing the border between Germany and Holland, he was aware of relief, and a sense of horror. He wanted literally to brush the dust from the soles of his shoes. It seemed to him that a dark shadow was forming in the centre of Europe, a shadow that threatened to grow and spread, until it smothered them all.

He took the Harwich ferry from the Hook of Holland. He remained on deck throughout the voyage, even though the sulphurous sky was spitting snow. Hunched in his coat, his mind darted edgily through the events of his weeks abroad. He had no doubt that war would come. Fascism, which fed off violence, needed war. They had a few years, he thought, no longer. He found himself wishing he could hold back the passage of time. Once he had longed for fame and recognition; just now, all he wanted was to keep Alix and Rory safe. He wondered whether they were right even to consider bringing another child into such a world. But it seemed to him that a child represented hope, and that without that hope one was just giving up oneself to the shadows.

He understood completely that war threatened both his family and his livelihood. That they would not survive the coming havoc unaltered. Thus the frenetic activity, thus the frequency of his journeys abroad. He must do what he could to ensure their survival.

Docking in Harwich, he caught the train to London. It was evening, and sleet trailed through the cold air. Walking through London's busy streets, Derry caught sight of a group of men spilling out of the Carlton Hotel. He recognized one of them immediately. Charles Lanchbury, in top hat and tails and white silk scarf. It was not until they passed beneath a street lamp, and he saw their faces illuminated by the yellow glare, that he recognized the others: Sir Henry Channon, and Ernest Tennant, and the German ambassador, von Ribbentrop. *Ribbentrop*. Derry watched for a while, and then, longing for Alix, he walked quickly home.

Four weeks later Alix was helping Roma in the shop. They were getting *Storm* ready for the January sales. They had heaved furniture into place, and had crawled around, fixing price tags to articles, draping lengths of fabric from poles.

Roma was standing on a stepladder, a hammer in her hand. 'We're almost out of string,' she said, through a mouthful of tacks. 'Do you think, Alix . . . ?'

Alix went into the office. She had spent the previous day touching up damaged pieces of furniture with paint. The room still smelt of turpentine. She stood still for a moment, trying to quell the dizziness that suddenly blurred her head. Then, as she reached up to the shelf where they kept the string, the floor swooped and rocked, and the room went greenish-black.

When she came to, she was lying on the carpet, a clutter of pens, papers and paintbrushes around her. Roma was kneeling over her, looking anxious, fanning her with a foolscap folder.

'Too much caviar?' asked Roma. 'Or perhaps the champagne . . .' The previous night they had belatedly celebrated the New Year.

Alix blinked. The floor no longer rocked, and the dark miasma had cleared. She shook her head. 'I think,' she said – and when her voice trembled she knew that it was with happiness – 'I think that I'm pregnant.'

CHAPTER FIFTEEN

In the early months of her pregnancy, Alix looked at Derry severely, and said, 'You won't *fuss*, will you, Derry?' She meant, you won't behave like Jonathan.

He did not fuss, even when Alix insisted on continuing to work for Roma. As soon as the nausea and faintness had passed, she went back to her murals and friezes. At half term, Rory came home to Owlscote. Cooking his tea, Alix took a deep breath and told him about the baby.

'The doctor thinks it'll be born in September. So I shall look like an elephant all the summer months, I'm afraid.'

Rory mumbled something unintelligible. Alix, turning thankfully aside from the horrible glistening fried eggs and fat pink sausages, glanced at him. He had shot up like a beanpole this year. There was a small sprinkling of spots around his chin and he no longer seemed quite in control of his gangling limbs and enormous feet.

She put the plate on the table in front of him, and said tentatively, 'Rory, you do know about babies, don't you?'

'*Mum!*' He looked at her, red-faced and anguished,

and then speared a sausage and ate it whole.

Years ago, the cat had given birth to kittens: Alix remembered Rory's astonishment and questions, and her own attempts to answer them honestly. Since then, she acknowledged, there were topics she had evaded, and questions that she herself had not known the answers to. Lacking brothers, she had known no adolescent males other than her own son. Looking at Rory, now teetering on the verge of adulthood, she felt ashamed of herself.

She must put matters right, she thought. 'I mean,' she said, 'about how babies get there and how they are born, and—'

'*Mum!*' he wailed again.

She sat down beside him. 'It's just that I knew almost nothing until you were actually born, Rory. I thought you might come out of my belly button.'

He sighed. 'Of course I know all that stuff. Everyone at school knows all that stuff. We did it in Biology with Parsons. And besides, Derry told me everything *years* ago.'

'Oh,' she said faintly, and reached over and ruffled his silky, fine hair. He grimaced only slightly and, relieved, she made herself a cup of tea.

Working in rambling country mansions and smart town houses, Alix hid her growing belly beneath a painter's smock. Through her paintbrush, nature also swelled and burgeoned. Fat cherubs fluttered around ornate fireplaces, and cornucopias of fruit spilled across cornices and mouldings. Then, when in the summer her ankles swelled and her back ached, Alix retreated to the little office behind the shop, and sat gilding picture frames, and painting swathes of flowers and shells around looking-glasses.

Yet, in the summer heat, she found herself longing for Owlscote. Derry, returning to London from Europe one afternoon, discovered her wilting and pale in the close, heavy city sun. When she demurred he insisted, packing a bag for her, driving her down to Wiltshire that very afternoon. She need not be bored, Derry pointed out. If she chose to keep on working, then she could just as well work at Owlscote. And she would not be lonely. Polly and Jonathan lived only twenty miles away, and would visit frequently. And he himself would spend as much of his time at Owlscote as possible. Every weekend, he promised. *Storm* could wait; even Berlin could wait. And besides, it was almost the end of the summer term, and Rory would soon be home.

Two men arrived every fortnight or so with a vanful of furniture and fire surrounds which they lugged into the Great Hall. Alix found new inspiration in Owlscote's library. She decorated a mirror with a border of Jacobean chevrons, and a wooden chest with white birds in flight, like the ones she and Edward had found in the mosaic in the desert. When her work was complete, the men would reappear, and take the finished pieces back to London.

Derry had tentatively suggested a London specialist, but Alix refused, preferring to give birth to her baby in a nursing home in Salisbury. During the final months of pregnancy, she endured, Alix thought, every possible ailment. Dr Arthur spoke to her of minor discomforts, and she swallowed down both her irritation and whatever useless concoction he prescribed. Her belly swelled, her face became rounder, even her *feet*, for heaven's sake, seemed to have become bigger. When she caught sight of herself in the mirror, she thought that she looked grotesque. Eventually she no longer fitted in the passenger seat of the car, and she could not stoop to weed the flower beds. The house, with its steep stairs and narrow, crooked passageways, began to tire her. Most of the things she liked to do – long walks, and tidying up the garden, and visiting the library in Salisbury, became impossible. She recalled working in the desert, digging in the sand, into the last month of her pregnancy with Rory. I am getting old, she thought, old and tired. It wearied her to move from library to kitchen to drawing-room. Plates and furniture remained undecorated in the Great Hall, her paintbox put away, her brushes clean and unused.

In the bath, she lay with her arm across her belly, feeling limbs struggle beneath her skin. A heel, pressing at her ribs; a tiny elbow, drawn from one side of her body to the other. Time seemed to have slowed, and she longed for the remaining weeks to pass. She wanted to see her baby's face, she wanted to say his name.

Two weeks later, Alix, waking early one Friday morning, was seized by a terrible impatience. She roamed around the house, which was empty because Rory was staying for a week with a friend in Bournemouth, tidying a shelf here, clearing out a drawer there.

Derry, returning from London, stooped and kissed her. 'I couldn't find anyone. I thought you were out.'

Alix was on the terrace, deadheading the roses. 'And where else would I be?' she said crossly. 'Riding? Ice-skating? Ballet-dancing?'

'I thought' – he leaned against the wall, watching her – 'that you might have gone shopping.' He added vaguely, 'Baby things,' and Alix made a contemptuous noise.

She looked properly at Derry. He was just the same, she thought indignantly, his black hair unsullied by the smallest hint of grey (she had found a silver strand that morning and had yanked it furiously from her scalp), his movements as easy and graceful as ever.

She clamped the jaws of the secateurs together, lopping off a stem. Dead petals drifted over the flagstones. She felt restless and irritable. The weather, she thought. The last interminable weeks of pregnancy.

He kissed the back of her neck. 'I could row you on the lake.'

'The boat would sink.'

'Nonsense.' He placed his palm on her distended belly. 'Ballast.'

They walked down to the lake. Derry helped her into the boat, and untied the painter. When Alix trailed her hand in the water, her fingers left a narrow V-shaped wake.

Suddenly, he laughed. 'I was propositioned last night.'

'Who?'

'Weaselly little fellow I met at a party years ago.'

'A *man*?'

The blue sky had begun to pale; Derry's face was shadowed. '*Alix*. It wasn't that sort of proposition. He suggested I join the Anglo-German Fellowship. It's supposedly a business organization to promote trade between the two countries.'

'"Supposedly"?'

Derry shipped the oars, and the boat glided into the centre of the lake. 'It's a bit more than that in reality. Ribbentrop – the German ambassador – uses the Fellowship to encourage political sympathizers.' His eyes narrowed. 'If it wasn't all so utterly dreary and vile, I'd *almost* be tempted. Charles Lanchbury is a member, you see.'

She looked up at him. 'Derry—'

'Don't you think it would *almost* be worth a great deal of boredom to see the expression on his face at some frightful dinner at the Carlton Hotel?' He shook his head. 'But I couldn't bring myself to. I had to decline. All those dull and ponderous Nazi-lovers . . .' Derry pulled at an oar, taking them away from the reeds. 'He's in Germany at the moment, actually.'

'Uncle Charles?'

'Yes. And your cousin Ella. At the Olympics. Dinner at Herr Goering's, no doubt. He is *courted*.' His voice was dry and contemptuous.

The gentle movement of the boat, and the cooling air, had begun to soothe her. Alix lay still, cushioned in the prow of the boat, her eyes closed. She said lazily, 'By whom?'

'German diplomats in London.'

'Why?'

'Because that's how it works. Ribbentrop gets to know Charles Lanchbury through the Anglo-German Fellowship, and Charles Lanchbury lets drop that he has friends in high places, so Ribbentrop thinks, how much *simpler* to bypass official Foreign Office channels and use Lanchbury to influence those in power—'

There was just the plash of the oars and, in the distance, the shriek of a barn owl.

'—because, when war breaks out, Germany would rather we were on their side than on France's.'

Alix stared at him. She remembered working at Fallowfield when the nursing home had first been set up. Furniture had been put into storage, and rugs stripped from the floor. She had scrubbed endless floorboards and helped install heavy iron beds in place of delicate Regency tables and elegant sofas. And then the ambulances had brought the patients from the field hospital to the nursing home. There had been sixty beds, and within an afternoon each had been occupied.

Derry said suddenly, 'You mustn't worry, Alix. I'm sure it won't come to that. If there is a war, it won't be anything to do with us. Germany might want war, but Britain doesn't.'

'*Derry*. Don't *lie* to me.' She glared at him furiously. 'I'm pregnant – I'm not a child, or an imbecile—'

'So stupid of me. I didn't mean to worry you.'

She ignored him. '*When*, d'you think?'

He was silent, and then he said, 'A few years, perhaps. And a lot could happen in that time.' He shelved the oars. 'It's just that so much of Europe is becoming intolerable, Alix.' He looked sad. 'Germany – and Italy – and now Spain . . .'

'*Rory*.' Her heart began to pound, and the baby kicked, protesting. 'You know how much he likes aeroplanes, Derry. And he's joined the air cadets at school . . .'

He said, 'I shall keep you safe, Alix. You and Rory and the baby. And Owlscote. I promise.'

'And the business?' She thought of her decorated mirrors, her *trompe l'oeil* fireplaces.

He began to row again, heading for the bank. 'Oh, there'll be no market for any of that.' Derry's voice was careless, his eyes dark and expressionless. 'The house sales will finish, too, and the art and antiques market will collapse. All this rushing about and buying and selling . . . war would put an end to all that.' She could not tell, looking at him, whether he minded.

A few nights later, Derry woke at midnight, and saw Alix standing at the window. She had not turned on the lamp; there was only the greyish light of the moon, but he saw how she held herself, and his heart began to hammer against his ribs.

'What is it? Are you ill?'

'Not *ill*.' Alix tried to smile. 'It's the baby, Derry.'

His mind became completely, untypically blank. He heard her say, 'Rory was early too. There's no need to worry. But I think we should go to the nursing home.'

He fell out of bed, then, and began to pull on his clothes, mis-buttoning his shirt, tripping over his shoes. He watched Alix move calmly around the room, folding a nightdress and placing it in the open case on the wooden chest, zipping her brush, comb and mirror into a bag.

'How does it feel? Is it awful?'

'A bit of a twinge.'

On the way to the nursing home, he concentrated on driving the car smoothly, slowing at each bend in the narrow road so that Alix would not be jolted. The head-lamps dyed gold the froth of cow parsley and nettles on the verge. Heading towards Salisbury, Derry realized that he hadn't thought much about the baby itself. Pregnancy had to some extent divided Alix from him; he had seen from the beginning that his own small, fleeting part in the whole affair was long past, and that the best thing he could do was to let her get on with it in her own way.

He could not begin to imagine what it was like, to have a new life grow inside you. Few of his closest women friends had children. He had asked Polly, and she had given him a typically matter-of-fact, practical reply that had told him little; he had held back from quizzing Alix, because he didn't want to bother her. He had understood that all he could do was to see that she didn't worry about unnecessary things, like money, or the state of Owlscote's roof. He had tried to distract her, taking her out for drives, buying her books and a gramophone. She had been fractious with him during the last few weeks, seeming to find his very presence an irritation, but that seemed to him entirely reasonable, the distribution of responsibility being so profoundly unfair.

By the time they reached the nursing home, he had calmed down – the drive (he always enjoyed driving) and the velvety darkness of the night had made things seem less threatening, more normal. He helped Alix out of the car, and took her bag from the boot. Then, inside the nursing home, the smell of antiseptic and floor polish assaulted him, and unease began to uncurl once more in his stomach. A nurse with purplish cheeks and a crackling blue uniform looked up uninterested from the reception desk. Alix had paused in the corridor beside him. He saw the way her fists clenched, and the way her face screwed up, and he called out, 'Can't someone do something?' and the nurse, irritation stamped across her features, came towards them.

'Are you having a contraction, Mrs—'

'Fox,' said Derry loudly. 'She's Mrs Fox.'

'Now, just breathe deeply, Mrs Fox, and we'll get you settled in a tick.'

Then some sort of machine seemed to click into gear, and Alix was led away, and Derry was made to fill in forms, and after what seemed like hours, the purple-cheeked nurse reappeared.

'It'll be some time yet, Mr Fox. You'd better go home and get some sleep. You may come back in the morning. Doctor says that baby won't be with us until midday, possibly the afternoon.'

He was disbelieving. 'But Alix—'

'Your wife is doing very well. She's quite comfortable.'

'I want to see her.'

The nurse looked shocked. 'That's not possible, Mr Fox. You may wait here if you choose, but really, it would be much more sensible to go home.'

With something akin to hatred, Derry watched the nurse's broad rear disappear down the corridor. The waiting-room was sparsely furnished, with a few tattered copies of *Punch* on the table. Expectant fathers, he thought, generally pounded up and down waiting-room carpets, or got drunk. Neither option seemed either appealing or appropriate. After a while, he stumbled outdoors, where the cold night air, after the muggy warmth of the nursing home, shocked him into thought. He wished he had cigarettes. He wished he had never inflicted himself on Alix. He remembered the expression in her eyes when she had stopped, hand on belly, in the corridor of the nursing home. Not a *twinge*, he thought savagely. He himself had never experienced agony, but he had wit enough to recognize it when he saw it.

Derry began to drive, but with no particular direction in mind. It was only when he glanced down at the speedometer and saw that the needle had hit seventy that he pulled in at the side of the road. *Idiot*, he thought. He wished that Alix had chosen to have the baby in London. He'd have felt better, surely, if she were in a London nursing home. Just now he wanted plush waiting-rooms, and letters after consultants' names, and the sort of reassurance only a great deal of money could buy, all the things he'd once professed to despise. And besides, in London there'd be Roma, Sophie and May to distract him from the company of his own zig-zagging, frightened imagination.

He sat quite still for a moment, trying to calm his nerves. The small noises of the countryside – the whisper of the leaves, the growing chattering of the birds – soothed him sufficiently to start up the car again. He saw that, in the distance, the night sky had begun to turn grey, announcing the dawn. He began to drive, slowly and carefully, understanding that whatever he did now impinged not only upon himself, but on Alix and on the child.

Because he could think of nowhere else to go, he drove back to Owlscote. But without Alix, the house was strange and unfamiliar. Alix was part of Owlscote; the two were inseparable. He knew that if he lost her, if the worst happened, the house would become unbearable. Dark shadows pooled in corners, and floorboards creaked as he walked from room to room. He did not know what he was looking for – some sort of omen, perhaps, that she might survive. Eventually, he curled up on the sofa, wrapped in his overcoat. He must have slept, because he thought at first that the ringing of the telephone was the shrieking of an owl. He ran out of the kitchen to the hall, and grabbed the receiver.

'Yes?' He could hardly speak. *Alix*.

'Derry . . . ?'

It took him a few moments to recognize Jonathan's voice. He leaned against the wall, his muscles trembling, the phone clutched in his hand.

'Derry? Are you all right?'

He said, 'Fine,' and then he thought *Idiot* again, and pushed his hair out of his eyes with the palm of his hand, and said: 'Alix is having the baby, Jon. And I had no idea it would be *so bloody awful*.' His voice shook.

Jonathan drove over from Andover, and scooped Derry up. Polly had had a feeling, he explained. Derry had nodded blankly, unable to imagine the prosaic Polly as the psychic sort, his own head besides filled with horrors.

Jonathan said reassuringly, 'It'll be all right, Derry – honestly, it'll be all right,' and drove him back to the nursing home. Walking down the corridor, they encountered the plum-cheeked nurse of the previous night. She had altered, though, her frowns replaced by smiles. 'Just in time,' she said. 'Baby was a little bit quicker than doctor thought.'

Derry ran his fingers through his uncombed hair, and stared at her. He heard Jonathan say something, and then he felt Jon take his elbow and steer him down the corridor.

Alix was in bed, propped up on pillows. Her face was greenish-white. He felt a dizzying wash of relief, as though he had been horribly close to disaster, and at the last moment had been let off. He heard her whisper, 'Look at our daughter, Derry. Isn't she beautiful?'

There was a cradle beside the bed. Such a little, shrimp-like thing curled up inside it. He laid his finger against the tiny, crumpled face, and then his vision blurred and he had to turn aside so that they should not see the tears in his eyes.

'She looks,' said Rory dubiously, 'as though she's got too much skin.'

'Nonsense,' said Derry, looking down at his daughter. 'She's just the right amount of skin. Haven't you, sweetheart?'

They were in Alix's bedroom at Owlscote. They had fled the nursing home, a place of cold corridors and unpredictable rules, after only three days. Alix had hissed, 'Derry, I have to go *home*!' and Derry had bundled her and the baby up in blankets and driven them both back to Owlscote.

'And you mustn't call her Josefina,' added Rory. 'She's too small for such a long name.' Josefina had been Derry's great-grandmother's name. 'She should have a small name. Like Anne.'

'Anne Fox. Too monosyllabic,' said Derry. He stroked his daughter's cheek with the tip of his finger.

'Elizabeth, then.'

'People would shorten it to Betty. Or Liz. Or Bess.'

'Marjorie.'

'*Madge.*' Derry made a face.

'Patricia. Hugh's sister is called Patricia, and she's a jolly good sport.' Hugh Hollingworth was Rory's best friend.

Alix said, 'She's called Emma.'

They both turned to look at her. 'Emma?'

'There's an Emma in my history of Owlscote. I thought of her as we came down the drive. She was an Anglo-Saxon princess. There's a legend that the owls flew down to guard her as she prayed at the chapel that stood here before the house was built. The name's not too long, and it suits her.'

The baby had begun to stir. Very carefully, Derry lifted his daughter out of the cradle. 'Yes. It does.' He smiled at her. 'Hello, Emma Fox.'

It was three weeks before she could walk instead of shuffling, soreness lingering between her legs. Dr Arthur took the stitches out, and when he had gone, Alix lay in a bath of salt water, tears streaming down her face at the memory of the humiliation and the pain. Her breasts swelled up, as hard as stone. She flinched when Emma's small mouth clamped round her nipple, and she developed a fever, which took days to shake off. Her nights were a watery, confused drifting between sleep and waking. She'd fall asleep as she was sitting up in bed, feeding Emma; she'd dream that Emma was crying, and wake to find her still asleep.

When Emma was a month old, she pushed the pram to the village. Her legs wobbled so much she had to stop and rest on the bench outside the post office. Passers-by, out shopping, stopped and peered into the pram. Women whose daughters she had once taught to draw, whom she had hidden from when she had first arrived here, walling herself up in Owlscote, offered her their congratulations. Mrs Ritson gave her a bundle of beautifully knitted baby clothes, and the vicar's wife suggested she drop by for a cup of tea. Touched, Alix had to blink away the tears that came nowadays so easily to her eyes.

She dreamed of Emma. When she closed her eyes, she'd see Emma's features imprinted on her inner eyelid. From several rooms away she would hear the smallest cry, the tiniest cough or snuffle. She had forgotten the way one's whole life centred around a new baby. Just as she had forgotten the pain of the stitches, and the way her breasts and belly ached, so had she also forgotten the pleasure and pain of that obsessive and all-encompassing love. The despair of being unable to settle Emma at night. The perfect contentment of sitting curled up on the sofa, her baby in her arms, her own smile reflecting Emma's wide gummy one.

Slowly, she began to feel well again. Her sagging stomach shrank, leaving her with a pattern of white stretchmarks down both sides of her body. The days settled down into something approximating a routine.

Derry said one morning, 'I may have to go abroad again. Just for a week.'

'Of course.' Alix remembered the conversation they had had on the lake, a few days before Emma's birth. She shivered.

'If you don't want me to go . . .'

They were on the terrace. The sun had just begun to peep over the horizon, washing meadows and lake with pink and gold. She said fiercely, 'I want Emma to have *everything*. I want her to learn to draw and to ride and to play the piano. I want her to go to school. I want her to have plenty of friends. I want her to have a dog and a pony and all the books she can read. I know those things cost money. I know you have to work.'

He put his arm round her. She imagined her daughter running, dark pigtails flying, down to the lake. The two of them walking through the woods, side by side. Most important of all, Emma would have parents who believed in her utterly, who never doubted her for a moment.

Polly's twins took turns on Rory's old rocking horse as Alix fed Emma.

'It used to take me *hours* to feed Nicky and Harry,' said Polly. 'That's all I seemed to do, the first few months. Feed one and then the other.'

'I have to tickle Emma's toes to keep her awake. Or she only takes a few ounces at a time. Rory used to gulp for hours, and then howl for more, and then have indigestion.'

'She's—' Polly broke off. '*No*, Nicky. You mustn't pull Harry's hair. You'll make him cry. I was going to ask' – she turned back to Alix – 'whether Emma's put on weight.'

'Two ounces, the district nurse said.' Alix put aside the bottle.

'Will you – I said *no*, Nicky.' Polly rose and disentangled the two howling little boys, and sat both, one behind the other, on the rocking horse's back. 'Will you go back to work?'

'Eventually, I suppose.' Alix dabbed the dribbles from Emma's chin with a muslin cloth. 'I tried to do a little the other day. The Great Hall's full of things I've never got round to. I tried to paint a border round a mirror – the easiest thing, Polly – but honestly, it was hopeless. I can't think why having a baby should have made me forget how to paint, but it seems to have.'

Polly smiled. 'I used to forget everything. I even forgot to make dinner once. I remember an awful day when Nicky and Harry were very tiny, and both of them had colds, and I was so tired that when they finally fell asleep in the afternoon, I fell asleep too. None of us woke up till six o'clock, when Jon came home. The daily help hadn't come in that day, and Jon found *Eva* trying to make dinner.'

Alix giggled.

'Bridge sandwiches, I think it was. She didn't know where anything was. She was cutting the bread with a butter knife, poor thing.' Polly sighed. 'You are lucky having a daughter, Alix. Of course, I adore the boys, but a daughter would be nice. Perhaps this one . . .' Polly patted her flat stomach.

'*Poll.*' Alix stared at her. 'Are you sure?'

Polly beamed, and nodded. Alix hugged her. Polly said, 'Jon wanted to stop at the twins, and I wanted six children, so we've agreed to compromise with four. I just hope it's not twins this time. Poor Jon would go completely grey.' Polly looked down at Emma. 'She's so

438

sweet. So tiny.' She fell silent, looking down at the baby.

'Poll?'

'Oh . . . nothing. I just wondered who you think she looks like.'

Emma had dark blue eyes, and a small feathery covering of dark hair. Alix looked down fondly at her daughter.

'I think she looks like Derry – she has his nose, don't you think? – but he thinks she looks like me. And Rory very tactfully says she's a mixture of the two of us.'

Rory had gone back to his boarding school in the middle of September. He had recently taken up photography, using an old camera of Edward's that he had found in the attics. Alix had been touched to notice that he had included a photograph of his baby sister in his school trunk.

There was a howl from Harry. '*Heavens*,' said Polly. 'You two.'

Alix glanced out of the window. The weather was fine and bright and cold. 'We'll take them out for a walk, shall we? Emma will drop off if I take her out in the pram, and the boys can work off some energy.'

Polly was making the Christmas cake; the twins were helping. Jonathan, coming home after work, kissed both her and the boys.

'Busy day?'

'Mmm. And you?'

'Quietish. Old Mrs Quest has changed her will again.' Jonathan prised the jar of glacé cherries out of Nicky's hands. 'Poll? Are you all right?'

'Yes. Of course.'

But he had noticed that she had paused before speaking. He said anxiously, 'You should sit down – all

439

this standing around can't be good for you – the wretched cake can wait . . .'

'I'm fine, Jon.' Polly attempted to smile. 'Honestly. Just a bit tired. I went to Owlscote today, remember.'

He saw then that Harry was showering the table with raisins, and that Nicky was licking peel off the lemon grater, so he said firmly, 'Bathtime. There's time for a battle if you're quick,' and watched them scoot off squealing to the bathroom.

Jonathan loved bathtime: the chaos of it, the mess and the shrieks of laughter. His was a secret, slightly embarrassed pleasure; his colleagues at work seemed to believe it appropriate to leave the care of their children to their wives and nursemaids.

He had washed flour out of the twins' hair, and had re-enacted the Battle of Trafalgar with three small wooden boats and a rubber duck, when Polly came into the room.

She said bluntly, 'It's Emma. She doesn't look right, Jon.'

'Another cold?'

Polly shook her head. He saw the fear in her eyes and felt an answering alarm. 'She just doesn't look right. She's so tiny.'

He lifted Nicky out of the bath. 'Alix and Derry are both slight. You wouldn't expect Emma to be a big baby.'

'She hasn't grown, Jon. She hasn't put on more than half a pound since she was born. Just think how these two shot up at that age.'

Nicky pummelled Jon with small, soaking fists. 'What does Alix think?'

'You know what they're like. They both think she's perfect. As all parents do.' Polly sighed. 'Alix puts down

Emma's slow growth to her own tiredness. She's started bottle-feeding her.'

Polly dried Nicky while Jonathan towelled Harry's damp golden hair. Jonathan glanced across at her. 'Poll?'

'And once or twice she hasn't seemed able to get her breath.' Polly's mouth was set. 'Alix said that the doctor thought it was a touch of asthma—'

'Derry had asthma when he was a child—'

'—but I'm not sure, Jon.' She made a face. 'We took Emma out for a walk in the pram, and when we got back to the house she'd gone blue around the lips. Talcum powder, please, darling.'

He handed her the talcum powder, and the warm, steamy air became perfumed and cloudy. 'Alix thought Emma must be cold,' said Polly, 'but I remembered a baby at home who didn't grow, and went blue sometimes. She was a dear little thing. Daddy spent a lot of time with the parents. She had something wrong with her heart, you see.'

Jonathan, buttoning Harry into his pyjamas, did not ask what had happened to the baby who went blue. He could not have asked something like that, with his two small sons in the room. It would have seemed to tempt Fate somehow, and besides, he guessed Polly's reply.

When the twins were in bed and asleep, he and Polly sat by themselves in the drawing-room.

'Do you think,' said Jonathan tentatively, 'do you think we should talk to Derry and Alix . . . say something?'

Polly was picking up toys from the playroom floor. She paused, her arms heaped with teddy bears and rattles, and said bleakly, 'I suppose so.'

'It's probably just a setback. If Emma's shaken off

that cold . . .' Yet Jonathan's voice drifted away, his sentence unfinished.

'I'll leave it for a little while,' said Polly. 'See how things go. And then I'll talk to Alix. Not to Derry.'

Jonathan imagined telling Derry that there might be something wrong with his adored baby daughter. Just the thought was appalling. He put the last of the rag books back on the shelf, and limped to the cupboard, and poured himself a large whisky.

Derry continued to rearrange things: a marble fireplace now stood in a shopkeeper's drawing-room, and Grinling Gibbons's carvings graced a factory owner's Scottish-baronial dining-hall. Throughout the autumn, his affairs seemed to be looping themselves into an increasingly complicated knot. There was his interest in Roma's shop, which, though time-consuming, provided him with most of his income. A month ago, he had gone back to Berlin. It had become almost a routine, meeting those broken, defeated people in Steffie Wolff's apartment, and exchanging money for a treasured ornament or jewellery. The price they must pay to leave Germany mounted steadily, the price they must pay to escape a life of constriction, humiliation and danger.

Attending a party in London in October, Derry had become acquainted with a West Coast American who had a gallery to furnish. He had also heard, through the usual grapevine of gossip and rumour, of the possible sale of a Berkeley Square palace – everything, down to the last teaspoon in the last Tudor buffet. And he had, via the friend of a friend, got to know the owner of a nice little hunting-box by the Tweed. The owner of the hunting-box was a recluse, and in the middle of a sticky divorce, and wanted a quick sale. Derry offered to help him out.

At weekends, Derry made phone calls, Emma balanced in the crook of his arm as he talked into the mouthpiece. She seemed to enjoy the sound of his voice; he saw her lids droop until she slept. His love for her had taken him by surprise. He had imagined leaving her to Alix for the first few years, and finding her interesting when she began to talk sensibly. But his feelings for his daughter had been instant and instinctive, a raw emotion that was frightening in its intensity. He had, he thought with sudden dazed happiness, everything he wanted, and his work, an intricate cat's cradle, to support them all.

And then, returning to London at the beginning of December, things started to go wrong. The gentleman with the hunting-box refused to sell, telling Derry that he had changed his mind. Because he could not buy the hunting-box, the owner of the Berkeley Square palace – who knew no greater pleasure than to stand thigh deep in ice-cold water, watching the salmon leap – refused to co-operate. And so Derry's American friend was unable to purchase the lovely, ancient furniture that he had set his heart on, and returned to his white-walled San Diego mansion in a huff. And Derry was left to count the cost of months of wasted effort.

A week later he discovered that the hunting-box had been sold anyway, for less than his Berkeley Square acquaintance had offered. Derry made it his business to find out the name of the buyer. It took him only a few days, and a few days more to learn that the owner of the hunt-ing-box was a member of the Anglo-German Fellowship, and an old schoolfriend of Charles Lanchbury's.

*　　*　　*

Alix said, 'Emma's fine, Polly. Look at her. She's perfect.'

'Of course she is. She's a darling.'

'It's that wretched cold, I'm sure. I thought she'd shaken it off, but it seems to have come back.' Alix, suddenly anxious, bent over the carrycot. She found herself remembering Rory's first illness, the measles he had contracted at eight months. Whereas Emma had been plagued by colds and sniffles almost from her birth.

'The doctor could prescribe a tonic, perhaps.' Polly sounded unconvincing. 'Mine gave the twins the most marvellous stuff after they had croup.'

Much later, Alix thought, that was when it started. That was when another cut was drawn across the pattern of her life, tearing apart both expectation and hope. Polly had said, D'you think you should take Emma back to the doctor, Alix? Just for a check up, to make sure she's all right, and at that moment a knife had touched her heart, a small, chill point, and someone had begun to twist the blade.

Half an hour later Polly left for Andover, and Alix looked down at her small, sleeping daughter, and thought, so ridiculous. Yet she could neither concentrate on the letters she had meant to write, nor eat her lunch. With a mixture of anger and fear, she went to the telephone.

Dr Arthur called that afternoon. He spent a long time examining Emma, a long time with his stethoscope pressed to her chest. She only whimpered a little at the cold metal: such a good baby.

'I should have thought the nursing home would have picked it up . . .' he muttered. 'It's supposed to be a good place . . .'

'Dr Arthur?' Alix's heart was pounding. She felt sick.

'There is a little murmur.'

'A murmur?' She could hardly speak. Her fingers, buttoning Emma's cardigan, shook.

'Her heart, you see. I'm sure it's nothing to worry about, Mrs Fox. These things often heal up on their own. But I'll arrange for you to see a specialist. There's a good man in London.'

She wanted to scream at him, If there's nothing to worry about then why should Emma see a specialist? And, Her *heart*. How can something be wrong with her *heart*?

But she only whispered, '*When?*'

'As soon as possible. Next week, I hope. I'll telephone you tomorrow.'

The Harley Street office was opulent, with heavy swags of velvet curtain at the window, and dark, deeply polished furniture. Mr Patterson, the heart specialist, sat back in his chair, his fingertips pressed together.

'There's a complicated name for your daughter's condition, Mr Fox, but I won't trouble you with that—'

'Tell me.' There was an edge to Derry's voice.

A small sigh. 'Emma's condition is known as the tetralogy of Fallot. Your daughter's heart has not one defect, but four.'

'And they are?'

'The pulmonary valve is narrowed. The septum is incomplete – in layman's terms, a hole in the heart. The right ventricle . . .'

Alix ceased to listen. The words continued, battering away at all her happiness and hope, and in her mind's eye she pictured her daughter's small, struggling heart, incorrect and incomplete. Looking down at Emma, she saw the now familiar faint purplish discoloration around her mouth.

The words stopped, and there was a silence. 'And the treatment?' said Derry. 'What is the treatment?'

'I'm afraid your daughter's condition is incurable, Mr Fox.'

'There must be something . . .'

A small shake of the head.

'So she'll stay small – she won't be able to run . . .'

Mr Patterson bent forward. 'The outlook for these children is very poor, Mr Fox. You have to understand that.' For the first time, a note of pity entered his voice. 'Many don't live to your daughter's age. It is to yours and your wife's credit that the infant has survived this long. Generally, they catch a cold, and pneumonia takes them. It's a gentle end, believe me. With the best care and with God's will your daughter may live a few more months, but I can offer you no more hope.'

Alix found herself out on the street. She had no recollection whatsoever of what had taken place between Mr Patterson's saying, *I can offer you no more hope*, and finding herself standing on the pavement, Emma in her arms. Disbelief and terror jangled together in her mind. There was rain in the air, and the first cold drops began to fall, dotting the pavement. People brushed past them, and traffic roared ceaselessly down the road. She and Derry were still, frozen, icy statues amid the everyday clamour and bustle.

She heard Derry say, '*Damnable* idiot . . . pompous *oaf*,' and then he hailed a taxi.

'Where are we going?'

'To get a second opinion, naturally.'

Hope fluttered. Alix held Emma very tightly. 'Yes. Yes, of course.'

They stayed three nights in the flat. Derry made telephone calls, and badgered and cajoled his way into the consulting-rooms of London's top heart specialists. When the fifth had said much the same as the first, Alix drew him aside.

'Derry, I think we should go back to Owlscote.'

'There's a man in Edinburgh, apparently. I phoned Sophie. She says that he's good.' There was a wild look in his eyes.

The anger that had for days tightened her throat and coiled in her stomach, flowered. 'Derry, I'm tired and Emma's exhausted, and I want to take her home.' Her voice was brittle.

He looked suddenly stricken. 'Yes. I'm sorry. Next week, perhaps. After a few days' rest.'

With the tip of his finger, he moved aside the shawl that half covered Emma's face. It seemed to Alix that the blueness had spread, ebbing down her daughter's tiny mouth to cover her chin.

Back at Owlscote, in familiar surroundings, Emma smiled and fed and slept, just as she always had. The visit to London receded, taking on a nightmarish quality.

The world beyond Owlscote became unimportant. Within the walls of the house, time seemed to have slowed, each beat of the clock measuring the rise and fall of Emma's lungs. At the end of every day Alix ached all over: the accumulated tension of feeling that she was permanently on guard, of feeling that if she let that guard fall, Emma might just slip away. Alix moved the cot into the bedroom that she and Derry shared. At night, she woke frequently, unable to go back to sleep until she had checked Emma's breathing. She remembered the specialist saying, *It is to your wife's credit that the infant has survived this long.* If she had achieved that small miracle, Alix thought, then she could achieve more. Her strength would keep Emma alive. She would keep her safe, and then the months might mount up into years.

Dr Arthur called every few days, and sat and talked to her, sharing a pot of tea. When he said, 'Emma seems to be holding her own,' or 'What a splendid job you've done with her, Mrs Fox,' she beamed at him, and felt stirrings of happiness. When he said gently, 'You must remember that Emma is a very sick baby,' Alix got up briskly and showed him out of the house.

She carried Emma with her wherever she went, cradled against her ribs, as though the steady beat of her own heart might give her daughter's failing one the strength it lacked. She avoided her friends, unable to bear the pity in their eyes. She's not going to die, she wanted to shout at them: I'm going to keep her alive!

She was patient only with her daughter; if anyone else said the wrong thing, or looked the wrong way, she snapped at them. She rejected brusquely all Derry's suggestions that they engage a nurse to help with Emma's care, or consult another specialist. When he tried to insist, she said coldly, '*I'll* take care of her. I don't need anyone else.' When he told her that he had arranged for a paediatrician to call at Owlscote the following week, they quarrelled bitterly. 'She's *my* child. Don't *interfere*.' Her words echoed against the rafters. 'I will not have her poked and prodded', she hissed, 'by some stranger in *my* house.' Emma whimpered, sensing her fury. Alix, frightened by her own anger, sat down,

448

cradling Emma, and whispered, 'It won't do any good, Derry. It's kinder not to trouble her,' and she saw him turn on his heel, his face white, and leave the room.

Everything hurt. It hurt when Emma smiled at her, it hurt when she cried. It hurt when strangers peered into the pram and cooed, 'So sweet! You must be so proud of her!' It hurt that friends no longer admired Emma, but remained mute, pity in their eyes.

It hurt to tell Rory. Another needlepoint scratched across her heart as he looked up at her and said, 'She won't die, will she, Mum?'

She heard herself mutter, 'I don't know Rory. I don't know,' and then she turned away, finding it unbearable that fate should inflict such pain on him, yet unable to lie to him.

She counted off the milestones. The strange, bitter-sweet Christmas they endured; the flurries of snow that marked the New Year. The sharp frost that solidified the water in the pipes. Rory's return to school; the helle-bores, with their curious green and crimson petals, blooming in the snow. These markings of the passage of time were all small, private triumphs. It seemed to Alix that the days, the hours, and the minutes persisted through her own effort of will.

In early January, Emma caught another cold. Alix fed her drops of warm milk from a teaspoon. They lived in the kitchen, the warmest room in the house. Alix put the carrycot by the battered old sofa, and slept there each night, bundled in blankets. Derry did not return to London after the weekend, but remained at Owlscote.

After a few days Emma seemed to recover. Alix looked up when Derry came into the room.

'She seems better. She drank two ounces of milk. Take her for a while, won't you, Derry, while I clear up.'

449

He cradled his daughter in his arms, adjusting Emma's bonnet so that it did not fall into her eyes. 'She looks pinker, don't you think?'

Alix was rinsing out bottles, cleaning rubber teats with salt. 'Dr Arthur thought she looked much better than yesterday.'

'I ought to go to London. Just for a couple of days. But if you want me to stay – if you think . . .'

She felt suddenly unbearably weary. She stood for a moment, her hands resting in the soapy water, staring out of the window.

'She's asleep.' His voice was soft. 'That's good, isn't it, that she's asleep? I'll put her in the carrycot.'

Alix herself fell asleep on the kitchen sofa before Derry left the house. She slept deeply and dreamlessly. When she woke it was already light, and the ice on the windows had begun to melt, thin streams of water trailing down the glass.

She knew instinctively that something had changed, but could not at first think what it was. She sat up, rubbing her eyes. She could not remember when she had last slept so long, so uninterruptedly. With sudden dreadful understanding, she bent over the carrycot. There was a terrible noise in her head, and it was a few moments before she understood that she was listening to her own howl of pain.

CHAPTER SIXTEEN

The funeral bewildered him. The blue sky and snow-drops in the churchyard, the utter inappropriateness of the sudden beginnings of a false spring. Throughout the service, Derry stood beside Alix, trying to force his mind to go blank. The headache he had had for days intensified, as if to fill the vacuum. Yet the thoughts intruded, of course. Jonathan's telephone call, his own drive back to Owlscote from London (he could not now remember one road, one turning, only the screech of the tyres and the blurring of his vision). The following day he had driven to Rory's school, to break the news to him. Jonathan had offered, but he had refused, knowing that it was something he must do himself. Rory's house-master had lent them his study so that they could speak in private. Derry remembered how Rory had struggled not to weep. He had ached for him, recalling the brittle pride of adolescence, and had put his arms round the boy and Rory had pressed his damp face against his shoulder.

After the funeral, people came back to the house and spoke to him, and he answered them, and made sure they had a drink and something to eat and didn't bother Alix too much. She was sitting on the sofa in the drawing-room, an untouched glass of sherry in her hand. The blank, dull look in her eyes alarmed him. Every now and then he'd find himself looking round for the cradle, or realizing that his ears had been straining to hear Emma's cry. Dressing for church that morning, he had found in his coat pocket a tiny white mitten. He had pressed it against his face, his eyes tightly closed, wanting, for the first time in his life, just to stop being, not to be there any more, not to have to endure the torment of recalling over and over again her absence.

When the guests began to drift away, Alix looked up at them and nodded, but Derry wasn't convinced that she saw them. Only when Jonathan and Polly left, taking Rory back to school en route, did she rise from the sofa. He saw her draw Rory tightly to her, as if she could not bear to let him go.

After he had said goodbye to the last of the guests, Derry went back to the drawing-room, but Alix was no longer there. He wandered through the house, looking for her. She was in the kitchen, standing at the window. Her gaze slid slowly from the sink, to the draining board and the dresser.

'I was going to clear up,' she said, 'but someone's already done it.'

All the dirty crockery had been washed up, put away.

'I should have been here,' he whispered. 'I'll never forgive myself for having gone away.'

She didn't reply. 'There was something I had to do,' he said. His voice sounded hollow, echoing. 'You do understand, don't you, Alix?'

He gathered her to him, but she lay limp and unresponsive in his arms, like a rag doll. The house itself seemed stilled and lifeless. Through the window pane, he could see the lake. It appeared to have been lacquered, so that its glassy surface reflected the hard, blue sky. When he looked down at Alix, Derry saw that her eyes were wide open, as cold and blank as the chilly waters of the lake.

After a fortnight, Derry went back to London. He went first to the office behind the Kensington shop. He was glancing through the post that had accumulated during his absence, when Roma came into the room.

'Derry! What on earth are you doing here?'

'Looking through the bills.'

She came to sit opposite him. 'I wasn't expecting you for ages. We are managing, you know.'

He shrugged. 'I thought I might as well make myself useful. It's been long enough.'

'Alix—'

'Prefers her own company just now.'

Roma came to sit opposite him. 'Derry.' Her voice was gentle. 'Something as dreadful as this – it affects people in different ways.'

'The doctor said that. And Jon. And Polly.' He tried to smile, but it was a peculiar sensation, a stretching of skin that seemed numb. 'And I couldn't stand the house. Owlscote. I'd begun to hate the place.' He shivered. 'I had to get away.'

Roma looked at him. 'Of course.' She squeezed his hand. 'Coffee?'

'I'd rather have brandy.'

She poured him a glass, and then left the room. Derry sat for a while looking at order books and invoices, but the figures seemed to jiggle into incomprehensible shapes, and the whole exercise – the gathering of artefacts from the four corners of the globe and the selling of them to over-indulged Londoners – seemed extraordinarily pointless. After a while he drained his glass and left the office by the back door, calling out a farewell to Roma as he went.

He found Sophie in her room by the Embankment. She was typing something long and full of footnotes; the room, with its single-bar electric fire, was chilly.

She didn't scold him or express surprise at his appearance, but told him to sit down on the fold-down bed, and offered to take his coat.

'I'll hang on to it, thank you, Sophie – it's damnably cold in here.'

'You look terrible, Derry.'

'Thank you, darling Sophie.'

She peered at him over half-moon glasses. 'Have you a headache?'

'A rather catastrophic one. Do you have any brandy?'

'Aspirin might be a better idea.'

'I'd prefer a brandy.'

She poured him a glass. 'If you want to talk, Derry, then we shall talk. But if you'd rather not, then we shall just listen to music, yes?'

He did not reply, and after a few moments Sophie switched on the wireless, and began to glance through a sheaf of notes. The music, a Beethoven piano sonata, began in a reasonably cheerful manner – something heroic in C major – but then quietened, becoming slower and softer, the sort of music that did not distract him one little bit, but focused his mind on thoughts he found unbearable. He heard himself saying, 'I think she blames me, you see,' and then Sophie reached out, and turned down the volume.

'Alix?'

'I was in London. When Emma died.'

He thought, that's the first time I have said it aloud.

When Emma died. He had put her in the past tense. He closed his eyes, his fingertips pressed hard against his throbbing forehead.

'She won't let me near her. Won't let me touch her. I've been sleeping in the spare room. She says she can't sleep if I'm in the same bed, but I'm sure she doesn't sleep anyway.'

'A little time to herself, perhaps – a little quiet—'

'I don't know whether just to stay away—'

'No, darling, I'm sure Alix wouldn't want that. A day or two perhaps.'

Derry hardly heard her. He had to explain because someone had to understand so that they might forgive him. And then perhaps he'd be able to forgive himself.

'I'd been having problems – money problems – for months. Something I'd spent a lot of time on didn't work out. And when Emma was ill, I just let matters slide. And then things came to a head, and I had a phone call and had to go to London.' He looked up at Sophie. 'You see, I could manage quite well when there was just the flat, but with Owlscote – it *eats* money. And I didn't want to worry Alix. I've still a few stocks and shares, but you know what the market's like at the moment—'

'No, Derry.'

'—Hitler sneezes and the City gets the jitters. I don't know what to do. I thought I might be able to sort something out, but I can't even seem to add up.'

'Why did you come back to London, Derry?'

He was silent, and then he whispered, 'Because there are all these things I can't bear to think of. And when I'm at Owlscote, I think of them.'

'Emma?' He nodded.

'It takes time, *Liebchen*.'

'So everyone keeps saying.' His voice was savage.

455

'People keep telling me I have to get through a day at a time. They don't seem to realize how much effort it is just to get through a *minute*.'

Sophie offered her cigarette case to him. The small black cigars were strong-tasting and pungent. 'You must be patient, Derry. You have suffered a terrible loss. To lose a child – it's the worst thing.'

'Does it say that in your textbook, Sophie?' His voice was sarcastic.

Sophie exhaled blue smoke. 'I had two younger sisters. They both died of starvation in Berlin, just after the war. That's why I chose not to have children. I saw how my parents tried to keep them alive. I chose not to put myself through that.'

He muttered, 'I'm sorry.'

'I'm not lecturing you, Derry. Just pointing out that I didn't even have the courage to try.' There was a silence. 'Grief takes many forms – I'm sure people have told you that as well. It is often expressed as anger. And often the anger is directed at those you most love.'

He looked down at his empty glass. 'Not to be able to *talk* to her – we've always been able to *talk* . . .' He stood up, stubbing the cigar out in his brandy glass.

'Stay a while, Derry. I shall make you supper.'

He shook his head. 'Things to do,' he said. 'People to see.' He looked at Sophie. 'But I'll go back to Owlscote tomorrow.'

Outside, walking along the street, he had the odd sense of not really existing, as though he moved in a world that had become as unfamiliar and strange as the bottom of the sea, or the surface of the moon. A ghost, looking on, invisible.

It was as though he had discovered that he took his reality from the people he was with, so that he became a reflection in their eyes, and was nothing in their absence. He felt the beginnings of panic, so he walked for a while until he came to a small square, edged with metal railings. There was a bench set among laurels and roses. He sat down on the bench and covered his face with his hands, and wept. The rain mingled with his tears. He wept for his daughter, who would never become a young girl, never become a woman, never have children of her own. He wept because she was alone now, in the cold ground. He wept for the joy of her birth, the transience of her short life, the cruelty of her death. He wept because he had loved her more than he could possibly have imagined, and because her damaged heart had irretrievably damaged his.

Alix woke up thinking that if she hadn't gone to the fair, then Emma wouldn't have died. Sitting up in bed, eyes wide open, she still heard the music of the carousel, and the gypsies' dancing feet.

After a while she managed to separate them, Emma and Charlie, and she got up, and dressed, and went downstairs. In the kitchen, she stood for a while, trying to remember what she was supposed to do. The anxiety of the dream lingered. She wanted to telephone Rory's school and check that he was safe and well, but she did not, because it was far too early in the morning and besides, she had telephoned only the previous evening.

There were a few pots and pans on the draining board – very few, because there was just the two of them, and neither of them ate much – so she put them away. Then she put on the kettle and made tea. She heard Derry's footsteps on the stairs as she warmed the pot, so she took out another cup. She said, without looking at him,

'Did you sleep well?' and he nodded, and said, 'Fine. And you?'

'Oh, fine.'

He stood at the window, drinking his tea. Alix sat on the sofa. She glanced at the clock, and saw that it was only ten past seven, and thought, fifteen hours to get through.

He said suddenly, 'You have to help me, Alix. You have to tell me if there's anything – anything at all – that I can do.'

When she saw the pleading in his eyes, she shrank away, pulling the folds of her cardigan around her. 'You don't have to stay here, Derry. If you need to go back to London, then go.'

They circled each other, she thought, like birds of prey, wary, waiting.

'I don't want to leave you on your own.'

She did not believe him. She thought that he longed to leave. 'I don't mind being on my own,' she said. 'I prefer to be on my own.'

'You'd rather I wasn't here?'

She considered explaining that it wasn't him exactly, it was the whole business of feeling and caring and being with someone else. But she was too tired, and it was far too much trouble to explain, so she said only, 'Yes.'

He put down his cup, and left the room. A few moments later she saw him walking across the lawn, skirting the lake, and heading for the chalk hills. She had noticed how he escaped from the house at the least opportunity. How he could hardly bear a morning, or an hour, trapped beneath Owlscote's roof. How eager he was to pass the time of day with the milkman, or the postman, or the old man who knocked at the door offering to sharpen knives. His restlessness angered and

458

exhausted her; she needed to be silent, undisturbed, permitted to curl up inside her shell again, left alone to decide whether, if ever, to come out.

Polly, serving Jonathan pork chops and cabbage, said, 'I went to Owlscote today.'

'How were they?'

Polly passed him the gravy boat. 'I took a cake, but the one I brought last week was still in the tin. It had gone mouldy. And the *house* – there are cobwebs, Jon, and the grates didn't look as though they've been cleaned for weeks. I thought I'd have a go at them, but Alix wouldn't let me.'

'Good,' said Jonathan. Polly was seven months pregnant. He looked sharply at her. 'Poll?'

'She was angry. Quite offensive, actually. She made it clear she didn't want me there.'

'Oh, *Polly.*'

'I don't mind – it hurts, because she's my friend, but I can put up with that. I'd do anything to help her get through this awful time, you know that, Jon. But I wondered whether it was because of this.' Polly patted her swollen belly. 'I can't *hide* it, can I? And I wondered whether Alix thinks I'm flaunting it.'

Jonathan realized that he didn't feel at all hungry. He put down his knife and fork. 'Perhaps you should stop visiting for a while. Just till things have had time to settle down. I'll go on my own.'

Yet he recalled the last time he had seen Alix and Derry together, their words like knives, scratching at raw wounds. Derry's grief, Alix's coldness and anger, their mutual inability to assuage each other's pain. How, if they passed on the stairs, Alix shrank back to avoid Derry's touch. How his gaze followed her, wounded, burning. Jonathan had come, in the months since Emma's death, to dread calling at Owlscote.

He looked at Polly. 'Did you see Derry?'

'Just for a moment. He was leaving for London. He works there three days a week, apparently.'

'How was he?'

'He looked awful.' Polly's voice was bleak. 'Jon, I never thought I'd say this, but I wish they'd part. For a while at least. They are destroying each other. I can hardly bear to see it.'

He went to her then, holding her to him, her face pressed against his chest, the unborn child between them, needing to feel the warmth, the reality of her, needing to block out the sudden dread that he, like Derry, might without warning lose everything.

The gifts of food and flowers had tailed away. Sometimes, in a half-empty larder, Alix came across a pot of homemade jam, now with a white bloom on its untouched surface, or a basket of apples, withered and brown. Once, in a little-used room, she found a vase of flowers, the stems blackened, the water stinking. There was a note with the flowers. *Thinking of you at this sad time.*

In her dreams she continued to muddle them up, Charlie and Emma. Charlie's heart stuttered and failed, and Emma wandered away into the woods. She slept badly, Alix supposed, because she did not tire herself physically during the day. She neither cooked nor gardened nor attended to the house She did nothing because to do anything seemed futile. She had put all her strength, all her will, into keeping Emma alive. Yet Emma, in spite of everything that she had done, in spite of the intensity of her love, had died.

Her anxiety for Rory persisted. Alix retained just enough control to know that her fears were irrational, born of the loss of Emma, and that other, older shadow. Yet she had to fight the impulse to telephone Rory each evening, or to withdraw him from school so that she could keep him at Owlscote, where she could see him, where he was safe. Her nerves jangled, and she found company exhausting, and new places frightening.

Derry suggested she accompany him to Salisbury one morning. Alix shook her head.

'Why not?'

'I'm happy here.'

'*Happy*?' Momentarily, the look in his eyes jarred her. He held out her coat. 'Only for an hour or two,' he coaxed. 'We'll go for a walk, then we'll have lunch. Then I'll bring you home, I promise.'

She thought, if he says, *It'll do you good*, I shall scream. But he did not, so she shrugged on her coat (it was a fine morning, but she was always cold now), and followed him to the motor-car.

In Salisbury, they wandered around the shops, and then went into the cathedral close. The great spire seemed to loom over her, threatening to tumble down and consume her. She recalled that she had even prayed for Emma – she, who had lost her childish belief in God when Charlie had disappeared.

'Horrible building,' she said, and shuddered. 'So dark and gloomy. I hate it here.' She began to walk very fast out of the close.

May was at home when the telephone rang. Mrs Ware, Bell Wood's housekeeper, was incoherent with distress and embarrassment, uttering a stream of disjointed phrases.

'Miss Lanchbury . . . in the post office . . . an affray, the policeman said . . .'

Seized by a mixture of resentment and anxiety, May caught the next train to Cambridge, and then a taxi to Bell Wood. The housekeeper appeared as she fitted her key to the door.

'Miss Lanchbury's in her room, Miss May. The officer drove her home. Your father's away, he's gone abroad. I knew there'd be trouble. Miss Lanchbury was so upset that he didn't take her. She's been a bit funny lately. But I never thought it would come to this. The police . . . in *this house* . . .'

May went to the kitchen, and put the kettle on. Over a cup of tea, she managed to worm the whole story out of the housekeeper.

Ella had taken to wearing brown shirts and armbands with swastikas. Ella hadn't the sense to keep her allegiances to herself, but sported her uniform in the village. She had gone to the post office to buy stamps, and she had (and May flinched) raised her arm in the Nazi salute. The postmistress's son, who was notoriously left-wing and had recently returned from fighting with the International Brigades in Spain, had been there, helping in the shop. He had tried to throw Ella off the premises. She (and May momentarily closed her eyes) had defended herself, hurling pens and rubbers, cards and envelopes, from their racks. The police had been called, and Ella had been escorted back to Bell Wood in a police car.

'Will they charge her?'

'I'm not sure, miss. They wouldn't say.' Mrs Ware added doubtfully, 'Will you write to Mr Lanchbury, miss?'

May shook her head. Then she went upstairs to Ella's bedroom, and tapped on the door.

'Who is it?'

'It's me. May.'

The door opened. 'Do hurry, May.' An urgent hiss. Ella's gaze darted up and down the corridor. 'I don't want any of *them* to see me.' Ella's voice was muted, secretive.

The door closed behind May. 'Who?'

'They're watching me. I know they are.'

May swallowed. She looked around the room. Ella's bedroom was unchanged since May had last seen it. The photographs, the flag – even, dear God, thought May, staring at the dressing-table, Adolf Hitler's *autograph* – all remained.

She found her voice at last. 'Ella, you must get rid of all this. What will people think? What will the servants think?'

Ella did not seem to hear her. She was looking out of the window. She said, 'I've Papa's rifle, you know, May. He showed me how to load it. Just in case.'

In case of what? thought May. In case the Germans invade? Or, more likely, if they don't?

She took Ella's arm, forcing her sister to turn and face her. 'In the post office—'

'He didn't like my badge, May. Look, I made it myself.'

She was still wearing the swastika armband. May, sitting on the edge of the bed, said wearily, 'Ella, these things offend people. You have to understand that. Wear them in the house if you must, but not in public, for heaven's sake.'

'In Cambridge, someone spat at me.' Ella's face was white and angry.

'You have to be sensible, Ella,' said May firmly. 'And it isn't sensible to antagonize people – to pick fights with them.'

'I threw a jar of humbugs at him.' Ella smiled. 'It was so funny – they rolled all over the floor.'

May rose then, and went to the window, and rested the palms of her hands on the sill. Ella's bedroom window looked out over Bell Wood's garden. May could see the lawn, and the lime walk, and the box circle, and beyond it, the lake.

She saw that it was pointless trying to reason with her sister, so she tried a different approach. 'They could put you in prison, Ella. You do realize that, don't you?'

Ella looked defiant.

'And if you were in prison, then you wouldn't be able to look after Papa, would you?' May's voice coaxed. As though she were talking to a child, she thought, or an imbecile.

Ella's pale eyes glared. 'I'll always look after Papa. You don't need to worry, May. I do everything for him.'

'Of course you do, Ella.' May's tone was conciliatory. 'But if you get into trouble, then you might not be able to look after him, might you?'

'I looked after Papa even when I was a little girl.' Ella smiled again. 'He knows he can trust me.'

She would have to go to the police station, thought May. As soon as she had extracted a promise of more reasonable behaviour from Ella, she would go to the police station.

'I've always done as I was told. Not like you and Daisy. Ever since your birthday—'

She would reassure the police that such an episode would never happen again. She would try to prevent it coming to court; if necessary, she would beg Mrs Morris, at the post office, not to press charges.

'—when Charlie was lost. I was a good girl, then. That's why I went in Papa's motor-car. Because he knew

464

he could trust me. Because he knew I wouldn't tell.'

It took a few moments for Ella's words to register. A sort of echo, May thought, from a very long time ago. They wrenched her mind from this room, crowded with all the dreadful paraphernalia of Ella's obsession, back to the past.

Bewildered, she stared at her sister. 'Wouldn't tell what, Ella?'

Ella's expression altered, becoming suspicious. 'Nothing. It doesn't matter. It's a secret.' She smiled. 'Papa and I have lots of secrets. Lots of special secrets.'

May blinked. 'Charlie,' she said. 'You told me that you didn't remember anything about the day Charlie was lost.'

'I know lots of things you don't know, May. Lots and lots of things.'

'About Charlie?'

'Perhaps.' Ella was smiling to herself.

May felt suddenly exhausted. Her long journey, and the anxiety provoked by the housekeeper's telephone call. The rest of the day stretched out appallingly before her, full of humiliating, self-abasing tasks.

Ella, she thought, was taunting her. Ella was inventing secrets, because that was how Ella shored up her fragile ego and reassured herself of her superiority over her younger sisters. She should arrange for Ella to see a doctor, acknowledged May, miserably. Perhaps a psychiatrist could rid her of her obsessions, her fantasies . . .

Then Ella said, 'Papa told Daisy to tell Alix that Charlie was in the motor-car. Papa's motor-car.'

For a moment May was unable to speak, and then she whispered, 'Ella? Papa said what . . . ?' Then she broke off. 'I don't understand.'

'On your birthday, May. *I* remember. I told you that I didn't, but I do. I remember everything. It's my secret. *Our* secret. Papa's and mine.'

Papa told Daisy to tell Alix that Charlie was in the motor-car. May struggled through the tangle of confusion and shock to think clearly. 'At the fair? Do you mean at the fair, Ella?'

'Of course.' Suddenly, Ella's gaze darted around the room. She muttered, 'You won't tell anyone, will you, May? It's our secret. Papa would be angry if he knew I'd told you our secret.'

'The fair,' said May. 'Tell me what happened at the fair, Ella.'

But Ella, who had begun to chew her fingernails, shook her head vehemently. 'I won't tell you. I can't remember. I've forgotten.' There was a hunted look in her eyes. She glared at her sister. 'Now you must go, May. I've work to do. Papa will be home soon, and I haven't finished my typing. You must go.'

May left the room. Walking down the avenue, back to the bus stop, she had to press her hands together, and to swallow down the cold fear that had begun to uncoil inside her. She tried to reassure herself. She told herself that Ella's secret was just another invention, that her disordered mutterings were only the consequence of her irrationality, her paranoia. Nothing more.

But the words lingered throughout the long, tiresome afternoon. Offering apologies on behalf of her sister at the post office, giving assurances of good behaviour at the police station, they echoed in her head. The possibilities that had begun to take shape in May's imagination were so dreadful, so appalling, that she was unable to bring herself to countenance them.

Papa told Daisy to tell Alix that Charlie was in the motor-car. That Charlie was in Papa's motor-car . . .

At Owlscote, Derry cooked Alix food she did not want to eat, and bought her magazines that she leafed through once, and then discarded. He drove her to Rory's school, so that she could attend Speech Day. She sat for a while listening to the headmaster, and then she stumbled out of the hall and walked back to the car.

Derry appeared a few moments later. 'Are you ill?'

'So dull. So pompous. You know I loathe things like that.' She wondered, fleetingly, why she could not tell Derry that she had not been able to bear it because Rory's headmaster had spoken of 'our precious children' and 'their promise for the future', reigniting both her grief for Emma and her fears for Rory.

But something in his eyes seemed to harden. 'And Rory?'

She did not reply. '*Someone* should be there for him.' He turned on his heel and went back into the school.

Later, heading home, they drove at first in silence. Halfway back to Owlscote, Derry drew the car into the side of the road, and lit a cigarette. A gentle rain drummed on the bonnet of the car. He said slowly, 'I should have thought – I should have thought that something like this would have brought us together.'

'Should you, Derry? How sentimental of you.'

He closed his eyes for a moment. 'What use is a marriage that works only in good times?'

'I don't know,' she said. 'I don't know.' Trees arched overhead, their bright green leaves beating and flapping in the breeze.

'I loved Emma, too, Alix. I realize it's worse for you because you—'

'Did you?' Her voice, like ice, cut through his words. 'Did you love her, Derry? You weren't at home when she died.'

She saw him flinch. 'I didn't know. I thought she was a little better. My God, Alix – if you knew how I've hated myself for that—'

'I can't understand why you don't just go back to London.' The words, a release for some of her anger and loss, began to tumble out. 'After all, you know you can't bear being in the same place for too long, can you, Derry? You know you can't bear being with the same people too long. Or being trapped in the same sort of *life*.'

She saw him blench. She felt a sense of triumph, the closest she had come to pleasure in months. He got out of the car, and stood, leaning against the bonnet. She said coldly, 'I know that you are longing to go away. You can hardly bear to be in the house.'

He swung round. 'Because of you, Alix. Because you don't want me there.'

'Why don't you admit it? You only wanted to marry me because you found out that I was engaged to someone else – and because you thought, all those years you were abroad, that I'd still be at Owlscote, waiting for you—'

'*No*.' His voice was a whisper.

'Oh, *Derry*.' She smiled. 'How you deceive yourself. You've always wanted what you haven't got. You wanted to be rich and famous because your father didn't think you were capable of that. You wanted Edith Carr because she was Jonathan's.' She twisted the knife. 'What have you ever done, Derry – what have you ever *wanted* – other than to satisfy your ambition, or your curiosity?'

Her words resounded, echoing against the trees. The outburst of emotion had exhausted her; sitting back in the seat, she watched the rainwater drip from the trees and slide down the windscreen. At last, she heard him say: 'And you, Alix? Why did you marry me?'

She could not reply. The words seemed locked in her throat. To acknowledge love was to acknowledge the terrible depth of her loss. To speak was to bring back the howl of agony that had issued from her throat when she had seen her baby, still in her cot.

Derry came back to the car. All the colour had gone from his face. She saw him flick his cigarette end into the undergrowth.

They drove back to Owlscote. Alix's anger had faded, replaced by a drowning weariness. She could not, stepping out of the car, remember what she had said to him. She knew that she had wanted to hurt, to make Derry suffer as she suffered, but exactly what she had said had become muddled and lost.

She went into the kitchen. She sat on the sofa, cradling one of the cushions in her arms, pressing it to her chest, shivering with cold and reaction. She heard Derry come into the room.

'I'll do what you want, Alix,' he said. 'I've had enough.'

Her throat was tight. She did not speak.

'I see that I cannot comfort you. That we cannot comfort each other.'

She whispered, 'You're leaving?'

There was the shadow of his familiar crooked smile. 'After all, we agreed ages ago that if it didn't work out, I'd go and not make a fuss. Well, it hasn't worked out, has it?'

She clutched the cushion tighter. 'No.' Her voice sounded odd, rough. 'I suppose it hasn't.'

'Does this count as an honourable failure, do you think?' Again, that unsettling smile. 'Perhaps not. Perhaps we shouldn't even give ourselves that small consolation. The point is that Emma is dead, and whatever we had seems to have died with her. Maybe we never loved each other as much as we thought we did. Maybe that's why it only worked when things were going well. Maybe you were right, Alix – maybe I wanted you because you were unattainable, and maybe you – well, God knows why you wanted me. Because I caught you at a low moment, perhaps, when there wasn't much else on offer. I don't know. And to be honest, I find that I don't much care. I've had enough, Alix. I'll do what you want. I'll leave you in peace.'

She saw him go to the window and look out at the lawn, the lake, and the trees that enclosed them. After a while, he left the room. The front door slammed as he walked out of the house.

There had been a finality about Derry's leaving that sometimes Alix had to veer away from thinking about, but on the whole, she was thankful of the solitude and silence of the house. She slept a lot, and walked down to the church often, and sat by Emma's grave, and thought of the girl she had imagined running down to the lake, dark pigtails flying.

At the beginning of the Easter holidays, Rory came home. Hugging him, a little of the tension and anxiety seemed to slip away from her.

Inside the house, he looked up at Owlscote's Great Hall, said, 'Coo, Mum. Ripping cobwebs. It looks like Count Dracula's castle.'

She looked up. Grey hanks were suspended from the ceiling. 'I hadn't noticed.'

They went into the kitchen. The room felt unusually chilly, and when she stretched out her hand above the stove, Alix found that it was cold. 'It's gone out. The wretched thing's gone out.'

'There's no coal.' Rory was peering into the scuttle. 'I'll get some from the outhouse.'

He came back a few moments later. 'There were only a few lumps left. Hasn't the coalman been?'

Alix couldn't remember. Any more than she could remember when she had last paid the bills or ordered milk or bread or any of the other things she was supposed to do.

'It doesn't matter, Mum. I'll get some logs. You sit down.'

He relit the stove, and made a pot of tea. The tea was very strong, and had tea leaves floating in it, just as Rory's tea always did.

'Shall I telephone the coal merchant, Mum?'

'Yes.' Then she thought, money, and went to the dresser where she kept her purse. When she upended it, a handful of coppers and sixpences fell out.

'I've got some cash,' said Rory. 'Uncle Jonathan gave me some pocket money. Do you think ten shillings would be enough?'

'I don't know. I expect so.'

He went to the telephone and placed a call. When he came back, Rory said: 'It's five o'clock. What shall we have for tea?'

Looking in the larder, Alix discovered half an onion and a few potatoes and a rather stale loaf of bread.

'Are there eggs?'

'I haven't looked yet.'

'I'll go.'

She made omelettes, and they toasted the bread. Afterwards, he said, 'I'll wash up. You do something nice, Mum. You could sit in the library – you could write your History.'

'My History's finished. There's nothing more to do.' She got up, and plunged the dirty dishes into the hot water. She heard Rory leave the room.

It seemed to Alix, scrubbing the plates, that everything she had once valued was finished. Emma had died, and she and Derry had parted, and Owlscote was fast returning to the decrepit state from which she had rescued it. And she, who had nursed wounded soldiers during the war, who had danced in the desert with Edward, who had run the guest house and had painted murals of boats and trees and river, now had no useful role to play.

And yet, there was still, of course, Rory. She wiped her hands on her apron, and went to his room. When she tapped on his door, there was a mumbled reply.

He was sitting at his desk, his back to her. 'Rory?' she said. 'Are you busy?'

He shrugged, but said nothing. She looked around the room. Model gliders hung suspended on lengths of cotton from the ceiling.

'Did you make all these? The aeroplanes?'

Another shrug.

'They're awfully clever. They're made of wood, aren't they?' When she touched a fragile biplane it trembled on its length of thread.

'Balsa wood,' he said. 'And tissue paper.'

'What's this one?'

Fleetingly, he glanced over his shoulder. 'That's a Sopwith Camel.'

He turned back to the desk, but Alix had seen his red-rimmed eyes. 'Rory?' she whispered. 'Are you crying?'

'Course not.' He sounded angry. She put a hand on his taut shoulder.

'*Mum.*'

'Is it because of Emma?'

A shake of the head. 'This stuff' – he pointed to the pot of glue – 'makes your eyes funny, that's all.'

He went back to his model. She watched him cutting tiny slivers of balsa wood with a razor blade, gluing tissue paper to struts that seemed more delicate than the cobwebs that hung from Owlscote's ceilings. She tried to think of something comforting to say. But her voice seemed to have become rusty with disuse, and after a while she quietly left the room.

Alix woke, as she so often did, in the middle of the night. She got up and pulled on her dressing-gown. She had become accustomed, sleeping badly over the past months, to wandering around the house at night. She'd walk through all the familiar rooms, and pet the cat, curled in its basket in the scullery, and make herself a cup of cocoa, and drink it, looking out at the moonlit garden.

But this time, she saw the cobwebs that Rory had pointed out in the hall, and the dull patina of muddy footprints in the passageways. The litter of crumbs and peel in the kitchen sink. The dust, like peachskin, on every surface.

She went into the library. She traced her fingertip across the top of the desk, marking a dark line through the dust. As the pages of her notebook waterfalled through her fingers, she heard the door open behind her. She looked round.

'Rory?'

'I saw the light.'

'I didn't mean to wake you.'

'I wasn't asleep. First day of the hols – the bed's always funny.'

'Of course.' Her heart ached for him.

'Are you all right, Mum?'

'I'm fine.'

'What are you doing?'

'I was looking at my History. I suppose I haven't finished it. I haven't written anything about your father.'

'At school, there's a book in the library with Dad's name in it. Something about Mesopotamia. We did it in Scripture.'

He had come to stand beside her. Alix thought how like Edward he had grown: tall and thin, a lock of brown hair falling continually over his forehead. His eyes were Edward's calm, solemn grey. His voice had settled down at last to Edward's gentle baritone.

'Where's Derry?'

'He's gone away.'

'Is he in London?'

'I don't know. I expect so.'

'We were going to go to Biggin Hill to see the planes. Derry has a friend who's in the RAF. He said he'd take me. When's he coming back?'

She saw that she must tell him. 'Derry's not coming back to Owlscote, I'm afraid, Rory.'

'Doesn't he like it here any more?'

She looked away, unable to bear the expression in his eyes. 'It's not that.' She struggled for the right words. 'Married people aren't always as happy as they're supposed to be. And Derry and I weren't happy.

Actually, we were making each other very unhappy.'
Yet she had begun, in the dark silence of the night, to
miss him. To miss the warmth of his flesh, the touch of
his skin, the sound of his voice.

'Will you get divorced? Hollingworth's aunt got
divorced.' Rory's voice was determinedly casual. 'It was
in all the newspapers.'

He has lost two fathers, she thought. She stood up,
intending to hug him, but he moved away.

'I'm tired. Going back to bed.' She heard him run up
the stairs.

In the flat in London, Derry sat alone, glass in hand,
looking around the room. It was filled, as it so often
was, with artefacts – vases, tapestries, books, pieces of
furniture – that he intended to sell on, either privately
or through the shop. He knew that soon – in a year, or
five at the most – all this would have become so much
worthless clutter. He knew that war would shake
them up – himself, the Lanchburys, even Alix in her fast-
ness at Owlscote – in a way that none of them could
escape. And he knew that when the storm eventually
passed, they would be left empty-handed, changed
beyond recognition, their friends and relations dead or
dispersed, their belongings scattered to the four corners
of the globe. Just then, he longed for the violence of the
storm. Not to have to think. He imagined himself caught
up in a whirlwind, robbed of thought and grief, no
longer able to love or to mourn.

In the evenings, he wandered from bar to bar,
from nightclub to nightclub. He gathered friends and
acquaintances, no-one he knew too well, no-one who
would see through the façade. He was witty, amusing,
thoroughly good company. He excelled himself, he

thought. He heard his own voice, drawing them towards him, and caught, reflected in the plate glass windows of the shops and cafés, his smile.

He came across May Lanchbury sitting in a corner of a small, dark Piccadilly pub. There were three others with her. She caught sight of him, and said, '*Derry*,' and he stooped and kissed her cheek.

'You're supposed to ask me how I am, May. And then, to ask after Alix. Only perhaps it would be better if you didn't, because actually I'm bloody awful, and Alix and I have agreed to part. So if you can think of some other topic of conversation . . .' He realized that they were all staring at him, and his words slid into silence.

May's friends tactfully rose and left. She took his hand. 'What would you like to talk about, Derry?'

He sat down beside her. 'I'd like you to tell me the gossip. The scandal.'

So she told him about the divorces and the love affairs and the fallings-out. Who was betraying whom, and who was trying to ensnare whom. He tried to listen, but the thoughts, the thoughts he could not bear to face, intruded, and after a while he said: 'Dance with me, won't you, May?'

There was a pianist, bent like a lover over his piano, and a tiny square of dance floor. May was soft and warm and comforting. It was good to touch someone again; since Emma had died, his arms had felt so empty. And May was a wonderful dancer, always perfectly in time with the music, her large, stately body sinuous and sensual as she moved.

He held her close to him. Her pale silky hair brushed against his face. He had longed to lose himself and now, breathing in her perfume, moving in rhythm with the music, he managed to forget, if only for a while.

At midnight, the pianist put away his music and closed the piano. He stood for a while, holding her, and then he heard her say: 'I could make you coffee, Derry. Or would you rather go home?'

He thought of his empty flat. He shook his head, and followed May out into the street.

Boiling water, grinding beans in the kitchen, May could, through the half-open door, see him. Derry was sitting on her sofa, his long legs flung out before him, his head propped on his fist. She felt a tremendous sense of pleasure and pride just in seeing him sitting there. It was as though he were hers.

She put the coffee pot and cups on a tray, and carried it into the sitting-room. When she handed him a cup, he thanked her, and looked up and smiled.

'I'm being a frightful bore, aren't I, May? Inflicting myself on you like this.'

'It's a pleasure, my dear vulture.' Only there was nothing hawkish about him now, she thought. Carrion, perhaps, as though the events of the last year had picked him over and left him bleeding.

'How long will you stay in London, Derry?'

'I don't know.' He shrugged.

'Owlscote . . . ?' she said tentatively.

He shook his head. 'I won't be going back.' He put down his cup and ran his hands over his face. 'Alix doesn't want me there, May. She made that quite clear.'

There was a silence. Then she said, 'And you?'

'I've had enough.' Derry's eyes were wide and bleak. 'Can't do any more. I suppose I should pick up the pieces, start again.' He looked at her. 'That's what I'm supposed to do, isn't it? That's what people say you should do.'

When she did not reply, he added, '*Move on. Put the past behind me.*' His voice was savage. 'Don't you agree, May?'

'I don't know, Derry. I've never married. I've never had a child.'

'You lost your mother. You lost your brother.'

Papa told Daisy to tell Alix that Charlie was in Papa's motor-car. Ella's words, which had haunted May since her journey to Bell Wood, echoed.

But she said, 'I was a child. It was different.'

She was unsure whether he had heard her. He said slowly, 'You see, there's the possibility that I was mistaken. That's the thing. There's the possibility that Alix married me just because she was at a low point. Because she was lonely, and because there wasn't much else on offer at the time.'

May's mouth was dry. 'I'm sure you're wrong, Derry. I'm sure Alix . . .' Her words faded away.

'It doesn't matter now, does it? It's over, and I should have the guts to accept it, shouldn't I?'

She took his hand in hers, squeezing it. After a while he turned to her. 'You're very sweet, May. Listening to this drivel.'

'Oh, that's my function in life, didn't you know? A shoulder to cry on. A sort of professional elder sister.' She could not keep the bitterness out of her voice. 'I'm in the wrong job, aren't I, Derry? I should have been an agony aunt, not a gossip columnist.' She pulled away from him.

'May – you're crying . . .'

It was true, there were tears in her eyes. He put his arm round her, drawing her towards him. She heard him say, 'You know I adore you, May.'

She looked up at him. 'Do you, Derry? As what?

Good old May – sensible old May—'

'Hush,' he whispered, and she felt his lips press against the top of her head. She closed her eyes very tightly, seized by a painful delight. Her head was in the hollow of his shoulder, and she was protected by the warmth of his arm. She thought she would have liked to remain like this for ever, pierced by such a mixture of happiness and longing. She knew that if she was careful, and if she made the right moves, he could be hers. She knew that, vulnerable and grieving, he needed her friendship, her generosity. And that friendship could lead to love. And that if she put up her face, then he would kiss her properly. And that she longed to feel his lips against hers.

Yet something held her back. And why, she railed against herself fiercely, should she not have him? She had waited long enough. She had *wanted* him long enough. His wife had, after all, sent him away. Why should she not capitalize on his loneliness, his need for comfort? Why should she, as capable of love and longing as any woman, be forced to remain a perpetual virgin?

But at the back of her mind, Ella's voice still echoed. *Papa told Daisy to tell Alix that Charlie was in Papa's motor-car.* Try as she might, May herself had been unable to remember every detail of that long ago night at the fair. She remembered the gypsy dancers, and their fast hypnotic music. She remembered the tiny monkeys in their knitted suits. She had cradled one, Ella the other. But she could not clearly recall what had happened when they had gone back to the motor-cars. Other things, things that she would have chosen to forget, she remembered in cold, unchanging detail. Yet the night at the fair remained dark, devoid of feature. She could not

479

be sure whether Ella fantasized, or whether she had let slip a terrible truth.

She heard Derry say wearily, 'I just couldn't bear it, you see, May. Owlscote. It seems so full of her.'

She said, with a sigh, 'Emma?'

'I still listen out for her cry. She's been dead almost four months, and I still listen out for her cry.'

May thought of Charlie, and how, a small girl, she had always expected him to come home. How, running to the nursery, she had for so long believed that he would be there, restored to them, sitting in his high chair, banging a spoon, laughing at her. And how, returning from that dreadful holiday in France, she had been certain that she would find him at Bell Wood, safely asleep in his cot. It had taken her a long time to learn that he would not come home, would never come home.

Derry's arm had slipped from her shoulder. Turning and looking up at him, May saw that he was asleep. She remained sitting on the sofa, motionless at his side, for a long time. The proximity of his body was a mixture of pleasure and pain. She knew now what she must do. Taking great care not to disturb him, she fetched a rug and tucked it around him. And went to her bed, alone.

CHAPTER SEVENTEEN

Alix began to tidy the house. A gargantuan task. A little
at a time, she said to herself. A little at a time.

The larder first. Dreadful old inedible things lurked
on dark, distant shelves. She found a tin of Emma's milk
powder, and wept as she emptied it into the bin.
There were potatoes with curling lemon-coloured
shoots, carrots with green fringes, and brittle, crackling
onions. She threw them into the wheelbarrow, and
Rory upended the barrow onto the compost heap. She
scrubbed the floor with washing-soda, and washed the
walls with Sunlight soap, and polished the tiny window
at the back of the larder until the narrow rectangle of
glass once more framed the distant copse.

After she had worked for an hour or so, she retreated
to the sofa, and sat, her heart pounding, nauseous with
tiredness. Yet she persevered. She cleaned the drawing-
room. There was a musty, sour smell about the room.
She couldn't think why she hadn't noticed it before. She
flung the rugs over the washing-line and beat them, and
swept the ash out of the grate. In the library, she perched
on stepladders, taking book after book from the shelf,
banging the pages shut in a small explosion of dust.

In the attics, she wandered among the dark shapes of

the fossils and flint axes. History imprisoned in stone. From the distant past, Derry's voice echoed. *That's not safety, Alix, that's self-immolation.* Sitting down amid the jumble of orange-boxes and tea-chests, she pressed the tips of her fingers against the bones of her face. She thought, it's how I bear it. How I have taught myself to get through it.

She gathered up the writing cases and diaries that had been put away for years in the attic, and went downstairs to the library. The paper was brittle and yellowed, but the handwriting was familiar. She took out of the desk the family tree that she had drawn up years before, and spread it in front of her.

'I'm writing about your father,' she explained to Rory. 'And about his elder brother.' Gusts of rain spat against the window panes.

'I was called after him, wasn't I?'

'Yes. He died at Passchendaele in 1917. I've found some letters from your Uncle Rory to your grandfather. Your father's father.'

Rory peered at the family trees. 'Where am I?'

'Here.' She pointed at his name.

'And Emma? Where's Emma?'

She whispered, 'I haven't written her in yet.'

'Can I do it?'

She handed him a pencil. She watched him carefully print his sister's name: *Emma Beatrice Fox.*

Rory squinted at the paper. 'I'm not sure how to do the other bit. Emma's father and my father. So it says that Derry was Emma's father and Dad was mine.'

'You put my maiden name – Alix Gregory – there. And Edward's there, and Derry's there.'

'Where does Granny go?'

'Just here. Beatrice Ada Gregory née Lanchbury.' Alix

looked at the sheet of paper, and then at her son, standing beside her, his tongue clamped between his teeth, his brow furrowed in concentration. She saw the fuzz of bristly hair to the sides of his jaw, and the way his long body towered over hers. He was no longer a child; he was almost a man.

She took a step into the dark. 'And, Rory, you must write down Granny's brother's name. He's called Charles Lanchbury.'

'Granny had a brother? Is he dead?'

Alix shook her head.

'He didn't come to Granny's funeral. Or to Emma's. People are supposed to come to their relations' funerals.'

'Granny and Uncle Charles didn't get on, I'm afraid.'

'They quarrelled? Like you and Derry?'

'Something happened,' she said carefully. 'A long time ago.' How odd, she thought, not to be afraid any more. Such an unexpected consequence of losing her daughter, to discover that she had been through the worst, and that there was nothing left to fear.

Looking down once more at the family tree, she saw them all: the Norths and the Gregorys and the Lanchburys and the Foxes, tied together, making a pattern. She began to tell Rory the story of Charlie Lanchbury.

The following day, Alix was weeding the front garden when she saw the woman walking down the drive. Fair-haired, pink-cheeked, and carrying an enormous bunch of pink and white tulips.

'Alix?' Pale blue eyes peered at her. 'Cousin Alix?'

Cousin Alix. She thought, Ella, May or Daisy . . . and then, looking once more at those pale blue eyes, she whispered, '*May.*'

'I should have telephoned, I know. And I apologize for turning up on your doorstep at such an unearthly hour, but I must be back in London this afternoon.' May thrust the tulips into Alix's arms. 'These are for you. And if you'd rather I went away, you must say so.'

'Of course I don't want you to go away.' Alix's voice shook. But she put aside her trowel, and went into the house, May following after her.

'It's lovely to see you, May – I'm just rather—'

'Stunned? That the dear little girl you remember has turned into such a substantial woman?' May smiled. 'I would have known you anywhere, Alix. You look just the same.'

'I have grey hairs,' she said wryly, 'and the beginnings of the most awful crow's feet.'

'So have we all, my dear, if we are seen in the wrong light.' May looked around. 'Such a glorious house! So wonderfully *Gothic*.' She paused. 'I came here for two reasons, Alix. One was to do what I should have done a long time ago – to offer my condolences on the death of your daughter. The other – the other was to ask you whether you can remember anything about Charlie.'

She was taken by surprise, but she said, 'Of course I can.'

'I mean, whether you can remember anything about my birthday. The day he was lost.'

'I remember everything, May,' she said simply.

She made tea in the kitchen. Boiling water, pouring milk, offering cake, Alix found herself glancing covertly at May, trying to see the young girl of her memories in the grown woman. She said, handing May a cup, 'I've told Rory about Charlie. You're his family too, after all. I kept secret what had happened for years. I was so ashamed, you see. I told only Derry.' There was

484

a silence. She wondered how he was, what he was doing.

Then she smiled. 'I remember the last time you and I had tea together. It was at your birthday picnic, May. We drank lemonade—'

'And the grown-ups had champagne.'

'We had to eat two plain slices of bread before we were allowed anything nice.'

'I had a wonderful birthday cake,' said May wistfully. 'There were strawberries on top. A little sugar house, and strawberries.'

'Such a happy day,' said Alix, 'until—'

'No.' May put down her cup and saucer. 'No, you're wrong, Alix. You've forgotten. It wasn't a happy day. Not at all.'

Alix stared at May. 'It was warm and sunny, and everyone was enjoying themselves—'

'No.' May shook her head vigorously. 'It was too hot. And so dusty and sticky, and everyone was cross.'

Now, when she looked back, there was a muddle of bright weather and old-fashioned motor-cars and chattering voices. But no laughter. Few smiles.

'Uncle Charles was cross with me. But he was always cross with me.'

'Papa was cross with everyone.' May looked troubled. 'He was cross with Ella for sulking, and when I was riding in the motor-car with Mama, he told me off for fidgeting. I remember that I wished I was in the other motor-car with you and Daisy and Charlie, but I didn't say so because riding with Papa and Mama was supposed to be such a treat.' May stared down at her plate. 'No-one could be happy when Papa was cross. And he was in a particularly vile temper that day.'

'Why? Because we were to go home early?'

There was a silence. Then May said, 'I've never told

anyone. But you must realize that you're not the only one to have secrets, Alix.' She sighed. 'I'm not even sure why I minded so much – or why I kept it to myself. Like you, I was ashamed, I suppose. Ashamed that I hadn't the family I wanted to have. Children do mind about such things. You see' – and Alix saw May take a deep breath – 'something awful happened.'

'Charlie?'

'Before Charlie. It was early in the morning. *I* saw.' Absently, May poked at the slice of cake with her fork. 'Papa hit Mama.'

They remained in Alix's memory, fixed and unchangeable. Charles Lanchbury in his high collar and suit and waistcoat and straw boater, Aunt Marie in her whalebones and silk tussore. Stern and distant and impervious to passion. It was as though those old, faded drawings had begun at last to move, to shift position.

'I'd woken very early,' said May, 'because I was excited about my birthday. I thought I'd creep downstairs and look at my presents. They always put them on the sideboard in the dining-room. But when I went past Papa and Mama's room, I heard them arguing. And then I saw him hit her. The door was ajar, you see. He hit her so hard that she fell to the floor. When she looked up she saw me. She didn't say anything, she just made a gesture with her hand, telling me to run away. There was' – and May's eyes were anguished – 'a horrible mark across her face. I ran back to my room. I was sick, actually. Louise scolded me. She thought it was over-excitement.' May looked across at Alix. 'Don't you remember, Alix, that Mama wore a veil all day?'

'I thought that was because of the sun. Aunt Marie had such soft white skin.'

'I have tried to forget, but I can't.' May's smile was

suddenly brittle. 'So annoying, don't you agree, that one cannot choose what one wants to remember. I still *mind*. How odd that I still mind.'

Trees painted dark smudges onto the lawn. Shadows moved and shifted.

'Do you know what they were quarrelling about?'

'What do married people usually quarrel about? Money . . . unfaithfulness . . .' May shook her head. 'I don't know. But we almost didn't go on the picnic. I remember crying because I was afraid we wouldn't go on the picnic.' A small smile. 'I always longed for my birthday. I was always certain it would be the best day of the holiday, and yet it was usually a disappointment. That was the most dreadful year, of course – and the last picnic – but my birthday was never as good as I expected it to be. There were always wasps, or awful grown-up food that made me feel unwell, and everyone was so bad-tempered. But that was my worst birthday. Even before Charlie was lost, that was my worst birthday.'

Looking up at Alix, she said fiercely, 'Happy days were when Papa wasn't there, you see, Alix. When Daisy and I were children, we were always so pleased when Papa went away. We weren't afraid any more. We weren't worried about making mistakes.'

There was a silence. May stood up and went to the window. Her back to Alix, she said, 'I remember the fair – the gypsies, the monkeys – but there are things that I've forgotten. I can't remember leaving the fair, Alix. I can't remember the cars. I can't even remember when I last saw Charlie.'

So long ago. It was as though it had happened to someone else. In another country, far away.

'I was drawing,' said Alix, 'and then I got lost.' The rain and the darkness of that evening seemed a distant dream. 'I couldn't remember how to get back to the cars. Then Ella found me, and I walked back with her. Ella went in the Daimler with your mother and father, and you were in the Boncourts' car with me and Robert.'

'And Charlie?' The words were a whisper.

'I thought Charlie was in the Boncourts' car, but he wasn't. I was going to get out and look for him, but then Daisy came and told me that Charlie was with your parents, in the Daimler. At least, that's what I thought she said, but I must have been mistaken. When I looked up, I saw that your father's car was already driving out of the village. That's when Charlie was lost, May, I'm certain of it.'

Silhouetted against the window, May remained motionless. There was only the drip of the tap, the tick of the clock. She turned round. 'I must go. The train . . .' Her voice tailed off. Her face was pale, her mouth set. 'I saw Derry last night. He told me that you'd parted. I was so sorry to hear that, Alix. Whenever I think of my own family – how *fractured* we are – I've always envied you for doing so much better than us.' The pale blue eyes, now dark and troubled, focused on Alix. 'Whatever griefs you've endured, you have a home, a husband, a son. Neither Ella nor Daisy nor I can say that. Not one of us has children. Daisy has been the only one to marry, and her marriage ended in a shameful divorce. And Ella, of course, is Papa's creature.' May's voice was bitter. 'We are become an anachronism, we and our kind. The world has no more use for us.'

She gathered up her bag and gloves. 'There was something else I came here to say. I'm about to be very presumptuous. It's just that Derry loves you. I may be a spinster, but that doesn't mean that I haven't loved, and it doesn't mean that I can't recognize love when I see it.

Derry loves you, and he needs you, Alix. He has never loved any woman other than you.'

Alix remembered sitting cross-legged in the desert, joining together fragments of mosaic. Fitting them together like a jigsaw puzzle. White birds taking flight against a black sky.

From a drawer in the attic, Alix took out her sketch-book, and unwrapped the tissue paper that enclosed it. She had not opened the book for twenty-three years, but now the pages parted and she saw the docks at Dover, and the beach at Le Touquet, all carefully sketched in pencil. And – she turned another page – Charlie and his sisters, playing on the beach. The girls' striped dresses were tucked into their knickers. Charlie's straw bonnet was tied with a blue ribbon. The expression on Charlie's face seemed to alter as she looked at it, a smile touching the corners of his mouth, and his hands, raised to catch a ball, beckoning to her, calling her to follow him.

Once more, she looked out of the window of the Boncourts' chateau, and saw the Lanchburys gathering on the forecourt. The chauffeur, waiting in the car; Uncle Charles, pacing the gravel. Aunt Marie, her face veiled, and the three little girls in their white muslin dresses. Uncle Charles's anger was not now with his niece, Alix, for keeping them waiting, but with his wife. Aunt Marie wore her veil not to protect her delicate complexion from the sun, but to hide the scarlet weal across her face. May's smiles and excitement were not in celebration of her birthday, but a terrible bravado that disguised the confusion and pain in her small heart. And Ella? Ella watched her father climb into the Daimler, her love and allegiance already fixed.

Disguises and concealments. The sun, passing behind

a cloud. White muslin dresses and pink sashes, flickering between black branches.

They had driven to the wood. One couple had loved, and another had hated. Louise and Robert, kissing behind the dogcart; Charles and Marie Lanchbury, their mutual detestation smouldering, inflammable, about to catch fire, like sunlight burning through glass.

The jewelled carapace of a snakeskin was moved aside to reveal not the lithe, living animal, but a coil of maggots, feeding on rotting wood. Charlie had ducked through brambles, played peekaboo behind hedges. The nursemaid had been sent home with the servants; the Boncourts, too, had returned to the chateau. Charles Lanchbury had played a game of cricket with his children. The three little girls, conscious of an unprecedented honour, had been clumsy with nerves and tiredness and fear, the ball slipping through their fingers, their button boots stumbling on the tussocky grass. Marie Lanchbury had watched, unable to join in the game. She had been bound by corsets, whalebone and straps, infantilized by lace and baby ribbon. Her body was hidden from view, because it was the property of her husband. As her daughters had run and played, Marie had known that they too would soon be imprisoned by their sex, their class. She had put up her hand every now and then to her face, and had felt through the fragile mask of the veil the bruise that ran the length of her jaw.

The game had not ended until shadows had begun to darken the forest. Then they had driven to the fair. There had been revulsion on Charles Lanchbury's face as they had made their way between the stalls and sideshows. They had been jostled by countryfolk in patched clothes, and the air had been heavy with the scent of bonfire smoke and unwashed bodies, and the damp, matted coats of dogs. The rain had washed the paint from the dancers' faces, and swilled ribbons and crêpe paper along the gutters. Marie had said, *I fail to see why we must mingle with such people. It is not like you, Charles. I realize that you wish to—*

Punish me? Hurt me? They had left the village, rain battering against the hoods of the cars, Charlie's fate, and Alix's own, already sealed. They had stopped at the crossing, and she had watched the troop train pass. She thought that she had seen the truth just then in those laughing faces caught behind the glass. For one fleeting, crystal-cold moment, she had seen the future.

At the chateau, they had discovered Charlie's absence, an absence already as profound as death. Her feet on the black and white tiles; the toy sword tap-tap-tapping against the banister as she ran upstairs to the nursery.

Alix remembered bending over the cot. But the old loss became confused with the more recent one, and she saw a baby, still and pale, her skin already chilled. She remembered that she had howled with pain. She had clutched Emma's body against hers, trying to give her warmth, and she had breathed into pursed blue lips. She had run to the telephone, the baby still held to her breast, her fingers slipping, slithering on the dial.

Alix put up her hands to her face. The tips of her fingers were washed with tears. She would have done, she thought, anything – *anything* – to keep Emma alive.

If I had been Charles Lanchbury, I would have searched for days and nights without cease. If I had been Charles Lanchbury, I would have woken every inhabitant of Herleville-aux-Bois and bade them scour the streets and the forest until they found him. If I had been Charles Lanchbury I would not have rested until I had found my only son. Nothing would have stopped me. Neither weariness, nor failure, nor war. My feet would have worn thin the soles of my shoes, and my voice, calling his name, would have echoed for eternity against those flat, golden fields.

Polly's baby, a girl, was born a few days later. Alix, visiting, held little Dorothy in her arms, closing her eyes, breathing that sweet, newborn baby smell, and remembering.

She found Jonathan in the garden. 'They're both having a nap. Dorothy's gorgeous, Jonathan. Absolutely beautiful.'

He looked anxious. Alix said firmly, 'You mustn't think that I mind. You really mustn't. I don't at all.' Which was not quite the truth, of course. Holding Dorothy had been an almost overwhelming mingling of pleasure and pain. She looked around. 'Where are the boys?'

'My mother's taken them to the park. Or they've taken her – I'm not quite sure.'

'I wanted to ask you something, Jon. I wanted to ask you whether you'd seen Derry recently.'

Jonathan thwacked a dandelion head with his walking-stick. 'Not *recently*. A few weeks ago.'

The path broadened out, circling a rose bed. Alix looked at him. 'Have you told him about Dorothy?'

'Not yet.' Jonathan looked despairing. 'To tell the truth, Alix, I don't know how to. To confront him with the birth of my daughter – well, it's rubbing salt in the wound, isn't it?' He took his penknife from his pocket and cut a mildewed leaf from the rose bush.

'I drove him away.' Alix knew that she had teetered on the edge of a precipice, and that she had allowed only Rory to drag her back from the chasm. 'I couldn't bear anyone near me after Emma died. I couldn't bear anyone to touch me. I couldn't bear anyone to *love* me. Derry needed me, and I sent him away.' Her voice was flat. 'Everything hurt so much that I didn't care. It was what I had to do. I almost enjoyed it. Hurting someone as I'd been hurt. It almost made me feel alive again.'

'And now?'

'I think about Emma all the time, Jon. Something like that doesn't ever stop hurting, but I suppose you begin to get used to it. We had her for a while, and then we lost her. Both of us tried so hard to keep her, but we couldn't. It was no-one's fault. No-one's to blame.' She looked at Jonathan. 'I miss Derry, Jon. I miss him so much.'

'Do you think that if you explained to him—'

'I said some awful things, Jon. Hurtful things.'

Jonathan began to cut roses, one by one, pink and white and yellow and red. Alix smiled. 'I remember the first time I met him, at Fallowfield. He was so bubbling over with energy and curiosity and *joie de vivre* – all the things I didn't allow myself to have. And then I married Edward, and I didn't see Derry again for years. And then – do you remember? – there was that awful party at the Rose Café.'

Jonathan smiled. 'Turkish cigarettes and punch like poison. It seems a long time ago.'

'The way our lives have fitted together, like the pieces of a jigsaw. I have to try again, don't I?'

'Yes,' he said. 'You do, Alix.' Then he heaped the roses into her arms. Travelling back to Owlscote, their perfume clung to her.

*　　*　　*

When Alix pressed the doorbell of Derry's flat, there was a long wait, and then a rattling of chain and bolt.

She followed him into the flat. He muttered, 'I wasn't expecting company . . .' and pulled back the curtains. Dustmotes fluttered in the bright light, settling on the boxes and tea-chests heaped in the corners of the room.

It was so hard to find the words. When they came, they were hopelessly banal.

'How are you, Derry?'

'Fine. I'm fine.'

She thought that they might stand there for ever, acres of silence and heartbreak between them. She wanted to go to him, and put her arms round him, but something in that taut, still frame stopped her.

Instead, she said, 'May came to visit me.'

He swung round. 'May Lanchbury? How touching. The family reunion at last.'

'We talked about the day that Charlie was lost—'

'Fascinating—'

'—and I knew, after I spoke to her, that I've probably never seen things as they really were.'

Derry ran his hands through his hair. 'Of course you haven't,' he said impatiently. 'I've known *that* for a long time. But it's a question of joining together all the pieces. And you've never possessed all the pieces.'

'May told me that Uncle Charles quarrelled with Aunt Marie – he hit her, Derry—'

'*Alix*. It's no longer my business. Don't you see?'

There was a silence. Tears pricked at the back of her eyes. But she had a message to deliver. 'Jon and Polly have a daughter,' she said. 'I went to see them yesterday.

She's a lovely little thing, Derry. She's called Dorothy.'

Derry's eyes lidded. He went to stand at the window, his hands on the sill, looking out, his back to her.

'You must give them my congratulations.'

She said, 'Come back to Owlscote, Derry,' and he turned to look at her.

'No.'

She could hardly bear to form the syllables. '*Never?*'

'It didn't work, did it, Alix?'

There was a silence. She felt cold and breathless. She thought, I love you, Derry, and I want you to come home, but the words, almost voiced, remained silent because, for the first time, she saw clearly, and understood the significance of, the boxes and cases standing around the room.

She knew then that he was going away. That she had driven him away. The boxes were sealed and labelled, but her sight had blurred so that she could not read the writing on the labels. She wondered where he would travel to this time: not, she supposed, to the Europe that he had begun to find so intolerable. To America, perhaps, or beyond that, to the East . . . She thought, not even to share the same country . . . the same continent . . .

She heard him say, 'Alix? Are you all right?' and she looked up.

She made herself smile. 'I'm fine. I have to go.' She would not, she thought, leave him with her tears. Then she left the flat.

After a few moments, he went back to the window and looked out. He searched through the crowds for her green sweater, her dark hair. You wouldn't think that someone could disappear so quickly, so completely. His fist slammed hard on the sill, and then he grabbed his jacket and ran out into the street.

He could not find her, even though he took a taxi, eventually, to Waterloo, and searched among the queues at ticket-office and platform. Knowing that he had lost her, Derry bought himself a drink in a pub just outside the station. From that pub he walked to another, then another, picking up company as he went.

At last he found himself in a bar in the Kennington Road. There were half a dozen of them, but he couldn't remember any of their names. The man on Derry's right was telling an interminable story about a policeman and a whore; the girl to his left was drinking neat gin and fretting because she had broken a nail. At the adjacent table there were black berets and clenched fists, and a balding, mustachioed chap banging on about the International Brigades in Spain. Someone passed round a cap ('Every little helps, comrade'), and coins chinked, and Spanish slogans were called out.

When the story about the policeman ended, its teller, staring at Derry, said, 'Well *I* thought it was funny,' and patted his pockets, looking for cigarettes. Then he rose from his seat. At the same time one of the black-bereted men, cap in hand, lurched across from the adjacent table. There was the crash of breaking glass, and coins spilled to the floor. The man with the black beret said, 'Clumsy bastard,' and Derry's friend said, 'Who are you calling a clumsy bastard?' and the girl with the broken nail shrieked, and the rest was inevitable.

At first Derry enjoyed himself. He found, perhaps for the only time in his life, a relief in thoughtless physical violence. But then he said something tactless, and found himself at the wrong end of a large, meaty fist, and the poky room darkened and became sprinkled with stars. His back was against the bar as he slid slowly down to the floor.

Through the greenish, spangled gloom he heard a woman say curtly, 'Leave him alone, Miguel. You'll kill him.'

He heard something muttered in Spanish. Someone crouched down beside him. 'Put your arm round me, Derry. Hurry up – I'd like to be out of here before the police arrive.'

He felt a shoulder jammed beneath his arm, and he managed to get to his feet. Mayhem had erupted around him. Out in the street, he tasted blood in his mouth.

'Hurry up, Derry.' Her voice snapped at him. 'I can hear sirens. Taxi!'

She pushed him into the cab. Derry's sight had cleared sufficiently to see her clearly.

'Mina,' he mumbled, staring at her. 'Mina Carr.'

'I don't know whether to be flattered,' she said, 'that you recognize me, or insulted. I have improved, haven't I, Derry?'

Of the lank-haired, bespectacled sixteen-year-old that he remembered, there was little trace. Mina Carr's dark hair fell in smooth waves, and her large brown eyes studied him, unimpeded by glasses. He attempted a compliment, but it hurt to speak, and he put up his hand to his face instead.

'My *teeth*—'

'Well, what on earth do you expect? So *ridiculous*.' Mina passed him a handkerchief. 'There isn't the faintest hope for the world until men learn to control their baser instincts.' She added curiously, 'And what on earth did you say to Miguel to annoy him so much? He hardly speaks any English.'

'My Spanish isn't bad,' he mumbled. He felt bruised and battered and foolish. 'After Jon's accident, I was in South America for a few years.'

'I know.'

He stared at her.

'I've followed your career with interest, Derry.'

His head ached far too much to work out the implications of that, so he shut his eyes and sank back into the corner of the cab, letting the movement of the vehicle soothe him. After a while, Mina rapped on the glass partition. 'Just here!' Paying the driver, she glanced back at Derry. 'Are you coming?' He followed her out of the cab.

He saw that they were in Bloomsbury. All tall Georgian windows and nice little parks with iron railings. Mina fitted a key to the door, and Derry followed her upstairs.

The drawing-room of Mina Carr's flat was well proportioned and light. It was filled with books – thousands of books – and posters. The posters bore Spanish slogans exhorting one to join a union or fight the nationalists, or Cyrillic lettering beneath pictures of bespectacled scientists and sturdy female tractor drivers.

'The bathroom's through there,' said Mina, 'if you want to clean yourself up.'

Surrounded by bottle-green ceramic tiles and yet more books, Derry plunged his head into a basinful of cold water, and came up gasping. Shaking the drops of water from his face, he stared into the mirror. He thought, you are too *old* for this, Derry Fox. Much too old. There was a bruise, shading rapidly from red to purple, on his forehead, and a cut at the side of his mouth. He did what he could to make himself presentable, and went back to the drawing-room.

The mantelpiece was crowded with photographs. Derry glanced at them.

Mina, coming back into the room, placed a tray on the table. 'That's Howard and Timothy. Edith's sons.'

He had picked up a snapshot of two small boys, resplendent in new school uniforms. He said cautiously, 'How is Edith?'

Mina poured out coffee. 'She's very well.'

'The marriage is . . . happy?'

'Oh, I wouldn't say *that*. I think we both know that neither of them got quite what they wanted. Poor old Marcus wanted a wife with a title, and Edith wanted – well, let's not go into that just now.' Mina's voice was tinged with irony. 'But on the other hand, Edith has the easy life she always longed for, and Marcus does love her, you know. He does care for her. And I've always thought it terribly bad for a person to have everything they want, don't you agree? There should always be *something* that one hungers for. Or one becomes smug and complacent.' She looked at Derry. 'But all that *floundering* – being engaged to Jonathan, and falling in love with you – was so untypical of Edith.' She offered him a cup. 'Cream, Derry?'

He shook his head. 'You sound as though you despise her.'

'Not at all. I'm very fond of my sister, and I adore my nephews, who are as boneheaded as Marcus and as beautiful as Edith. It's just that passion can leave such debris in its wake, can't it?'

He remembered sitting in the hospital waiting-room after Jonathan's accident, and his slow, sickened understanding of what had happened. He shivered.

'You don't approve of passion, then?'

Mina frowned. 'There are different sorts of

passion . . . Naturally, I approve of political passion. But passion between men and women – it depends whether you mean love, or whether you mean sex.'

'Both, I thought,' he said mildly.

'I thought for a long time that love was the pre-rogative only of the beautiful. The yellow-haired and blue-eyed.' She looked at him. 'Thoughts like that are the burden of the younger, plainer, sibling.'

Jon and Polly have a daughter. She's called Dorothy. Derry recalled the stab of black jealousy that he had experienced: that Jonathan should once more have what he had wanted so much. It galled him that the rivalries of childhood lingered. Because of his anger and envy, he had been prickly and offensive to Alix, who had asked him to come back to her.

He smiled crookedly. 'I suppose we have that in common.'

Mina stirred sugar into her coffee. 'Though we've done well, haven't we?'

'*You've* done well. I've fouled things up pretty thoroughly.'

'Modesty doesn't suit you, Derry. As I said, I've followed your career with interest.'

He looked up at her. 'Why?'

'Because, years ago, when I was sixteen, I had the most frightful crush on you.'

He blinked, and put aside his cup. 'Mina—'

'You asked, Derry.' She shrugged. 'I've always wanted things. I'm not like Edith – nothing has ever come easily to me. I have to plan and to scheme, and eventually – sometimes – I get what I want.'

'So you rescued me—'

'For your *beaux yeux*. Yes.'

'*Oh.*'

'It's all right,' she said. 'I grew out of it a long time ago. I was curious, though, to see what you'd become.' She refilled her cup. 'Pretty girls and plain girls are often thought to be a different species. Yet we have the same hearts.' She smiled. 'I don't write that in my books, of course. It wouldn't be *modern*. Too romantic.' She held up the coffee pot. 'More coffee, Derry?'

His head was a fuzzy mess of confused thoughts and alcohol. He passed Mina his cup. He saw how she squinted, her face a few inches from the pot, as she poured. He said, 'You can't see. You still can't see, can you, Mina?'

'I can see clearly six inches in front of my nose. Without my glasses I ignore old friends in the street and trip over paving stones.'

'Why don't you wear them?' Yet he knew her answer.

'Such a cliché, the ugly girl in her glasses. The handsome hero doesn't notice the mousy little heroine until she takes her spectacles off. I went through a stage of telling myself that I didn't mind. I'd wear my glasses everywhere, and choose my clothes for their warmth and their price, and I'd cut my hair myself. Because of Edith, you understand – anything to be different from Edith. But I wanted love, and I realized after a while that you have to make certain concessions for love.'

You have to make certain concessions for love. He himself had made no concessions. He had allowed his pride and his grief, and the envy of Jonathan that he had believed long ended, to drive Alix away once more. He had not told her of his reasons for selling the Chelsea flat; now, sitting in Mina Carr's drawing-room, he remembered the boxes and tea-chests, and knew suddenly, what she must have thought. He wanted to groan out loud his regret, to beat his bruised head against a wall.

Mina was still speaking. 'I've become quite good at managing without my spectacles, actually. I can tell this blur from that blur, and I can even cross the road without being run over by a bus. But *men* – I can't tell whether or not I like them until I'm so close that it's rather too late.'

He stirred his coffee. 'What on earth were you doing in that awful pub?'

'We hold our meetings there.'

'"We"?'

'The Succour for Spain group. More appropriate than some plush West End hotel, don't you think?' She looked at him. 'What were *you* doing there?'

He said honestly, 'Getting plastered, I suppose.'

'Why?'

He did not reply. Mina said, 'I heard that you'd lost your daughter. And I assume that you've parted from your wife.'

'Alix came to see me this morning. She wanted me to come home. What would be the point?' His voice was savage. 'What have I to give her? I couldn't even father a healthy child.'

'What was wrong with your daughter?'

'Her heart. There was something wrong with her heart.'

'These things are random, Derry. You know that. As so much of life is.'

'Do you think so? I've always believed I could control things. Manipulate things.' He shook his head. 'Not any more. It leaves me without a direction, you see. I can't see where to go.'

Mina began, 'There are a great many worthwhile causes—' but he interrupted her.

'I'm afraid I've never had much of a passion for politics. Not enough *belief*. All my passions have been personal.'

'The personal and the political will soon be indistinguishable, don't you agree, Derry?'

He glanced quickly at her. 'Yes, of course. But it'll be a year or two, don't you think, before Europe erupts again.'

'What will you do?'

'When war breaks out? I don't know.'

'Marcus and Edith will go to America. Edith told me that Marcus has already moved some of his money.'

'And you, Mina?'

'Oh, I'll stay here.' She smiled. 'Such wonderful *material*. I suppose I shall milk cows or become a bus conductress or whatever it is that women do in wartime.'

He said softly, 'Sometimes I long for it . . .'

She glanced sharply at him. 'You aren't a *sympathizer*, I trust?'

'With the Nazis? Good God, no.'

'There are those who are. The Londonderrys—'

'Sir Henry Channon. Sir Barry Domvile.' And Charles Lanchbury, he thought. 'I know. I've met some of them.'

'You move in interesting circles, Derry. I prefer to observe from a distance.' Mina folded her hands together, watching him. 'When war comes, it will be important to know who those people are, and where their loyalties truly lie. Some of my friends make it their business to know that sort of thing.'

He thought of the streets of Berlin, and Mosley's thugs, marching through the East End. 'I've never found autocracy remotely appealing,' he said slowly. 'All those uniforms and marching and having to do what you're told. Like a particularly hideous boarding school. Though to be frank, I've recently felt quite attracted to the death and destruction aspect of war. Appalling, isn't it, when one considers what's going on in the world . . . in Spain . . . in Abyssinia . . .'

'We all have destructive impulses. Employ them,' said Mina crisply, 'for something useful.'

Which got them neatly back to lack of direction, Derry thought. He tried to remember what he had wanted, leaving school, aged eighteen, all those years ago, so full of energy and ambition and bloody-mindedness. He muttered, 'Such a hotch-potch – my career, as you generously call it. Why on earth didn't I become a doctor – or a teacher – or a solicitor, like Jon? Then I'd know what I was supposed to do.'

'Because that wasn't what you wanted. And because it wouldn't have suited you.'

He rose and went to the window and looked out. It was late evening, and in the unrelieved darkness he could not see the garden below. He knew that he, like Mina Carr, had always wanted things. He had wanted to make his mark, or to be better than Jon, or to win his father's approval. He had adopted new personas, and had explored new avenues: he had, as Mrs Kessel had long ago expressed it, reinvented himself. Over and over again. And then, at last – a safe shore, glimpsed through the clouds – there had been Alix and Owlscote and Emma. He had needed nothing more, and yet somehow he had lost them. He had not, as he had once promised Alix, kept them safe. *Hell is when everything you know, everything that is familiar and beloved, is taken away from you.* The words of the old woman in the French market place echoed.

He heard Mina say, 'Are you hungry?' and he turned back to her.

'I haven't eaten for hours. I should go.'

She disregarded him. 'I'll make sandwiches.' She went into the adjacent kitchen. He heard cupboards opening, and the clink of knife and plate.

He wandered around the room. On an occasional table, he found a book, its pages pristine, unopened. He picked it up. It was entitled *Ashes of Roses*. On the dust-jacket was a picture of an etiolated young woman; Mina Carr's name was on the spine.

He held it up. 'Your latest?'

She glanced through the doorway. 'To be published in a fortnight's time.'

'I read *The Girl in the Yellow Dress* when I was in South America.'

She was buttering bread. 'I can never bear to read any of my work once I've finished it, but I'll always be fond of that book. It allowed me to buy this flat.'

'Was it your first novel?'

She shook her head. 'My second. My first was published just before Edith married Marcus. It was about blood and lineage – the principal characters were aristocrats.' Mina sawed at a loaf of bread. 'It was simply *seething* with illegitimate children and unfaithful wives. Blue-eyed parents with brown-eyed children, and ladies of the manor having love affairs with under-gardeners.' She smiled. 'Now, if I'd confined myself to *that*, it would probably have sold rather well – wealth and scandal always do. But I'm afraid I introduced a dreary political subplot, and a rather lengthy rant about women's inheritance rights, so it didn't sell at all.'

She came back into the room, and placed a plate on the table in front of him. 'Ham and mustard – I hope that's all right.'

He said, 'Yes. Perfect,' and she peered at him, eyes narrowed.

'Derry, you've gone quite white.'

'Have I?' He felt dazed.

'Is your head hurting?'

He stared at her, his eyes at first refusing to focus, as though he was concussed, as though he, like Mina, was short-sighted. 'Say it again, Mina. The plot of your novel.'

She looked bewildered, but she said, 'I can't remember it exactly – I wrote it a long time ago – but there was a landowner with two children.' She frowned. 'A girl and a boy. The boy was illegitimate—'

He said, 'Blood and lineage – inheritance rights – of *course*.'

'Do sit down, Derry. You look as though you're going to pass out.'

He did not sit, but went back to the window. The clouds had moved away from the face of the moon, so that he could see clearly at last. His gaze travelled from the wrought-iron bench, to the small circular pool, and to the roses, their petals clenched and grey and papery. He heard Mina say, 'You should eat. I'm sure you'd feel better if you ate something.'

'I'm fine. Honestly.' He saw that he must offer some sort of explanation, so he said to Mina, 'It's just that something I've been puzzling about for ages has just begun to make sense.' He was almost afraid, he realized, of losing track of it: afraid that if he looked away, the clouds would block his view, blurring everything once more.

Back at Owlscote, Alix wandered round the house and gardens, recognizing that she had sometimes found it easier to love stone and mortar than changeable, mutable human beings. Tonight, the house offered no solace. Doors creaked as she peered into empty, lifeless rooms; her History, spread out on the desk in the library, seemed no more than a collection of half-forgotten names.

The following morning, rising early, she took out her brushes and paints. Her hands were clumsy as she started to work, but slowly, persevering, she began to recover her skill. She painted wreaths of flowers onto the bowed fronts of chests of drawers, and *trompe l'oeil* packs of cards spilling across occasional tables. She painted a Greek frieze around a clock face, and butterflies dancing across the lid of a chest.

She made a telephone call. 'Roma? It's Alix.'

'*Alix*. How lovely of you to call. How are you?'

'I'm fine. There are some things here for Ted and Jack to collect.'

'You've been working?'

'Yes. Some of them aren't very good, I'm afraid. I'm rather rusty.'

'I'm sure they're all *wonderful*. I'm so pleased that you've started working again. Derry has been so busy, and I need all the help I can get.'

'Has he gone?'

'Gone? Who?'

'Derry.' She felt cold.

'Gone where? Oh—' Roma's words were lost in a crackle of static.

'Sorry, Roma – I missed that.'

'He's been away for a few days, but I expect him back any moment.'

Alix was bewildered. 'But the flat . . . ?'

'You know that he's moving? I told him he was mad. I said that—'

Another crackle. She loathed telephones. 'Roma, where is Derry going to? Is he going back to South America?'

A peal of laughter. 'Goodness me, no. Nothing so exotic. He has rented a room. In Islington, for heaven's sake. Quite beyond the pale.'

'So he's not leaving the country?'

'You sound rather odd, Alix. Are you all right? This wretched line . . . No, of course Derry isn't leaving the country.'

More crackles. The coldness had dissolved; now, the sudden hammering of Alix's heart mingled with the static on the telephone wire. She shouted, desperately, 'Then why is he selling his flat?'

'Oh' – Roma was vague – 'something about freeing up capital. Making changes to his investments. Hasn't he been to see you yet?'

'See me?'

'He told me that he was going to. He said he had a gift for you.'

'What sort of gift?' Her legs were shaking; she had to lean against the wall.

'He was rather mysterious. He wouldn't say. Is it your birthday? He told me that—' The hisses and clatterings became more intense, a rainstorm of interference, drowning Roma's words, until the phone cut off, until there was only the tick of the clock, and the mew of the cat, begging for her supper.

Derry went to Berlin once more. There, he visited Steffie Wolff. He bought from her a silver flagon and a string of river-pearls. The pearls, opalescent and misshapen, trailed through his fingers. She gave him a gift, too, a small, silver fox. 'For your firstborn son.' He did not want to accept the gift, because he saw that her flat was becoming stripped and bare, but she pressed it on him, and saw him off with a kiss and a smile.

He headed back to England the following day. He arrived in Dover in the early morning, and travelled north, pausing in London only to pick up his car. At first, there was sun and blue skies, but as he continued up the Great North Road into East Anglia, steel-grey clouds gathered on the horizon. The sky seemed to press closer to the earth, enclosing town and countryside and all the creatures that scurried between them.

He found himself in a landscape of gentle rise and fall, and fields threaded with hedgerow. The darkly leaved branches of the trees were silhouetted against the heavy sky. Through the windscreen of the car the road spread out before him, becoming narrower, winding around copse and thicket, the fields punctuated at intervals by sparse villages of terraced houses and flint-walled churches. Then, beyond meadows and chalk knolls, he caught sight of parkland, railings, and ornamental trees.

He slowed the car at the tall wrought-iron gates, braking in the shadow of a horse chestnut. There was a long driveway, palisaded with trees. Bell Wood, the Lanchburys' home for three centuries, stood at the end of the driveway, a vast oblong house, built of the pale yellow brick that this part of Cambridgeshire favoured.

Bell Wood's gate creaked as Derry opened it, and his

feet crunched on the gravel. He stood for a while, looking up at the house, and then he walked to the garden. There was a peculiar stillness to the landscape. It seemed frozen in time, preserved in the act of its dying, like an insect trapped in amber. He walked through a rose garden, where drifts of red and white petals carpeted the ground, and then he made his way along an avenue of limes. Their leaves gave off a heady scent, and a few keys whirled to the grass. The row of trees debouched into a circular box hedge which soared twelve or fifteen feet above the lawn. He was caught about by green leaves, cocooned in hedgerow. Crossing the circle, he saw the lake. He stood for a while, noticing how the fringes of willow stooped to touch the smooth, silvery water, and how the eye travelled to a distant vista of chalk escarpment. His gaze came at last to rest on an artfully placed pavilion set on the skyline. He knew now to what lengths a man might go to keep all this. He knew now that one might feel that this land, these stones, were part of blood and bone. He knew, but neither understood, nor forgave.

Derry walked back to the car. He knew also what had happened to Charlie Lanchbury, and why. It was to do with loss and love and pride and blood. Charlie's disappearance, and the injury that Alix had suffered in consequence, had not been accidental, but had been planned, coldly and deliberately. He, who had endured the loss of a child, vowed there and then that for Alix, and for Charlie, there would be vengeance. But he would wait, and he would watch the millstone grind slowly.

Meanwhile, he would offer to Alix two gifts. The first of them, the pearls, were wrapped in silk, safely in the inner pocket of his jacket. His second gift was the gift of truth. He thought that Alix, by speaking to May, knew most of the story already. All he could do was to fill in the last of the gaps.

Derry started up the car and headed for Owlscote.

PART FIVE

MAY–JUNE 1940

A House-Cooling Party

CHAPTER EIGHTEEN

Sometimes – catching sight of newspaper hoardings in Salisbury, or talking to her neighbours in the village – Alix had to remind herself to conceal her contentment. Her serenity did not match the sense of foreboding that had seized the country. The events of the closing years of the 1930s rang like a death-knell: Munich and Kristallnacht, and the occupation of Czechoslovakia. At the beginning of 1939, the German army had invaded Poland, and Great Britain and France had declared war. British troops had been dispatched to the Continent, and an uneasy, precarious calm had followed. And then, in the April of 1940, Germany had occupied Denmark and invaded Norway.

Though Alix understood what these events meant to her, and what they meant to the world, they did not touch the core of her. Her life marched to a different, more tranquil rhythm. Its beats, gently drumming her contentment, were her reconciliation with Derry, and the birth of her second son (a strong, healthy baby – eight pounds and bawling his delight at his first sight of the world) in the late spring of 1938. She had longed for another baby even while grieving for the daughter she had lost. She had celebrated her third child's birth and infancy with the echo of Emma's brief, poignant life always in her heart.

She and Derry continued, Alix thought, to be careful with each other. They had an awareness of each other's wounds, and an understanding of the ease with which the skin could be pierced. As so much that was familiar fell away, they held fast to each other, the absences that war imposed on them punctuated with letters and telephone calls. She treasured the pearls, his gift to her. They seemed to her to be an acknowledgement that one day, when the war was over, they would need to start again. She remembered sitting beside Derry on Owlscote's terrace as he had given her his other gift. His suspicions had matched hers. Their differences she had kept to herself. Derry believed that Charlie Lanchbury was dead. In Alix's heart there remained a small stubborn kernel of hope, a candle still lit for an infant whose features she could not now recall. He would be twenty-eight now. She pictured him, tall and strong, his coppery hair cropped short.

Derry had joined up at the beginning of the war. Shortly afterwards, Roma had closed down the interior design business. The sale of art and antiques and country houses, which had blossomed between the wars, had ground to a halt. In 1939, the Compensation Defence Act had permitted the requisitioning of houses for government purposes. All over the country, large houses and mansions, that had until then known only graceful, muted existences, were requisitioned. Alix had waited, anticipating the inevitable. Now, walking around the reedy fringes of the lake, she saw, looking up, that Owlscote had already altered: the black-out on the windows, the criss-cross of tape on the glass, and the khaki-clad figures teeming in and out of doors. It did not trouble her. She had never owned Owlscote, she thought. Time, and fate, had permitted her only to borrow it.

One of the soldiers, the nice one who had made Patrick a paper boat, was changing the lock on Owlscote's front door. He looked up when Alix approached.

'A child could open these. And a lot of our stuff's terribly hush-hush, you know.'

'I'm almost packed,' she said. 'And my lift is here. But Patrick's still having his afternoon nap, I'm afraid.'

'No hurry, Mrs Fox. Though best to leave yourself plenty of time. The blackout, remember.'

'I wondered' – she hesitated – 'I wondered whether I could have a last look round before I leave.'

The corporal shot a quick glance down the drive. 'Don't see why not. I'll have to accompany you, though.'

'Of course.' Alix spoke to Polly, who was waiting in the car, and went into the house. There was only a narrow passage through the hall, between the filing cabinets and tables and chairs. The corporal remained a tactful few steps behind her as she walked from room to room, pausing at the library, where she had written her history of Owlscote, and in Rory's old room where, until only a few weeks ago, his model aeroplanes, ghostly miniature foreshadowings, had hung from the ceiling. The Great Hall, where she had danced with Derry before the first fancy dress party, was now filled with neat rows of desks. In the kitchen, the battered old sofa, horsehair extruding like a fungus from the holes in its upholstery, was being dragged out of the door by two uniformed clerks.

'Dreadful old thing,' said the corporal. 'Expect you're glad to see the back of that.'

Alix smiled politely, and went upstairs. The corporal said, 'These old places are always so cold. Stone walls, and they never seemed to bother much about heating, did they?'

She paused at the top of the stairs, looking out of the window at the lawn and the lake and the copse. She said, 'I always meant to put in radiators, but I never got round to it.'

'And lonely, too. Me, I like to be near a cinema and a pub.'

She thought of all the people who had passed through Owlscote's doors. Beatrice and Jonathan and Polly and Maddy and Roma. The paying guests. The party-goers. If she closed her eyes she could almost hear laughter, and the click of a high-heeled shoe on a polished floor, and the rustle of a beaded dress. When she looked around her, the bright wraiths disappeared, replaced by khaki uniforms and grey-green War Department furniture, and rooms that were already unfamiliar.

'I won't bother with the rest of the house,' she said. 'I'll just dress Patrick, and then we'll go.'

Alix went into the nursery. He had begun to stir, to shift, smiling in his sleep. When she bent over the cot and softly said his name, he opened his eyes and, looking up at her, laughed.

In Knightsbridge, Edith Wenlock, coming out of Harrods, found herself face to face with Derry Fox. Encumbered with bags and gas-masks, they stood motionless amid the rivers of people rushing along the pavement.

Derry found his voice first. 'Edith, how lovely to see you. How are you? You look wonderful.'

She indicated the bags. 'Shopping – so exhausting.'

'Mina told me you were going to America.'

'We sail next week. Marcus doesn't see the point in exposing the boys to all this tedium and danger.' Edith looked at Derry. His hair had begun to grey round the temples, and his eyes, those dark eyes that she had once thought able to see into her soul, were red-rimmed and tired.

'You're in uniform, Derry,' she said. 'How patriotic.'

'Just a desk job at the Admiralty. Nothing heroic. Are you staying in London, Edith?'

'At the Ritz. We've closed up Marblehurst. Hail me a taxi, would you?'

They stood by the edge of the pavement. 'Your sons,' he said. 'How old are they now?'

'Timothy's eleven, and Howard is eight. They'll miss England, I suppose.' There were few taxis on the streets, and all that drove past were occupied. 'And you, Derry? Have you children? You married . . . she lived in the middle of nowhere . . . I can't remember her name . . .'

'Alix North,' he said. 'We have a son, Patrick. He was two a fortnight ago. And I have a stepson, Rory, who's at school.'

Derry raised his arm again. Edith found the courage to say his name. 'And Jonathan? How is Jonathan?'

'Happily married with four children. Two boys and two girls. They live in my mother's house in Andover.'

'The accident . . . His leg . . . ?' She bit her lip.

'Oh, Jon's fine. He'll never run a marathon, of course, and he can't even consider joining up. Which Polly, his wife, thinks is a blessing in disguise. And I'm inclined to agree. After all, Jonathan did his bit years ago.'

A taxi drew up by the kerb. Edith said, 'Give them all my best wishes, won't you, Derry?' She climbed into the cab.

The driver headed off into the traffic; Edith did not look back. Instead, she took out her compact and checked her face. And had a sudden irresistible impulse to claw her fingernails, making four scarlet stripes across the familiar perfection of her skin.

There were now nine people living in the Andover house. Because there were only four proper bedrooms, Eva shared her room with Dorothy, while Alix and Patrick had the attic room that had once been occupied by the Foxes' live-in maid. The new baby, Jane, slept in a crib in Polly and Jonathan's room.

The noise – five children under the age of seven – began in the early hours of the morning. From her attic bedroom, Alix could hear Jane crying for her early morning feed. She would pull the blankets over her head, close her eyes, and drift thankfully back to sleep. Patrick would wake her at around seven o'clock, rattling the bars of his cot, jumping up and down, making the springs rattle and creak. At mealtimes, it was bedlam. The baby cried, the twins fought, and Patrick and Dorothy dipped bread soldiers into their boiled eggs and, pressing their fingertips into the yellow goo, drew squiggles round the borders of their plates.

Both Rory and Derry managed to be there for Eva's sixtieth birthday party. All eleven of them ate sandwiches and cake in the large dining-room, spilling out through the open French windows onto the lawn. The children sat at the table, and the adults balanced plates on their laps. Sunlight flickered on the lawn and on the polished parquet floor. Several conversations went on at once.

'How are things, Jon?'

'Fine. Perfectly fine.'

'I wondered – with petrol rationing—'

'Oh, I walk to work. Such terrific weather, isn't it, Derry? I don't need the car. I tried a bicycle – I'm working three evenings a week for Civil Defence, manning a telephone exchange – did I tell you?'

'He fell off the wretched bike in the blackout.' A whisper. 'He is *exhausted*, Derry.'

'Nicky, *no*. Nice little boys don't do that.'

'But *Granny*—'

'Eat the cake, not just the icing, Nicholas old chap.'

'Jane's crying.'

'Jane's always crying. She's just a cry-baby.'

'I'll just slip upstairs and feed her . . .'

'Don't worry, Poll – I'll hold the fort.'

'I can't see the point of staying at school. If I'm going to join the RAF—'

'In the summer, when you've taken your exams.'

'*Derry*—'

'To please your mother, Rory. And to humour me.'

'More tea, anyone?'

'I saved the icing sugar. Polly iced the cake.'

'It looks wonderful, Mother.'

'Polly and I are digging up the herbaceous border. We've planted masses of beans and peas.'

'Auntie Alix, Jemima is chasing the hens!'

Alix went outside, into the garden. She shooed the hens from the vegetable patch, and scooped Jemima the cat into her arms. Looking back at the house she saw them all: the children, now escaped from the table and rolling around the floor, or scrambling onto an adult's knee. Rory, tall and handsome, playing with the twins. Eva Fox, still beautiful, sipping tea from a bone china cup. Derry and Jonathan, laughing over something.

She thought, my family. She recalled, for the first time

in many years, why she had so longed to go on holiday with the Lanchburys. Not just for the adventure of visiting France, but because she, an only child, had imagined and envied the warmth and busyness of large families. She thought of her early years of isolation at Owlscote, and how, a long time ago, she had needed silence and sanctuary. She needed them no more.

Derry, waiting outside the newspaper offices, met May Lanchbury as she came out of the building.

'Have you time for a drink, May?'

She glanced at her watch. 'A quick one.' She looked at him. 'How are you, Derry?'

'Busy,' he admitted. It was seven o'clock, and he had only just left his desk at the Admiralty. 'There's some sort of a fuss on.' He grinned. 'A state of affairs which will, I expect, continue for some time to come.'

They walked to a small, crowded bar in Piccadilly, where he bought gins and tonic and squeezed into a corner table beside her.

'How's Alix?' she asked. 'And the baby?'

'They're both very well. Blooming, in fact. Last weekend, I had to sing "Pat-a-cake, pat-a-cake" twenty times. No-one has ever admired my singing so much.'

'Someone told me that Owlscote has been requisitioned. Have Alix and Patrick moved out yet?'

'They're living with Jon and Polly now. We're no longer permitted to visit Owlscote without an escort.'

'Don't you *mind*?'

Derry shook his head. 'I've never felt much for places, I suppose. I thought Alix would mind terribly, but she seems to have accepted the inevitable.' He looked at her. 'And you, May? And Bell Wood?'

'It's been requisitioned, too, but by a boys' school. They were originally evacuated to the east coast, but then they were told to move again.'

'Have you been there?'

May shook her head. There was a lull in the conversation; she sipped her gin.

'Your sisters? How are they?'

'Daisy's in Kenya now. Have you heard that she married again?' May scrabbled in her bag for her cigarette case. Derry noticed, lighting her cigarette for her, how her hands shook. 'As for Ella – it's a long time since I've seen Ella.' She smiled, but the smile did not reach her eyes. 'The newspaper – I'm so busy, you see. I've been promoted. I write lengthy pieces about keeping the home fires burning. And besides . . .' May left the sentence unfinished, and once more smiled that fleeting smile. 'And I am an ARP warden. I have a tin hat, and a very unflattering pair of overalls.' She looked down at her glass.

'And your father?'

She looked at him sharply. 'I haven't spoken to Papa for years.'

He smiled. 'Not even Christmas and birthdays?'

She shook her head. 'Not even Christmas and birthdays. Especially not birthdays.' Her voice was bitter. She looked away from him. 'Why did you want to speak to me, Derry?'

'To warn you.'

Again, that sharp blue gaze. 'Warn me?'

He said gently, 'They will intern traitors, you see. And potential traitors.' The bar was crowded; he had lowered his voice.

May licked her lips. 'My father?'

'He has kept unwise company over the past few years.

And the authorities can be rather indiscriminate in their suspicions.'

She stared at him, eyes wide. 'What are you saying, Derry?'

'That you should distance yourself. From your father. And from Ella. Although,' he added, 'it sounds as though you've done so already.'

She muttered, 'Anyone can see that Ella harms only herself – that she is insane—'

'But your father, May . . .' He paused. 'As you say, your sister's clearly deranged. And she is your father's puppet. She may escape unscathed – I don't know. But your father's a different matter.'

She whispered, 'How do you know all this?'

'Oh,' he said easily, 'you know me, May. I listen to the gossip. I find things out. And I talk to people.'

The silence extended. He saw her understanding in her eyes.

'*Why*, Derry?'

'Because of Alix,' he said.

She closed her eyes. Her fingers were knotted together. She whispered, 'You *know*, don't you, Derry?'

He thought of the pieces he had put together over the years. His discovery that May and Alix were cousins. Jonathan's accident, and Alix's description of the loss of Charlie Lanchbury. His journey to northern France with May. The trail that they had followed, which had led them to a memory of a child in ragged lace and velvet.

He saw the expression in May's eyes, and he paused, momentarily wanting to spare her. Then he thought of Alix, and the burden that Charles Lanchbury had imposed on her.

'I know that your father was responsible for Charlie's disappearance. He made sure that Charlie became separated from the rest of the party in Herleville-aux-Bois. And then, I suppose, though he pretended to look for him, he didn't. And the war played into his hands. Can't search for your lost son when there's a war breaking out around you, can you?'

May had gone pale. She closed her eyes tightly. He said, 'You knew too, didn't you, May? That's why you don't speak to your father any more, isn't it? And that's why you've avoided me.'

'Partly,' she said. She smiled, a tremulous stretching of the lips. 'Partly.' Her hands cradled her glass. 'Ella told me. A few years ago.'

'Ah,' he said. 'I always wondered what Ella knew. So strange that you, the younger sister, should remember so much, while Ella should claim to remember nothing. Years ago, I wondered whether to speak to her, but I had a suspicion that my fatal charm wouldn't have worked on Ella. As she is' – and his gaze met May's – 'so utterly devoted to your father.'

'But I don't know', she said carefully, '*why*?'

'Charlie wasn't your father's son.'

He saw her frown. 'This is what I think happened,' he said. 'Your parents quarrelled violently on the morning of your birthday. I'm convinced that they quarrelled because your father had found out that your mother had a lover. Had had a lover for some time. Charlie – the sole heir, your father had believed, to his name, his blood, his lands – was not his son.'

'You're guessing, Derry. You can't *know*.'

'But it adds up, doesn't it? And it's the only explanation that makes sense. There were always so many things that didn't seem right. Your father's search for Charlie was so peculiarly half-hearted – remember that we discovered in France that Charlie had still been alive at the end of August – and not far away from Herleville. And then Daisy let slip that your mother had had love affairs. And you yourself told me of your father's belief in the importance of lineage. It all fell into place. Charlie didn't even *look* like the rest of you. He was red-haired, whereas the rest of the family is fair.' His eyes narrowed. 'My money's on the chauffeur. Didn't Louise call him Ginger? I bet he had red hair. I'm not quite sure about the mechanics of it all, but my guess is that Charlie became mixed up in the crowd around the cars at Herleville, and your father made sure to drive off without him.' He looked at May. 'What did Ella tell you? That she knew that your father had lied to Alix? That she protected her father?'

Her silence was the only answer he needed. At last she spoke.

'Alix.' Her voice was dull. 'Does she know?'

'We talked about it a few years ago, when we got back together after Emma died. Alix had worked most of it out herself. I just filled in the last few gaps.'

'She must hate me.' May's eyes were pale sapphires in a blanched face. 'She must hate all of us.'

'Alix? No. That would be making the same mistake your father made, wouldn't it? Judging and condemning a person by their name and blood and descent.'

Her cigarette had burned down almost to her knuckles. He slid the stub from her hand, extinguishing it in the ashtray.

'What will you do, Derry?' Her voice sounded odd.

'Nothing. Someone else will do it for me.' He looked across at her. 'Another drink?'

She shook her head, and rose to her feet. 'I think I should go.' She looked down at him. 'You know', said May, 'that I loved you, Derry.'

He said simply, 'Yes. And I'm sorry.' But he did not think that she believed him. He watched her thread her way out of the crowded pub.

Alix was hoeing rows of beans when she saw Derry, framed in the open French windows. She ran towards him.

'*Derry.*' They kissed. 'I didn't know you were coming.'

'Someone gave me a lift. Where's Patrick?'

'Having a nap. He and Dorothy are in disgrace. They seem to have taken a vow to be the most dreadful children in Hampshire.'

'What have they done?'

'They cleaned the bath with custard powder. Polly was collecting the boys from school, and Eva had one of her funny turns, and by the time we'd noticed, the bath was yellow.' She looked at him. 'I know – you can't help laughing – but it took ages to get it off.'

He said, 'You've heard the news, I assume?'

At midday, watching the children eat scrambled eggs and stewed apples, Alix and Polly had listened to the announcement on the wireless. That morning, the German army had invaded Holland.

She nodded. Derry lit a cigarette. She saw how tired he looked. 'How's London?'

'Emptying. Everyone's going to the countryside.' He smiled. 'There are house-cooling parties.'

'Our friends?'

'Not Roma, of course. It would take more than the German army to make Roma leave London.'

'Sophie?'

'May be interned.'

'*Derry.*'

'Yes. An enemy alien. Unutterably bloody, don't you agree?'

She put her arms round him, hugging him. She felt his lips touch her forehead.

'How long have you got?'

'Not much. Half an hour.' He stroked her bottom. 'And those trousers are very fetching.'

'They were yours once, I think. I found them in a chest of drawers in your old bedroom.'

'They look a lot nicer on you.' He threaded his hands beneath her blouse, caressing her bare skin. 'I suppose we'll give poor old Patrick some sort of complex if we go upstairs . . . ?'

'Probably.' She kissed him again.

They sat on a bench beside the roses, his arm round her shoulders. She wondered whether the roses, too, would have to be dug up.

'Do you think . . .' She could not finish the sentence.

'What?'

'People are talking of invasion,' she said bluntly.

When he did not immediately reassure her, she felt, in spite of the warm sun, chilled. She heard him say, 'We're not ready, you see. We've had eight months to think about it, but we're not ready.'

'But – *France* – France will hold out . . .'

He did not reply. Early that morning, German aeroplanes had dropped parachutists into Holland, billowing white silk mushrooms, floating down towards green fields and neat gardens.

He took her hand. 'I came down here to tell you that if the worst happens – if I can't manage to get to you because I'm stuck in London – or for whatever reason – then you must go away. I've brought the addresses of some people I know in Scotland and Wales. And petrol coupons. But now that I'm here' – he looked around the sunny garden – 'it all seems rather . . . *inappropriate*.'

She smiled. 'You know that I won't go, Derry. You know that I wouldn't leave a single one of them – Polly or Eva or Jon or the children. And I can't really imagine all nine of us hauling off to the Shetlands or wherever.'

There was a silence. Then he said, 'I rather thought you'd say that. Still, I had to try. And I'm probably just being pessimistic.' He stood up. 'I must go.'

'When will I see you again?'

'I don't know. Alix . . .'

'Yes?'

He shook his head, enfolding her in his arms. 'I'll phone every night, that's all.'

After he had gone, she realized that it was too terrible to imagine: fleets of enemy ships cutting through the English Channel, bombs raining down from that cloudless sky.

Like a whirlwind, the German army swept through Holland, Belgium and Luxembourg. On 13 May, Panzers crossed the French border at Sedan. In Bapaume in northern France, Louise Desvignes dug a deep hole in the orchard of the farm, placed a box containing gold coins inside it, and covered it with earth and turves, so that the ground appeared undisturbed. She had already picked open the seams of her corsets, and had sewn her jewellery into the lining. Then she helped her mother-in-law pack the car, so that they could flee south. Old Mme Desvignes grumbled. 'The second time in twenty-five years. And both times the boy hasn't been here to help. I deserve better than this. I'm an old woman, and should not have to endure such journeys.' Louise gritted her teeth, and wondered at the fate of her son, in the army of the Meuse.

By 20 May, the German army had reached Amiens. On the same day, a code clerk at the American Embassy in London was arrested. He had been passing secret documents to Nazi sympathizers in London. On 22 May, the British government gave itself the power to arrest anyone likely to endanger the safety of the realm. Doorbells rang unexpectedly in the early hours of the morning, papers were burnt, bargains made.

In Wilmersdorf in Berlin, Steffie Wolff took a last look around her apartment. It was not the treasure-cave it had once been; the walls and mantelpieces were bare. Everything of value had been sold to help her friends and family escape from Germany, or given away to those she loved. Steffie opened the bottle of champagne she had kept for the occasion. She swallowed the pills. Hard and cold, they scratched her throat. Then she went to bed. She hoped that they would believe that she had died naturally in her sleep. Strange, she thought, propping herself on pillows, closing her eyes, how greatly one desired propriety and dignity, even in death.

Derry was working at his desk in the Admiralty when there was a tap at the door of his office.

'That chap you asked me about. Lanchbury.'

'Yes?'

His colleague closed the door. 'He's in Wormwood Scrubs.'

'You've arrested him?'

A nod. 'He'd been in contact with that Yank at the Embassy. Passing stuff to Berlin, via Mussolini.'

Derry stood up and went to the window. Silver

barrage balloons twisted and turned in the blue sky. 'How did he take it?'

'Oh, like a gentleman, of course. They all do. Told us he wouldn't be in the Scrubs for long – that Britain will have to make peace with Hitler, and then chaps like him will be in charge.'

'That's not', said Derry thoughtfully, 'impossible.'

'No. Though I'd take care who you say that to. Defeatism, you know. Anyway, thanks for your help.'

Derry had expected to feel elated, triumphant. He felt neither. He thought of Mina Carr, and their chance meeting in the pub, and their subsequent occasional contact. *It will be important to know where people's loyalties lie. My friends make it their business to know that sort of thing.* He said, 'Do you think that I might talk to him? To Charles Lanchbury?'

His colleague blinked. 'Could be tricky. But I'll see what I can do.' He looked curious. 'What's your interest, Fox?'

'Oh,' said Derry. 'Family business.'

There was a silence. Then, 'He'd better hope that Hitler gets a move on. I shouldn't think Lanchbury'll see the year out. He's in his seventies, you know. Health's a bit rocky by all accounts.'

The door opened and closed, leaving Derry alone. Family business, he thought, and went back to his desk.

Polly said, 'Jane wakes me up at half past five each morning, and I think first how awful it is to wake up, and then that it's going to be another lovely day, and then I remember, and I think, oh, *heavens*. It just doesn't seem real, does it?'

It was 26 May. Earlier that day, all the Foxes – from Eva to Jane – had attended the service in St Mary's

Church. Similar services had been held all over the country to pray for the safety of the British Expeditionary Force, struggling for its survival in northern France.

Now it was late evening, and Jonathan, Eva and the children were in bed. Only Polly and Alix remained awake, sitting in the drawing-room. The floor was littered with toys. Children's sandals were scattered by the French windows.

Polly took a bottle of gin and two glasses from the cupboard. 'You find yourself thinking such awful things, don't you? Wondering whether you should bury your jewellery.'

'Or sharpen the bread knives.'

'Quite.' She handed Alix a glass. 'I'd like to think that if we were invaded, then I'd do something – that I'd fight. But then I realized how stupid I was being. How I was deceiving myself. How can you fight when you have four small children?'

'No-one's expecting you to man a machine gun, Poll.'

'I was thinking', said Polly, 'more of hoes and pitch-forks.' She sounded upset.

Alix extracted a teddy bear from the seat of her chair. 'It'll be all right. Really. It'll be all right.'

'Are you sure? After all, *you* came to church, Alix. And I didn't think you believed in God.'

The blackout material taped to the windows sealed them away from the garden and the sky; for once, all the children were quiet.

Alix said slowly, 'To be honest, what I feel most of all is anger. And disbelief, I suppose, that something so beyond my control should threaten me. I feel that my life had just about got on an even keel. I didn't even mind giving up Owlscote – well, I could bear it. I thought, it doesn't matter as long as I've still got Derry and Patrick and Rory. And I was so worried when Derry joined up, and so relieved when he wasn't sent to France. But now – well, Rory will join the RAF, you know, Polly, as soon as he can. And as for the rest of us . . .' She did not finish her sentence. The German army had bombed Rotterdam when it had invaded Holland. Thousands of civilians were rumoured to have died.

Polly looked pale and tired. 'I almost wish that I hadn't had Jane. When you think of what's happening in Holland – in Belgium – in France – it seems almost *wrong* to bring a child into such a world.'

'Oh, *Poll*.' Alix hugged her. 'Here – drink up.' She topped up Polly's glass and her own. 'Get pickled. That's the best thing to do. We'll get pickled, and grow our vegetables, and look after the children, and make sure that Eva isn't bothered too much and still has her tea in a bone china cup.'

Polly giggled and blew her nose. 'Jane will get drunk.'

'Then she might sleep through the night at last, and that would be worth celebrating, wouldn't it?'

After Polly had gone to bed, Alix went out into the garden. Because of the blackout, the darkness was complete. Stars sprinkled the inky sky. For a moment, closing her eyes, wrapping her arms around herself, she imagined herself back at Owlscote, listening to the sounds of the countryside – the whisper of leaves, the flap of a bird's wing.

With fierce intensity, she knew that she wanted them here, with her, now. Derry and Rory and Patrick, the small family that she had fought so hard to keep together. She wanted them under her eye, so that she could see that they were safe.

*   *   *

'What-ho, Fox! Know anything about boats?'

Derry glanced over his shoulder; Nicholson, who worked in a nearby office, was standing in the doorway.

'A bit. Why?'

'They're shouting for small craft to be taken to Sheerness. The *Elizabeth*'s moored at Kingston. I'm going to take her down. Could do with a hand.'

Derry yawned and stretched. 'Why not? Though I warn you, I'm a lousy sailor.'

Travelling through London, Nicholson said, 'Lovely day for a sail. Beats shuffling pieces of paper.'

Derry thought privately that shuffling pieces of paper was really rather pleasant. He had joined up the previous September partly because all his other occupations had, with the outbreak of war, inevitably dried up, and partly out of conviction. The desk job had not been unexpected. Asthmatics who had turned forty tended not to be first choice as frontline troops.

They had reached the boatyard. 'She's been under wraps since last summer,' said Nicholson affectionately. 'Haven't had a chance to work on the poor old thing – this bally war, you know.'

They heaved off tarpaulins and swept away the dirty puddles that had gathered on the deck and on the roof of the cabin. Water gurgled sullenly in the bilges. Paint peeled from the *Elizabeth*'s bows.

'Compass is a bit wonky,' said Nicholson cheerfully. 'Always meant to get it fixed, but . . .' He rapped the glass. 'If you give it a good thump it always comes up trumps.'

The outboard motor, after a few moments' silent protest, coughed stubbornly into life, and they set off down the Thames, threading through locks and beneath bridges. They were beyond the Isle of Dogs when

Nicholson, glancing at Derry, said: 'I say, are you all right, old chap? You look a bit washed out.'

'I told you I was a rotten sailor.'

'Not on the *Thames*. No-one can be seasick on the *Thames*.'

I can, thought Derry, and changed the subject. 'I assume they're going to take the boats over to France.'

'That's the gist of it. Navy takes over at Sheerness.' Nicholson offered a packet of cigarettes to Derry, who shook his head. 'She'll be ferrying those poor sods back to Blighty before the night's out.'

'Do you think' – Derry tried to be tactful – 'do you think she's up to it?'

Nicholson was indignant. 'Course she is! Lovely little craft.' He patted a blistered plank. 'Taken her across the Channel myself a good few times. There's a smashing little restaurant in Deauville – *Antoine's* – do you know it? Impresses the popsies no end, giving them their grub in France.'

The warehouses and cranes that lined London docks were replaced by mud-filled creeks and acres of featureless marshland. Derry had discovered a long time ago, on his first stomach-churning voyage across the Channel with Mrs Kessel, that it was best to think about something else. He recalled his interview with Charles Lanchbury, which had taken place the previous afternoon in a small, bare room in Wormwood Scrubs, with a prison warden standing just beyond the door. Lanchbury had looked old and ill. Yet his pride and conviction had lingered. At first, Derry had feared that Lanchbury would not speak at all, and that he himself would never be certain. Then he had asked, 'Why Alix? Why blame her?' and Charles Lanchbury had smiled his reptile's smile, and had spoken.

'Because she was there. Because it was convenient.'

He had stood up then, and had walked around the room, unable to bear the sight of the man. The warden had put his head round the door, suspicious, checking. Lanchbury had said, 'Don't you want to know how it was? Aren't you curious?' and Derry had bowed his head.

'The idea came to me when we were picnicking in the woods. Just – lose the brat. That was why we went to the fair. The darkness – the crowds. When we went back to the cars, I saw him wander away. Then it was easy. I told my daughter to tell the girl that the brat was with us. And I made sure we drove away quickly. The next day I sent them all back to England. A few weeks later a fellow claimed to have found the creature – tried to sell him back to me. I sent him packing. Then I went home. The grieving father.' There was a silence, and then Charles Lanchbury had repeated slowly, 'He just wandered away. It was easy. I was lucky, wasn't I?'

Derry, wanting to retch, had swung back to him. 'Yet you had no more children. Why?' Lanchbury had not replied. Derry, understanding, had said, 'Oh. How galling for you. You couldn't, could you?' Looking back, he had, for the first time, seen emotion in those cold blue eyes, and he had asked curiously, 'Did you regret it? After all, an heir of dubious provenance is surely better than no heir at all. Did you ever regret what you'd done?'

Lanchbury had rapped imperiously on the table, and demanded to be taken back to his cell. Now, Derry, standing on the prow of the *Elizabeth*, recalled how he himself had felt, leaving the prison. A sickness more virulent than the one he suffered now, a sickness that bit into his soul. He had wanted to call the man back, to make him understand the enormity of what he had done. To force him to acknowledge that the loss of a child is a terrible thing, an outrage against nature.

The boat, threading through mud flats, made open sea. Derry breathed in lungfuls of salty air. The chill wind touched his skin. He felt as though he was being washed clean.

They reached Sheerness by the late afternoon. Heading round the Kent coast, Derry and Nicholson had raised the sails, and the *Elizabeth* had caught the wind, carrying them forward at an increased pace. They had become part of a flotilla of small boats. All kinds of craft were heading for the port: fishing smacks, cockle boats, lifeboats, wherries, passenger ferries, barges. 'Like the bloody Armada,' said Nicholson, his eyes wide. Derry, awed, agreed.

Sheerness was a muddle of threading their way through the hundreds of boats in the harbour, looking for someone in charge. Then a lot of waiting around; Derry, thankful to have reached dry land, wandered about the quayside, leaving the paperwork to Nicholson. Throughout the day, craft gathered at the port. There was an air of emergency. Although the newspapers and wireless had so far been uninformative about the fate of the British Expeditionary Force, working in the Admiralty – even in a rather obscure section of the Admiralty – one picked up a great deal. The phoney war had turned into a rout. Both the BEF and the French army were in retreat. Thousands of soldiers were stranded on the beach at Dunkirk.

Derry was sitting on a bench, half dozing in the sunlight, when Nicholson called out to him.

'What-ho, Fox! Haven't anything arranged for

tonight, have you? No popsy warming the bed?'

Derry opened his eyes. 'What had you in mind, Nicholson?'

'A little jaunt to France.' Nicholson was grinning. Derry stared at him.

'They haven't', explained Nicholson, 'enough Navy wallahs to go round. So I said I'd take the old *Liz* across myself. You'll come, won't you? You speak the lingo, don't you, Fox? Might come in handy.'

Derry thought, the odd smattering of German might be handier. But he stood up. 'Of course I'll come.'

They were given charts and told to form convoys. They set off at nightfall. Part of such a vast fleet, it wasn't hard to find the way. Like slipping into the traffic at Piccadilly Circus, said Nicholson. The white ribbon of the Kent coast faded into the distance as the *Elizabeth* wallowed and dipped. 'Lovely calm sea!' shouted Nicholson. Derry's stomach, as he studied the charts, also lurched and dipped.

Then there was a quiet bit, when a thin mist slid over the surface of the waves, curtaining the other lightless craft from them. There was only the chug of the engine and the small slap of water against the bows. They took turns at the tiller, one hour on and one hour off. Derry almost enjoyed the grey, chill peace. But he began to realize how cold he was, and how tired. Nicholson had kitted him out with a jersey and a mackintosh, but even so, even with the good weather and it being almost midsummer, the cold still bit into his skin. He thought about Alix, and about Rory and Patrick. How he wouldn't tell Alix what Charles Lanchbury had said to him. *She was there. It was convenient.* How he wished he'd had the chance to phone her before leaving for

France, to tell her that he loved her. Though she knew that. He understood what it meant, this armada. It meant desperation. It meant defeat.

He must have slept, huddled on the deck, because eventually he opened his eyes and saw a strip of red on the horizon. He was about to call to Nicholson, to tell him that it was sunrise, but something stopped him. Such a dark, angry red. Not the colour of the sun.

Nicholson had come to stand beside him. Derry heard a muttered word.

'Hell.'

'Yes.' It seemed to him an apt description. As they drew closer Derry could see the tongues of flame that leapt from the crimson gleam on the horizon, and the smoke that intermittently blacked out the red. The city of Dunkirk was on fire.

'Damn and blast it,' said Nicholson, hurrying to the tiller.

Every size of ship, from destroyer to rowing boat, was funnelling towards the port. The sea seethed with craft. It seemed inevitable to Derry that they should tumble into each other, bow against bow, wood against metal, capsizing, sinking. In spite of a night without sleep, his mind became focused and alert as they wove through ships and debris. Like one of those fairground games, he thought, where you thread a loop along an electrified wire, trying not to touch it.

'Beach shelves gradually,' muttered Nicholson. 'Half a mile. That's why the destroyers are anchored well out. Sandbanks, you see. Can't see why they couldn't have chosen a better—'

He broke off. They could see, at last, the beach. The red glow from the flames illuminated the long strip of sand. An immense black serpent coiled the length of the beach. Derry did not at first understand what the serpent was. Then he saw that it was composed of men. Line after line, an endless curling pattern in the sand. The lines extended into the sea. Soldiers stood up to their knees, waists and shoulders in water. Derry's heart seemed to pause. The defeated armies of Britain and France waited for rescue on the beach at Dunkirk.

May was at the office when she received the telephone call. As she put the receiver down, one of her colleagues said, 'Are you all right, May? You look frightful. Not bad news, is it?' She thought of saying, *Actually, my sister has shot herself*, but instead shook her head and pleaded a summer cold. Though they would know soon enough. She went to speak to her editor.

The next day, May caught the train to Cambridge. There were endless dreadful things to be done – the police station, the undertaker – and she endured them all with an emotionless efficiency she would have once thought alien to her.

The police sergeant showed her Ella's wristwatch and jewellery. May said, 'I'd like to see the body.'

'It's not necessary, miss.'

'I'd like to.'

'Bit of a mess, you see. Better if you just tell me whether these things belonged to her.'

May looked down at the desk. A wristwatch, a gold crucifix, the onyx brooch that she herself had once given Ella for her birthday. She was beyond tears, gripped instead by an awareness of the essential dreariness of life, its greyness, its lack of magic and mercy.

'These were all Ella's.' May looked up at the sergeant. 'Please tell me what happened. She was my sister. I'd like to know.'

'Miss Lanchbury shot herself early yesterday morning. She used your father's rifle. She was in the garden. One of the evacuees heard the shots.'

'Where?'

'A sort of lawn, with a hedge round it.'

The box circle, thought May. 'You said *shots*. How many shots?'

The man looked uncomfortable. 'Two, miss.' May looked at him. 'The first just winged her shoulder. The second – well, she put the gun in her mouth.'

May closed her eyes. She heard, eventually, the clink of cup and saucer.

'Drink this, miss. It'll make you feel better. There's plenty of sugar in it. Half our ration.' He had a kind smile. He was trying to comfort her.

She drank, thinking of Ella, and how Ella, of course, had muffed it. Thinking of those last unendurable moments of her sister's life, between one shot and the next.

She put the cup down. 'Her things. Can I go to the house and sort out her things?'

'We looked through Miss Lanchbury's room yesterday. We had to, you understand, miss, in case there was a note.' May looked up. He shook his head. 'Nothing.' Again, he seemed uneasy. 'We found . . . certain books and materials.'

'She was insane,' said May. 'Ella was insane.'

'Some of what we discovered may have to be shown at the inquest. Evidence, you know.'

May understood that he, like Derry, was warning her. She picked up her hat and gloves.

'I'll give you a lift, if you like, miss,' said the sergeant. 'It's on my way. Buses are few and far between.'

She would have preferred to be alone, but she

accepted, forcing a smile. He dropped May off at Bell Wood's gates. The alterations to her childhood home were immediate and shocking. The pupils from a boys' elementary school had been billeted on the house. An impromptu game of football, with cast-off sweaters for goalposts, was taking place on the lawn. Small boys swarmed up the chestnut trees beside the drive. In the courtyard, men were unloading desks and blackboards from vans. The old walls echoed with shouts and curses and conversation.

In Ella's room, May folded olive-brown shirts and jerseys, and packed up pairs of sensible black-laced shoes. The WVS could use them all. There was only one photograph remaining on the chest of drawers. It was the snapshot of their father, which had had pride of place on Ella's dressing-table, next to Hitler and Goebbels, all the heroes of Ella's diseased imagination. May slid the photograph out of the frame. Then she tore it into tiny fragments, scattering the pieces out of the window.

Outside, she walked through the garden. She saw how the lawn had been scuffed and scarred by children's boots, and how footprints trampled the seedlings in the flower bed. As she watched, two boys fought each other, roaring with laughter, falling against a hedge, making a scar of broken branches, scattered with leaves. As May entered the avenue of limes, the walls of greenery blocked off all sound. Inside the circle of box she stood for a while, looking up at the high green hedges and the blue sky.

She thought, there is nothing left of us. We never were much – we were naive and overconfident and un-prepared for the world – and now we are nothing. The Lanchburys and their possessions had been scattered to the four winds. She wondered whether any of this would have happened if she hadn't, years ago, met Derry Fox. Yet she knew that one had to look further back than that. She knew that the seeds of their destruction had been sown in 1914, on the day that Charlie had disappeared. She understood that they were being punished, and that their punishment was just.

May clasped her arms around herself, remembering. She remembered the dancers in the French village square, the ribbons of their tambourines making bright arcs in the light of the bonfire, and the rhythm of their drumming feet. And she remembered dancing with Derry in the café in Piccadilly, and the ecstasy of the warmth of his body against hers as they had moved together to the music.

Then she turned and headed for the drive. She would never, she knew, see Bell Wood again. She thought that she would marry. Her colleague at the newspaper – a kind, pleasant, easy-going man – had been asking her for years. She would marry and, if she were lucky, she would have children. May put up her face to the sun, letting its rays dry her tears.

Dunkirk was a holocaust. German artillery shells pounded the beach, and the Luftwaffe strafed the sea. Black smoke from burning oil cast a pall over the water. Flames rose from the city, and reached into the sky. Bodies lay, imitating postures of repose on the sand, or making fluttering macabre movements at the water's edge. Once, reaching into the sea, Derry came across the carcase of a horse. The noble eyes looked up at him, wide open and reproachful.

The smallest boats went in close into shore, picking up the swimmers and the men on rubber dinghies and on rafts, and those who had waded into the shallows. Then they transported their passengers to the small ships – the ferries and pleasure steamers – who in turn took them to the destroyers, waiting half a mile out to sea. Or that was the intention. Only it wasn't as easy as that, because men who were up to their necks in freezing water tended to panic and grab at the ropes flung from the boat, threatening to capsize it. And the barrage from land and sea rendered you unable to hear the sound of your own voice, let alone the voices of those who cried for help. And the debris in the sea – the empty barrels, the kitbags, the wrecks, and the drowned, swollen men – were an obstacle course, heaving and crashing at the fragile bows of the *Elizabeth*.

He had not slept, Derry calculated, for more than three hours in forty-eight. He had last eaten – he could not remember when. He could not eat; there was nothing to eat; he hadn't time to eat. At dawn, after he and Nicholson had ferried countless cargoes of men back to the larger boats, they cut back across the Channel, a party of exhausted French *poilus* on board. And then, pausing at Ramsgate to make repairs to the *Elizabeth* and refuel, they put out to sea again with barely a respite. At Ramsgate, Derry had longed to change his mind, to turn round, to go home. He knew, though neither of them spoke of it, that Nicholson felt the same. Yet they remained on board the boat.

Sailing back to Dunkirk, Derry remembered himself, at eighteen years old, longing to be significant, longing to take part in events of world-shattering importance. He wanted to laugh. He did not know whether this would be remembered as a shameful disaster, or as a glorious defeat. Both, perhaps, but he understood, even then, that it would be remembered. But that didn't matter: what mattered was that he was cold and tired, and sometimes so frightened he had to force himself not to curl up into a ball in the bottom of the boat.

Drawing towards the French coast, it was the same as the first time. The same crimson light on the horizon, the same ranks of waiting men, seemingly undiminished by the armada of boats that had shipped soldiers from the beach the previous day. The same tortuous, winding route around the wreckage that littered the shallow water, and the fishing boats, yachts and lifeboats that reached out to the men standing in the sea. Derry, helping soldiers climb into the *Elizabeth*, felt faintly comforted by the sameness of it.

Until, that was, the launch's engine coughed, spluttered, and fell silent. Derry glared at Nicholson.

'What-ho,' said Nicholson uncertainly.

They had just unloaded a boatful of soldiers onto a waiting passenger ferry, and had returned to the shallows once more.

'The engine—'

'She can be a touch flighty.'

Derry wanted to hit him. Nicholson was crouching in the wheelhouse, a spanner in his hand.

'Can I do anything?'

'If you could just hold this – watch out, it's hot . . .'

The engine juddered, and then fell silent again. Looking up, Derry saw that to the east, the sky was becoming lighter. He thought of pointing out that unless the engine started working again soon, the tide would go out and they would be grounded on the sand, a tempting target for whichever Stuka or Messerschmitt felt inclined to take pot-shots at them. But he supposed that Nicholson knew that already.

After a while, Nicholson, not looking up, said, 'Hitch

a ride, why don't you, old chap, on one of the other boats. This could take a while. I'll see you back at the office.'

Derry never knew quite why he chose to stay. He was cold and hungry, and the place was unendurable, and Nicholson possibly one of the most irritating men he had ever met.

But he said, 'Oh, shut up, Nicholson, why don't you, and fix that bloody engine,' and remained crouched on the deck, peering at the oily tangle of nuts and gaskets.

Belgium had capitulated, and Calais and Boulogne had fallen to the enemy. Royal Navy warships had been sunk in the English Channel. Throughout the south of England, rumours abounded of boatloads of ragged troops arriving back at coastal ports and resorts.

Derry had not telephoned for three days. He had promised to phone every night. Alix made calls. May Lanchbury, she discovered, had left the newspaper; there was no forwarding number. Maddy had taken the children to her husband's draughty Scottish castle. Roma was breezy, dismissive. 'You mustn't worry, Alix. Derry'll turn up. Always does, the wretch.' Alix ran her fingertip down the list of names in her address book, and thought, people are going away. Everything is changing.

She asked the operator to be put through to one of Derry's colleagues in the Admiralty. The line whirred and paused, waiting. She thought she had been cut off, but then a voice said, 'Hello?'

'Sandy, it's Alix Fox.'

'*Alix.* How are you?'

'Very well. I'm trying to find Derry.'

A silence. Then she said desperately, 'You see, he

hasn't phoned. And he always phones. Have you seen him?'

'Er, no.'

She knew that he was hiding something from her. '*Sandy!*' Her cry made the line reverberate. 'What is it? Is he ill?'

'No, no. It's not that. Hang on a moment, Alix.' She heard a door closing. 'It's just that this isn't all quite out in the open yet. And one has to be careful.'

She struggled to keep her patience. 'Sandy, do you know where he is?'

Looking round, she saw that Jonathan had come into the room. Her anxiety was reflected in his eyes. As she listened to Sandy's reply, she felt dazed, sick.

She put the receiver down. Jonathan was staring at her.

'Derry has gone to France,' she said.

Derry walked along the beach at Dunkirk. A thick black pall of smoke hung over the sands. He thought he could feel the heat from the burning city on his face. Debris littered the shore: an open wallet, brown coins like clams stuck at odd angles into the wet sand. A pullover, neatly darned on one elbow. A mess-kit, the two metal tins clinking softly as the movement of the waves spun them one against the other.

The *Elizabeth* waited, her engine repaired, becalmed on a spit of sand. Nicholson had remained on board the *Elizabeth*. It was worse – just – to remain inactive, a sitting target, than to walk through this hell on earth, so Derry had taken to the beach. Apart from the wreckage, the sea was now empty of ships. The fleet would return at nightfall. Because of the smoke from the burning oil tank, the sands were temporarily safe from the attentions of the Luftwaffe. The smoke blocked out the sun, and choked Derry's lungs. The noise of the barrage was infernal, as German troops blocked off the escape corridor and moved into the perimeter of the city, aiming their artillery at the beach and tightening the noose that trapped both French and British soldiers. It seemed to Derry that he was walking through an underworld, crushed between a darkened sky and the surreal litter on the sands.

Some of the waiting soldiers had dug foxholes in the dunes, so that only their heads and shoulders protruded. Others waited in those interminable winding snake-coils on the shoreline, braving the artillery fire so that they should not lose their place in the queue. A game of soccer took place on the impacted sand. Broad Yorkshire accents filtered through the clamour of the barrage. 'To me, Reg!' 'Over here, tha' daft bugger!'

He realized after a while what it all reminded him of. It was as though he had found himself at some final, terrible party. The milling crowds, the huddles of people, the endless changing unfamiliar faces, the noise and clamour and tension and tedium, bore an eerie echo of all yesterday's parties. Stukas played hide-and-seek behind the clouds, and columns of men hokey-cokeyed into the seawater. As he walked, his mind, hallucinating with tiredness, flickered from one reality to another. He was at Owlscote, strolling beside the lake, and Miranda Hughes, wearing a scarlet dress, was beckoning to him. He was at a party in South Molton Street, and the clash of mortars was the clash of the jazz band's cymbals. He was in some vast, dark, cavernous room, weaving between endless ranks of guests, evading the hands that reached out to him, escaping the voices that called out to him.

He shook his head, struggling to clear it, and was back on the beach once more. Not far from him, a voice called out, '*Shar-lee! Viens ici!*' He saw a small group of French *poilus* sheltering beneath the sweep of a sand-dune. Their uniforms were ragged and torn, their faces blackened by smoke. They were cooking something in a billycan over a small fire. The scent of the food was intoxicating. As he watched, Derry saw another soldier crown the dune and run towards them. The smoke from the burning oil had begun to clear, and the rays of the sun caught his coppery curls. He had two bottles of wine, one in each hand.

They called out his name again. '*Oh, Shar-lee. Shar-lee, mon brave.*'

It was because Derry was very tired, and very frightened, that it took him so long to recognize the name they were calling.

Charlie.

Because he had good French, because he had not spoken to them in the awful bastardized travesty of their language used by most of the Englishmen they had encountered, they invited him to share their food. There was stewed chicken, washed down with the red wine that Charlie had brought. After he had eaten, the hallucinations retreated, and he felt better. The *poilus* told Derry something of their story. They were part of the French rearguard that had defended the corridor to Dunkirk, enabling so many English soldiers to escape across the Channel. Early that morning, they had been ordered to abandon their positions, and retreat to the beach. The German army would follow in their footsteps within a day, two at most. Then they would be trapped, taken prisoner at best, and at worst—

A shrug. A finger drawn across the throat.

In Dunkirk, they had filched a chicken from an abandoned hen-coop, and onions and pulses from a gently smouldering *épicerie*. Now they lay propped on their elbows in the sand, passing round a bottle of wine. Derry watched and listened. He watched Charlie, in particular. It was not possible, he told himself, that this was Charlie Lanchbury. He wondered how many other red-haired, blue-eyed Frenchmen might bear that name, but his mind, fuddled by fear and exhaustion, could not find an answer. It was also not possible that he himself should meet Charlie Lanchbury on a beach in northern France, almost twenty-six years after his disappearance. Any moment, and Charlie would take photographs of a red-haired father and mother from his pocket, and display them proudly. Or offer an explanation for his English name: *in honour of my uncle in Devon* . . . or, *I was born in London* . . .

But Charlie, in reply to Derry's question, shrugged and said, 'It's my name, that's all. I don't know where it came from.' A small shiver – a ghost's fingerprint – ran down Derry's spine.

'Your surname?'

'Leconte. Charlie Leconte.' They shook hands. Charlie passed Derry the wine bottle.

So he watched the sea, and watched Charlie, and saw, as the smoke cleared, the Stukas black against the blue sky. And the tide, edging lazily back towards the shore. When he explained about the boat, the four *poilus* looked at each other, and shrugged some more, and gathered up their things and followed Derry down the beach.

He heard the *Elizabeth*'s engine, an uncertain rattling, as he waded out to sea. Nicholson looked up as he climbed onto the deck.

'Don't know how long she'll last. Might be best to get out of here while the going's good.'

Though it was evening, the sky was not yet dark. Derry said, 'I've some passengers.'

'The more the merrier.'

They headed out of the port. Enduring the terrible obstacle course once again, he forgot to wonder about Charlie Lanchbury. There were the hulls of abandoned ships, stuck at oblique angles in the sand. There was the debris floating in the shallow water, the corpulent, bloated bodies bobbing against the *Elizabeth*'s hold, and the metal containers that might be oil drums, and might be mines. There were the Stukas, winging through the sky like angry insects. Derry crouched at the bow, calling directions, while Nicholson steered. Adrenalin pumped through Derry's veins. His entire body ached with nerves. The shapes in the water fleetingly adopted different guises. An old tyre uncoiled like a sea-serpent. A corpse's white eye winked at him.

Then they were out into open sea, and Nicholson was saying, 'Can't wait to be back in Blighty. Met a stunning little girl at the flicks the other night—' and suddenly, out of nowhere, an aeroplane screamed down, silver fire snouting from its guns.

The noise erased all thought. Derry just threw himself on the deck, his forearms folded over his head. When the Stuka had gone, he waited, knowing that any moment chill salt water must begin to seep up through the deck.

But he heard a voice whisper, '*Merde*,' and he turned round. His palm touched dry wood. There was a lace-work of holes in the deck, but the body of the boat seemed to have suffered little damage. He wanted to laugh. He said, his voice trembling, 'Nicholson, I think we've got away with it,' but Nicholson did not reply. He drooped over the tiller, as though exhaustion had claimed him at last. Derry crawled over to him.

Nicholson was dead. There was a neat hole in his forehead, and a surprised expression on his face. Derry thought, I never even knew his Christian name. Then he remembered Nicholson's popsies and what-hos and grating cheerfulness, and he wanted, momentarily, to weep. But he heard one of the *poilus* say, 'He's hurt. François is hurt,' and he glanced up.

One of the Frenchmen was slumped face down on the deck. Another – the young boy whom Derry guessed to be about Rory's age – was stooped green-faced over the handrail. The fourth crouched by the wheelhouse, his face contorted in pain. Charlie was bending over him.

Derry said, 'Your friend . . . ?'

Charlie shook his head. 'And François has been shot in the shoulder. Have you bandages?'

'The first aid box . . .' He tried not to think, scrabbling through broken glass and splintered wood, of his situation. Somewhere in the middle of the Channel, in sole charge of a boat with an unreliable engine, and two dead men and one wounded on board . . .

He focused instead on Charlie, who was undoing François's tunic. And on the scarlet seeping through the rough cloth. And on the mess the bullet had made of the man's shoulder. They splashed disinfectant over the wound, and bandaged it as best they could.

'Was there any wine left?'

'In Armand's pocket.'

Derry offered the aspirin bottle. 'It's the best we've got, I'm afraid.'

'François? Drink this. It'll make you feel better.'

The wounded soldier's head rested against Charlie's shoulder. Derry fed him aspirins, washed down with wine.

He stumbled back to the tiller. When he glanced at the compass, he saw that the needle had jammed. He thumped it with his fist, but it did not move.

'What's up?'

'The bloody compass has stuck.'

'Are there charts? We can manage', said Charlie, 'with the stars and charts.'

The sky began, at last, to darken. Tiny pinpoints of light pierced the greyness. The port of Dunkirk was long ago lost in the curve of the earth's surface. The Stukas too had gone. As Derry stood in the wheelhouse, the milky greyness intensified, a faint mist spreading over the surface of the water.

He heard Charlie say, 'It's so peaceful. So quiet.'

The absence of sound, after the terrifying clamour of Dunkirk, rang in Derry's ears. He found himself listening to the silence.

'How's your friend?'

'Poor François. It's his first time at sea.' Charlie's hand stroked the wounded soldier's matted hair. 'And Emile, too – you hadn't seen the sea until yesterday, had you, Emile?' The boy nodded, his eyes wide and glazed with fear. 'They're both farmers, you understand.'

'But you're not?'

Charlie shook his head. 'I'm a teacher. But I've always been fascinated by the sea. Most unusual for an inland Frenchman.'

Again, that curious shiver to the skin. François moaned, so they held the wine bottle to his lips.

'Where do you come from, Charlie?'

'Crévecoeur. Do you know it?'

Derry was aware of a flutter of disappointment. Not Bapaume, then, or Herleville. 'How old are you?'

'Twenty-eight. More or less.'

Derry's heart seemed to pause. 'More or less?'

'I was adopted.'

Charlie was taking off his tunic, spreading it over François. François moaned again. Emile, crouching beside them, tore at his fingernails with his teeth. Derry said softly, 'Tell me.'

'There's nothing much to tell.'

'It would pass the time.'

'And it's going to be a long night, isn't it?'

'It would take our minds off things.' Derry glanced at the boy.

'Have some wine, Emile – there's a little left.' Charlie passed the bottle to the boy.

'If you're twenty-eight,' said Derry, 'that would mean you were born in 1912 or thereabouts. Were your parents killed in the Great War?'

'I've always assumed so. The nuns told my mother that I was found wandering at the roadside, ten miles or so south of Bapaume.'

'Bapaume . . .' he muttered. Disbelief and a growing certainty fought in his tired brain.

'So the nuns took you in?'

'And then, in the war, they moved south, to be with their sister convent in Crévecoeur.' Charlie's voice was low and level, so as not to disturb François.

'And then . . . ?'

Charlie smiled. 'My mother found me.'

'Your adoptive mother?'

'Yes. She did rough work at the convent. She had lost a son in infancy, and her husband had been killed at the Marne.'

'She just . . . picked you out?'

'My big blue eyes, she said.' Charlie smiled. 'My mother always tells me that I reminded her of the baby she'd lost.'

It was quite dark, now. The lights of the boat were extinguished so as not to attract the attention of further enemy aeroplanes. Waves slopped against the *Elizabeth*'s bows.

'Did the nuns ever try to trace your parents?'

'How could they? There were a hundred children in the orphanage. In peacetime, there were a dozen, maybe two. They struggled just to feed us.'

'Your life before the orphanage . . . Do you remember anything?'

A small shake of the head. 'I was very young. Not much more than a baby.' A chuckle. 'The nuns had a nickname for me, my mother said. They called me *le petit prince*. Because I had such good manners – I didn't push and grab like the other children – and because, when they found me, I was wearing what had once been good clothes.'

Velvet and lace, thought Derry. They sat for a while in silence. Emile wiped his nose on his sleeve, and bit his lip. François's eyes had closed. For a while, Derry drifted in a half-world between sleeping and waking. He knew that he must say, *Charlie, there's something I should tell you*, but he was unsure whether he had already spoken the words aloud, unsure whether a minute or an hour had passed since Charlie had spoken.

He heard Charlie say, 'To tell the truth, I never think about it,' and he opened his eyes.

'But your real parents—'

'It was a long time ago. Your parents are the people who love and care for you, don't you think?'

'But aren't you curious?'

There was a silence. Charlie said slowly, 'Whatever happened, it happened to another person. I am no longer that person. And besides, I am a fortunate man. I have a mother who adores me, and whom I too adore, and I have a beautiful fiancée. I love my family, and I love my country. What more could I want?'

Careful not to disturb the wounded man, Charlie took something from his pocket and handed it to Derry. Derry looked down at the photograph.

'This is my mother,' said Charlie, 'and this is Juliette, my fiancée. Isn't she beautiful?'

'Very beautiful.' His voice echoed in the emptiness of the sea. A small face looked up at him, a hand shyly shading one side of her face. The older woman's comfortable, generous features were creased in a smile. The two women stood outside a small, brick house.

'Your home?'

'Yes.' Charlie's smile faded. 'I hope they're well. I hope they're safe.'

Derry went back to the wheelhouse. He opened his mouth to speak, and then he closed it again. He thought of the Lanchburys. The events of the last quarter-century had all but extinguished them from the face of the earth. Dispersed, dead or dying, there would be none of their name to follow them. The new world made by this war would struggle to find a place for their kind.

Whatever Charlie had once been, he had become something more. Derry watched him for a while, as he cradled his comrade's head against his shoulder. The only sounds were the purr of the engine, and the slide of wave against bow. A curious sense of calm washed over him. The Lanchburys and their story had slipped into the past they belonged to. The future was Alix and Rory and Patrick, and the different world that the war would make. He saw that of all the things he had once longed for – fame, and recognition, and the chance to make his mark – only love endured. The boat drifted through silent seas, making for England.

In those strange, early June days, fear and delight mingled. Some of Alix's fears were too vast to contemplate – the possibility of invasion, the possibility that, her army stranded in France, Great Britain might not be able to defend herself. As the newspapers began, at last, to tell of the tragedy and triumph unfolding at Dunkirk, and as the numbers of soldiers rescued – fifty-three thousand one day, sixty-eight thousand the next – began to mount up, one anxiety was alleviated while another, with each passing hour, intensified. Every knock at the door, every ring of the telephone, made her pause, her knuckles pressed against her teeth, adrenalin rushing through her veins.

Her delight was in her son. In the morning, waking, the first beat of her heart would accompany her rush of love for Patrick, the second her anxiety for Derry. She treasured the private joys of those dawn hours. She knew that in Patrick she had been given a second chance, and the beginnings of a new life. Patrick, Rory and Derry had enabled her to bear her uprooting from Owlscote, and the loss of the life that she had become accustomed to. In the early hours of the morning, Patrick's plump fists would thump against the guardrail of the cot, and his bare feet would bounce up and down on the mattress. Alix would lift him out of the cot and into her own bed, so that he did not wake the rest of the household. He would lie curled up with her quietly for a few moments, and she would begin to drift off to sleep again. Then a small finger would touch her face, or soft wet lips plant a kiss on her forehead. When she opened her eyes he would laugh, a liquid chuckle that always made her, no matter what the hour, smile too. And he would seize her hands, clapping them together. 'Pat-a-cake, pat-a-cake, baker's man . . .'

By day, working in the house and the garden, or playing with the children, she managed to distract herself. Speaking on the telephone to Rory, she heard the yearning in her son's voice. 'In *France*? The lucky *swine*.' She could not share Rory's envy; she feared for Derry. By night, her anxieties crowded round her, and she dreamt of gunfire, and the ruined towns of northern France, and a small boat, drifting empty and alone on a vast expanse of sea.

Early one morning, she dreamed that she was walking through the watermeadows beside Salisbury Cathedral. Derry was beside her, and Patrick's hand curled inside hers. Rory strolled ahead of them. Swans, doubled by their perfect reflections, floated on the river, and willows bent to touch its smooth surface. All around them, children played: on the path, and on the grassy banks of the Nadder, and among the trees in the copse, their shadows flickering on the mossy ground, their laughter half heard beneath the sunlit leaves.

She awoke, smiling. The telephone was ringing. She slid out of bed, and ran downstairs.

She snatched up the receiver. His voice said her name. Then he said, 'I've a story to tell you, Alix . . .'

THE END

FOOTPRINTS ON THE SAND
by Judith Lennox

The Mulgraves are a rootless, bohemian family who travel the continent, staying in crumbling Italian palazzos, Spanish villas, French vineyards – belonging nowhere, picking up friends and hangers-on as they go, and moving on when Ralph Mulgrave's latest enthusiasm dwindles. Faith, the eldest child of the family, longs for a proper home. But in 1940 Germany invades France and the Mulgraves are forced to flee to England. Faith and her brother Jake go to London, while Ralph reluctantly settles in a Norfolk cottage with the remnants of his family.

In the intense and dangerous landscape of wartime London Faith finds work as an ambulance driver, and meets once again one of Ralph's retinue from those distant and, in retrospect, golden days of childhood. Through war and its aftermath it is Faith on whom the family relies, Faith who offers support and succour, and Faith who is constant and true in her love.

'Judith Lennox's writing is so keenly honest it could sever heartstrings'
Daily Mail

'A compelling story of courage, resilience and enduring love, of family bonds, hope and redemption'
Home and County

0 552 14599 8

A SELECTED LIST OF FINE NOVELS
AVAILABLE FROM CORGI BOOKS

THE PRICES SHOWN BELOW WERE CORRECT AT THE TIME OF GOING TO PRESS.
HOWEVER TRANSWORLD PUBLISHERS RESERVE THE RIGHT TO SHOW NEW RETAIL
PRICES ON COVERS WHICH MAY DIFFER FROM THOSE PREVIOUSLY ADVERTISED IN
THE TEXT OR ELSEWHERE.

Transworld titles are available by post from:

Book Service By Post, PO Box 29, Douglas, Isle of Man, IM99 1BQ

Credit cards accepted. Please telephone 01624 675137
fax 01624 670923, Internet http://www.bookpost.co.uk
or e-mail: bookshop@enterprise.net for details

Free postage and packing in the UK. Overseas customers: allow £1 per book
(paperbacks) and £3 per book (hardbacks)